An hour or so later, when gorse and brambles, myrtle and creeping willow had finally given way to barren rock, Morag halted once again and drew out the sandwiches that Isa had given her. She settled herself with her back against a boulder to admire the view. From this height she could see far out over the loch to where miniature fishing boats cut a swathe across the mirror-black waters which perfectly reflected the hills of the Ardamurchan peninsular. Far off to her left the Corran Ferry, its funnel belching black smoke, traversed the loch, crossing the path of the noonday steamer returning from the south. To the right it was possible to follow the line of the canal which bisected the valley to the east of the town.

# Fields of Heather

## Mary Withall

*Mary Withall* (signature)

**CORONET BOOKS**
Hodder and Stoughton

First published in Great Britain in 1998 by Hodder and
Stoughton
First published in paperback in 1998 by Hodder and
Stoughton
A division of Hodder Headline PLC

A Coronet Paperback

10 9 8 7 6 5 4 3

A CIP catalogue record for this title is available from the
British Library

ISBN 0 340 71746 7

Typeset by Hewer Text Ltd, Edinburgh
Printed and bound in Great Britain by
Mackays of Chatham PLC, Chatham, Kent

Hodder and Stoughton
A division of Hodder Headline PLC
338 Euston Road
London NW1 3BH

For Andrew who has climbed many mountains

# Chapter 1

With a joyful whistle the steamer drew in to the pier at the head of the loch and disgorged her passengers. At this late period in the season the number of tourists was greatly reduced, but Morag Beaton noted with interest a group of young men carrying skis and snow sticks, in addition to their huge rucksacks. No doubt they were hopeful that the promised snow would indeed visit Scotland's highest peaks over the next twenty-four hours and give them a few days' sport before the accepted start-date for the skiing season.

She glanced anxiously at the fob watch attached to her lapel. It was well past noon and her appointment was for two o'clock. Should she satisfy her craving for hot tea and a sandwich, in the expectation of hiring a cab to take her to the hospital, or should she forget the refreshment and simply walk? A quick investigation of the contents of her purse helped her make up her mind. She had to consider the cost of a night's stay in the town, before catching the steamer the following morning.

She fumbled busily with the contents of her over-large leather handbag, satisfying herself for the twentieth time that all her documents were still in the pocket where she had stored them. With a quick glance at the paper carrying her father's written instructions, she turned to the left and headed up the slope towards the main street of the old highland town.

Morag approached the coming interview with uncharacteristic anxiety and indecision.

Until now all her appointments had been within the university hospital in which she had trained and where she was well known to the staff. This would be different. Today she was going to

1

be in competition with a number of others, perhaps more experienced and almost certainly, male. Ashamed to admit to her apprehension, she had refused her mother's offer to accompany her on the journey from Eisdalsa. Now she rather wished that she had agreed to having her as a companion.

Millicent Beaton had quite fancied a trip on the steamer. It was so seldom that they had a chance to visit anywhere other than Oban or Inverary and there were some good shops in Inverlinnhe, selling traditional highland woollens and fine tweeds. Her daughter was, however, adamant that this next step upon a career that was already a monument to perseverance against extraordinary odds, should be taken unaided and alone.

As Morag stepped into High Street which ran parallel with the water, a blast of wind from the north-west nearly carried away her close-fitting hat. Clasping her hand to her head, she struggled against the sudden blast, stepped on to the cobbled roadway, and darted between the traffic: a mixture of handcarts, horse-drawn waggons and the occasional motor lorry. When she was halfway across, she was startled by the sudden hooting of a horn, and a large limousine, travelling far too fast in the busy, narrow street, swept past her, throwing up muddy water from the rainstorm of the previous night. She cursed in unladylike fashion, and glanced up to find that the vehicle had stopped and the driver was leaning out of his window, looking back to see what had happened. He was a dark young man, with heavy eyebrows and a square-set jaw, and at this moment he was scowling . . . at her.

'Can't you look where you're going?' he yelled. Regardless of the mess he had made of Morag's stockings, he continued to rail at her. 'I don't know what this town's coming to, tourists wandering all over the place as though they owned it! The rules of the road apply here as they do elsewhere, you know!' he concluded, pulling back his head and preparing to drive off.

'In that case,' she observed, coolly, 'surely you should be driving with due care and attention to the other traffic and pedestrians using the road?' She too had a driving licence, and had read the motorist's code laid down by the Automobile Association. 'You were going far too fast!'

He lifted his chin in exasperated fashion, let in the clutch and lurched forward, narrowly missing a horse-drawn baker's cart which had emerged from a side road during their exchange, and was now drawn up before a small café.

Morag glanced down at her legs. Her stockings were filthy. Well, that decided it, she would have to go into the café, order a cup of tea and make use of their lavatory. She couldn't appear at the interview in this state. She pushed open the door and walked in.

There was only one other customer seated at a table close to the window. As she entered, he half rose from his seat with an anxious expression.

'Are you OK?' he enquired, and then when she appeared bewildered by the question, 'I saw what happened out there. Did that bastard hit you?'

'Oh . . . no. Just ruined my clothes.' She made to pass by to another table, but he stood up properly now to inspect her muddy skirt, the back of her coat and her wet feet.

'Look, there's a radiator here. Why don't you sit down and dry off?' Then, when she hesitated, 'I'll move if you would prefer . . .'

'Oh, no, please don't disturb yourself. And thank you,' she replied graciously, sinking into the proffered seat. As her companion had suggested, the radiator was very warm and soon her clothes began to steam. The mud would probably brush off when it was dry.

'You're quite certain he didn't injure you at all?' The other customer demanded a second time, with a note of disappointment in his voice. Really, she thought, he might almost have wished it were so!

She smiled weakly in response and gave her order to the proprietor who, having completed her transaction with the van-driver, had moved over to their table.

'Just a pot of tea, please,' Morag requested, 'and a round of toast.'

'It's time that young idiot was up before the Sheriff,' her companion insisted. 'Just because his old man owns half the town, he thinks he can carry on like some medieval baron. Just let him put one foot out of line and I'll have him!'

Then, in response to Morag's puzzled expression, 'I beg your pardon,' he said, hurriedly, 'Magnus Glendenning, senior reporter on the *West Highland Gazette*.' Again he half rose from his seat and offered his hand.

'Morag Beaton,' she replied, taking it. 'Is there so little happening in Inverlinnhe that you have to go out looking for news?'

He was struck by her candour and replied with a laugh, 'It's true that there isn't much happening on the surface in this sleepy backwater, but you'd be surprised what a mire of intrigue and subterfuge there is behind the scenes!'

'Sounds just like the village I come from.' She grinned, then busied herself with her tea and toast for a few minutes, leaving an awkward silence in which he pretended to study his paper.

'Are you just passing through?' he enquired, when she had replaced her cup and wiped a stray crumb from her lips.

'Hopefully not,' she replied, glancing out at the watery sun of a December afternoon. There was a smile in her grey eyes as she looked back at him and noticed his obvious interest on hearing that they might possibly meet again. Morag might be thought a blue-stocking by her contemporaries, but that didn't mean she was averse to polite advances from the opposite sex.

'I am attending an interview for a job,' she explained. 'That's why I was so upset about the mud.' She looked at her watch and was startled to see how little time she had left to find her way to the hospital, and she had yet to try and tidy herself.

She looked around for the sign which said 'Ladies'. Her companion glanced in the right direction and she rose to go.

She was tall for a woman, and moved with a grace which was uncommon amongst the females of Magnus's acquaintance. Most young girls these days seemed to try over-hard to be as boyish as possible, he reflected. Their underwear was designed to make them flat-chested, their fashions aped masculine attire: shorts in summer and slacks in winter. Instead of dinner gowns they wore, as often as not, pyjama-like evening trousers. Most of the time, he thought, disgruntled, it was difficult to distinguish one sex from the other.

This young woman, on the other hand, wore her knee-length beige tweed skirt with style, and her loose-fitting topcoat, in a warm rust colour, complemented her auburn hair. When she emerged a few moments later, still brushing at the hem of her coat, he was struck again by her finely sculpted profile which was enhanced by the cloche hat she wore. He stood up as she approached.

'How is it now?' he asked, examining her coat from every angle.

'I think I've removed most of the mud,' she replied. 'My shoes were a mess but I've managed to wipe them off a bit. I'll just have to tuck them out of sight as much as possible.'

'If you go in smiling, they'll be so busy looking at your face, they won't notice.' He grinned as he opened the door for her.

'Oh, I haven't paid for the tea,' she cried, suddenly remembering.

'I settled it for you,' he told her. 'I hope you don't mind?'

'You really shouldn't have done that.' She gave him a rather mischievous smile. 'I don't know what my mother would say about my accepting tea and toast from a complete stranger!'

'If you don't tell her,' he replied, with a sagacious air, 'she'll be none the wiser.'

Outside, they found that the afternoon had turned much colder, and there was a distinct feeling that the dark clouds gathering above Beinn Mart were filled with snow rather than rain. Morag examined the sky anxiously, and shivered a little.

'Where are you making for?' Magnus enquired. He had studiously avoided direct questions about her purpose for being in the town. Long experience of interviewing had taught him that the best material came from people who did not realise they were being cross-examined.

'I have to get to the hospital,' she told him. 'Can you direct me?'

'I can do better than that,' he declared. 'I have to visit someone there myself . . . a hill-walker who is recovering after being lost on the mountain for twenty-four hours.'

'I suppose you meet a lot of those?' Morag observed as she allowed him to take her arm. He guided her along High Street until, after making a right-hand turn, she found that they were climbing the steep slope to the next plateau, some two hundred feet above the loch.

On this level, the houses were substantial villas which must have been built towards the end of the previous century. Each had a piece of garden to the front, where even now the dead flower heads of vast hydrangeas, and the occasional rose and fuchsia, still flowering, gave an indication of summer splendour. Many houses had glass conservatories attached, either by design or as an afterthought, to the front elevation. These provided a panoramic view over the loch to the mountains beyond, for those visitors confined to the house by the unpredictable highland weather.

This was the territory of the Bed and Breakfast trade, upon which fifty per cent of the town depended for its livelihood.

Morag was forced to pause for breath. Magnus gladly slackened his pace. His love of good food and alcoholic beverages of all kinds had given him a figure which would have sat ill upon a man ten years his senior. He must have weighed fifteen stones at least, and his belly struggled to escape over the top of his loose-fitting Oxford bags. His skin was bad, surprisingly so since by his brogue Morag would have guessed that he had spent his life in the Western Highlands, where the rain seemed to soften and polish the skin to a healthy glow. By contrast with his countrymen, Magnus's pallor was yellowish. In the coming weeks and months she was to wonder how she had ever got into conversation with such an outwardly unprepossessing character. Perhaps it had something to do with his smiling eyes and beautifully modulated voice. Later she would bless her own good instincts for sensing, below the surface, the kind-hearted, witty, intelligent fellow who was the real Magnus Glendenning.

'Been nursing long?' he demanded, as they set off again up a further steep slope to the next terrace.

'Nursing?' she echoed, sounding surprised at the question.

'You said you were going for a job at the hospital . . . I naturally assumed you were a nurse.' He seemed embarrassed now. Had he presumed too far perhaps?

'Oh, yes,' she replied vaguely. 'But . . . no, I have applied for the post of house surgeon.'

Magnus came to a halt, staring at her in astonishment.

'A surgeon? I knew that there were a few women doctors about,' he hastened to add, 'but it had never occurred to me that they would be allowed . . . er . . . would wish to become surgeons.'

Morag laughed lightly. 'It's merely a matter of snipping and stitching,' she replied, amused at his discomfiture. 'Actually women can make quite good surgeons . . . it's much like dressmaking if you think about it!'

He was silent for some time. As they plodded on, his mind ran over the members of the Hospital Committee whom she would undoubtedly encounter that afternoon. They were a pretty reactionary bunch on the whole, and the man in whom most of the power resided was the senior consultant, Sidney Maynard. He was a bachelor and noted misogynist who had been most vociferous during the campaign for women's suffrage, writing endless vitriolic letters to the Press on the subject. Magnus could not believe that he would accept the appointment of a female assistant without protest.

Should he mention it? He covertly regarded the girl who was labouring up the last of the slope beside him. She looked tough enough to withstand the kind of onslaught which would no doubt come from Maynard. To have reached this position in her career, she must have fought a few such battles already. He would let her gauge the situation for herself, and keep his fingers crossed for a successful outcome.

'Here we are,' he declared, gasping thankfully as they passed in through an imposing gateway and paused at the gate-keeper's office to report their arrival.

'Afternoon, Angus,' Magnus greeted the man. The reporter was obviously a frequent visitor.

'Oh, aye, Mr Glendenning . . . you'll be wanting a word with yon walking gentleman,' observed the old fellow.

'Yes, that's about the size of it,' Magnus agreed, then added, 'The young lady has an interview with the committee.'

'Oh, aye?' Angus gave Morag a strange look. 'You will be wanting the boardroom, miss. Wait now and I will come and show you the way.'

'No need, man,' Magnus interrupted, cheerfully. 'I'll show her myself.'

They walked on along the path of granite chippings, and the elderly gate-keeper shook his head in disbelief. Women doctors indeed . . . whatever next?

The small ante-room was hardly more than a corridor off the main passageway which ran from front to back of the building. There was no window and a single unshaded electric light bulb did nothing to relieve the gloomy atmosphere. On a row of hardback chairs sat three men, each in his own way demonstrating a degree of anxiety. Morag took her place on the one remaining chair and smiled at them.

A young man of about her own age half rose, politely, and murmured a greeting.

He was very pale and appeared quite agitated. His nervous gesture of invitation to her to take a seat was exaggerated by his unusually long arms, although she noticed that these were, in fact, quite in proportion to the rest of his lofty stature. His hair was so fair as to be almost white, and curled close to his head in a manner which seemed somehow undignified in a man. He looked tousled, like a small boy who had managed to escape the attentions of his nursemaid. Morag warmed to him instantly, and regretted that they must be in competition for the same job.

The other two doctors stared straight ahead, too wrapped up in their own concerns to acknowledge her arrival.

Morag had expected to find other candidates for the post, although she had been led to believe that there was not a large queue of people wanting to come and work in this somewhat remote hospital. It was hardly an ideal stamping ground for the really ambitious practitioner. She wondered if they were all seeking the same appointment, and addressed the friendly young man to that effect.

'I believe there are to be two appointments made,' he explained. 'I am an anaesthetist, myself.'

The doctor at the far end of the line snorted his disapproval. Clearly he was of the opinion that lesser mortals, which was how he regarded all anaesthetists, should not be appointed in company with real medical men. He brushed the knees of his pinstripe trousers as if disassociating himself from such lowly company, and stared at Morag over the top of his gold-rimmed spectacles. No doubt the female was also after the anaesthetist post . . . it was about all women doctors were good for. He cast his glance over the fourth candidate, noted his somewhat crumpled appearance and over-anxious demeanour and concluded that there would be no contest. Relaxing in the certainty that his journey had not been wasted, he picked up an ancient *Lancet* from the pile on the table and began to read.

'Mr Anstruther.' A woman with iron-grey hair and wearing a clinging knitted suit, emerged from the boardroom carrying a sheaf of papers. A string of amber beads, which she wore in two substantial loops around her neck, bounced up and down upon her ample bosom as she walked.

She scanned the row of pale faces, looking enquiringly from one to the other. He of the gold-rimmed spectacles rose grandly to his feet, cast a deprecating glance at his fellow candidates, and followed the woman into the boardroom.

Morag smiled faintly at her neighbour. 'I imagine he is also a candidate for the house surgeon's post,' she observed. 'He clearly has little regard for anaesthetists.'

'Pity the poor anaesthetist who's expected to work with him, then!' It was the first time that their colleague had spoken. He was an elderly man, nearer sixty than fifty, Morag estimated. His right cheek was heavily scarred, and the corner of his lower eyelid was dragged down on to his cheek, giving him a lopsided appearance.

'Oh,' said the younger man, 'I take it then that you are also a candidate for anaesthetics . . . that makes three of us for the same post.'

He looked quite crestfallen. The other fellow might well be turned down on grounds of age, and since he wore the scars of battle, they might think him something of a risk, but the girl was a 'looker' and probably brilliant . . . all the women doctors he had ever met were high fliers. They had to be, or they would never have gained a place in medical school to begin with.

Morag quickly allayed his fears.

'I am a candidate for the post in surgery,' she told them. The older man seemed unmoved by this announcement, but the other could barely contain his amazement.

'I've never met a woman surgeon before,' he said at last, recovering from the surprise. 'Wherever did you find a hospital to train you?'

'I trained in Edinburgh,' she replied, 'following in the footsteps of Elsie Inglis, Louise McIllroy, Francis Ivens, and many others who proved their worth during the war.'

'Oh . . . I hadn't realised . . .' the younger man murmured, but his veteran colleague nodded in agreement.

'They did a fine job, those women,' he declared in ringing tones. 'Never did get proper recognition for it, either. You don't hear anything now of the work they did in the most appalling conditions in Serbia and Russia.' He leaned across and laid a hand on Morag's knee. 'Good luck to you, miss. It's time places like this recognised the value of women to the medical profession.'

She smiled back at him, grateful for his support.

Soon the first candidate emerged, looking rather red and a little less composed than he had when he went in.

'Dr Beaton,' he addressed Morag, 'they will see you now.' He held the door open to allow her to pass through and closed it silently behind her. After the dimness of the corridor, the interview room seemed excessively bright.

'Ah, Dr Beaton, please take a seat.' The Chairman indicated a chair, centrally placed before a semicircular table of massive proportions.

He introduced the members of the committee one by one, but

of them all, Morag registered only the senior consultant in surgery, Sidney Maynard. He had a long face, with an exceptionally high forehead which was accentuated by a nearly bald pate. She was reminded of sketches of Martians from H. G. Wells's book, *The War of the Worlds*. It was his hands, however, which caught her attention. They rested in relaxed fashion on the table before him, the long tapering fingers with their immaculate nails a sure indication of his profession.

His eyes were small and piercing. She felt he could see right through to her very soul. Although his face was quite expressionless, she could sense his almost tangible antagonism and shuddered involuntarily.

A tall willowy figure rose from his seat at the far end of the table and adjusted the window which had been left open a fraction. In contrast with the other men in their dark city suits and stiff white collars, he wore tweeds, his heather green Norfolk jacket set off by a colourful silk cravat. He was a man in his middle years, prematurely grey, Morag thought, but wearing his age well. From his tanned skin and the deeply etched wrinkles about his eyes and mouth, she judged him to be a man who spent a great deal of his time outdoors.

'I do believe the temperature has fallen a few degrees since we started,' he explained, putting Morag instantly at her ease. He was rewarded by her smile of gratitude.

The interlude had given her an opportunity to relax a little. Practising the method taught her long ago by her father, she allowed her muscles to loosen, beginning at her fingers and toes, until her limbs felt quite heavy and she was breathing easily. The tense feeling with which she had entered the room had quite left her.

'Dr Beaton, 'the Chairman Graham Fraser began, scanning the documents spread before him,' you come highly recommended by your tutors at the Royal. It seems that you have been a gold medal winner on no less than three occasions during your training.'

She inclined her head, modestly, but made no reply.

'I also have a recommendation from the Medical Officer for

Health for the County of Argyll. Mr Michael Brown is, I believe, a relative by marriage?'

'My uncle,' she confirmed.

'But most important of all, ladies and gentlemen,' he swept his glance around the table, 'Dr Beaton is the latest recruit to a succession of medical men bearing her name, who have long been a byword in this part of the country.'

Fraser had done his homework well, thought Maynard, with grudging admiration. It was clear to everyone that he favoured the girl . . . saw the appointment of a women surgeon as a 'first' for the West Highland Hospital, making him appear progressive in the eyes of the electorate. Fraser had his eye on becoming Lord Lieutenant one of these days.

'I will ask Mr Maynard, our senior consultant surgeon, to open the interview.' Fraser sat back, easing himself into the comfortably upholstered armchair, and beamed delightedly.

'There is no doubt as to your theoretical knowledge, Dr Beaton,' Maynard began, 'you have clearly proved to the satisfaction of your mentors that you can remember the words . . . but how are you when it comes to watching the blood flow on the operating table?'

There was a little squeal of apprehension from the one female member of the committee, she of the knitted suit and dangling beads.

'I am sorry,' Morag answered coolly, 'I am afraid I don't understand your question?'

'Dammit!' the surgeon exploded. 'Most of the young women of sensitivity whom I know would faint at the first sight of blood, let alone feel themselves able to take a scalpel and cut into living flesh!' Then, appreciating the indelicacy of his outburst, he apologised to the single woman member, who had turned quite pale. 'Pray excuse me, Miss McKinnley.'

'Do you have male nursing staff in your operating theatre, Mr Maynard?' Morag asked, with an innocent air.

'What . . . ? Of course not,' he blustered. 'How do you mean?'

'It is just that I fail to see why you should feel that it is permissible for female nurses to witness operations, but not for female surgeons to carry them out,' Morag explained, carefully.

The pleasant-faced man at the end of the table nodded, approvingly.

'Tell me, Miss Beaton,' Fraser tried to steer the conversation into less dangerous waters, 'do you feel that you have had sufficient experience of the kind of surgery most often practised here at the West Highland? There are many accident cases, often quite traumatic, with people injured on the roads, the water or in the mountains. I think I am correct in saying that much of the work here is of an emergency nature?' He raised an eyebrow in Maynard's direction and that gentleman nodded sagely in agreement. 'Cases for which surgery can safely be delayed are often conveyed to Inverness or Edinburgh for treatment.'

'I spent several months in the accident wing of the Edinburgh Royal,' Morag responded, 'receiving serious injury cases on a day-to-day basis. In addition, I grew up on the west coast, where my father's practice covered a very large area of hill country. He dealt with accidents to walkers climbers and sailors, as well as tending the ordinary people of the parish, many of whom were quarry workers and fishermen. From the age of ten I accompanied him on his rounds, and in later years acted as his apprentice when I was on holiday from school.'

This appeared to satisfy all but Maynard himself.

'You have all had an opportunity to read these letters of recommendation, lady and gentlemen.' The Chairman glanced at his colleagues. 'Are there any further questions for Miss Beaton?'

Maynard, who detected that the battle to see off this interloper was by no means won, replied icily, 'We are told that Miss Beaton possesses all the necessary qualifications but we have yet to see proof of this. Do you have your documents with you, madam?'

Morag fumbled with her bag for a few moments before withdrawing a sheaf of papers. Fraser, leaning forward to take them from her, noted with satisfaction that Maynard had not insisted upon seeing the previous candidate's papers. He was clearly clutching at straws now.

He glanced through the documents himself, finding there everything that her letter of application had listed. Without comment he passed them to Maynard, who shuffled through them and could not fail to be impressed by the level of attainment recorded. He would have passed them back immediately to Morag, had not the other members demanded an opportunity to examine them.

'Perhaps we may keep these for the time being, Dr Beaton?' Fraser suggested. 'If you would care to wait in Matron's office while we discuss your application, I think we will be able to give you an answer before you leave this afternoon.'

She was not quite sure how she reached the door. She was aware of the pleasant gentleman who had not spoken a word since closing the window, hurrying to open it for her, and hoped that she had expressed her thanks. Now, as she stood outside with her hand still on the knob, she felt herself trembling from head to foot.

'You look ghastly,' said the young anaesthetist. 'Was it really that bad?' He forced her to sit down and would have thrust her head between her knees had she not prevented him.

'I'm all right, really,' she assured him. 'It was just that the tension built up a bit . . . you know how it is.' She smiled reassuringly and he took his seat beside her.

'That other fellow was whisked off by the matron to see round the hospital,' he told her. 'I think they expect you to join up with them.'

'Oh, very well.' Morag was by now quite recovered. 'Did you see which direction they took?

'Well, lady and gentlemen, how shall we play this?' Fraser beamed upon his committee. He was highly delighted with the previous candidate, whose presence at the interview had been entirely at his own insistence. Maynard had been all for throwing Dr Beaton's letter of application into the waste-paper basket.

'We can discuss the post in surgery now, or we can wait until we have seen the anaesthetists and then make decisions on both appointments.'

'As there is nothing to discuss, we may as well make the appointment at once, and send Mr Anstruther upon his way rejoicing.' Maynard sat back, lacing his slender fingers on the table before him, anxious to be done with the business. If they could only get a move on there might yet be time for a round of golf on the town's nine-hole course before it was dark.

'Now, just a moment . . .' Fraser began to protest, but the surgeon interrupted him.

'Oh, come on, Graham,' he chided, 'don't be a bad loser. You've interviewed your little girl . . . given her a bit of a hearing as it were . . . and you've shown willing with regard to the appointment of females to the staff. What more do you want? Why, we can even give it to the Press if you want: progressive Hospital Board includes woman candidate on short list for surgeon's post. Or something of the kind. That should satisfy your objective.'

'I don't know what you are implying,' Fraser protested. 'I found Dr Beaton to be entirely satisfactory in every respect. You cannot deny that her qualifications are quite outstanding for one of her years. On paper hers is a far better application than any we are likely to attract from male candidates . . . as we have already discovered.'

'On paper.' Maynard brushed the argument aside with a dismissive shrug of his shoulders. 'It takes a man to deal with the kind of work we have here.'

There was a feeble 'Hear, hear' from further along the table, and Sidney Maynard beamed upon Miss McKinnley. As she leaned forward to acknowledge his approval, the amber beads crashed against the table's edge. Fraser, looking up at the noise, thought she wished to speak and invited her comment.

'Oh . . . I . . . only wanted to say . . .' she sought for words, 'that I agree with every word of dear Mr Maynard's. I am sure that most of the ladies of my acquaintance would prefer a male doctor.' She simpered in girlish fashion which hardly befitted a woman nearer to sixty than sixteen! Not for the first time, Graham Fraser wondered how it was that Georgina McKinnley, owner of the Inverlinnhe Temperance Hotel, had managed to find a place on the committee.

15

'Ahem.' A wiry little individual who had remained silent throughout the proceedings now tapped his pencil on the blotting pad before him to command attention.

'Mr Treasurer?' Fraser was thankful to invite this intervention.

'I would draw the attention of the committee to the question of the salary to be paid to the appointee. Mr Anstruther is a man in his forties, with a wife and family to support. He is going to demand a salary appropriate to his age and experience. Dr Beaton, on the other hand, is seeking her first appointment and, I suspect, is more interested in gaining employment than in the recompense she is likely to receive for her work.'

Having completed his observation, the Treasurer removed his spectacles and polished them busily. The Manager of the Inverlinnhe branch of the Royal Bank of Scotland was a shrewd person, as his profession demanded. His business was to assess the integrity of his clients and he prided himself on being able to spot an imposter at a hundred yards! He had not been at all impressed by the pompous Mr Anstruther. He thought that the girl had a good, honest face and felt he would be happy to have himself or his wife treated by such a person. He knew, however, that the argument about the salary would weigh heavily in her favour and was willing to let his recommendation rest there.

Graham Fraser, anxious for any support for his female candidate, was quick to take up the point.

'What the Treasurer says makes a great deal of sense,' he insisted. 'We can offer Dr Beaton a contract on far more favourable terms to ourselves than a man such as Anstruther is likely to accept.'

There was a general nodding of heads at this point and Sidney Maynard was quick in his attempt to reverse their opinion.

'Oh, is that what it comes down to?' he demanded, angrily. 'Which surgeon will be the cheapest? I hadn't understood. I thought we were here to appoint the best house surgeon for our hospital . . .' He made an elaborate attempt to rise from his chair, suggesting he was about to quit the meeting in disgust. Fraser, however, motioned him to return to his seat.

'Come now,' he said, smoothly, 'there is no need for rancour.

Let us try to settle this matter amicably.' Then, as though it were an afterthought, he added, 'I had anticipated that once the appointments were made this afternoon, we might find time to discuss the next stage in the upgrading of the operating facilities in the surgical wing . . . since we are all met together so conveniently.'

He smiled benignly at Maynard, who knew he was defeated. There was no way in which he would get the improvements he wanted without the full support of the Chairman. If, on the other hand, the committee approved the plans, they could be put into motion immediately after Christmas.

'Mr McRae, you have had nothing to say upon the appointment of our new surgeon?' The attentions paid to Morag Beaton by the gentleman at the far end of the table had not escaped the Chairman's notice. He could do with just one more word in the girl's favour before he moved to the vote. He was not disappointed.

'Thank you, Mr Chairman,' McRae began. 'I have listened to Mr Maynard's argument this afternoon with despair. He has put forward nothing to commend the male candidate to you, other than his gender, yet he dismisses the undoubted talents of Dr Beaton because she is a woman. Mr Maynard tells us that surgery is an unsuitable occupation for a female doctor. Let me tell you that there are hundreds of ex-servicemen who are only alive today because of the ministrations upon the battlefield of the doctors of the Scottish Women's Hospitals. As one who came into their hands at the hospital at Royaumont, I can assure you that no wound was too horrible, no case so hopeless, that these women flinched from their duty. I am appalled to find that in 1931, little more than twelve years on, their efforts are so disregarded. I hope – nay, I insist – that this committee considers this doctor's application upon its merits, having no regard whatsoever to the fact that she is a woman!'

In the silence which followed McRae's outburst, more than one of the men seated at the table had the grace to hang his head in shame. Quickly grasping the initiative, Graham Fraser called for the vote. Maynard stuck to his guns, as did his simpering acolyte.

Of the rest, only one other voted against Morag. This was a grey-haired, ancient gentleman who, having dozed throughout the discussion, was startled out of his slumber by Fraser's call for 'those against'.

Morag had caught up with Anstruther as he was inspecting the hospital in company with the matron. They had passed through rooms where the patients lay neatly in their beds, lined up with a precision reminiscent of the days when Miss Nightingale herself, using a theodolite and a yard measure, was said to have laid out her wards. They had visited the dispensary and the operating theatre, where the startlingly good order of the place rather suggested staff with a lot of time on their hands. This did not have the appearance of an efficient, constantly used operating theatre of the kind Morag had become accustomed to during her training in the city. She felt she might be fearful of moving an instrument here, lest she put it back in the wrong place!

Anstruther beamed as he regarded the premises. 'Splendid, splendid,' he crooned, rubbing his hands together with pleasure. 'I can see that we shall be able to perform very well in these circumstances!'

Matron moved about the operating room, pointing out certain prized pieces of equipment, seemingly unaware that many of them were twenty-five years out of date. Things had moved on since the hospital was opened by Queen Alexandra in 1904.

Morag found the matron's devotion to some of these obsolete pieces more excusable than Anstruther's apparent indifference to them. Could it be that he did not realise that no one nowadays used a guillotine for amputations, because the instrument left bone protruding from the stump and the proper fitting of a modern prosthesis was made almost impossible? The guillotine method had been useful in the days when amputations were performed without anaesthetics, but today the surgeon could take his time and carry out a decent job. As for the administration of anaesthetics . . . surely a Clover's original inhaler had gone out of use during the war?

'Of course,' Matron was saying, in answer to some query from

Anstruther, 'I like to ensure that my gentlemen have everything to hand that they can want. The Theatre Sister, Miss Dunwoodie, keeps a very close eye on the supplies and I do not believe you will have any cause to complain.'

No doubt in *her* mind who is going to get the job, thought Morag.

'For how many days a week is the theatre in use . . . on average?' she now enquired, giving the woman some reason to acknowledge her existence, at least.

'Wednesday is general ops day,' came the rather dismissive reply. Turning to Anstruther, Matron elaborated: 'The patients are admitted on Tuesdays and prepared for surgery overnight. Of course, a surgeon may be called upon to operate at any time in an emergency . . . our peak period for such work is between January and April according to the length of time the snow remains for skiing on the hills. There is a growing secondary peak for accident admissions, I might add . . . so many people are taking up hill walking these days with little idea of the danger they can encounter. All I say to them is, don't get yourself into difficulties on a Thursday . . . that's Mr Maynard's day for the golf course.' Her laugh was a high-pitched titter which ended in a groan like that of a dying klaxon. It was just as well, thought Morag, noticing the lines about the woman's mouth, that such demonstrations of levity were probably few and far between.

'We have seen the most important areas of the hospital,' Matron went on. 'Perhaps you would care to take a cup of tea in my room?' She cast a glance in Morag's direction as she spoke, feeling obliged, no doubt, to include the second candidate in her invitation. Somewhat reluctantly, Morag trailed behind the pair, wishing that the matter of the appointment would be settled and she could be on her way. Not really concentrating on where Matron and Anstruther were headed, she lost sight of them and, rounding a corner, walked straight into Magnus Glendenning as he emerged from a side ward.

'Hallo again,' he cried, obviously delighted to see her. 'How did it go?'

'I'm still waiting to hear,' she told him, 'but it seems both Matron and Mr Maynard have already made up their minds.' She grinned, trying hard not to show her disappointment.

'I could have told you that Maynard would be pretty difficult to convince,' he said. 'But I didn't want to put you off right at the start.'

'His attitude is pretty well par for the course,' she replied resignedly. 'Mr Fraser, and a number of other members of the committee, seemed rather more inclined to consider my application . . . anyway, it looks as if we shall know at any minute.'

She had caught sight of the pleasant gentleman from the committee – was it McKay – or Mallory? He was approaching purposefully.

'Ah, there you are, Dr Beaton, we're ready for you now.' Recognising Glendenning, he paused to shake the reporter's hand.

'I enjoyed your piece in the *Gazette* last week,' he commented. 'What you say is quite right. If we want people to use the town as a tourist centre, we must make visitors feel welcome, not treat them as an interference to our comfortable way of life!'

He had placed his hand under Morag's elbow and was steering her towards the boardroom as he spoke. She glanced back at Magnus, thinking she would not see him again.

'Thank you so much, Mr Glendenning,' she called.

'Always happy to be of service, ma'am,' was his reply.

Outside the boardroom she found the younger of the two anaesthetists, still waiting.

'Have they not seen you yet?' she asked concerned that he had been kept waiting so long. 'Oh, yes,' he replied, eagerly. 'Actually they have sent the other fellow away and asked me to remain behind, so I'm rather hopeful . . .'

'Come along, Dr Beaton.' McRae held open the door, allowing her to slip inside in front of him.

'Ah, Dr Beaton,' Fraser welcomed her in friendly fashion. 'Do take a seat.'

She perched on the edge of the chair upon which she had sat

previously, awaiting the inevitable string of explanations as to why they could not appoint her . . .

'Well, now, Dr Beaton,' Fraser leaned forward to hand back her little sheaf of qualifications, 'we are all so impressed with these, and the recommendation of your sponsors, that we have decided to offer you the appointment of assistant surgeon. Now, what do you say to that?'

Tongue-tied for a moment, she tried to register his exact words . . . was he really offering her the job?

'Of course, we are mindful of your youth and inexperience,' Fraser continued, 'and for this reason feel obliged to offer an initial salary of one hundred and fifty pounds per annum, together with all your living expenses, laundry charges and so on. After a probationary period of one year, we will be prepared to review your stipend.'

Morag was no fool. It was a derisory amount, but who was she to quibble . . . it was a job, wasn't it? She was going to be a fully fledged surgeon.

'Well Doctor,' Maynard demanded, cuttingly, 'do you want this post or don't you?'

'Yes,' she replied, resolutely. Then, addressing Fraser in particular, she added, 'And thank you for the trust which you have placed in my capabilities.'

'We shall look forward to seeing you on the second of January.' He shook her by the hand and McRae opened the door, also shaking her hand as he did so.

'Well done.' He grinned. 'We don't always make such sensible decisions.'

# Chapter 2

❧

The bright light brought her instantly awake.

'The ambulance has arrived, Doctor . . . there are two casualties.'

'What kind of injuries?' demanded Morag, swinging her legs over the edge of the couch and pulling on her overall, which was crumpled and soiled from the previous day's activities. When on night duty she tended to snatch her sleep fully clothed and ready for instant action.

'One fractured lower leg, one head injury . . . according to the first-aider who went with the mountain rescue team.'

'Very well, you'd better alert the theatre staff, Sister . . . the fracture will have to be dealt with right away. Do we know at what time the accident happened?'

'About eighteen hours ago,' the nurse called back over her shoulder as she hurried off to wake the theatre sister.

Morag detected a tremor of anticipation in the night sister's tone. What was it about these people? she wondered. Did they think her incapable of acting on her own, was that it?

Since the day in early-January when she had taken up her post as house surgeon, they had seemed to be forever hovering expectantly over her, waiting for her to make her first mistake.

In a sense she could forgive Sidney Maynard his doubts. Any consultant with the reputation of the hospital to maintain, must surely view each new member of his team with some scepticism until whoever it was had proved his worth. He made no secret of his feelings about women surgeons in general but, to give him his due, had been civil enough across the operating table and seemed, while concentrating upon an operation in progress,

23

to disregard her sex and rely more and more heavily upon her support. He had even, on one occasion, complimented her on her suturing, although he did qualify this with a curt: 'Only to be expected in a woman, I suppose!'

No, it was the attitude of the nursing staff which she found so objectionable. Both Christine Kemp, the matron, and the theatre sister, Violet Dunwoodie, seemed to hold some sort of a grudge against her. Was it because she had, in their opinion, stepped beyond the bounds of a woman's natural role in the hospital? Did they perhaps resent another woman's having superior knowledge and responsibility, by reason of her education and training? Morag suspected that this was not the whole reason for their dislike, though. What then? Could it be that these dried up spinsters received a sort of sexual gratification from their purely clinical contact with male physicians and surgeons, and resented being deprived of an additional man upon whom to lavish their devotion?

She shivered, and pulled on a woollen cardigan over her white coat. She would be stripping down for theatre in a short while . . . best get warmed up properly first.

The staff quarters were in the old country house which had formed the basis of the original hospital. Rooms which once had been well-proportioned, with high ceilings and huge windows, were now subdivided to provide a series of nearly rectangular boxes, each having some peculiar kink or odd alcove in the walls as a result of unimaginative partitioning of the space. The windows were ill-fitting and although they commanded an excellent view either across the loch to the front, or along the glen to the rear, each room had only a part of a window and it was impossible to open one without first obtaining the agreement of the next-door occupant!

Another unfortunate result of this arrangement was that the small gap between the end of each partition and the window was sufficient to allow all sound to penetrate from one living space to the next, so that the rooms afforded no more privacy than the pupils' cubicles in a boarding school!

As it happened, Morag had not wanted to open any windows

since her arrival. The snow had lain thick on the ground for the first two weeks of January and the outside temperatures had remained below zero until well into February, conditions which delighted the skiers and mountain climbers, but spelt trouble for the staff of the West Highland Hospital. Not only was the number of casualties with which they had to deal vastly increased, but water supplies were interrupted by frozen and burst pipes, while deliveries of coal for the boilers had been delayed by stormy seas.

Obviously the welfare of the patients came first. Junior hospital doctors and probationary nurses had to make do with piling coats and spare blankets on their beds, or spending as much time as possible in the wards in order to keep warm.

Morag quickened her step as she pushed open a swing door and crossed, by way of a covered walk, to the hospital building. The still frosty air was thick with fumes from the incinerator; she found herself choking and coughing as she pushed open a heavy door which gave access to the main corridor.

The building, a model design for its period, was built in the shape of a letter E, in which the main wards occupied the long side and faced over the town and Loch Linnhe, while the top and bottom arms contained the kitchens, staff dining-room and laundry to the south and the accident admissions unit, theatre and recovery room, to the north. The central arm of the E was made up of the old house and its covered access.

In the small courtyard formed between the theatre block and the walkway, Morag noticed the town's single motorised ambulance drawn up before the emergency entrance. A number of people were grouped around the open door to the admissions area. It was bad enough to have to turn out in the middle of the night to attend to the injured . . . she wished she did not have to encounter, in addition, anxious relatives and members of the Press.

Morag hurried past the assembly and pushed open the door into the theatre ante-room. She was not, however, so quick that she could ignore the buzz of interest from those who recognised the new lady doctor and noisily pointed her out to others less well informed.

The fracture case was laid on a trolley in the ante-room, with Eddie Strachan, the new anaesthetist, already in attendance. He looked up as Morag entered and smiled a welcome.

They had been appointed on the same day, and had shared the usual tribulations of the uninitiated during their early weeks at the West Highland Hospital. Perhaps because of this, a camaraderie had developed between them which provided the one ray of brightness in Morag's otherwise dismal world. She was a friendly girl, who had always enjoyed the companionship of a wide circle of her contemporaries. Under the eagle eye of the senior nursing staff, however, even those younger women in the hospital who might have offered her the hand of friendship, were loath to be seen fraternising with the female surgeon. Had it not been for Eddie's support, she felt she might have given up after that first awful month in the job!

'What have we here?' she asked, reaching for scissors to cut away the strapping which was wound around a make-shift splint.

She looked into a pair of anxious brown eyes and smiled disarmingly at the mountaineer. From his grey pallor and the two or three days' growth of beard, he might be mistaken for a man of thirty years or more, but when she had examined him more closely and heard him speak, she realised that he was, in fact, barely out of his teens.

She uncovered the wounded leg, exposing a compound fracture of both tibia and fibula, just above the ankle. It was not the worst break she had ever seen, but it was the most complex she had had to deal with on her own.

The broken ends of both bones had penetrated the skin and in the eighteen hours since the accident, suppuration had begun to set in. The first aid rendered had immobilised the leg satisfactorily, but little effort had been made to cleanse the wound, and there was a clear danger that gangrene might develop.

'It's at times like this that I wish we had that X-ray machine they keep promising us,' she observed, examining minutely the angle of the broken bones, trying to assess the degree of reduction which would be required. To do a good job, she would have to

26

make a fair-sized incision on either side of the break. This would of course render even more tissues open to infection, but it was the only way to ensure a perfect resetting.

'Look,' she said to Eddie, 'you carry on with your preparations . . . it will be quite a long operation, he will need to be under for an hour at least.'

He nodded, looking up from his notes. He was busy calculating the strength of anaesthetic required, according to the bodyweight of the patient.

'Before I scrub-up,' Morag continued, 'I'll take a look at the head injury. He's probably only concussed. If it were anything more serious, after eighteen hours he would almost certainly be dead.'

She swept back out into the corridor, ignoring the throng of people, full of anxious enquiries, and made her way to the first of a row of cubicles off the waiting area. Here she found the night sister, taking the blood pressure of someone similar in age to the lad Morag had just seen. Despite the grime from the recent ordeal on the mountain, Morag could see that the second patient was in fact a singularly beautiful girl.

When she saw Morag, the patient's face became wreathed in smiles.

'Oh, hallo, Doctor,' she said, trying to raise herself on her elbow but sinking back on to the pillow in her weakness. 'I hoped I might see you. My father has told me so much about you . . .'

Morag, nonplussed, looked inquiringly at the nurse.

'Miss McRae's father is a member of the Hospital Board, Dr Beaton,' the nurse volunteered, 'and a prominent landowner in the district,' she added, in respectfully hushed tones.

McRae . . . of course. Her friend on the interviewing panel. Now that she examined the girl more closely, she could see in those dark good looks the resemblance between father and daughter.

'Well now, Miss McRae,' Morag addressed her patient, 'I understand you had a crack on the head. Whereabouts, exactly?'

The girl placed a hand tenderly on the back of her skull and

Morag, parting the thick black hair carefully, examined the area for damage. There was undoubtedly some severe bruising, but the skin showed no sign of laceration and there was nothing to indicate that Miss McRae would suffer further consequences from the blow.

'You are going to have a headache for a few hours, but there's no sign of any major damage,' Morag observed, comfortingly. 'Do you feel well enough to tell me what happened?' she asked, concerned now for the young man, who was in no condition to describe their accident in detail.

'I'm afraid it was all my fault,' said Miss McRae, suitably contrite. 'I argued with Richard about which way we should take around a bluff, and caused him to lose concentration for a few seconds. He slipped and fell amongst a scree of boulders. We were roped together so I took the strain, hoping to lessen his impact on landing, but the rope broke and I fell backwards and cracked my head on the rocks. I must have been unconscious for a while, because when I came round I could hear Richard calling me from below. Once I had stopped seeing double, I struggled down the slope to where he was lying. It was then that I realised his leg was broken. There was nothing for it but to dress ourselves in all our spare clothing, rustle up a warm drink on our little spirit stove and pray that someone would come to find us.'

Recalling the events of the past hours seemed suddenly to bring home to the girl the extreme danger from which she and her companion had been rescued. She began to shake, uncontrollably.

'I'll give you some laudanum to help you sleep.' Morag said, placing a thick blanket around the girl's shoulders. 'Sister will see that you are tucked up comfortably. What you need more than anything is a long rest. After that, I think you should be well enough to go home.'

As she wrote out the necessary prescription for the sister, Morag said quietly, 'Keep her warm and let her stay here undisturbed until morning. If she should vomit, or show any sign of distress, let me know immediately. I must go now and sort out this fractured leg.'

The night staff had been busy in her absence. By the time Morag had completed her personal preparations, the male patient had been stripped and washed and was already under the anaesthetic. The sweet smell of ether hung on the air. She looked inquiringly at Eddie Strachan.

'He's a powerfully built young man,' the anaesthetist explained. 'I thought it best to use a mixture of ether and nitrous oxide initially. I'll switch to open ether once you get started.'

She nodded her agreement, bending over the injured leg and examining it carefully. Now that the wound was properly exposed, and the surrounding area cleaned with carbolic solution, it was possible to see more clearly the degree of displacement of the bones and the extent of the inflammation which had set in.

She set about cleaning the wound itself, using a stronger solution of the carbolic now that the patient was asleep and unaware of her activities. When she was satisfied that she had removed any possible source of further infection, she took a sharp scalpel and, feeling along the length of the fractured fibula, made her incision along the line of each of the displaced sections of bone, extending the open wound by several inches on either side. With the damage properly exposed she could see that the break to the tibia was clean, which meant that a single extension to reposition the shattered fibula should set both bones satisfactorily if she used a metal plate to stabilise the join. She gave her instructions to the theatre sister who, not trusting her assistants to select the right-sized plate for sterilisation, bustled away to find the necessary equipment.

Morag worked steadily for a few moments, clamping off damaged blood vessels and applying retractors to hold aside larger vessels and nerves which might become damaged in the process of setting the bones.

'There are a few fragments of loose bone here,' she said to the theatre staff indicating the broken ends of the fibula. 'I shall try to reposition them, but it will need two of you to pull the ends apart and hold them in position until I can get the fragments set in place.'

As she spoke she lifted three small pieces of bone away from the area, and laid each carefully in a kidney dish, in the order in which she would use them. They were thin, sharply pointed slivers, which must be laid back in exactly the correct position if they were to regrow *in situ*, without leaving any unsightly protrusions. Since Sister Dunwoodie had not reappeared, she would have to proceed with the aid of the remaining nurses. She indicated where each of them should take her grip, one on the foot and heel, the other just below the knee. 'When I say pull . . . pull the bones apart with a steady tension,' Morag instructed. 'Remember, I will need several minutes to do my part, so be sure you are standing in as comfortable a position as possible. Once we begin, you must not relax your grip until I say so.'

The senior of the two nurses had witnessed innumerable settings of broken limbs. She doubted Morag's ability to make the kind of job of it that Mr Maynard would have done. What a pity for the young man that he had been brought in in the middle of the night!

Mary Neal was serving her first spell of duty in theatre, however, and this was her only experience to date of a serious fracture. She looked very worried when Morag, satisfied that she had everything in position for this tricky part of the operation, asked if they were ready.

Both nodded, the more experienced woman in somewhat exasperated fashion. She wondered what the surgeon was making such a fuss about.

Although Mary had indicated she was ready, Morag, sensing her disquiet, smiled encouragement at her. 'Just a few minutes,' she urged, 'but you must hold very still while I work.'

The nurses lent all their strength to the broken limb and the severed ends of both bones moved apart just enough for Morag to ease the clean edges of the broken tibia into position, so that they would come together neatly when the stress was removed. Now she worked rapidly to reposition the badly displaced fibula, bringing together the shattered ends and laying each of the loose fragments in place, as one would fit the pieces in a jigsaw puzzle.

She looked up to see the strain in the faces of the two nurses.

'Just a few moments longer,' she breathed, reaching for a spool of fine silver wire from which she cut short lengths which she used to splice the sharp fragments into position.

'Now, very slowly, relax your hold.' As the edges of the bones slipped into place, Morag watched anxiously to see that the joins were as perfect as possible. There was a sigh of relief from all round the table as Morag straightened up, finally satisfied. She had been unaware that she had been holding her breath while she worked. She must remember to relax a little more next time . . .

'I think this should do the job, Doctor,' declared Sister Dunwoodie, importantly, reappearing just as the most crucial part of the operation had been completed. When she saw how far the team had progressed in her absence she looked at first disconcerted, and then angry.

Oh, well, she told herself, after the first flush of annoyance had passed. At least I shall have a good excuse if things go wrong with this case. She rather hoped they might.

To give her her due, Sister Dunwoodie had indeed selected exactly the right silver plate for the job. In a matter of minutes, Morag had the holes drilled and the plate screwed into place with two screws into each of the free ends of the tibia. Now she was ready to close the wound. Once it was carefully dressed, she signalled to Strachan to turn off the electric fan used to waft carbolic-laden air throughout the theatre.

'When he is in the ward,' Morag said to Sister Dunwoodie, 'I'll come along and set up the traction. The wound could even now develop gangrene. It will have to be dressed twice a day until we are quite sure . . .'

Violet Dunwoodie moved her head curtly, in what Morag took to be a nod of agreement. The theatre sister was obviously annoyed that the surgeon had continued with the operation in her absence. Morag wondered why the woman made working together as a team so very difficult. What on earth was she doing absenting herself from the theatre for so long, anyway? She resisted the urge to make any further enquiry, feeling that enough antagonism had been generated between them for one session.

The nurses moved the patient on to a trolley and wheeled him away. Eddie Strachan was busy clearing his station and replenishing his supplies of chemicals and equipment, in readiness for the next emergency.

'That was the neatest piece of bone surgery I've seen since I've been here,' he observed, grinning, as Morag removed her white surgical mask and withdrew the skull-hugging cap which she wore in the theatre. As she did so her unsecured locks of burnished copper fell to her shoulders.

Eddie had never seen her like this before. She was a very striking woman even if, as those of his colleagues who considered themselves experts on the subject frequently insisted, she was too tall. But her grey eyes were deeply sunken now, and dark shadows under them indicated that she had had very little sleep in the past twenty-four hours.

'It's only five-thirty,' he observed. 'If we don't take too long up in the ward, there may be time for you to get a couple of hours shut-eye before breakfast.' He held open the door and allowed her to pass before him into the corridor.

They were immediately engulfed by the sea of people waiting for news of the victims of the accident. Recognising among them her reporter friend from the *West Highland Gazette*, Morag demanded to know what they were all doing there.

'Don't you know who your patient is?' Magnus Glendenning asked, incredulously.

'Other than that his name is Richard, no,' she replied, too weary to be very interested.

He mentioned the name of a young man, someone whom she vaguely remembered as being a cousin of the King.

'Now do you see why his accident has caused such a stir?'

'Yes, I see.' Morag swept a hand wearily over her forehead and turned to the company in general.

'Well, all I can tell you is that the young man has sustained multiple fractures of the right lower leg, he has undergone surgery and has just been taken up to the ward where I am needed at this moment.' She looked around at those who were busily scribbling in their notebooks, glancing up just in time to be caught by the flashlight of a camera.

'Oh, please, I don't think that the authorities would approve of photographs being taken within the hospital building,' she protested. To Magnus she said, 'If the photographer is anything to do with you, please see he doesn't use that. I have enough difficulties already without being labelled a publicity seeker!'

Glendenning, realising that Morag was near the end of her tether, turned to his colleagues and lifted a hand for silence. 'Dr Beaton has told you everything there is to tell for the moment. I think she should be allowed to carry on with her duties, don't you?'

The crowd began to disperse, so that when Eddie Strachan reappeared at last, with a reluctant night porter in tow, intending to remove the reporters, the job was all but done.

'Thank you.' Morag smiled gratefully at Magnus. 'I suppose we shall be getting a lot of this in the next few days. Just ask them to approach the hospital authorities for bulletins next time,' she begged, stifling a yawn.

Magnus had thought often of the striking young woman whom he had met in the café on that cold December day. He was not prepared to let her out of his sights again without making some effort to build on that casual acquaintance.

'Look, I know you are tired now, but I would like to see you again sometime,' he told her. 'Do you have an afternoon off?'

'Not often, and usually they come without warning,' she replied, ruefully. 'If I ever get more than a day to spare, I shall have to go to see my parents. I haven't been home since I started working here.'

He seemed disappointed. Rummaging in his pocket, he brought out a dog-eared card bearing his name and the telephone number of the *Gazette*. 'Give me a call if ever you are at a loose end,' he suggested. Adding diffidently, 'Please.'

She slipped the piece of card into her overall pocket.

'You will have to excuse us,' Eddie interrupted. 'Our patient is waiting.'

Morag smiled wearily at Magnus and reminded him about the

photograph. 'It really will do me no good at all if they print that,' she insisted.

'I'll do what I can,' he replied, knowing full well that the story would break in the next day's papers, and all material, relevant or otherwise, was sure to be incorporated.

Morag arrived late on the wards the following morning. The limited supply of hot water in the residents' bathroom had been drawn off already, and the bath she had taken had been almost cold. The chilly dowsing had served to wake her up, at least.

The frosty expressions on the faces of the nursing staff did nothing to warm her as she entered the male surgical ward, intent upon visiting her important patient of the previous night.

A quick glance around the ward showed her that he was not present. Turning to the staff nurse, who had followed her in, she demanded, 'Where is my tib-fib fracture?'

'Mr Maynard has had him transferred to a private ward,' was the starchy reply. 'He seemed surprised you had not ordered it in the first place.'

Ignoring the hint of criticism, Morag swept out into the corridor and made her way to the small group of single rooms reserved for those patients who could afford to pay for the privilege of occupying them. In moving the young man, they could have interfered with the traction apparatus which she had assembled so carefully the night before. She was anxious to assure herself that no damage had been done.

Beside the door to the first of the private rooms she found a uniformed policeman seated on an upright chair. This must be where her patient had been taken. As she approached, the policeman rose to his feet and barred her way.

'I'm sorry, miss, only authorised personnel are permitted to enter.'

'What on earth are you talking about, Constable?' Morag demanded. 'I'm Dr Beaton, the surgeon who performed the operation on the patient . . . now kindly allow me to pass.'

'My instructions are to allow entry only to those people who have been named by Mr Sidney Maynard.' He scanned a piece of paper in his hand and not finding any Dr Beaton on the list, suggested, 'Perhaps you should speak to the gentleman yourself, miss?'

'I most certainly shall,' she responded angrily, and turning on her heel, she made for the chief consultant's office.

Sidney Maynard was juggling with both the telephones on his desk when she burst into his room. His secretary, Miss McArdle, half rose to prevent her, but seeing that a storm was brewing, wisely kept her head down and got on with her typing.

Into one mouthpiece Maynard fired a terse rebuttal. 'No, I am sorry, the hospital has nothing further to say about Mr Ashley Keynes's condition. A bulletin will be issued at noon, after my colleagues and I have made our rounds.' He slammed down the telephone and spoke rather more politely into the other handset. 'I am so sorry, my Lord, the Press are most insistent, and if one does not provide them with answers they simply make something up. Yes, my Lord, I can assure you that your son is progressing satisfactorily, and is receiving every care that the hospital is capable of providing. I'm sure that he will be fit enough to be transferred to the hands of his own doctors in a day or two . . . not at all, my Lord, it is a pleasure to have been of service.'

Maynard was smiling broadly as he replaced the receiver, but when he looked up and saw Morag standing glowering at him, it was his turn to be angry.

'Dr Beaton, I do not know what form of etiquette existed in your previous employment, but here at the West Highland it is usual for junior members of staff to wait to be invited into my inner sanctum.'

'I demand to know why I am prevented from seeing my patient . . . *my patient* . . . by a policeman waving a piece of paper from which my name has been excluded,' she responded, bitterly.

'Frankly, Doctor, I would have thought that the reason was obvious,' Maynard responded icily. He indicated the pile of newspapers spread on the desk before him as he continued, 'We do not seek sensational publicity for the work we do here, young woman. Headlines of this kind do not depict a side of the hospital which the board would wish to present to the public.'

He pushed forward the most lurid of the journals whose headline read. **WELL DONE, GIRLIE! Woman Surgeon Treats king's cousin – Marquis of Nairn's son rescued in climbing incident**. Below the banner was a blown-up photograph of a bleary-eyed Morag still wearing her theatre gown . . . just about the most unattractive image of herself that she had ever seen.

'I was not responsible for the presence of the Press in the hospital last night, Mr Maynard. I would suggest it was the duty of the night porter to see these people off the premises, not myself. I was caught unawares on leaving the theatre to follow my patient up to the ward.' Her tone had softened now that she had seen what the newsmen had done. Maynard was fully justified in his annoyance, but must understand that the offence was not of her making.

'That is as maybe,' he responded, his manner remaining cold and aloof.' You gave out information; something my staff are strictly forbidden to do in such circumstances, and you posed for a photograph . . . such as it is.'

'The photograph was taken without my consent,' she protested. 'In fact, I demanded and received an assurance that it would not be used. As for giving out information, there was so much wild speculation going on that it was clear, as I overhead you say yourself not a moment ago, that if the reporters had no real information they would make it up for themselves. I thought it best to give a brief description of the injury, just to get rid of them.'

'Nevertheless, what you said has filled two columns of the *Glasgow Chronicle*, in addition to covering the front page of this rag.' He pointed savagely at the lurid headline and the photograph that she had already seen. Underneath it she caught sight of the *West Highland Gazette*. Her own photograph, she noted, had not been used, but she was interested to see a picture of her patient with his arm around Miss McRae, and that she was described as the young man's fiancée.

'I fail to see why this situation, which is not of my making, should necessitate my exclusion from Mr Ashley Keynes's case. It was I who performed the surgery, after all.'

'That is of course a further matter of contention, Miss Beaton. You should know that for patients of this calibre I am always on call. Why was I not notified when Mr Ashley Keynes was admitted?'

Now she understood the reason for his anger. Important patients were his prerogative, especially since he could demand an outrageous fee for his services.

'At the time, Mr Maynard, I was concerned only for the welfare of my patients. Having recorded their names on admission, I gave their identity no further thought until the surgery was completed and both of them had been attended to. I would point out that the casualties were admitted at four o'clock in the morning and that I had a skeleton staff of nurses at my disposal to attend to two patients, both with considerable trauma.'

'As to the staff at your disposal,' he took up her argument, 'I understand from Sister Dunwoodie that you quite deliberately carried on with the operation in her absence, relying on the help of only a nurse and a probationer.'

'Sister insisted upon leaving the theatre to fetch the plate I required as she was unwilling to send one of the nurses. I was not in a position to wait about while she did whatever it was she found to do . . .' Morag wondered if Dunwoodie had been talking to the reporters and had known all along who their patient was. Perhaps that was why Maynard was now, apparently, so well-informed . . . it would explain why the theatre sister was so long away from her post, too. She would have had to scrub-up all over again before returning.

'Well,' Maynard concluded, his manner somewhat less aggressive now that he had had his say,' perhaps we should go and inspect the damage. I hope I shall not have to reset the bones, Dr Beaton.' He left this threat hanging in the air as she followed him along the corridor towards the private wing.

Morag was convinced she had done her part properly, but could not guarantee that in moving the patient at such an early stage, adjustments would not be required to the traction.

Before they entered the patient's room, Maynard turned to her once more. 'Remember, Doctor, in future you leave the Press to me, and you make every effort to discover who your patient is when you admit him, even if it is the middle of the night!'

Observing hospital protocol, he stood aside as Matron advanced along the corridor with her train of nurses, anxious not to miss this encounter with aristocracy. She it was who was the first to sweep into the room, beaming.

'Ah, good morning, Mr Ashley Keynes,' Sidney Maynard said, taking the chart proffered by Matron. 'And how are we feeling this morning?'

'Fine, thank you, Doctor.' The patient, having winced at Sidney's over-hearty manner of address, added hastily, 'Thanks to this young lady.' Richard Ashley Keynes smiled up at Morag, who although attempting to make herself as inconspicuous as possible, was once again the focus of attention.

'I think we had better take a peek at the wound, Matron,' Maynard said, glaring in Morag's direction. 'Just to make sure . . . you understand?'

Morag held her breath while the bandages were removed. The flesh around the sutures was a healthy pink colour and although Maynard examined the leg from every angle he could find nothing out of place. He then examined minutely the structure she had put in position to apply traction and made a small alteration to the tension.

He patted Richard Ashley Keynes reassuringly on the shoulder. 'We'll have you knocking hell out of them on the rugby field again before you know it, sir.'

'In time for next season, do you think?' Richard asked anxiously.

'I can see no reason why not,' beamed Maynard, 'now that you are in my personal care.' He nodded curtly to Morag, and as he left she overheard a murmured exchange with the policeman.

She was not prevented again from entering the room of their distinguished patient, although Maynard made it very clear to everyone who was in charge of this very special case. When the time came for the Hon. Richard Ashley Keynes to leave the hospital in a wheelchair he was collected by his father, the Marquis of Nairn, in a specially adapted Rolls-Royce limousine.

This time it was Sidney Maynard and Matron Christine Kemp who appeared in all the newspapers, bidding him farewell.

The following morning, Morag was called over to the reception desk as she was passing.

'Chap in chauffeur's livery left these for you, Dr Beaton.' The elderly porter handed her a magnificent bouquet of red roses – a flower seldom seen in florists' shops in the Highlands in winter.

Mystified by such largesse, she read the label:

*From a grateful patient*

There was no doubt in the mind of the Hon. Richard Ashley Keynes just who had prevented his becoming a cripple for life.

# Chapter 3

The green and white charabanc came to a halt where the road made a steep incline, leading to the head of the pass. The passengers had been quiet, almost moribund, for much of the journey. All morning they had gazed zombie-like at the rain which streamed down the windows obscuring the view. Even when the rain eased, there had been little improvement in the outlook, for here in the mountains the fine mist was slow to lift from the lochs and glens, and the peaks above them were shrouded in dense cloud. For those who had come specifically to see the wild scenery of the north, the excursion had, so far, been a great disappointment.

The driver cut the engine. In the sudden silence which followed, the passengers' heads were raised in anticipation and a buzz of excited conversation ensued at this interruption to their boredom.

Although it was still impossible to see much of the road ahead, the sun was at last making a valiant attempt at breaking through the fog. The passengers at the rear of the vehicle were now able, by turning in their seats, to observe the whole panorama of the valley from which they had been ascending steadily for the past twenty minutes.

The driver rose to his feet and turned to address them.

'Yon road-up ahead,' he indicated over his shoulder, 'it's verra, verra steep,' he began, in thick Glaswegian tones. 'I shall have to ask one or two of the fit 'uns to get out and walk to the head o' the pass.'

They were slow to respond. He would need greater persuasive powers than this if he was to lighten his load sufficiently to get the coach up the steepest part of the incline.

'There's a fine view of the gorge further up,' he persevered. 'You'll nae see it near sae guid frae the coach.'

A young man who had come aboard in company with a rather frail-looking elderly gentleman was the first to volunteer. His companion rose to join him but the other dissuaded him.

'It's a long walk uphill, Uncle,' he said, 'I really think it will be too much for you.'

Reluctantly Gregor Campbell watched his nephew descend from the coach followed by the handsome young woman with red hair who appeared to be travelling alone. He settled back in his seat and allowed his eyes to close.

Free for the Easter weekend, Morag Beaton had debated with herself whether she had time to travel home to Eisdalsa and back with only two days' leave at her disposal, and had decided she would prefer to use the opportunity to see something of the local countryside and perhaps get in a little hill walking. The wet weather had made the latter idea less enticing and she had elected at the last moment to take this bus tour. After so long staring out, trying to get a glimpse of the view so tantalisingly obliterated by the mist, she relished the opportunity to stretch her legs.

Not to be outdone, the three youths who had been entertaining the whole coach for much of the journey with their amusing banter, also climbed down to the road. They had been living under canvas for a week and had chosen to come on the excursion in order to get out of the rain for a spell. Now, with the sun shining, they were only too pleased to escape from the dull atmosphere on board the charabanc.

Seeing the adults preparing to walk up the mountain, Malcolm and Jenny Pritchard demanded to be allowed to accompany them.

'Oh, I don't know, dears . . .' Their mother hesitated. Malcolm, nearly thirteen, was quite capable of walking the distance, but Jenny was only nine.

'It's all right,' Morag called out to the anxious woman, 'we'll see they come to no harm.'

'That's reet!' one of the lads called out in his broad Yorkshire accent. 'The doctor will take care of them!'

Although there had been very little interchange between the majority of the passengers, the group towards the rear of the coach had engaged in a certain amount of conversation. After sustained if good-humoured probing from the boys, Morag had revealed to them that she was a doctor from the hospital in Inverlinnhe. The young man travelling with his elderly companion had been persuaded to introduce himself as Adam Inglis, and had told them that he worked in the Borough Engineer's office.

As Jenny and her brother alighted on the road, they were followed by two more of the younger passengers, eight-year-old Ian and his twin sister, Molly.

Throughout the dreary journey, the two older children had entertained each other with various games, in which the twins too had quickly become involved. Now they insisted that they should be allowed to accompany their newfound friends.

With her load thus lightened, the charabanc crawled on up the steep incline. Very soon it overtook the walkers, who were given assurances from the driver that he would be waiting for them around the bend at the head of the pass.

Those on foot soon found that although the going was steep, the effort had been well worthwhile. They could see so much further from outside the coach, enjoying to the full the grandeur of the splendid scenery all about them.

The charabanc was now out of sight. The roar of its engine, tackling the higher slopes in bottom gear, had died away as the vehicle rounded the bend. The only sounds remaining were the natural noises of the mountains. The wind sighed and whistled around the boulders, and from the woodland in the valley below, the occasional drumming of a woodpecker was followed by a series of trills. Almost at the eye level of the walkers, a skylark hung above a peat bog which was some two hundred feet below where they stood on the road. Suddenly the bird ceased to utter its liquid chirrup and silently plummeted to earth. The children watched, spellbound.

'It's like being on top of the world,' breathed Jenny.

From every quarter there came the constant murmur of water rippling over rocky stream beds as it found its way downwards, between heather-strewn banks of brown peat.

It took the party some time to reach the head of the pass. When at last they rounded the bluff, there was no sign of their coach. The road at this point clung tightly to the sheer cliff, and from its outer edge, which was guarded only by a low dry-stone wall, there was another sheer drop into the gorge below. The little party gazed, awestruck, at the sight of so much water roaring through the narrow valley, foaming white and leaving a fine mist along the bed of the river. Every few hundred yards a waterfall tumbled down the mountain slopes to join it. The roar of falling water blotted out all other sounds.

'Come on.' Adam Inglis shouted. Grasping hold of Jenny to prevent her going too near the edge, he appealed to Morag to hurry the others along. 'We really should be moving on,' he insisted, 'the driver will be waiting.'

Morag was surprised to find that she did not resent the manner in which he had taken command of their situation. Used to fighting continuously to maintain her position in a man's world, she usually recoiled from men who presumed to tell her what to do. Adam Inglis, however, had an air of natural authority which however he wielded with a certain charm. She found herself responding in an uncharacteristically willing way to his request.

She would not have described him as handsome, exactly. He had a broad brow and the rather square features of the Nordic races. His hair, probably light coloured, was darkened by the liberal use of lotion. It was slicked down close to his head and parted centrally in the manner of the day. His eyelashes and brows were so lacking in colour that they merged with his deeply tanned skin. Had it not been for his deep brown, almost bovine eyes, his sharply pointed nose and the pleasant curve to his mouth he might have been described as quite plain.

His stocky build and impressively broad shoulders made him appear rather shorter than he was. She suspected him to be a man of enormous potential energy, one in whose company a woman could feel safe, whatever the circumstances.

'Come along, twins,' she called. 'Hurry up, Malcolm, we must be getting along.' She dared not hustle the older boys but they came along anyway, quickly catching up and overtaking Morag and her charges.

Adam led the party, urging them to hug the inside edge of the road until there was sufficient space for a verge on the outer edge. After a further half mile, this verge became wide enough for the parking of vehicles.

This surely must be the place where their driver had intended to wait, yet there was no sign of the charabanc . . .

Gregor Campbell, deserted by his nephew, had dozed off. His monotonous low-pitched snoring was punctuated by an occasional tuneful grunt, which made the Pritchards in the seat across the aisle smile at one another.

With their children having joined the walkers, it was a pleasant change to be on their own, even if it was for just a short while. Helen Pritchard snuggled into her husband's side and he placed an arm comfortably around her shoulders.

The droning of the engine changed pitch as the vehicle reached the head of the pass and made the turn, exposing to view a magnificent gorge, cut by the river deep into the ancient rocks of the north-west Highland plateau.

'What river is that?' John Pritchard asked his wife.

Helen traced the watercourse across the map which she held on her lap.

'It says, *Allt Easach*,' she told him.

Roused by the sound of their voices, Gregor Campbell opened one eye, glanced out at the scene and leaned across the gangway. 'It means the river of waterfalls,' he told them.

As the charabanc crept cautiously along the narrow track, allowing those passengers on the off-side of the bus an unimpeded view of the gorge, two of the smaller children, sitting up front beside the driver, called to their parents in the seat behind.

'Just look, Mummy . . . lovely waterfalls!'

Gregor Campbell and John Pritchard exchanged triumphant glances.

The delighted exclamations of other passengers were tinged with apprehension, however, and not a few of them were relieved when the ledge carrying the road widened sufficiently to allow for a grassy verge to separate it from the extreme edge of the gorge.

At this spot, on the inside of the bend, a wide stream fell some eighty feet from an overhang of rock into a deep pool. Here the water gathered, before passing beneath the track and plunging in a succession of waterfalls to join the foaming river, a hundred feet below.

The road had been built a century before, for the passage through the mountains of sheep and their drovers, men on horseback and the occasional farm cart. Little account had been taken over the years of changes in the nature of the traffic which it must carry.

The driver decided that this was a good place to pull over, and await the walkers.

He steered his heavy vehicle on to the soft green verge, easing forward until the entire length of the charabanc was clear of the road. As he did so, the child beside him leaned forward eagerly, nudging her sister, and pointing.

'Look!' she cried, more interested than alarmed.

The driver followed her pointing finger and saw, to his horror, that a great crack had appeared in the ground beneath the wheels of the bus.

There was no time for him to haul back.

As the soft ground crumbled before it, the heavy vehicle lurched forward and was launched into space.

For a few seconds the charabanc was airborne. Then its wheels made contact with the steep scree slope, and for an instant the driver thought that he might regain control. He applied the handbrake, hauling back with one hand while the other fought to control the direction of descent.

The bus careered downwards.

There was a tearing of tyres, but its speed was not diminished.

He forced his foot down on the clutch pedal, and attempted to pull the engine into reverse gear. There was a fierce screaming of torn metal, but the bus plunged onwards.

Nothing could stop them now.

The scree ended abruptly in a moraine of huge rocks covered in dense undergrowth. The vehicle plunged, bonnet first, into this pile of boulders, its rear end tipping forwards until it was almost vertically above the front. The next instant it slammed back, leaving the rear axel pivoted on a pinnacle of rock.

The sound of the impact echoed and re-echoed between the walls of the gorge, but there was no one to hear it save a small herd of red deer on a high bluff opposite the road. Startled, they lifted their noses to the wind, then galloped over the rocks and out of sight.

A pair of oystercatchers rose from their perch beside the river, threw up their curved red bills and flew, screaming, over the surface of the water, white underwings flashing a warning to other creatures.

Inside the vehicle all was still.

The driver, impaled upon his steering column, had died on impact.

From the front passenger seat, the two little girls had been thrown through the shattered windscreen. Like a pair of rag dolls they lay sprawled upon a pebbly strand, beside the river.

Those seated towards the front were cut by glass or crushed by the collapsed seating. Mercifully, the parents of the little girls who had died were themselves unconscious.

Adam Inglis's uncle had miraculously suffered no injury, other than a tap on the head which had knocked him out for a few minutes. He came to suddenly, and tried to stand. As he shifted his weight, the entire body of the vehicle rocked dangerously. Those further forward, with the strength to do so, yelled at him to sit still.

Across the aisle from Gregor Campbell, John and Helen

Pritchard remained clinging to one another, just as they had been before the accident. Now, cautiously, Helen eased herself free.

Her arm felt wet. She sat upright, gazing at her sleeve in horror. It was soaked in blood.

At first she thought it was her own. She ran her fingers along the arm and wriggled her fingers. It was a trifle numb but there appeared to be no serious damage. Where then . . . ?

She turned to John, suddenly aware that he had not spoken a word since the accident.

His head was thrown back against the seat, a deep gash oozing blood from his forehead. On his left-hand side, where he rested against the window, the sleeve and front of his jacket were darkening slowly, as the thick woollen material soaked up quantities of blood.

For a moment, Helen stared at him, uncomprehending, then suddenly she began to scream. 'My husband, he's badly injured . . . someone help me, please!'

Gregor leaned across the aisle and grasped her hands. 'All right, my dear,' he tried to reassure her. He peered at her husband, felt along the damaged arm and knew that they must act immediately if they were to save him.

'From the amount of blood, it looks as though he has severed an artery,' he decided. 'We shall have to apply a tourniquet. Do you have a scarf or a tie we could use?'

He looked around frantically. The other passengers were all similarly engaged in trying to patch up themselves and their neighbours. No one responded to his request.

He pulled the leather belt out of his own trousers, and handed it across to Helen Pritchard.

'Get it right up, under his armpit,' he instructed her, 'then tighten it as hard as you can.'

She took the belt and turned in the cramped space. She tried to lift John's arm to position the strap. He yelled out in agony.

'I can't.' Helen, despairing at her own weakness, turned back to Gregor. 'Please, can't you do it?' she pleaded.

He summed up the situation. 'Only if we change places . . . Look, you slide out of your seat on to the floor and lie flat.' Helen did as he said, stretching herself out cautiously along the aisle. The bus moved slightly, but quickly came to rest once more. Gregor was now able to slide across the aisle into her seat.

The tourniquet was quickly set in place. He waited for a few minutes, closely examining the sleeve all the time. It seemed to him that the spread of blood had ceased. He took out his watch, waited for a few more minutes to pass, then slackened the tourniquet a little. Immediately, he could see fresh blood appearing through the material, and tightened the belt again.

'You will have to look after this, my dear,' he told Helen. 'Every four minutes you must loosen the strap and allow a little blood to flow.'

'Will he be all right, do you think?' she pleaded.

'Of course,' replied the old man, wishing he felt more convinced of his prediction. 'He'll be fine just as soon as the ambulance arrives.'

The children, running on ahead now that the going was easier, were the first to catch sight of the waterfall. With squeals of excited anticipation they hurried on around a low bluff, which until now had hidden the next part of the road from view.

Suddenly the shouting stopped.

Adam and Morag, following close behind, froze in horror when they came upon the children. They were standing perilously close to the edge of a huge crater formed at a point where the verge widened to allow vehicles to park.

Adam, grabbing at Molly's hand to pull her back out of danger, now saw for himself what had riveted their attention.

At the foot of the scree, bent and twisted almost beyond recognition, their motor bus lay poised upon a pile of huge boulders, only a few feet above the fast-flowing river.

'My God, what's happened?' demanded Tom, the Yorkshire lad, coming up behind them with the other two.

Speechless, Adam pointed into the gorge, while Morag, placing an arm around each of the twins, guided them away from the ghastly scene.

Malcolm and Jenny Pritchard clung to each other for some

minutes until the boy, thrusting his sister aside with a curt, 'You wait here,' began to descend, following the path gouged out by the stricken bus.

Adam, momentarily stunned by the chaotic scene, suddenly realised that Malcolm could be in extreme danger.

'No, Malcolm, wait a minute!' he shouted. 'We have to think this out. Come back up here while we decide what must be done.'

Malcolm hesitated. 'I must get down there . . . my parents . . .' he protested.

'I know, lad,' said Adam, more gently, understanding the boy's need for action. He knelt down and found a handhold, so that he could reached out to help Malcolm back on to firm ground. After a brief struggle, the boy was hauled to safety. He went over and sat disconsolately on the low wall beside his sister.

'Someone should go for help.' It was another of the campers, Percy, who spoke. He took a few steps to the next turn in the road, and surveyed the countryside which was now visible at the far end of the gorge.

'Look,' he cried excitedly. He pointed into the far distance where a red corrugated-iron roof indicated the presence of a barn or croft house. Even as they watched, a steady plume of smoke sprang from the single chimney at the gable-end of the building. The house was occupied.

'Right,' Adam decided, 'someone must go for help while the rest of us climb down to see what can be done for those poor people.'

He dared not even hint at what they might find when they got there. It was clear that it would be a miracle if anyone were left alive.

Between them the three young men agreed that Percy should be the one to go to fetch help; he was a long-distance runner of some experience. They watched until he trotted out of sight around the next bend in the road, then Adam turned to where Morag hovered beside the children, doing her best to reassure them.

'Now please don't worry,' she said, seeing tears coursing down the cheeks of both twins. Molly, white as a sheet, grasped her brother's hand as though fearful he too might go away and leave her alone. 'Mr Inglis will climb down right away and see what we can do to help the people in the bus. You will have a very important job to do. You will have to wait here until someone comes to help. Now, promise me that you will be good children, look after each other and do exactly as you are told.'

She turned away, no longer able to bear their misery, anxious only to be off down the scree slope to where she might be able to do some good.

'You'd better stay here with the youngsters,' Adam suggested to the youngest of the campers, Dave. 'Stop any vehicle which comes along and see if you can get the children a lift to the nearest police station . . . that's Inverlinnhe. Ask the driver to report the accident. After that you had better stay on here until someone sends a rescue squad. You will be able to direct them down to us.'

Dave, himself only just past his fifteenth birthday, was relieved not to have to witness the devastation below. He nodded his agreement and went over directly to the children.

'The descent looks more difficult than it is,' Adam said, turning to Tom and Morag.

'I've done quite a bit of hill walking,' she reassured him, 'I can tackle a scree.'

Tom said nothing but went to the edge of the drop and began to search out the best way down.

'We'll need to be careful,' warned Adam, 'our movements could cause a further avalanche . . . we might bury the bus in rubble if we're not very careful.'

They walked on along the road for several yards before beginning their descent. After watching her take the first few steps into the shifting scree, Adam seemed to be satisfied that Morag knew what she was doing and left her to her own devices. This she appreciated. There was nothing more irritating than having a man fussing over her every movement.

Tom was the first to arrive at the bottom. Fearful of what they were about to find, he turned and waited for the others to catch up.

As they approached the stricken vehicle, the roar of the water blocked out all other sound. They could see no movement aboard the bus. Nothing to indicate that there was anyone alive at all.

Noticing what seemed to be a bundle of clothing among the rocks beside the stream, Adam went over to inspect it.

There was no doubt that the two children were dead. He felt like retching, physically sick at the sight of the lifeless little bodies. Steeling himself for other horrific sights to come, Adam returned to the others, shaking his head as Morag tried to pass him and look for herself.

'It's no use,' he told her, gently. 'There's nothing that you can do for them.' Ignoring him, she pushed past, determined to make her own examination. After a few moments she returned.

'I shall be required to declare them officially dead in my report,' she explained. 'And for the death certificates.'

He nodded. 'I hadn't thought . . .' he said, lamely.

They were relieved to see some movement at the windows as they approached the coach. Some of the survivors waved, thankful to see a sign of rescue.

Tearing his hands on a tangled mass of brambles, Tom tried to scramble on to one of the boulders to reach the door of the vehicle.

Adam hauled him back.

'We'll have to support the bus somehow before anyone can go up there,' he shouted in the boy's ear. 'No wonder they're all so still – see how she rocks!'

The vehicle was perched on a pinnacle of stone on which it swayed alarmingly whenever there was the slightest movement from inside.

'There are some big branches down there in the stream bed,' Adam yelled above the roar of the waters. 'We can use them to shore her up so we can get the people out.' He cast around, hoping to find something with which to tie the timbers securely.

Anticipating his need, Tom said, 'There's a length of rope in my rucksack. We'll have to get them to throw it down.'

'They'll never hear us above the noise of the river,' said Adam, desperately. 'How can we make them understand what we want?'

It was then that Tom remembered the map in his jacket pocket.

He pulled it out and spread the large sheet across a boulder, with its blank white back face up.

Morag fished in her pocket for something to write with and came out with a thick black pencil. Adam took it from her and in a practised hand executed a bold neat notice.

## REAR SEAT – ROPE

Helen Pritchard leaned across her husband's body in order to read the sign. She waved excitedly and then turned to say something to the old gentleman across the aisle.

Gregor Campbell eased himself round so that he could take a better look at the rear end of the coach. The seat where the campers had sat was completely crushed; no doubt the rucksack they had brought with them was somewhere in all that twisted metal.

He moved slowly but as he shifted his weight, the bus lurched sickeningly. Everyone gasped.

He paused for a moment to regain control, then eased himself forward again. Once he reached the pivotal point, the rocking ceased. Everyone breathed more freely.

Cautiously he tugged at the haversack, easing it out just a few inches, enough to get his fingers around the securing strap. Now he could begin to extract the contents, one article at a time. A woollen jersey, a metal water bottle, nearly full, and a first aid box, were passed back to where others waited anxiously to help in any way that they could. Then Gregor's fingers encountered the rope he was searching for.

Someone reached forward, caught the end and drew it away, along the length of the aisle. Once the rope was entirely freed, it was a simple matter to recoil it. Standing at the shattered window, Gregor waved to attract the attention of the men down below.

Adam caught the coil as it came flying through the air towards him.

It seemed like hours since Dave had managed to wave down a sleek black limousine, chauffeur-driven, with a single gentleman passenger. When they heard of the accident, the gentleman had come to the edge of the chasm with Dave and viewed the scene with dismay.

'What can I do to help?' he demanded eagerly.

'Would you be so kind as to take the children to the police station in Inverlinnhe and report the accident?' he pleaded. The kids had really been very good. Using all his ingenuity, he had devised a number of word games to divert them, but in every case after a few minutes of fevered activity they had abandoned the game and lapsed into an anxious silence. It would be better for them as well as for himself if he could have them taken off his hands.

The gentleman had kindly agreed to give the children a lift. As he helped her into the car, Jenny had turned to Dave and flung her arms around his neck.

'You will come and find us, won't you?' she pleaded. At the back of her mind lurked an unspoken fear that she and Malcolm were now all alone in the world.

'They'll look after you at the police station,' he tried to reassure her. 'You'll be warm there, and they'll give you something to eat, I expect. Cut along now, little 'un. I'll see you just as soon as we get your mum and dad out of there.'

He had watched the magnificent vehicle glide silently into the gathering dusk, wishing that he too might have been able to relinquish his vigil but knowing it was his job to stay put until help came.

He stamped his feet to try to get some life into his cramped toes.

It would soon be dark. If the rescuers didn't come soon, they wouldn't be able to see to get the people out.

He sensed rather than heard the approach of the vehicles, for the sound of their engines was drowned out by the noise of the waterfall.

When they came into view at last, the youth's heart sank. A single police car preceded an ambulance and a fire engine, carrying only ladders and winches. A second police car brought up the rear.

'Is this all you've brought?' he demanded of the burly police sergeant who emerged from the foremost vehicle.

'Aye, sonny. This is us!' was the cheerful reply.

'But there are thirty people down there,' he insisted, despairingly. 'most of them are probably unable to walk, let alone climb!'

'Oh, aye . . . so your friend suggested.' The officer followed Dave to the edge of the road and peered into the gloom. The scene below was almost obscured by a white mist which had settled over the valley as the sun went down.

'Dinnae fash yersel', laddie, there's more of us makin' their way along by the river It'll be all right now, son. We'll soon ha' them oot o' there!'


It had taken Adam and Tom the best part of an hour to make the bus stable enough to allow the escape of the more mobile passengers. When only the most severely injured remained on board, Adam helped Morag up into the coach to do what she could to assist them.

Gregor Campbell greeted her arrival with relief.

'We have done our best,' he told her, 'but I'm afraid that the couple in the front are in a very bad way. Fortunately one of the passengers was carrying a little laudanum so we have managed to calm the woman. She was in terrible pain.

'Her husband appears to be having difficulty breathing.'

'It was their daughters who were thrown out, wasn't it?' Morag inclined her head in the direction of the river bank. 'Do they know?'

The old man shook his head, 'The mother has asked about them a couple of times, but I've said nothing.'

'Probably just as well,' Morag agreed, and went to examine the father of the two girls. As Campbell had suggested his breathing was very laboured. She felt certain that his ribs must be crushed but there was nothing that she could do for the man until someone came to release him from the tangle of metal which pinned him to the floor. She felt for his pulse and found it to be very feeble. If the rescuers did not arrive soon, it would be too late to save him.

'What about the driver?' she asked, beginning to climb forward to where a man's body could be seen trapped between the dashboard and the driving seat.

Gregor caught hold of her shoulder to prevent her moving closer. It was a sight which had sickened him; there was no need for the woman to be distressed also.

'Dead,' he insisted, when she made to throw off his restraining hand. 'The poor man made a valiant attempt to slow our descent. Without his efforts, I doubt if any of us would have survived.'

'I must see for myself,' Morag insisted, gently moving the old gentleman aside. Satisfied that the driver was indeed dead, she moved among the injured passengers, checking their condition and murmuring a word of encouragement from time to time. There was little else she could do.

It was quite dark by the time the cutting gear and lifting tackle had been lowered to the river bank and the firemen eventually released the last of those trapped in the wreckage.

Within minutes of the driver's body having been lifted out of the web of torn metal and laid gently beside those of the little girls, someone spotted a line of torches carried by the rescue squad which was approaching alongside the river. Stretchers, carried in by the men or contrived from branches and coats, were used to carry out the more seriously injured. Percy had accompanied the rescuers back to the scene, and when they were ready to leave, he and Dave volunteered to carry one of the stretchers.

Because she was concerned to see the most seriously injured safely conveyed to hospital, Morag decided to walk back with them, beside the river. Meanwhile, Tom and Adam assisted Gregor Campbell, tired now and on the point of collapse, to clamber up the scree slope to where the police car awaited them.

When at last the rescue party reached the road at a point beyond the farmhouse they had seen in the distance, Morag was relieved to be able to settle back in one of the police cars and begin to plan how she would deal with the casualties once they reached the hospital.

Sidney Maynard was attending a function at Inverary Castle. The event, to be attended by Royalty, had been the main topic of conversation for weeks and she was only too aware of the importance her boss attached to it. Even were she to have Maynard telephoned, he could not reach Inverlinnhe before dawn. She would have to make do with assistance from the local practitioners.

The nurses and porters mustered the hospital's entire complement of trolleys and wheelchairs, in order to convey the casualties as quickly as possible to the reception centre which Morag set up in the surgical wing of the hospital. As the patients arrived, she made a rapid assessment of the priority cases, those requiring immediate surgery as opposed to others who might safely wait a little longer.

She assigned the management of treatment for minor casualties to the two younger local practitioners who had offered their services. Their more mature colleague, who had introduced himself as Gordon McDonald, agreed to assist her in the theatre.

The bodies of the driver, the two little girls and their father, who had died soon after having been cut free from the wreckage, were laid out in the morgue.

Morag feared that the wife would be joining them before morning.

Both the woman's legs and her pelvis were crushed. She had suffered a ruptured spleen and it was a miracle she was still alive on arrival at the hospital. Morag calculated her chances as so slender that, having administered a liberal dose of morphine for the pain, she decided to attend other cases first; those for whom there was a greater chance of survival.

Helen Pritchard had walked out of the valley, alongside her husband's stretcher. She came in through the main door at that moment, supported by Mary Neal. At the sight of the theatre nurse, Morag's expression brightened.

'Mary, it was good of you to come in . . . on your leave day too,' she greeted her.

'I came as soon as I heard,' said the young nurse. 'Sister Dunwoodie's already prepared the theatre. Which patient is first?'

Morag closed the wound in John Pritchard's arm, and looked up to find Gordon McDonald regarding her with a mixture of admiration and amazement.

He had been a newly qualified doctor at the outbreak of the Great War. Nothing in his training had prepared him for the scenes he was to witness on the battlefield, or for the butchery which was all he could achieve for his fellow men in those appalling conditions. What he had been obliged to witness and perform had turned him, irrevocably, from the path of surgery when he returned to civilian life. He had not been inside an operating theatre since the day he hung up his cap with the RAMC badge on it.

'I would have had no hesitation in amputating,' he murmured. 'Instead, you have performed a minor miracle. I should say there is every possibility this patient will keep his arm.'

Together they had inspected the damage to the crushed right arm and Morag had insisted she should save it if possible. With painstaking accuracy she had separated the tissues surrounding the main vessels and nerves, bringing together severed ends or tying off those which could not be repaired. The fractured humerus would soon mend, but tendons had been torn from their attachments and ligaments cut by glass. It would be weeks before they would know if John would ever again be able to use his arm properly. Had it not been for the careful attention given to the tourniquet by his wife, and later by their rescuers, Mr Pritchard would at the least have lost his arm, and in all probability have bled to death.

Morag stood back, peeled off her surgical gloves and passed a hand over her perspiring brow.

'Who's next?' she enquired of Violet Dunwoodie.

'The crushed pelvis,' the sister replied. 'If she's still alive.'

Even the theatre sister had been forced to admit to a grudging admiration for the way this female surgeon had performed in such stressful circumstances.

She had heard of the accident while enjoying an evening off in the home of a friend and immediately reported for duty, arriving to find a situation reminiscent of a field-dressing station. Amongst the casualties Morag Beaton worked swiftly and methodically. Under her direction, the local doctors were carrying out the treatment of the superficial cuts and minor fractures, and despite their being all three her senior by several years, seemed willing enough to take her orders.

Violet very quickly ceased deliberating about what dear Mr Maynard would have done in the circumstances and, professional that she was, rallied her nurses in support of the young surgeon.

Morag went into the ante-room to wash-up and re-gown, only to find that Eddie Strachan, who had gone out to fetch the next patient, was already stripping off his own gown.

'Too late,' he told her. 'She died while you were dealing with Mr Pritchard.'

'I was afraid she might,' Morag replied. 'In a way I hoped she would. Does that sound awfully callous?'

'Her chances of survival, even with surgery immediately after the accident, were very slim,' he tried to reassure her. 'The prognosis for her recovery was poor . . . maybe, with the support of her family, she would have overcome her injuries. But without them, I don't think she could have survived.'

'Perhaps I should have taken her into theatre first . . .' Morag faltered.

'Nonsense!' Gordon McDonald had joined them, having over-seen John Pritchard's transfer to the recovery room. 'There is one theatre, and only one patient can be attended to at a time. Naturally you select for priority treatment those with the greatest chance of survival. If you hadn't dealt with Pritchard when you did, he would certainly have lost his arm. You cannot continue to agonise like this over every decision you make, Dr Beaton. If you do, you'll end up a patient yourself!'

\*    \*    \*

For the three men who had climbed back to the road, the journey to the hospital seemed interminable.

Adam and Tom had crammed themselves into the rear seat of the black saloon with Gregor propped between them. As the car proceeded towards Inverlinnhe, Adam grew more and more anxious about his uncle.

The final effort to reach the road had been too much for the old man who had dozed off almost as soon as the policeman had handed him into the rear seat, and tucked a blanket around him. It was hardly surprising he should feel fatigued, and for the first few miles Adam was merely pleased to see him so relaxed after his ordeal. It was when his uncle's breathing became shallow and rather noisy that he had begun to worry. Then, while apparently unconscious, Gregor began to moan, clearly in considerable pain.

Adam leaned forward to attract the driver's attention.

'I think Mr Campbell is ill,' he said. 'Could you go a little faster?'

'Let's have a look at him first,' said the driver, easing the vehicle to the side of the road and drawing up.

He opened the rear door and flashed a torch in Gregor's face.

'Does he have heart trouble?' demanded the policeman.

'If he does, he has never mentioned it,' replied Adam, alarmed.

'See if he has any pills, or a wee phial of some kind,' said the driver. 'Heart patients often carry something with them.'

Adam searched the old man's pockets, his fingers eventually closing upon a small bottle which proved to contain some minute white pills.

The policeman examined the contents intently by the light of the car's headlamps. Finally satisfied that these were the pills he was looking for, he thrust one of them into the old man's mouth, under his tongue.

'There,' he said,' that should help him. Now hold tight, I don't intend to waste any more time!'

With klaxon roaring, the police car reached the town with

amazing speed but they were pleased to find that by the time the black Wolseley pulled up in the hospital courtyard, Gregor Campbell had all but recovered. They helped him from the car, and Adam insisted that he agree to be wheeled in a chair into the reception area.

'Is this the last casualty?' demanded Christine Kemp. The matron had been on duty for more than twelve hours and was beginning to feel the need of a little rest.

'I'm not a casualty . . . just very tired,' he protested, but Matron put on her 'I know best' expression and reduced him to silence.

'My uncle appears to have survived the crash without injury,' Adam explained. 'In fact, he was a tower of strength while we were trying to release the victims from the wreckage. He is just exhausted . . . oh, and he did seem to have a problem breathing earlier on. The policeman made him take one of his heart pills, just in case.'

'What we should do with you, Mr Campbell,' declared Christine Kemp,' is get you into bed for a good long rest.'

'Oh, leave me be, woman,' he replied irascibly, 'get on about your business. There's plenty of others will be grateful for your mollycoddling.'

Pushing her aside he threw down the blanket which had been placed over his knees and struggled to his feet. Seeing Helen Pritchard seated only a few feet away he went over to her.

'Mrs Pritchard,' he said taking the chair beside her,' How is your husband? Is there anything I can do to help?'

'John is in theatre . . . I'm still waiting to hear how he is.' She glanced up in alarm as the doors to the corridor swung open. It was only one of the porters returning from the wards with a wheelchair. She slumped back in her seat, disappointed. Remembering her other concern she turned to the elderly man.

'I don't know what they have done with my children,' she said, almost hysterical at the thought that she had not set eyes on them since they had left the coach, hours before.

'Don't you fret,' he tapped her knee in a fatherly fashion, 'I'm sure they are being well looked after. I'll go over and have a chat with that policeman. maybe he can tell us something.'

He moved across to where a police sergeant was carefully nothing the statements of one of the survivors of the crash.

'Excuse me,' Gregor interrupted, 'the lady over there, Mrs Pritchard, is anxious about her children, a boy about eleven or twelve and a little girl. Would you know anything about their whereabouts? They weren't on the coach at the time of the crash.'

The sergeant completed his laborious note-taking before answering.

'I'll need to make a call to the station,' he said at last. 'Just you wait here a minute.'

He wandered away and Gregor found himself involved in a discussion about finding somewhere to stay for the night.

'We were expecting to take the train back to Glasgow tonight,' the tourist explained, 'It was meant to be a round trip: Glasgow – Inverness – Inverlinnhe – Glasgow. Now it seems we must find somewhere to stay for the night.'

'I know a couple of nice little boarding houses which might have accommodation,' Gregor told them. 'When the sergeant has finished with the telephone, I'll see if I can get through to someone.'

The sergeant returned.

'The children are waiting at the police station to be picked up by their aunt. The message for Mrs Pritchard is not to worry about them at all, they are both safe and quite happy.'

'She'll be relieved to hear it, Sergeant.'

Campbell thanked him and went to tell Helen the good news.

A few moments later he was speaking animatedly into the telephone.

'They can do you a double room at the Rowan Tree. It's at the far end of the High Street. You can't miss it,' he told the worried tourists.

As they gathered their belongings together and made for the exit, Campbell spotted a pair of elderly ladies whom he recognised from earlier in the day. One had her arm in a sling. The other had a wad of bandage over one eye. Both appeared to be very worried.

'Now ladies,' Gregor approached them with a warming smile. 'You look as though you could do with a helping hand. Tell me, what's the trouble?'

Adam watched his uncle passing from group to group.

Organising everyone as usual, he thought, and smiled. There didn't seem to be much wrong with the old boy now, whatever had ailed him earlier on.

Suddenly sick with hunger and weary to the bone, Adam sank on to the nearest chair and groaned inwardly as he watched Magnus Glendenning approaching him across the hall. The last thing he wanted at this moment was an interview with the Press.

'Why, hallo, Adam,' Magnus greeted him. 'What's the Assistant Borough Engineer doing here at this hour, might I ask? Could it be that there are some consciences pricking down at the Town Hall concerning the state of some of the mountain roads?'

# Chapter 4

Magnus had managed to interview the three campers before they finally decided there was nothing more they could do by remaining at the hospital, and had gone off to their tent, pitched up in the glen. He thought he had a pretty fair picture of all that had taken place during that fateful afternoon. By the time he was free to seek out Adam Inglis in the reception area, even the small army of anxious relatives seemed to have dispersed.

'Have you any comment to make on the cause of the accident?' he demanded of the engineer.

'There was not a great deal of time to ascertain why the road collapsed . . . no,' Adam replied, sourly. 'I had other things on my mind!' He was tired, every muscle in his body ached, and he wanted nothing else but to crawl home to his bed. He had, however, promised Morag that he would wait until she was finished in the theatre, just to make sure there was nothing further that he could do to help. Otherwise he would have walked away when Magnus approached him.

There was no love lost between the staff of the Council Offices and the Press. Those employed by the Local Authority were not responsible for the decisions of the elected members of the Council, they merely carried out orders. Nevertheless, when things went wrong it was to the Council's staff, rather than the committee members, that the Press went for explanations.

Magnus was not willing to be put off easily.

'Those young men seemed to think that the rain of the past days had something to do with it,' he persisted. 'What precautions were taken to ensure that the roads remained safe, despite the increased volume of water flowing off the hills?'

Adam knew it was unwise to say anything at this stage, but he had had a long day, and would have done anything to get Glendenning off his back. The truth was that throughout the long drive in the police car, he had been going over in his mind the reasons for the accident. The more he had thought about it, the angrier he had become.

When he had taken up his post as assistant to the Borough Engineer the previous autumn, Adam's first duty had been to report on the condition of those roads which were the responsibility of his department. What he had discovered had appalled him. Since the end of the war, which had provided a convenient excuse for doing nothing to maintain any but the major roads used by the Military, consecutive Councils had placed road maintenance so low on their list of priorities that the department had been unable to afford any but the most urgent repairs. Some of the engineering structures on those mountain roads had been built by Wade's army in the eighteenth century, and as far as Adam could make out, other than an occasional patching with tarmacadam, little improvement had taken place since then.

'Excess rainwater clearly had a hand in the final collapse of the road,' he admitted to the reporter, 'but had the conduit been in good order, it should not have caused a problem.'

'Are you saying that the accident was caused by lack of maintenance?' Magnus demanded.

'I am saying that these conduits are constructed to handle excessive volumes of water,' Adam repeated. 'The fact that they did not do so on this occasion must be a matter for investigation.' Even as he made his reply, he could read in his mind's eye the headlines in the next edition of the *Gazette*: **'Assistant Borough Engineer Demands Investigation into Roads . . . neglect was cause of charabanc tragedy . . .** His boss would be hauling him over the coals for this.

Fortunately, at this moment the interrogation was interrupted by the appearance of Morag Beaton and Mary Neal, still clad in surgical gowns. Both of them looked weary. It had been a long night for everyone.

Adam rose to greet Mary as Magnus addressed her companion.

'Dr Beaton, have you time to talk to me for a few minutes, just to confirm the condition of the survivors and the final number of those who died?'

Morag, surprised that her new friend was already acquainted with Mary Neal, speculated upon this rather than concentrating upon Magnus's questions. Anyway, she had no intention of wasting what little remained of her energies in discussion with Magnus Glendenning. She had already been warned about speaking to the Press.

'Mr Glendenning,' she replied sharply, 'please address your enquiries to the hospital almoner when he comes on duty at nine o'clock. I am sure that he will be able to tell you everything you wish to know.'

She passed by with a warm smile for Adam. As she turned away into one of the wards, the young engineer remarked, 'Well, at last I've met your lady surgeon. She was magnificent at the crash but I can see what you mean about her being a tough bird! Mind you, it's only to be expected. I mean, no ordinary female would want to do a job like that.'

'Oh, she's not so bad as that,' Mary replied, 'she's had an exceptionally tiring day. As for her work . . . well, I don't believe Mr Maynard could have done any better in the circumstances.'

'That's not what you were saying a few days ago.' Adam recalled a previous conversation they had had about Morag Beaton when the nurse had been repeating Violet Dunwoodie's opinions of the female surgeon.

'It's a woman's privilege to change her mind,' Mary replied, smiling faintly. 'Look, I have to go now.'

'May I see you again, soon?' demanded Adam.

The girl smiled. 'Are you sure you're willing to risk it? You obviously find some females intimidating . . .'

'I'm willing to take a chance if you are,' he responded, stoutly. 'How about next Sunday?'

'I'll see if I can change my duty with someone,' she replied. 'I should be on stand-by for emergencies.'

'Let me know,' Adam concluded, and before Glendenning, who had been listening with interest, could resume his interrogation, the engineer strode off along the passage, making for the main door.

'Forgive me.' Magnus placed a restraining hand on Mary's arm. 'Am I to understand you have been attending the victims of the accident? Can you give me any details of what happened? Was the lady doctor actually on the bus?'

Mary replied, hesitantly, 'I believe that both she and Mr Inglis were with a small party of people who volunteered to walk up the steepest part of the road, to lighten the load. They were fortunate not to be on board when the bus went over the cliff.'

'So it was they who first helped the injured passengers? I have heard nothing but praise for the way the rescue was managed.' Magnus was exaggerating a little. He had only just heard about the accident but a number of the less seriously injured passengers had mentioned to him how Morag had attended to them until the rescue party arrived.

The girl blushed prettily, proud that Adam should be singled out for praise.

'They tell me that once the rescuers arrived, the doctor insisted upon walking out of the valley with the stretcher party, is that right?'

'I am sure that she felt it her duty to remain with her patients until they reached the hospital.'

'Very commendable,' Magnus affirmed, scribbling busily in his notebook.

Just as Mary turned to follow after Morag, Glendenning tore out the sheet he had been writing on, folded it twice and wrote on the flap.

'Would you be kind enough to give this to Dr Beaton for me?' he begged. 'I fear I owe her an apology.'

Mary took the note, wished him' Good evening', and hurried away. She found Morag visiting each of the admissions whose injuries had not required surgery, checking to see that her volunteer assistants had done all that was necessary for the patients. She was standing with the night sister beside the bed of an elderly gentleman when Mary joined them.

'Mr Campbell was not injured in the crash,' Morag was saying, surprised to find him in the ward. 'I understand that he did a splendid job keeping the other passengers calm till help arrived.'

She studied the chart for a few minutes before continuing, 'It seems he had a mild seizure following his exertions.'

'Mr Campbell spent a long time in reception helping some of the other victims of the crash to sort out their affairs,' the sister told her. 'After everyone had gone, Matron insisted that he must have a night under observation before being discharged. She asked me to find a bed for him.'

'Mr Inglis was telling me that it was the final climb back to the road which was a bit too much for him,' Mary observed. 'He's Adam's uncle, you know . . . well known locally as a mountaineer. He even had a shot at the Matterhorn in his younger days.'

Morag was tempted to continue any discussion involving Adam Inglis but as they stood gazing down upon the prone figure of Gregor Campbell, she noticed a darkened area just above his ear where the white hair had thinned sufficiently for the skin to show through.

'Hallo,' she remarked, stooping to get a better look. 'That's a nasty bruise.' She glanced again at the chart. No mention was made of any injury, yet clearly Mr Campbell had sustained quite a blow, presumably during the crash.

'No one suggested he was unconscious at any time after the crash,' Morag remarked, thoughtfully, 'but I suppose it's possible he was knocked out for a while. By the time we were on the scene he was fully alert – and very active.'

'I believe he used to be a Boy Scout.' Mary smiled.

'I can well imagine it,' replied Morag, laughing.

Their conversation was halted by a sudden alteration in the old man's condition. His intake of breath became shallow and erratic and he began snoring loudly in a manner which alarmed the surgeon.

With a small pocket torch, she examined each of Gregor Campbell's eyes and was disturbed to find that not only did the pupils differ in size, but that there was no involuntary conjunctival reflex.

She took the patient's chart from Mary Neal and found, as she expected, that his temperature had been a few degrees below normal ever since he was admitted to the ward, several hours before.

'It's a subdural haemorrhage,' she decided, 'caused, I suspect, by his activity following the knock he received in the accident. The pressure on his brain will have to be relieved . . .' She glanced at her watch and made a rapid calculation. 'This is something that can't wait any longer.'

'Wouldn't it be better to leave it until Mr Maynard gets here?' Mary asked, and then, seeing Morag's angry expression at her suggestion, hastened to qualify her remark. 'Oh, I'm not implying you are not able to do the operation, Dr Beaton,' she insisted. 'It's just that we are all very tired . . . perhaps a fresh team would do a better job?'

Her words faded to a mumble when she saw that Morag had indeed appreciated her concern and seemed to share it.

'You're right, of course,' the doctor agreed, 'but unfortunately Mr Campbell has been neglected for too long already. If I do not relieve the pressure immediately he will almost certainly die. I don't think he can wait half an hour, let alone four or five.' She was beginning to realise how remiss she had been in not summoning Sidney Maynard at once . . . she had not appreciated the length of time which it would take them to treat all the victims of the crash. The local practitioners must surely have left by now. It was up to Morag alone to do what she could to save the patient.

Mary Neal was torn between concern for the woman surgeon, whom she had come to respect more and more during the course of the evening, and the man who had done so much to help his fellow passengers. Young and inexperienced as she was, Mary was well aware that once she had him under the knife, any failure on Morag's part to save the old gentleman would place her career in jeopardy.

'Get word to Mr Strachan that we have one more patient for surgery,' Morag instructed. 'He will most probably be in the recovery room with Dr Pritchard.' Mary was gone in an instant. With the assistance of the night nurse on duty, Morag shifted Gregor Campbell outside, still in his bed. Together they pushed him the length of the deserted corridor and round the corner into the theatre's ante-room.

'All right, Nurse,' Morag said. 'You may get back to your ward. I can manage on my own until the theatre staff arrive.'

She waited impatiently for Eddie to reappear. Anaesthesia would be a matter of a local injection of cocaine to desensitise the area of operation. To administer ether to this patient would not be possible. While she waited, Morag prepared her patient by shaving the area of the left temporal bone, and exposing the full extent of the bruising. As she worked, the old man continued to snore, noisily.

Eddie Strachan arrived, looking bleary-eyed. He had crept into his bed only minutes before being roused again by Mary, and even his normally pink complexion was grey with fatigue. Morag regarded him anxiously, noting the signs of exhaustion.

'I'm sorry, Eddie,' she began, 'it really is imperative that we do this decompression immediately ... it has been neglected for far too long.'

'Mary explained,' he replied, splashing water on to his face to wake himself up properly. 'You know how it is when you're wakened after falling into that first real sleep.'

Within minutes, Violet Dunwoodie had also arrived on the scene, and with her one of the relief nurses who had come on duty early, having heard about the accident.

'Is this really necessary, Dr Beaton?' she demanded, taking a quick glance at Campbell. 'Matron assured me that this patient was merely suffering from exhaustion.'

'If you will take a closer look at Mr Campbell's head, Sister Dunwoodie,' Morag replied icily, 'you will see that he has sustained a severe blow to the temporal region which explains his shallow breathing, weak pulse and low temperature ... these are the symptoms of a subdural haemorrhage – to relieve which I intend to carry out immediate surgery.'

Violet Dunwoodie, stunned by Morag's abrupt reply, made no further protest. She sprang into action and within minutes the theatre was made ready for the operation. Eddie administered the local anaesthetic.

Soon Morag was able to begin her task by laying open the scalp in an arc above the left ear. The semi-circular flap she had cut was eased free of subcutaneous tissue to expose the skull. As she reached for the trephine, her hand trembled a little . . . it was the first time she had performed this operation unsupervised. She took a deep breath before continuing.

A circle of bone came away to expose the fibrous sheath covering the dura mater. She pulled aside the fibres using retractors and, on the exposed surface of the tough covering of the brain itself, made her incision in two directions at right angles, to form a cross. As the skin pulled apart under the pressure from below, a star of brain tissue appeared, glistening where light fell on the cerebral fluid which bathed it. This fluid oozed rather than gushed out, but the effect of decompression was spectacular. Almost immediately, the patient's vital signs began to creep back to normal. The pulse was beating strongly now, and colour was returning to the old man's skin as other involuntary activities of the body resumed at their normal pace. His breathing became quieter and the unnatural snoring ceased.

The team gathered around the operating table exchanged triumphant glances, and as Morag began to suture the layers covering the brain, Eddie applied an oxygen mask to assist the patient's breathing.

Morag, watching the colour returning to Gregor Campbell's face, was relieved to see the old gentleman open his eyes. He looked confused, his glance wandering over the brightly lit, clinically bare room.

'You are all right, Mr Campbell,' she assured him, smiling down at him confidently as she held his wrist. His pulse was quite normal. 'You had a severe concussion, and I have had to release the pressure inside your head. It's really nothing to worry about.'

'Thank you, Doctor,' he murmured, and closed his eyes again.

Thinking they could safely leave their patient to recover on his trolley before returning him to the ward, the surgical team repaired to the scrub-room and engaged in banter of a kind which Morag had not experienced since leaving her Edinburgh alma mater. There was an air of satisfied euphoria about them all, even Violet Dunwoodie, who was forced to concede that Morag's diagnosis had been correct. She could not wait for a chance to rib Matron about her mistake!

When they were finished, Morag said, 'I'll just check on Mr Campbell, Sister, then you can have him taken back to the ward.'

She knew the instant that she re-entered the theatre, that something was wrong. It was quiet . . . too quiet.

She leaned over the table and took the patient's wrist between her fingers. There was no pulse. Lifting the lid, she shone a torch into his eye and was dismayed to find that there was no response in the pupil.

Shouting for aid, she began frantically to apply artificial respiration, but in her heart she knew that it was to no avail. After a few minutes, Eddie Strachan closed his hands tightly over hers and drew her away.

'It's no use . . . he's gone.'

'Matron did suggest he might have had a heart attack following the rescue,' Violet divulged, rather belatedly.

Morag recalled the term 'seizure' in the notes. She had assumed this had referred to a period of unconsciousness due to the blow on the head. She should have thought about his heart . . . after all, he was a very elderly person.

'I never checked for a chronic heart condition,' she said, dismayed. 'I should have known that someone of his age might well have angina . . .'

'You had no alternative but to operate,' Eddie told her, firmly. 'It was a risk that had to be taken, no matter what.'

He looked across at Sister Dunwoodie, seeking confirmation.

'You did all you could,' the sister assured her, and meant it. 'Come along, dear,' she continued, addressing Morag in a more kindly manner than any of them had heard her use to the assistant surgeon before. 'It's been a tough night. You should try to get some sleep before the boss arrives. There will be a few questions asked about this. You must be fit and ready to answer them.'

Bright watery sunlight falling on her pillow had no effect upon the sleeping figure of Morag Beaton, but a persistent tap-tapping on her door roused her eventually.

'What is it?' she called, completely disorientated. What time was it anyway? She tried to make a grab for her watch, only to brush it off her bedside table on to the uncarpeted floor. When at last she managed to retrieve it, she found it had stopped and the glass was smashed. Sighing, she replaced it on the table and sat up, drawing the covers around her. The sun might be shining, but it was still cold for April.

Mary Neal poked her head around the door.

'Sorry to wake you, Doctor,' she said, 'but Mr Maynard has arrived and is breathing fire ... he wants to see you immediately.'

'Come in,' invited Morag, throwing back the covers and combing a hand through her tangled locks. As she wiped the sleep out of her eyes, she asked, 'Why should he be breathing fire?'

'It's the newspapers again,' the little nurse explained. 'There's a piece about the fine work done by the rescue services, and a whole lot about how well the hospital coped with the help of the local doctors, in the absence of the chief consultant.'

No wonder Sidney Maynard was angry, thought Morag, the wrong kind of publicity again. She knew now that she should have summoned him at once, Royal occasion or no.

'Your friend Mr Glendenning has been very complimentary about you . . . Oh, I nearly forgot,' she continued, and pulled from her pocket a crumpled piece of paper. 'He asked me to give this to you, last night. I forgot all about it.' She handed over the note and Morag read it hurriedly as she dragged on her white coat.

*Please meet me in the bar of the Long John Hotel, after nine o'clock, any evening this week.*
*Magnus Glendenning*

Morag screwed up the note angrily, and threw it in the waste-paper basket. She certainly would meet Magnus Glendenning in the Long John ... to give him a piece of her mind! His reporting methods had brought her nothing but trouble since she had taken up her post here. Why couldn't he leave her alone?

On this occasion she remembered to allow Miss McArdle to announce her arrival. Maynard's secretary, whose expressionless face as usual betrayed nothing of her employer's disposition, rose to her feet when Morag entered her small ante-room of an office. Wordlessly, she pushed past the woman surgeon in order to tap on the glass-panelled door which separated her master from the outside world.

'Come!' It was an imperious style of invitation which Morag had associated, since her childhood, with being hauled over the coals. Even her beloved grandfather, David Beaton, had used that tone with her on the rare occasions when he had felt obliged to reprimand her.

Lucy McArdle stepped inside and announced, 'Dr Beaton is here, Mr Maynard.'

Morag distinctly heard him clear his throat. Could it be that he too was nervous about this encounter?

'Very well,' he barked at last. 'Show her in.'

In an instant, Morag was inside the sumptuous office with the door closing soundlessly behind her. He left her standing in the centre of the Persian carpet for sufficient time to assert his authority. Then he nodded towards a severely plain, upright armchair which stood in front of and slightly to one side of his immensely impressive and very modern Charles Rennie Mackintosh desk, of some dark-coloured wood which Morag did not recognise.

On her previous visit to this room, she had been so annoyed that she had hardly noticed her surroundings. Today she was to find herself absorbing every detail, as though this might be her last opportunity to do so!

'Dr Beaton, I believe we had an understanding about when,

and under what circumstances, I was to be summoned to the hospital?'

'Yes . . . I realise that I should have let you know what was happening last evening,' she began, 'but it seemed pointless to call you from such a distance, when the casualties required immediate treatment. I myself returned from the scene of the accident about eight o'clock, and the first ambulances were arriving within minutes. I had managed to alert three of the local men . . . I thought it unnecessary to take you away from such an important function when the crisis would surely be over by the time you arrived.'

'I should have been informed, Dr Beaton. How do you think it appears to our Board of Directors, and to those who so generously donate funds to the hospital, to read in the Press that, at a time of crisis, their senior consultant was wining and dining in blissful ignorance, a hundred miles away?'

'You were not to know that the accident would occur,' she pointed out, stiffly.

'Of course I was not,' he exploded, 'but that is not the point. Had I known of the problem I would have come away immediately, and at least have been seen to do my best to be here . . . do you understand?'

She understood only too well. It was a revelation to Morag to realise just how insecure in his position Maynard was. He seemed to be inordinately disturbed by any whiff of scandal, any hint of criticism. She was quite unused to such behaviour in the medical men amongst whom she had grown up. Her father and grandfather were both physicians of considerable standing; her grandfather had been Chief Medical Officer for Argyll before his retirement in 1920, and her uncle, Michael Brown, held the same position now. Their activities had often warranted comment from the newspapers, some of it adverse. They had laughed at the unreasonable, and written to complain of the libellous, soliciting an apology for the more outrageous cases of misreporting. She had never known any of them to tremble at the effect that such coverage might have upon

their reputations. Did Maynard have something to hide? she
wondered.

She was truly sorry that she had upset her boss by not
summoning him immediately. She could see now that it might
appear she had been determined to prove she could manage a
crisis without him.

'I'm afraid that I panicked,' she told him. It was partly the truth.
'I knew you could not possibly be here in time to do any good,
and I knew how much you had been looking forward to the
event at Inveraray.'

'You sound more like a wife than a colleague,' he remonstrated.
'Only a woman would allow personal considerations to cloud her
judgement.'

There, he had said it. His resentment at her appointment had
surfaced at last, and he was not going to let it rest now that he
had the bit between his teeth.

'Well,' he snapped, 'your arrogance has cost the hospital its
reputation, and one respected citizen of the town his life!'

'Mr Campbell, do you mean?' How had he got hold of that
story so quickly? she wondered.

'Precisely. Perhaps you can tell me how it is that an eighty-
year-old patient could have been kept waiting four hours for
an examination, after which he underwent major surgery to
the brain without any account being taken of a chronic heart
condition?'

He was very well informed for so soon after his arrival. Morag
could not help suspecting that there had been a deputation
waiting for him, eager to absolve themselves of any responsibility
in the matter.

'Mr Campbell did not complain of injury to anyone,' she replied
carefully. 'He was instrumental in keeping the casualties calm
after the accident, and in my opinion was largely responsible
for the survival of many of them. When all the injured had been
removed from the scene, he complained of feeling tired and had
to be assisted up the steep cliff to the police car which then brought
him to the hospital. It appears that during this journey he had an
attack of an unspecified nature. There being no medical person

available at the time, the constable on duty administered one of Mr Campbell's own amyl nitrite pills. Mr Campbell appears to have made a complete recovery. So much so that on his arrival at the hospital he refused Matron's advice to rest overnight and instead spent some time assisting other victims of the crash to sort out their affairs.

'It was not until hours later that he showed signs of distress, and Matron suggested he should bed down in the ward for the night. By then all three of the GPs had left, and I was in theatre. It was after midnight before I first saw Mr Campbell, by which time he was showing acute symptoms of cerebral compression and it was obvious that immediate surgery was necessary.'

'From your notes it seems that no attention was paid to his heart condition . . . the patient has received treatment for angina over a period of some ten years. Did you not know that?'

'By the time I saw him, Mr Campbell was already unconscious. In the middle of the night there was no way I could have consulted his own doctor's records. I did what had to be done, and I am truly sorry that the poor man died.'

'There will be an inquiry into Mr Campbell's death, of course. I shall write my report to the Procurator Fiscal immediately. There will also be a Hospital Board to enquire into your handling of this case. Until such time as the actions which were taken last evening have been properly investigated, you may consider yourself under suspension.'

'I'm sorry,' Morag responded. 'What does that mean?'

'It means, Doctor, that until such time as the board sees fit to reinstate you, you will absent yourself from the wards and operating theatre. You may continue to live in the hospital if you wish, until the outcome of the enquiry is known. Should you decide to leave the premises, kindly inform my secretary of your whereabouts. Good day.'

Morag continued to stare at him while remaining rooted to her chair. Eventually he rose and went to stand gazing out of the window, his hands clasped decisively behind his back.

Further argument seemed pointless. She rose, stared at the consultant's back for a few seconds then stalked out of the room.

She was too stunned even to notice the sympathetic glances of both Miss McArdle and Matron Kemp, who unable to contain her curiosity about the outcome of Morag's interview, had found an excuse to visit Maynard's secretary at this precise moment.

Not knowing where she was going, or why, Morag strode the length of the main corridor and threw open the swing door to the main entrance. Before she could reach the outer door, a hand caught her firmly by the shoulder and hauled her back.

'Morag . . . what is it? What's happened?' It was Eddie Strachan who had halted her flight.

'I've been suspended!' She spat out the words in fury.

'You've what?' Eddie took a step back, his expression of disbelief quickly giving place to anger almost on a par with Morag's own.

'What possible reason could Maynard have for taking such a step? Doesn't he know what went on here last night?'

Everyone had been a little on edge that morning. The whole team on duty the previous evening, and in addition a number of off-duty staff, had worked long into the night to deal with the influx of casualties. In suspending Morag, Maynard appeared to be censuring them all.

'The grounds for suspension are that I took an unnecessary risk, operating on Mr Campbell without ascertaining that he had a chronic heart condition of ten years' standing.' Morag had calmed down a little by this time, and was beginning to see that Maynard did have a point. She could hardly question his right to order an enquiry.

Eddie was not prepared to be so understanding.

'It's outrageous,' he declared. 'No one could have done a more professional job than you . . . I should know, I was there every minute of the time. Perhaps if His Majesty had not been whooping it up with the aristocracy down in Inverary, he might have been here doing the work himself!'

'That's just the sort of remark which is going to put me out of employment for good,' declared Morag, but she was beginning to smile a little. She found Eddie's championship of her cause very consoling.

'Look here,' he suggested, 'I have an hour or two free. Why don't we go into town and have a bite of lunch? We can begin to plan our strategy . . . if there is to be an enquiry, we shall have to muster all our defences.'

'I will come to lunch with you,' Morag agreed, 'provided we go Dutch. As for the other . . . I think before you begin planning a campaign for my restoration, you should consider your own position very carefully. There would be no point in both of us losing our jobs, would there?'

Luncheon with Eddie, taken in the same little café where Morag had met Magnus Glendenning on her first visit to Inverlinnhe, had given her a breathing space in which to assess her position. He suggested it would be best if she were to continue to occupy her room in the staff quarters, since Maynard had agreed to this. Eddie persuaded her that it was important to show her face around the hospital. If she disappeared for weeks, people would begin to become hazy about what actually had happened on the night of the disaster. Her presence should act as a constant reminder that they were all of them under scrutiny, in one respect or another.

Morag had managed to persuade him that a quietly conducted campaign for support would be preferable to some of the wilder notions he had put forward initially. A march through the town of hospital staff carrying banners demanding **Reinstate Our Lady Surgeon** might alert the Press, but would definitely not impress the members of the Hospital Board.

She spent the afternoon writing to her father. There had been so little time since taking up her new post to communicate with any of her family and friends that she often felt isolated from her previous life. With the prospect of several weeks of inactivity before her, it seemed reasonable she should go home for a few days, despite Eddie Strachan's sage advice about remaining in and around the hospital. She needed the counsel of experienced medical men . . . and where better to find it than at home?

Writing down what had occurred on the previous evening helped to clarify her recollection of events, and when she had finished she felt she had a sound case to put forward in her own defence.

When she had the letter ready for posting, it was time to think about going to meet Magnus Glendenning in the Long John Hotel.

Her anger at the way in which the reporter had treated the happenings of the day before had faded somewhat since she'd had time to study the *Gazette* for herself. She was satisfied with the way in which he had written his account of the scene of the accident, and appreciated the manner in which he had praised the actions of all parties in caring for the injured on the spot, and in summoning help.

Her main bone of contention was that he had made so much of her own part in the affair, largely by emphasising the fact of Maynard's absence from the scene. She supposed she should be thankful there had been no reporters from the city broadsheets, though. At least there were none of the idiotic headlines that had appeared on that other occasion.

# Chapter 5

❦

The Long John recalled the name of a Highlander of mighty stature who had, according to tradition, led his clan in battle against the marauding Campbells of Argyll. The giant's broadsword rested in the town's museum and historians confirmed that John of the Glen must have been all of seven feet tall to have wielded it.

The ancient clock in the Episcopalian church tower was striking nine as Morag pushed open the door to the public bar and almost stumbled as her feet encountered three worn steps down to the stone-flagged floor. It took a few moments for her eyes to adjust to the dim lighting. There were no more than half a dozen customers gathered at the bar, and it was clear they had been engaged in heated discussion prior to her entry. The sudden appearance of a female in this essentially male preserve had immediately put a curb on their conversation. Morag approached the bar amid a disconcerting silence.

'Yes, madam?' the landlord enquired, accepting her presence with greater aplomb than did his clients.

'I was expecting to meet Mr Glendenning,' she told him. 'Has he been in this evening?'

Wordlessly, the landlord nodded in the direction of the inglenook at the far end of the room. For the first time, Morag observed the two figures hunched before the dying embers of a fire, lit more for decoration than from necessity. It had been a warm evening.

Magnus and his companion had been so absorbed in their discussion that they were unaware of the hush which had descended upon the gathering. When he heard his name, however, Magnus lifted his head and noticed Morag for the first time. He rose unsteadily to his feet, waving his pewter tankard in her direction.

'All hail, Daughter of Galen,' he cried, and made a sweeping bow which might well have graced the stage of Glasgow's King's Theatre.

Discomfited by his greeting, and anxious to put an end to the speculation which her presence there had already created, Morag hurried towards him and sat down unceremoniously.

His companion, the young photographer whom she recognised as having been present on the night when the Marquis's son had been brought in to the hospital, half rose from his chair, looking painfully embarrassed.

'You probably won't remember Donald,' Magnus said. 'Let me introduce you both,' he went on magnanimously. 'Dr Beaton, Mr Donald Fergusson . . . Donald Fergusson, Dr Beaton.' He slurred his words, so that it was only too clear to Morag that the tankard of ale before him was not his first of the evening.

'You must have a drink,' he insisted. 'What will it be? A Sidecar perhaps . . . a Manhattan . . . champagne?'

'A whisky and water, thank you,' she replied firmly.

She had learned early on that she was safe with a drink she knew, and whose strength she could gauge.

Magnus rose and made his way unsteadily towards the bar.

'I gather you were none too pleased with the photograph I took of you?' Donald observed. When he saw her scowl, he hastened to add, 'It was pretty dreadful, wasn't it? I was all for scrapping it, but my editor insisted.'

'At least it didn't appear in the *Gazette*.'

'Oh, no . . . not the Inverlinnhe paper. I work for the *Glasgow Evening Clarion* . . . a newspaper which appeals to the more sensational tastes of its readers.'

'I'm not sure I should even be talking to you at all, then,' Morag replied. Nevertheless, she felt herself warming to this rather pleasant young man.

'There we are, children!' Magnus, unstable as he was, had managed to carry three glasses and a jug of water on a tray, without spilling a drop.

'It comes of long years of practice,' he explained, as they regarded the feat with some surprise.

'How much water?' he demanded; the jug poised above Morag's glass.

'The same again,' she replied.

'What a sin to treat the *uisge-beatha* in such a fashion,' he declared, as he handed her her glass.

'Donald . . . a toast if you please.' He raised his tankard to Morag: 'To a daughter of Galen, divinely tall and most divinely fair!' he misquoted deliberately.

'That's twice you've mentioned Galen,' Donald interjected. 'Are we supposed to know who you're talking about?'

Magnus challenged Morag with a raised eyebrow.

Despite her annoyance, she could not help laughing.

'Galen was the father of medicine,' she explained, for Donald's benefit, her eyes twinkling.

'I thought that was Hippocrates,' said the photographer.

'He gets all the credit,' Morag replied, 'but Galen, the physician to Marcus Aurelius, was the first to make a systematic study of medicine and to write it down for others to share.'

Magnus applauded with a loud, slow handclap.

'I knew you would not let me down.'

'I'm hardly likely to forget,' she said, 'I was brought up on a diet of medical history . . . my Great-uncle Angus has spent his lifetime studying the ancient physicians of Mull and Islay, and my Uncle Stuart translated the Beaton manuscript – a medieval herbal, which was published during the war.'

'That was something I was wanting to ask you,' Magnus declared. 'Are you related to those famous Beatons who were physicians to the Lords of the Isles?'

'That is what my Uncle Angus believes,' she replied. 'He claims he has found evidence of a continuous line of succession, but you know how difficult it is to trace family history. Each individual was known by several different names . . .'

Donald could see that this conversation was going to last the night, and he had work to do. 'You'll have to excuse me,' he said, standing up and offering Morag his hand, 'I have an assignment at the Assembly Rooms this evening. It was a pleasure meeting you, Dr Beaton.' He hesitated for a moment before continuing, 'Look, I really am sorry about that photograph of you . . . it never occurred to me the editor would want to print it.'

'Of course, if you hadn't taken it in the first place, he wouldn't have been able to,' she replied briskly, but could not sustain her resentment in the face of such boyish contrition.

'Goodnight, Mr Fergusson,' she went on, taking his hand and shaking it in friendly fashion. 'I hope we meet again, but preferably not in the hospital, and not in the early hours of the morning!'

Alone with Magnus at last, Morag was now free to carry out the real task she had set herself for this meeting, but before she could muster her protest, he forestalled her.

'They tell me that there's trouble up at the hospital,' he remarked.

'Indeed there is,' she replied. 'Thanks to you.'

'Oh, come now, you can't hold me responsible for the extreme sensitivity of Sidney Maynard,' he protested.

'There was no need to make so much of his being absent from the hospital at the time of the accident,' Morag remonstrated. 'How was Mr Maynard to know that his presence would be required in such dramatic circumstances? You made it sound as though he had deliberately stayed at the Duke's dinner, despite having been called back. The truth is, I was at fault for not sending for him. Anyway, that's not the reason for my suspension.'

'What do you mean, suspension?' Magnus was instantly on the alert. Morag could not help marvelling how this man, clearly under the influence of drink, could sober up so quickly when there was a story to be had. She pondered the wisdom of telling him her problems. Oh, well, the damage was done now, she would have to rely upon his discretion . . .

'The old man, Mr Campbell, died following a brain operation.

There will be an investigation, it being death in suspicious circumstances.'

'Gregor Campbell, do you mean?' Magnus was surprised. He did not have the old gentleman on his list of casualties. In fact, on the basis of reports from other passengers on the ill-fated bus, Campbell had been hero of the hour.

'I didn't even know he had been injured,' he declared.

'That's just the point,' Morag confessed. 'No one knew he had suffered a blow to the head until well after midnight. Even then it was quite by chance that he began to show signs of distress at the very moment when I was visiting the ward. Had I not been there at the time, he would just have slipped away unnoticed until the day staff came on duty.' She had gone over this in her mind so many times. Would it have been better if Gregor had been allowed to die without her intervention? Would she not still have been accused of neglect then?

'Is it usual to suspend a surgeon pending such an inquiry?' Magnus asked. It seemed a drastic measure, considering how often such situations must occur.

'Only when there is a possibility that the doctor has behaved unprofessionally, or has neglected his duty,' she advised him. 'Had Mr Maynard been better disposed towards me, I think I would have been allowed to continue working until the enquiry was completed. As it is, he has seen fit to put the worst possible interpretation upon the facts, and considers it to be in the best interests of the hospital to suspend me from my duties until such time as my name is cleared.'

Magnus was looking contrite and genuinely concerned.

'If anything I have written has contributed to this situation, I am truly sorry,' he told her. 'You may rest assured that you will find the weight of the Press behind you, if things do go badly . . .'

'Oh, no, please! No more headlines. At least, not until the hearings are over and done with. I have no shortage of supporters wanting to proclaim my innocence in the streets of Inverlinnhe. I can't think of anything more likely to work against my cause than further publicity of that kind.'

'It's for you to choose, of course.' Magnus now appeared

completely sober. 'But remember, if you need help . . . I shall be behind you one hundred per cent.'

She rose to go.

'Oh, come,' he declared. 'The evening is yet young. Won't you have another drink?'

'No, really, I don't think so,' Morag protested. 'And if you will forgive me for saying so, you have had enough for one evening.'

'What else is there for a lonely bachelor?' he enquired.

'I must get back to the hospital,' she asserted, ignoring his plaintive tone. 'I have to catch the steamer for Eisdalsa at eight-thirty in the morning.'

'Going home to mother?' He had not meant it to sound so disparaging.

'Only because this is an opportunity which has not come my way since I started working here,' she retorted, sharply.

'Well said,' he applauded. 'Perhaps you will allow me to show you some of the less well-known charms of Inverlinnhe life, when you return?'

'Perhaps.' She was smiling again. How this man angered yet amused her. In his presence she seemed to swing constantly between one emotion and its opposite.

As she moved towards the door he followed her, placing a hand solicitously beneath her elbow.

'Oh, there's really no need to see me home,' she protested. 'It's still quite light outside.'

'Nonsense,' he insisted, 'I can't let you wander the streets alone at this hour.'

She glanced at the great Parliament clock above the bar, and was astonished to see that it was nearly eleven o'clock.

Outside, a chill wind, blowing off the mountain from the north-east, where snow still lingered in the corries, had dispelled the warmth of the day. The sudden change of temperature had a marked effect upon Magnus. He staggered and would have reeled into the gutter had she not grasped his arm firmly.

'It seems to me,' Morag said, 'that it is I who should see you home . . . not the other way about.'

'No, I can't have that,' he protested. Nevertheless, he had to concede that there was little hope of his being able to accompany her on foot up the steep slopes to the hospital.

'Let's call a cab . . .' he slurred, and began to wave his arms wildly in the direction of the cab-stand further down the street.

It seemed the only thing to do. With his weight fully upon her now, Morag steered the reporter along the pavement, fighting to keep him on his feet. Under the reproachful eyes of the cabby, she was at last able to set him down beside the car.

'Where to, miss?' the driver asked.

She had no idea, and Magnus was in no condition to tell her.

'I was hoping you would take the gentleman home,' she began to explain, 'but I don't know his address.'

The cabbie looked at her strangely. One might expect this kind of thing in Glasgow, Morag supposed, but Inverlinnhe . . . She would not have been surprised if he had refused to help her.

'It's all right, miss. Mr Glendenning and I are old friends.'

Without another word, the cabbie hauled his hapless fare up off the curb, where he had subsided, and forced him into the back of the cab.

'I'd be obliged if you would come too, miss,' the man requested. 'You never know with these characters. If he comes to suddenly he might try to interfere with my driving.'

How could she refuse? It was the least she could do for the obliging cab driver. She climbed in beside Magnus and placed her arm behind his neck to ensure he did not injure himself when the vehicle started up. Magnus's dark, shaggy head fell forward to rest comfortably upon her bosom. If the cab driver noticed the somewhat intimate nature of their position, he made no sign. She supposed he saw worse in the course of his duties.

They drove out along the main road to the east, as far as the canal, where the cabbie turned off, taking a narrow lane which ran alongside the water. At the second of a series of lock gates, he pulled up beside a single-story building with slate roof and whitewashed walls, reminiscent of the cottages in her own home village.

'Here we are, miss.' The driver spoke to her over his shoulder. 'I'll give you a hand with him.'

Together they staggered to the door. Magnus, barely able to stand, was supported between them. As one long practised, the driver searched Magnus's pockets for a key, unlocked the door and pushed it open. He left Morag holding the inebriated reporter propped against the doorpost until he could find a lamp and set a match to the wick. Instantly the room was bathed in light.

The sudden brightness seemed to rouse Magnus who opened his eyes, fixed them somewhat inaccurately upon a galvanised bucket standing beneath the sink, and lumbered across the room, managing to deposit most of the ensuing vomit in the intended receptacle.

When he had finished, he rolled over on the floor, moaning. Morag had followed him to the sink and now began to loosen his tie and collar before turning him on to his side.

'You done this before, miss?' enquired the cabbie, impressed at the efficient manner in which the young woman had dealt with such an unpleasant situation.

'Well . . . in a way, yes,' she replied. 'I'm a doctor.'

Of course, the driver knew who she was now. He had seen her picture in the *Clarion*. It was hardly surprising that he had not recognised her earlier, because the photograph had hardly done justice to her handsome looks.

Magnus was still only semiconscious as he lay groaning on the cold stone flags.

'Can we lift him, do you think?' Morag entreated. She glanced around the room for somewhere to deposit Magnus. An elderly sofa occupied most of the length of one wall. 'How about that?' she suggested.

Together they hauled Magnus to his feet once more, and made him as comfortable as was possible on the unyielding horsehair upholstery. Morag crouched beside him, lifted an eyelid in order to judge his level of consciousness, felt for a pulse in his neck, and slipped a hand inside his shirt to feel the steady rhythm of his heartbeat.

'He'll sleep now,' she pronounced, looking up into the anxious face of the friendly cab driver. Mr Glendenning was a regular client whom he had brought home on many occasions somewhat the worse for drink. He had never seen him in quite such an inebriated state as this, however.

'I'm sorry to rush you, miss,' he said, glancing at his wristwatch. 'But it's after midnight, and I really must get back into town There is a big affair at the Assembly Rooms this evening . . . they'll be turning out about now.'

'Oh, I am sorry,' she apologised. 'We are keeping you from your work.' She searched in her handbag and pulled out a ten-shilling note. 'You have been very kind,' she said. On a sudden impulse, she asked, 'May I know your name? I am sure Mr Glendenning will wish to thank you for himself, when he is able.' They both looked in the direction of the figure on the couch and exchanged smiles.

'Charlie, miss . . . just tell him Charlie brought him home. He'll know.'

'Will this be sufficient?' She pressed the note into his hand.

'More than enough, miss,' the driver replied. 'But won't you be wanting to get back to the hospital?'

'No,' she said. 'I can't leave my patient alone in this helpless state. If he should be ill again, I need to be here to help him.'

Charlie nodded, understanding her dilemma. Nevertheless, he would be leaving this young woman alone in the house with Magnus Glendenning, whose reputation with young females was a source of much speculation around town. He scribbled something on a piece of paper and tucked it behind the telephone handset. 'It's the number of the cab-rank', he explained as he let himself out.

# Chapter 6

For some time, Morag busied herself tidying up the cluttered little room. Magnus slept soundly, snoring occasionally but otherwise so deeply asleep that nothing she did seemed to disturb him.

When she had removed the evidence of his recent sickness she cleared the cluttered table, pumped up some water using the old-fashioned wooden handle beside the sink, and washed up the pile of dirty dishes. Then she set about stacking the heaped papers and books which littered the floor and every other flat surface in the room.

When she was satisfied with the living room, she went through to the second room where she found Magnus's bed unmade and his clothes strewn about in much the same manner as his papers. She pulled the covers straight and turned back the rather grimy sheet, leaving the bed ready for its occupant should he waken for long enough to be led to it.

Between the two rooms which comprised the living accommodation was the original closet, which in earlier times would have been half store, half alcove to house a second bed, in the kitchen.

The storage part was closed off by a crude door which, when opened, revealed a conglomeration of articles unlikely to have seen the light of day for generations. A glengarry with the familiar red and white checquered band of the Argyll and Sutherland Highlanders fell at her feet.

She picked up the cap and examined it thoughtfully, before stuffing it back on to the heap of folded uniform clothing which occupied the top shelf. Magnus must have been in her father's regiment . . . she should have realised he belonged to that generation which had fought in the war.

She closed the door rapidly on the tottering pile before everything spewed out into the tiny entrance lobby.

Returning to the kitchen-living room, she took another look at Magnus, regarding him with greater sympathy now that she appreciated he might have good reason for his heavy drinking. She should have thought of that. Had not her own dear father spent the last decade trying to stave off the effects of his experiences in France?

Dr Hugh Beaton had gone to war a strong reliable figure, a pillar of the community. Two years of ministering to the wounded in field hospitals had changed him into a trembling wreck of a man, indecisive, constantly worrying about trivialities, and leaning heavily upon her mother to get him through the day. Thankfully the Eisdalsa practice was not demanding, and he was able to spend much of his time on the family's smallholding where he seemed to be more at ease amongst the beasts and the growing crops.

On her return from university, Morag had been horrified to find that her father was no longer able to face a waiting room full of patients without a shot of whisky to 'perk him up', as he described it. His medical judgments were sound enough, she was convinced of that, but he no longer had faith in his own decisions. He could not hold a scalpel without his hand trembling, which meant that the most trivial of operations had to be transferred to the hospital in Oban. There was no doubt in her mind that her father would shortly be forced to retire.

She should have realised that Magnus might be similarly affected and shuddered to think what fearful scenes filled his dreams and drove him to seek oblivion at the bottom of a whisky bottle.

It was nearly one in the morning before she felt able to sit down and take a rest. As soon as she settled into the one rather uncomfortable armchair, Magnus stirred. It was almost as though the sudden silence disturbed him more than her former activity.

He groaned loudly, opened one eye, and looked at her in some surprise.

'What . . . ?'

'Am I doing here?' she finished the sentence for him. 'You passed out on us in the taxi and I thought I had better stay with you until you were safe to be left alone.'

'Oh, God,' he moaned, as he tried to lift his head. He sank back and would have dropped off again had she not insisted.

'Come on, let's get you into your bed. You can't sleep properly on that thing.'

'Thirsty . . .' he muttered, stretching his hand out towards a conveniently placed bottle.

'Not for that you're not,' she declared, removing the whisky from his reach and setting it down on the now relatively clear sideboard.

'If you want a drink,' she went on,' I'll make you something hot.' She had placed a half-filled kettle on the hob some time before and forgotten she had done so. In a matter of moments she had set out two cups and found a bottle of Camp Coffee Essence. It was revolting stuff, but in her explorations so far she had not come across the usual tea caddy. This would have to do.

'Sugar?' she demanded, stirring the dark liquid and looking about her for some sign of a milk bottle.

'Condensed milk,' he murmured, and nodded towards the wall cupboard where she found a small stock of tins. This kind of thing was all right for camping out, but it was no way to live . . . no wonder he spent so much of his time in cafés and bars.

They sat companionably for a few minutes, sipping the sweet steaming liquid.

Magnus regarded her strangely, trying desperately to recall just how he came to be here in his own home alone with Morag Beaton.

'How . . . ?'

'. . . did we get here?' She sought to enlighten him. 'A friend of yours . . . one Charlie? . . . brought us in his taxi. He was very concerned about leaving me here. Goodness knows what he thought you might get up to. The condition you were in, I knew I was perfectly safe.'

He was in too much pain from his pounding head even to smile at the suggestion that her honour might have been threatened. A frown did cross his brow, however, when he gave the matter a little more thought.

'There could be talk, you know. People are very ready to draw the wrong conclusions in circumstances like this.'

'I *am* a doctor,' she declared haughtily. 'I was quite simply attending to my patient in his hour of need.' She spoke lightly, but if she too felt some concern, it was not for herself.

There had been evidence of blood flecks in the vomit she had cleared up earlier. It might be nothing at all – just strain from the excess of alcohol taken perhaps – but on the other hand it could suggest a more serious problem. This was hardly the time to mention her worries to Magnus, however.

'Come along now.' She used what her brothers called her 'nanny' voice. 'Let's see if we can get you into bed.'

When he tried to rise it was clear he was still very unstable and was obliged to lean heavily on her as they struggled into the tiny bedroom. He sprawled across the bed, quite exhausted by the effort, and Morag suspected his condition arose from something more serious than ordinary drunkenness. As his head hit the pillow he rolled over and faced the wall. She decided to leave him as he was for the time being, and after covering him with the blanket, she crept out of the room. A few hours' sleep should make all the difference to him.

Only when she had turned down the lamp in the kitchen and settled herself on the horsehair sofa to rest, did she remember that she had intended to take the early steamer for Eisdalsa that morning. There was no way now in which she could get back to the hospital, change her clothes and catch the steamer. She put the thought right out of her head and, despite the discomfort, after a while dropped into a dream-filled shallow sleep from which she frequently awoke. She would lie listening for any sounds of Magnus moving about next door and then, hearing nothing, drop off again.

\*     \*     \*

A ray from the bright morning sun, which had managed to penetrate a gap in the skimpy curtains, fell full upon her face. Morag woke suddenly from her first real sleep of the night. Her head ached unbearably and for a moment she was confused about her surroundings. Suddenly she was fully awake, remembering where she was and what she was doing there.

She crept into the other room where Magnus lay sprawled untidily across the bed, still deeply asleep. She felt for his pulse . . . nothing to worry about there. She turned up his eyelid and watched for any discrepancy in reaction between the two pupils. Satisfied at last that the man's stupor was due merely to alcohol and not some life-threatening coma, she straightened the covers and left him to sleep while she dialled the taxi rank.

When, at last, the cab drew up outside, she was relieved to find that the driver was Charlie. At least she did not have to offer him any explanation for being where she was at nine o'clock in the morning.

'Good morning, Doctor,' he greeted her. 'How is your patient this morning?'

If there was just the hint of sarcasm in his tone, she chose to ignore it.

'I think he'll live,' she replied, eyes twinkling. Then, as she settled herself inside the cab, 'Will you take me to the hospital, please?'

'Yes, ma'am!' Charlie replied, and tucked a rug around her knees before closing the rear door. Even though it was early May, the air was still cool at this time of day.

The partition between the passenger seats and the driver's cab was open, she noticed. Clearly Charlie enjoyed conversing with his clients.

'You mustn't judge him too harshly, miss.'

The cabbie might have been reading her thoughts, so close was his observation to what she was thinking.

'He had a bad time in Flanders . . . we all did . . . but some of us were affected more deeply than the rest. He's a very sensitive man, is Mr Glendenning. The trouble with those of us that came out of it in one piece,' he continued 'is that we feel guilty, if you can understand that. We don't know why we were saved, and not the others . . .'

She nodded, trying to understand but not really grasping what he meant.

The cab swung through the hospital gates, depositing her at the side entrance where she hoped to enter the building unobserved. As she stepped out of the car and turned to pay her fare, Charlie, accepting the proffered coins, grinned at her.

'Don't worry, Doctor, your secret is safe with me,' he said, tapping the side of his nose with his index finger. 'Any time you need a cab, ring the number you used this morning and ask for me. If I can come, I will.'

She thanked him warmly and pushed open the door into the casualty department.

Morag strode past the reception desk, nodding a good morning to the uniformed porter who held open a door for her. She hoped that her appearance at this hour would go unnoticed. The consultants would be on their ward rounds and most of the nursing staff would be engaged in the morning ritual.

She reached her own room without further encounter, stripped off her clothes, which were soiled and crumpled from the night's experiences, and bathed her face in tepid water. When she emerged again half an hour later, she bore the appearance of one who has woken late in the knowledge that she has a full day of inactivity before her.

She had dressed in a plain tweed suit and carried a small haversack slung over one shoulder. Her shoes were tough brogues which she had often worn when walking in the hills around her home.

On her way to Sidney Maynard's office, she slipped into the kitchen and begged a couple of sandwiches and a flask of tea from Isa McClachan.

'I thought I would go for a hike up the glen,' she explained. 'If I can't work, I might as well take advantage of my few days of freedom.'

'It looks as though it will be a fair day,' Isa agreed. 'But you

watch out for any mist settling in. It can overtake you quite
unexpectedly, you know.' She added a packet of biscuits and a
couple of apples to Morag's rations. 'Just in case you get caught
out longer than you planned,' the cook explained.

The kindly woman, who ran the hospital kitchens with the
efficiency of someone trained in one of the noble houses of
Perthshire, had taken to Morag right from the start.

Most of the medical staff regarded the ancillary workers in the
hospital as a lower form of life and scarcely acknowledged their
existence, except to make demands upon their services. Morag
Beaton was different.

She seemed to understand that the welfare of the patients
depended as much upon the efficiency of porters, cleaners and
kitchen assistants as it did upon the chief consultant himself.

To Morag, a child of a large family where compromise
and co-operation were essential to peaceful co-existence, this
behaviour came quite naturally. She was entirely unaware of
the esteem in which the hospital's non-medical staff held her.

At Maynard's door, she hesitated before tapping lightly. Lucy
McArdle looked up as she entered and greeted her with a half
smile. A wave of sympathy had gone around the hospital in the
wake of Maynard's harsh decision to suspend Morag until the
result of the inquiry. Those who knew what things had been like
in the emergency unit on the night of the bus disaster, considered
his reaction to have been most unfair.

'Mr Maynard said I was to let you know where I would be if
I left the premises for any length of time,' Morag explained. 'I
shall be walking up the glen and taking the mountain path . . .
starting this late, I can't expect to reach the summit, but I would
like to see how far I can get.'

'Take care,' warned the secretary. 'It's not a very good idea
to go up there alone.'

'Oh, I know my limitations,' Morag assured her. 'I shall be
back before dark.'

As she made her way through the oak wood and along the narrow
track which skirted the mountain stream, Morag breathed deeply

of the heavy perfume of hawthorn blossom. A few stray bluebells and even a primrose or two still flowered amongst the loose leaf litter, reminding her that a prolonged winter had set back the earlier-flowering plants so that now two seasons had merged into one, giving an unprecedented display of colour. As she crossed the stream by an ancient humpbacked bridge and began the steady ascent of the well-trodden path to the summit of the Ben, she came suddenly out into the open and found herself surrounded by freshly sprouted heather and the brown fronds of last year's bracken. Here and there bright green shoots of new growth gave promise of the season's bounty.

Morag eased her haversack on to the other shoulder and continued on until the path began to climb more steeply and the lush foliage of the plateau was left behind.

She was above the treeline now and the air had become decidedly cooler. Grateful for having had the foresight to include in her pack a lightweight showerproof coat, she slipped this on over her jacket and rested for a few moments on a convenient boulder, relishing the solitude and the silence.

A small party of walkers was following her tracks up the path, shouting and laughing as they approached. Not wishing to become involved with people who appeared insensitive to the spirit of the place, Morag slipped around the boulder, remaining out of sight until they had passed. They were young people, three boys and two girls. Scantily clad in shorts and short-sleeved shirts, the boys moved on ahead of the girls, who were already beginning to make heavy weather of the climb. One of them was dressed sensibly enough in slacks and wore a woollen cardigan over her cotton blouse. Her shoes were low-heeled for walking, in contrast with the totally unsuitable footwear of her companion, who teetered along upon flimsy court shoes which made her progress over the stony path painfully slow, and probably unsafe. This second girl wore a dress of some thin silky material. The skirt blew up around her waist at every gust of wind, so that she was obliged to assign one hand permanently to the task of maintaining decency.

Only when this ill-assorted party was quite out of sight did Morag re-emerge and carry on up the mountain track.

An hour or so later, when gorse and brambles, myrtle and creeping willow had finally given way to barren rock, she halted once again and drew out the sandwiches that Isa had given her. She settled herself with her back against a boulder to admire the view. From this height she could see far out over the loch to where miniature fishing boats cut a swathe across the mirror-black waters which perfectly reflected the hills of the Ardnamurchan peninsular. Far off to her left the Corran ferry, its funnel belching black smoke, traversed the loch, crossing the path of the afternoon steamer returning from the south. To the right it was possible to follow the line of the canal which bisected the valley to the east of the town.

The wind was stronger now and quite chilling. She decided to put on her spare jumper and was grateful for the warmth of the tea from her thermos flask. The day was still clear although patches of white cloud were beginning to gather and to darken. She glanced up over her shoulder and was surprised to see that the summit, whose outline had only a few minutes before been sharply etched against the sky, was now shrouded in mist.

It was time to descend.

Carried upon the wind she heard a cry. Could it be a sea bird so high and so far from the loch? More likely a buzzard, or maybe even a chuff? These latter birds had once been common among the more remote cliffs and headlands of the Islands of Lorn, but hunted mercilessly for their black plumage, so valued by the Victorians, were now nearly extinct. She trained her eyes on the cliff, hoping for a glimpse of the bird, but saw nothing.

Lowering herself on to the path she began the steep descent . . . how much more difficult it was to go down than to climb up! Her progress was slowed by the unstable nature of the loose stones beneath her feet. At a particularly awkward place she was obliged to sit down and lower herself from rock to rock on her bottom. In this fashion she managed to reach the foot of the slope without mishap. Before she could regain her feet, however, she was showered from above by a hail of stones, dislodged by the incautious descent of a young man who was rapidly overtaking her.

As he caught up with her, she prepared to give him a piece of her mind. According to hill-walking lore one was expected to have a care for others as well as for oneself.

When she saw the boy's expression, however, she relented. He might have been expected to be red-faced and perspiring from his exertions, but instead his skin was grey with anxiety and his eyes stared wildly. He gave every appearance of having had a terrible shock.

'What is it?' she asked. She recognised him now. He was a member of the little group that had passed her earlier in the day.

'One of our party . . . a young girl . . . slipped and fell over the edge . . . we can't reach her from above . . . she isn't moving!'

He sank down on the rock beside her, suddenly exhausted, all the fight gone out of him.

Morag unstrapped her bag and drew out the thermos of sweet tea, which by now was nearly cold. She poured what remained into the cup and handed it to him.

'Drink this,' she ordered, firmly.

Unquestioning, he swallowed the tea and handed back the empty cup.

'Now then,' Morag demanded, 'how far are we from where your friend fell?'

'It can't be all that far from here.' He glanced around, anxiously. 'She must have fallen about seventy or eighty feet . . . over there.' He pointed eastwards to where a great bluff of rock obscured any further view of the mountainside. 'We were on our way down . . .' he continued, haltingly. 'It was getting too misty to see clearly and the girls were complaining of being cold . . . I told Fran she should have been wearing stouter shoes, but it was Billy, you see . . . she wanted to dress up for him . . .'

The boy, his first spurt of adrenaline already expended, was shivering now both from shock and cold. He was becoming confused in his thinking. She must get him moving again.

'Here, put this on,' Morag commanded, slipping out of her

waterproof coat and placing it over his shoulders. Silently he obeyed. 'Now, stand up here beside me, and we'll see if we can plan the shortest route to where she fell.'

They glanced up the path in the direction from which the boy had just come, then allowed their gaze to sweep across the face of the sheer cliff on the left-hand side.

'I think she must be about thirty or forty feet further up on the far side of that jutting-out piece of rock,' he decided. 'She fell into this huge basin, gouged out of the mountainside.' He was obviously unfamiliar with the term 'corrie'. His ignorance of the language of the mountains seemed to indicate why the expedition had been so ill-equipped.

'And where is the rest of the party?' Morag demanded.

'I told them to stay up above, from where they could keep an eye on Fran . . . in case she moved . . . and so they could direct the rescue party.'

It seemed to be the first sensible move the young people had made.

'Look,' Morag said, coming quickly to a decision, 'I am a doctor. If your friend is still alive, I may be able to help her.'

The look of relief in the boy's eyes was almost more than she could bear, for even if they were able to reach the casualty, Morag had nothing with her with which to render first aid, and scantily clad as both the casualty and the rest of the party were, they might all freeze to death before help could be summoned.

'Well now,' she said easily, trying to keep him calm, 'I suppose we had better introduce ourselves. I am Dr Beaton . . . please call me Morag.'

'I've heard my father speak about you, Dr Beaton,' he said. 'I'm Andrew McDonald . . . Andy.' Then he added, 'Fran is my sister.'

Morag remembered the GP who had helped her with her surgery on the night of the charabanc disaster. She placed a comforting hand on the boy's shoulder. 'Well, come along then, Andy,' she ordered, briskly, 'let's see if there is a way around that bluff.'

They studied the area on her map. At this height the footpath skirted a slope of loose scree, on the far side of which was the base of the bluff which hid the corrie from view. The scree slope descended into a dense scrub of heather and bracken.

Undoubtedly, the quickest route was straight across the scree slope, but the safest would be to descend to the heather belt and then to make their way around the base of the bluff through strewn boulders and dense bracken, where hidden streams and gullies might well impede their advance.

'We are going to cut across the scree towards that small pinnacle of rock . . . do you see?' Morag decided. She pointed to the needle of rock which marked the end of the spur. 'Have you ever tried to walk on scree before?'

Andy shook his head.

'It will feel strange at first; with each step you take, the ground will give way beneath your feet. The secret is to keep moving, with the fastest, lightest steps you can manage. That way you won't sink in too deeply.'

The boy nodded in understanding and made to return her coat.

'You wear it for the moment,' she told him. 'We may need it for Fran, later.'

With Andy following close behind her, Morag struck out across the scree. As she had explained, the going was hard. If she paused for a moment to rest, her feet would sink deep into the loose stones and it took an enormous effort to release them. With ten or twelve yards left to go, she took a deep breath and managed in a few swift strides to reach the sheer wall of rock.

A narrow ledge ran around the bluff about fifteen feet from the base. To a seasoned climber, reaching it would present no problem at all. For Morag, who had done plenty of walking in the mountains but had never attempted more than the easiest of climbs, it was a considerable challenge.

'Have you ever done anything like this before?' she asked her companion, indicating the way they must go.

He shook his head. 'No, not really,' he replied, 'but I've a head for heights and I'm quite good at gym.'

She studied him carefully. He was looking better now. The scramble across the scree slope had given him something else to think about other than his injured sister.

Her initial reaction had been to send him on down the mountain to fetch help, but it was important to find out first if the girl was still alive, and also to make some arrangement to get the rest of the young people off the mountain. He had said that the others were above the spot where the girl had fallen. In that case she could direct them herself . . . once they had found Fran. 'Watch where I put my fingers and feet,' she instructed him. 'Use exactly the same holds.' Morag found her first handhold and placed her toe in an indent. Grasping a protruding piece of rock, she pulled herself up on one leg. With her face pressed tight against the rock face, she drew up her other foot and sought blindly for the next toehold. She found it and reached again for a small cleft in the rock into which she could get her fingers. Pulling herself up with one hand, she sought above her head for the next hold. She turned to Andy.

'Now you,' she said, and waited until he had taken his first firm grip on the rock before moving on up the sheer face. It seemed a long time before they were standing side by side on the ledge. On examining her watch, Morag was surprised to find that the climb had taken them only a few minutes. The ledge which was to take them around the bluff to the corrie on the far side was nearly eighteen inches wide in places, and provided a firm footing even for inexperienced mountaineers.

At the point when they lost sight of the scree slope and the footpath they had left, they had their first view of the corrie. Morag was in the lead as they rounded the corner. Before her, the outer edge of the path had broken away and a gap of several feet appeared to make further progress impossible. The stiffening breeze caught her unexpectedly and for a moment she was in danger of losing her footing. She froze, face pressed against the rock wall.

Oh God, she thought, I can't move backwards or forwards. I shall have to stay here for ever.

In a voice which sounded far more calm than she felt, she said to Andy, 'I can't go any further, the rock has broken away. I don't think I can cross the gap.' She felt his hands on her shoulders, and the warmth of his body as he slid past her and reached the broken part of the ledge.

'I think I can jump it,' he said. 'It's really not very wide.'

Morag looked down. The track they were on had been rising steadily while they were rounding the bluff. The ledge was now something like thirty feet above the base of the cliff. If Andy fell from here he would be badly injured.

'I don't think I should allow you to attempt it,' she said doubtfully. But he had said that he was good at gym. His legs were young and strong . . . maybe he could make it.

'She's my sister,' he replied simply. 'I have to try!'

Without further protest, Morag backed away from the gap to allow Andy to take a run before leaping into space. He landed on the far side on all fours, well away from the crumbling edge. After examining his hands ruefully where they had been scraped on the jagged rock, he lifted his head and smiled triumphantly.

'That was easy,' he cried. 'Now you.'

He stood with arms outstretched, waiting to catch her as she jumped. There was nothing for it but to follow him. Screwing up her courage, Morag measured the gap with her eye, took a few steps backwards and tried to imagine she was leaping across level ground. She felt his arms tight about her as she landed, stumbled, and fell forward with the boy beneath her.

They came up laughing, forgetting just for a moment everything but the fact that they were still on the ledge and that neither had suffered serious injury.

Morag glanced across to where a patch of snow still lingered close under the back wall of the corrie. At its centre she could see the girl, her pale-coloured dress nearly lost in the whiteness surrounding her.

The ledge was noticeably wider now that they had turned the corner and were moving along the wall of the corrie itself. Soon it became a level path and in a matter of minutes Morag found herself on firm ground and able to make progress across a heather sward to where the stricken girl lay motionless.

The snow may have kept her warm, she told herself, knowing in her heart that, poorly clad and severely injured, there was little chance Fran could last out even if she were alive when they reached her.

As she approached the body with Andy close beside her, they heard a shout from above and looked up to see a row of anxious faces peering down at them out of the mist. Every sound was amplified by the proximity of the rock walls of the corrie. Morag breathed a sigh of relief. At least they could communicate clearly with those above.

Andy shouted up at them.

'I found a doctor!'

'Fran's alive,' one of the young men called. 'We've seen her moving.'

Together they struggled through snow which became deeper as they approached the girl.

Morag began to hope. If the snow was deep enough, it might have broken her fall sufficiently to save her.

Andy had run ahead and had crouched down beside his sister. As she came up to them, Morag could see the relief in his eyes. It was bad enough that any one of his friends should have suffered this fall, but his sister . . . if she died he would bear the responsibility for the rest of his life.

Morag crouched down beside the slender body. One leg was splayed out at an awkward angle and was clearly broken; her right shoulder had collapsed . . . a broken collarbone. Morag felt gently for a pulse. The movement roused the girl to semiconsciousness. She stirred, moaned incoherently and opened her eyes.

'Fran . . . Fran, it's me! Andy! This is Morag . . . she's a doctor . . . you'll be all right now.'

Morag looked up at him sharply. 'That coat . . . take it off and spread it on the ground.'

As Andy did as he was asked, Morag's hands moved over the girl's body, seeking for further broken bones. There was blood on her dress from a deep gash in one arm, made no doubt during her descent. There was nothing sharp enough to have caused the cut on landing. Fran had bled profusely for a while as the reddened snow around her upper body indicated, but the flow had ceased some time before. Her neck and skull seemed to be uninjured.

'Give me the belt off that coat,' Morag ordered.

As Andy struggled with numbed fingers, she examined the broken leg, trying to decide how best to straighten it.

'You'll have to help me,' she said as the boy handed her the belt. 'I am going to lash the broken leg to the good one, but first I must move it into position. When I tell you, I want you to grasp both ankles firmly and lift, so that I can get the belt underneath . . . OK?'

He nodded.

As she pulled the shattered limb into position the girl screamed. The sound echoed around the corrie, disturbing a golden eagle on her nest. With a great flapping of broad wings she took to the skies, hovering above them, suspicious of their intent. Convinced at last that the intruders were no threat to her young fledglings, the magnificent bird swooped down to her eyrie and all was still once more.

In seconds Morag had the two legs strapped firmly together.

'Now we must lift her on to the coat.' Morag took the upper part of the body, fearful of doing further damage to the broken collarbone, while Andy gently placed his hands under the good leg. Together they lifted the fragile girl on to the coat and Morag wrapped it around her. It was water and windproof. Perhaps they would be able to get her warm enough . . .

'We can't move her without a proper stretcher,' she said, 'so we are going to have to construct a snow shelter . . . you'd be surprised how warm they can be. But first of all we must do something about your friends up there.'

The three figures were fast disappearing in the mist which had advanced down the mountain with alarming rapidity.

'Can you still see to follow the path?' Morag yelled.

'Yes,' came the reply, deadened by the moist atmosphere.

'Then make your way back down. Is there anyone with warm clothing?'

'Yes.'

'When you get below the bluff, you'll find my map, marked with the position. Leave one of your party there with as much clothing as you can spare. They must guide the rescuers ... the rest of you, take the map and get on down to the nearest telephone. Call the police and an ambulance.'

Their spokesman waved his hand in acknowledgement and they disappeared from view.

'Come along, Andy,' Morag said wearily. 'We have to begin digging.'

It was no easy task to burrow into the hard-packed snow with nothing but their hands for tools, but the exercise did at least help them to keep warm. Together they gouged out a square hole nearly four feet deep, as close to where Fran lay as they could manage without disturbing her. When they had finished, they moved her gently, with Morag supporting her fractured leg and Andy taking the main weight of her body.

Out of the cold breeze, and wrapped in Morag's waterproof coat, the injured girl began to respond immediately to the change in temperature and quickly recovered consciousness. She seemed to take Andy's presence for granted.

'I knew you'd come,' she murmured. 'All the time I was lying here I was praying ... please God, let Andy find me and I'll never, ever borrow his things again without permission!' She smiled weakly as he rubbed her frozen hands and kissed her lightly on the forehead.

'Just stay alive until we can get you to hospital,' her brother replied, 'and you can have my drawing instruments and even my slide rule, whenever you want,' he assured her, his voice choked with emotion.

Morag, who was busily patting down the snow walls of their tiny shelter to make sure that they would not collapse in on them, was impressed. 'Can your sister use a slide rule?' she asked, surprised that such a young girl should be conversant with logarithmic tables.

'Better than I can,' he replied, gallantly. 'She's a whiz when it comes to anything to do with mathematics.'

Morag settled herself alongside Fran so that the girl was receiving body warmth from both her companions.

'I was hopeless at maths myself,' she confessed, and her admission brought a weak smile to the girl's face. 'I used to have to get my best friend to do my maths prep for me, and in exchange I did her biology drawings.'

'Did you always want to be a doctor?' Andy demanded, and Morag sensed more than a casual interest in her response.

'My father, grandfather and great uncle Angus too were all medical men ... Beaton doctors go back quite a few generations. But I'm the first woman in the family to have entered the profession.'

'My dad expects me to follow in his footsteps,' Andy explained, 'but I'm not sure that I'm up to it.'

Morag understood his reservations. 'It's very hard work,' she said, 'there isn't a lot of time for anything else once you start training, but I can recommend it as a worthwhile job. There is a great deal of satisfaction to be gained from being the one who knows what to do in an emergency.'

Fran moaned and seemed to be dropping into unconsciousness once again. Morag leaned over her and began rubbing her hands, arms and the good leg. She glanced up at Andy who was looking anxious.

'We must try to keep her conscious and shifting about just a little ... to keep the circulation going. Massage and move her limbs from time to time. She doesn't seem to have any pain on that side.'

They talked on as the light began to fade. Once the sun had sunk below the rim of the corrie the air became noticeably colder and they huddled closer to Fran to conserve what warmth there was. Morag emptied the contents of her rucksack and found the packet of biscuits which she had slipped in at the last minute, a slab of chocolate and the empty thermos flask.

'If I fill this with snow and sit on it for a while, perhaps it will melt,' she suggested, and proceeded to do so. They had already tried eating handfuls of snow but it was an unsatisfactory way of obtaining a drink.

Andy nibbled a biscuit, trying to make it last as long as possible, while Morag persuaded Fran to eat a little of the emergency chocolate she always carried with her on hill walks. Fran was reluctant to try at first, but the doctor persisted and was gratified to succeed at last.

Morag began to hum the tune 'The sun has got his hat on', hoping that the teenagers would join in with her, and Andy did so without hesitation.

It was a popular song of the day, currently on everyone's lips, and Morag was pleased to see that even Fran was mouthing the words, trying to join in.

Andy went through the entire repertoire of the *Boy Scouts' Campfire Songbook* and to their immense delight Morag taught them the medical student's version of certain popular hymns:-

> Hark the herald angles sing,
> Beecham's Pills are just the thing . . .

So engrossed were they in this entertainment that they did not hear the rescuers until they were nearly upon them.

It had grown quite dark by the time the first torches were seen reflecting off the rock walls of the corrie. The men were on the same track which Morag and Andy had negotiated hours before. She supposed they had picked up the marker left on the main path and followed in her footsteps. Nevertheless, while it was perfectly possible for strong healthy climbers to get around the bluff, she failed to see how they were going to manipulate a stretcher along that tortuous path. She climbed up out of the snowhole and stood waving until she was caught in a beam from one of the torches. The snaking line of black shadowy figures and flickering lights rapidly approached them across the snowfield.

In a matter of minutes they had Fran wrapped in blankets and lashed to the stretcher they had brought with them. Grateful for the additional warmth of a heavy wool jacket which someone had draped over her shoulders in the first few minutes of their arrival, and warmed from within by the drink of hot sweet tea produced from a thermos flask, Morag began to feel the 'pins and needles' associated with her own circulatory system warming up, and was forced to hop about in the snow until the sensations receded. Andy seemed to have withstood the ordeal better than either of the others and was happily greeting a number of old friends amongst the party.

Out of the darkness came a voice which seemed vaguely familiar.

'If you feel able, Dr Beaton, we are ready to move out now.'

The tall figure before her was wearing a hooded jacket similar to the one she herself had been given, and a woollen scarf which covered the lower part of his face. This he pulled down as he noted her puzzled expression, and she recognised the man she had not seen since the charabanc crash: Adam Inglis.

'I can't tell you how pleased I am to see you, Mr Inglis,' Morag exclaimed as he took her arm and led her gently to the edge of the snowfield. They seemed to be returning by the way that she and Andy had come and she could not help but express her concern about her patient's ability to sustain the journey.

'Do you think you can get the stretcher around the bluff?' she demanded doubtfully.

'Trust us, Dr Beaton,' was the reply, 'we know what we are doing.'

Instead of taking the sheep track as she had anticipated, the party moved forward to the edge of the corrie, to a point where the ground fell away in a precipitous cliff. It was too dark now to see the bottom of the drop, but Morag remembered it as being a good thirty feet down to the next area of level ground.

Some members of the party busied themselves with roping the stretcher while others assisted two of their colleagues to abseil to the bottom of the cliff, to receive the stretcher as it descended. Morag watched this procedure with interest, glad that she herself would not have to go down that way.

Two men handled the belaying ropes while another, separately roped, accompanied the stretcher in its descent. Morag peered over the edge to watch as Fran was lowered carefully, the stretcher held away from the sharply jutting rocks, and was impressed by the ease and competence with which the operation was carried out.

'All right, Doctor.' Adam Inglis had returned from supervising operations and was now holding in his hands the loose end of a rope. Without explanation he began to tie it around Morag's body. She pulled away in surprise.

'You don't expect me to go over there?' she exclaimed, suddenly terrified that that was exactly what he expected of her.

'You saw how it's done,' he replied casually. 'There really is nothing to it . . . we do all the work. All you have to do is lean back away from the rock and walk down the cliff as though you were on flat ground. If you find you must swing outwards to avoid a jutting piece of rock, then push off firmly but don't swing out too far . . . and flex your knees and ankles as you swing back.'

Morag found herself trembling with fright. Andy McDonald appeared suddenly, already roped himself.

'Come on, Doc,' he cried encouragingly, 'I'm going to try. If I can do it, I'm sure you can!'

That was enough for Morag. It was as though one of her brothers had challenged her. Throughout childhood and beyond, she had battled constantly to prove that she could do whatever any boy could. If Andy was willing to have a go, she would try too.

Adam Inglis roped her up and led her to the edge of the cliff where he turned her round with her back to the drop. He also gave her a stout pair of gloves to avoid chafing to her hands. With her legs astride a doubled rope, Adam reached down and pulled both strands together up and over her right thigh, across her chest and over her left shoulder.

'I feel like a trussed chicken,' she said, trying to sound nonchalant.

Adam placed one rope in her left hand. 'That's your guiding hand,' he explained. The second rope he pulled round and across her back, placing it firmly in her right hand. 'And this one controls your descent. As you lower yourself, play out the rope with your right hand, allowing it to slip easily through your left. If you want to slow down, hold both ropes firmly then ease them through your fingers a little at a time until you regain your rhythm. It's up to you how fast you travel!'

He could see that she was trying very bravely not to show how afraid she was, and had to admire her pluck.

'Now then, I have already tied a safety rope around you which I shall belay as you descend. If you should slip, I shall be here to stop you from falling, OK?' She nodded, silently, eyes wide with terror.

He led her backwards until they were both standing on the very edge. 'Lean back, allowing your guiding hand to take the strain,' he ordered.

There was nothing else for it. Used to taking instruction and relying upon the experience of others, Morag breathed deeply and let the air out slowly. Having thus forced herself to relax, she did as he suggested and found the rope straining in her hand as she leaned out into the dark pit beneath her feet.

'Now, walk down the wall!' he ordered.

And she did.

Just a few minutes more and she was standing safely upon firm ground.

'There, that wasn't so bad, was it?' demanded Andy, emerging from the gloom. 'I must say, you did jolly well. I was as nervous as anything the first time!'

'Do you mean to say this *wasn't* your first time?' Morag demanded, spitting out the words to relieve her inner tension.

'Well, no, not exactly. I did some a while back . . . with the Scouts . . . but never in the dark before,' he added hastily.

'Where have they put Fran?' she demanded, setting aside the matter of the boy's deception. She might never have attempted the drop had it not been for him egging her on!

Andy helped her release the last of her ropes before taking her to a sheltered spot, a shallow cave in the cliff wall. She knelt down beside the girl who appeared to be sleeping comfortably. Morag tested for vital signs. Fran was warm and perspiring freely under a mountain of blankets. Her colour was good and apart from the fractures she seemed none the worse for her ordeal. Thankfully the breaks were clean and there had been no penetration of the skin which meant that there was no risk of gangrene. The girl should recover very well, provided they could get her to hospital soon.

Sounds from above indicated that the remainder of the rescue party was now descending.

In moments, Adam Inglis was beside Morag, anxious to know if she had hurt herself during in the descent.

'You gave me a bit of a fright,' he said, rubbing at his shoulders which had borne the brunt of her momentary loss of control.

'Oh, I'm fine,' she insisted, appreciating his obvious concern. 'In fact, once I got going I began to enjoy it.' 'Well, if that's the case,' he fell into step beside her as the party moved away, 'you will have to come out with us on one of our training exercises. A doctor would be a useful member of our team.'

Morag was inordinately pleased at this suggestion. It seemed that he really was anxious to see more of her. A warm glow of happiness descended upon her, dispelling the discomfort which she had been feeling. Suddenly she discovered that all her senses were heightened. He turned on a narrow part of the pathway, offering his hand to help her over an awkward boulder. She thrilled at his touch, glad that she had returned the gloves he had given her for the descent. As her feet found the level ground once more she willed him to continue to hold her. As though reading her unspoken thoughts, he placed an arm about her shoulders to guide her down the rough path. Gladly she allowed herself to relax within his firm grasp.

As they followed in the wake of the rescue party Morag spoke of Adam's uncle for the first time since his death.

'I'm so very sorry . . . about Mr Campbell,' she faltered. 'You must miss him very much.'

'Yes,' Adam replied, his voice had a hollow ring. 'He was like a father to me you know. My own dad died during the war.'

'I do hope you don't . . .' she found it so difficult to put her worst fears into words.

'Look, I should have told you . . .' Stopping suddenly he turned to face her, 'There is no blame attached to anyone for my uncle's death. I watched him when we were waiting in the reception area that night. There was absolutely nothing to indicate that there was anything wrong with him. I doubt if he would have allowed you to examine him, had you mentioned it.

For an instant, he caught her in the beam from his torch. The look of relief which he saw in her eyes made him realise how she must have agonized over the events of that evening. He was suddenly filled with an extraordinary feeling of compassion for her.

'I'm sure that you did everything humanly possible to save him,' he told her firmly. Then taking her by the hand he led her on down the slope towards the lights of the vehicles in the valley below.

He released his hold on her, murmuring something about speaking to the police sergeant, and left her to supervise the transfer of her patient to the ambulance.

Before she climbed in herself, Morag waited, hoping to be able to have one last word. She could see that Adam was already occupied with the other members of his team in checking and loading the equipment.

Disappointed, she climbed in beside Andy McDonald and his sister and seated herself on the spare stretcher as the ambulance driver closed the doors on them.

# Chapter 7

❦

Gregor Campbell had lived for most of his long and distinguished life in the town of Inverlinnhe. It was hardly surprising therefore, that on the day of his funeral the roads should be choked with the volume of traffic making its way to the Episcopalian Church of St John which occupied a commanding position in the centre of the town.

Mary Neal had prevailed upon Morag to accompany her to the service, despite Morag's reservations about attending uninvited. While she had no reason to believe that his family bore her any ill will over the manner of his death, Morag herself was very conscious of the part she had played during Gregor Campbell's last hours. She had no wish to prove an unwanted presence at the wake.

'Adam is the chief mourner,' Mary insisted, 'and he told me himself he does not blame you in any way for his uncle's death. Besides, it is considered a mark of respect for a man's doctor to attend his interment . . . to stay away is to put doubt in the minds of those who might otherwise support you.'

'I didn't know you were that well acquainted with Adam?' Morag said huffily.

She was quite put out to think that he had spoken so intimately of her involvement with a third party, even if that person was the nurse who had been present at the time of his uncle's death. Mary should know that it really was not her place to enter into such a discussion with the hearing pending. This was not the time to remonstrate, however. Morag was in too much trouble herself to wish to antagonise yet another of her colleagues.

And Mary was certainly right about the need for her to

be present at the funeral. Morag could not argue against such logic.

The two women managed to slip in at the back of the church while it was no more than half full. When the cortège arrived at last, there was not a seat to be had, and late-comers were obliged to stand in the aisles. Morag was reminded of similar events which had taken place at Eisdalsa over the years. There the community was so small and close-knit that each member's passing was felt by them all, and everyone in the parish would attend the funeral. Here, she might have expected things to be different. Only when her one good friend on the Hospital Board, Duncan McRae, rose to give the eulogy, did she begin to understand how much the old gentleman had meant to the townsfolk of Inverlinnhe.

'. . . as a founder member of the Municipal Council, as a member of the town's Golf Club and Highland Games Committee, he was known to many. As a brave soldier who fought alongside many members of the Highland Light Infantry from this town, he was known to those few who are left to tell tales of the African campaign. He saw service in India and was decorated for bravery on two occasions.

'The younger people of the town knew Gregor Campbell for his work with the Boy Scout Movement, and his unstinting efforts to raise money for a town swimming pool.

'It was only what we had come to expect of him, that he devoted his last few hours on this earth to the rescue of his fellow travellers in the terrible automobile accident of ten days ago. Injured himself, as it later transpired, he nonetheless used up all his strength in caring for his fellows and directing their rescue, before himself succumbing to heart failure . . .'

Mr McRae brought his tribute to a close and the congregation rose for the final hymn. Morag cast a glance sideways at Mary and was distressed to find her companion's eyes filled with tears. She herself had met Adam's uncle only on that one occasion when the bus crashed. Mary must have known him well to be so deeply affected. Morag wished she herself had had the chance to get to know the old man.

They were filing out into the churchyard, gloomy now that

the bright weather of the earlier part of the day had given way to a heavy mist which was slowly descending from the mountain tops. Morag shuddered, remembering her recent night out in just such conditions, and her eyes were drawn to a point high up on the Ben.

Inverlinnhe's main cemetery was a recently acquired plot of land lying to the east of the town, on the slopes of Beinn a Mart, but Gregor Campbell's family had for generations been buried in a private mausoleum in St John's churchyard, and it was to this eighteenth-century black basalt monstrosity that the congregation now repaired.

The committal service ended as the first drops of real rain began to fall. All about them people bustled and fidgeted as they attempted to shelter from the downpour. Mary was obliged to huddle under Morag's dainty umbrella made, unfortunately, more for elegance than practicality.

At the lych-gate they were forced to wait behind a queue of those paying their respects to the chief mourners. Adam looked strained as he accepted the murmured condolences of the endless stream of people. When at last his glance fell upon the two women, his eyes lit up and he stepped forward to greet them both.

'Mary, my dear, I hoped you would be here.' Adam grasped her hand and the nurse brushed his cheek with her lips. Turning to Morag, he shook her firmly by the hand. She wished she knew him well enough to follow Mary's example, but confined herself instead to a few murmured words of condolence.

'I hope your own difficulties will be resolved very soon,' he told her.

She nodded, accepting his unspoken absolution and would have moved on had he not continued, 'Dr Beaton, I have not told you yet how much I admired what you did to save Gordon McDonald's daughter the other night. How is young Fran getting on?'

Morag, still banned from any contact with the patients, could only turn to Mary to give him an answer.

'It will take a long time, I'm afraid, but they tell me she is going to be fine.'

119

The queue was growing impatient behind them, and it was time to move on.

'You will come back to the house?' pleaded Adam.

Morag looked doubtful. 'Oh, I would not want to intrude . . .' she faltered, and turned to Mary. 'You must go, of course,' she said. 'I can make my way back alone.'

'I wish you would come too,' Adam insisted. 'There is something I want to discuss with you . . .'

Surprised and oddly gratified by his insistence, she relented. 'Then I shall be pleased to accompany Mary.'

The family home of the Campbells was one of the imposing three-storey villas which had sprung up all over the Highlands during the 1880s and 1890s, wherever a major railway link was established. Perched on the second terrace above the main street, the house, sturdily built of blocks of local granite, commanded a view of the railway pier and the eastern end of the loch.

When the mourners' limousine pulled up outside the gates, and its various passengers alighted, the rain stopped as suddenly as it had begun. A faint breeze, whipping up from the west, began to dispel the mist and within minutes tiny patches of blue sky appeared between the overcast grey clouds.

The garden seemed as dismal as the house itself, with its heavy rhododendron bushes and tall pines blocking out the light and much of the view from the ground-floor windows. On this occasion the gloom seemed appropriate, though, and it was with hushed voices and muffled steps that the guests entered the large marble-tiled entrance hall.

Gordon McDonald approached them as Morag and Mary stood uncertainly, just inside the door to the main reception room.

'Good morning, Miss Neal,' he greeted Mary, then turning to Morag took both her hands in his, trying to find some way to express the emotion which he felt.

'I can find no words which are adequate to thank you for saving my daughter's life, Dr Beaton. Andy told me everything that happened . . . how you took charge of things. Why those children were stupid enough to go on the mountain so ill equipped, I shall never understand. It's not as though they are strangers to the district. At least the experience frightened Andy sufficiently for me to be able to extract a promise from him that he will learn to climb properly before venturing up there again . . .'

'Perhaps I, too, should take some lessons.' Morag smiled, wryly. 'I have done a great deal of hill walking, but I have never tackled anything quite like that before. I was too cold and tired at the time to appreciate everything the mountain rescue people were doing. All I know is that they got us out of that corrie with far less trouble than Andy and I had getting in!'

'My wife is very anxious to meet you, Doctor, to thank you herself, and I know that Andy wishes to see you again. I wonder . . . will you join us for luncheon on Sunday? I gather you have no duties at the hospital just at present.'

The comment came easily – its delivery gave her no clue as to the GP's opinion in the matter of her suspension. Eddie and she had discussed the possible witnesses upon whom she should call during the enquiry. This might be an opportunity to sound out Gordon McDonald.

'I would be delighted to meet your wife, Dr McDonald,' she replied, 'Thank you for the invitation.'

'Please,' he insisted, 'call me Gordon . . . and I believe we know each other well enough now for me to address you as Morag?' He smiled at her so warmly that she found it impossible to be offended.

'Of course . . . Gordon,' she replied, while Mary Neal, glancing from one to the other, envied Morag the ease with which she could associate with her male colleagues when nurses like herself were always made to feel inferior.

Across the room, Morag caught sight of a familiar figure, signalling to her by raising his whisky tumbler. She excused herself and threaded her way through the throng of people towards him.

'Well, if it isn't the fair physician!' Magnus greeted her. 'I wanted to interview you about your exploits on the mountain the other evening but they said you were sleeping it off . . . for two days?'

'I am surprised you were capable of interviewing anyone,' she observed, dryly. 'The last time I saw you, a regiment of banshees would not have woken you!'

'Ah, yes, I owe you an apology for that night. I had to seek out Charlie before I could piece together exactly what happened.' He lowered his voice, and steered her towards the window where they would not be overheard.

'In fact, I have a suggestion which might make amends for my puerile behaviour. Did you ever manage that visit to your parents?'

'No, unfortunately too much has happened since that night. I've put the idea of a trip home right out of my head.'

'Then you must allow me to take you there on Friday. We could return on Saturday.' When she threatened to argue, he raised his hand to prevent her. 'I shall hire a car and take you home . . . a night in Oban will suit me very well as it happens. There's a meeting of Municipal Council Officers for the area which should be worth a paragraph or two in the *Gazette*.'

Morag, unable to think of a suitable excuse could only agree. 'Thank you, Magnus, that would be absolutely splendid!'

'I'll pick you up from the hospital at ten then,' he said as, catching sight of someone he particularly wanted to interview, he darted away.

'Let me replenish your glass for you,' suggested Adam Inglis, approaching with a half-filled decanter.

'No, really . . . nothing more, thank you,' Morag stammered, suddenly shy.

I can't tell you how pleased I was to see you at the church,' he went on.

'I wish I had known your uncle,' she responded. 'By all accounts he was quite a character.'

'McDonald assures me that the operation you performed should have saved his life,' Adam observed. 'Had his heart not given out, would he have returned to normal, do you suppose?'

'It's hard to tell,' she answered, honestly. 'With someone of his advanced years, a brain operation is likely to have unlooked-for side effects . . . a stroke maybe, or partial loss of one or more of the senses. It is impossible to say.'

'Well,' Adam assured her earnestly, 'I believe that my uncle would have thanked you for trying. And . . .' as she made to protest '. . . I am equally certain that he would be the first to have declared a good innings completed satisfactorily.

'Whatever the outcome of all these investigations and inquiries, I want you to know that I am absolutely certain you did everything in your power to save him. If there is any justice in this world, you will be exonerated.'

She lowered her eyes, unable to meet his steady gaze. If only she felt as confident as he obviously did.

'It is because I am convinced that you will be practising medicine here in Inverlinnhe for many years to come that I want to put to you a proposition arising from that experience on the mountain. Our team of volunteers was able to find you and get you down . . . it's something in which we are very well practised . . . but we all of us agreed the girl would have died had it not been for your presence at the scene.'

'I did what any doctor would do,' she replied. 'An amateur competent in first-aid procedures, could have done much the same.'

'I don't think so,' Adam replied. 'It was not just the treatment you gave to Fran's injuries. It was building the snow house, and the two uninjured people lying on either side of her to keep up her body temperature, that saved her. We talk about these matters amongst ourselves but you carried out the right procedures instinctively, which to my mind makes you the best person for the job.'

'What job?' Morag looked up inquiringly, unable to suppress her curiosity.

'We want to offer you the post of medical officer attached to our mountain rescue team.'

'But I can't climb, and I know next to nothing about mountain lore,' she protested weakly, because she already knew she was going to allow herself to be persuaded. She was determined to get to know Adam Inglis properly, and what better opportunity could she hope for than this?

\*　　\*　　\*

By mid-morning on the following Saturday, Morag and Magnus Glendenning were bowling along the road to Oban, having left the town on a route which ran parallel with Loch Linnhe. The Ballachulish ferry which would take them across the bottom end of Loch Leven was crowded with summer tourists; two charabancs were in the queue ahead of them.

When at last it was Magnus's turn to steer his motor car down the ramp and on to the raft-like vessel, Morag held her breath, fearing that the rather large open tourer would run off the farther end of the deck. Magnus came to a skilful halt, his wheels just touching the further gate. Two motor cycles, with sidecars attached, pulled up beside him, their drivers and passengers exchanging excited speculation about the mountainous heaps of white mineral material which lined the shore at the head of the loch, completely obscuring the view of the village beyond.

'That's the aluminium works owned by your Hospital Board Chairman, Graham Fraser,' Magnus explained to his passenger. 'See those great pipes coming down the mountainside . . . they carry water to the turbines which generate electricity for smelting the ore.'

Morag, a child of an important quarrying community herself, was no stranger to the science of geology.

'I had no idea there was any bauxite in these parts,' she observed.

'There is none,' he replied. 'The industry was set up after the war to give employment to returning ex-servicemen. It was the cheap hydro-electricity which encouraged the enterprise. The ore is imported from Spain, amongst other places.'

By now the motor cyclists were listening intently to their discussion and one of the women observed tartly, What a pity to spoil the scenery so with all that waste material . . . it really is disgusting.' She turned her back on the aluminium works and indicated the heaps of slate waste on the southern shore of the loch, where a once successful quarry producing roofing slates was now sinking into decline. 'There too,' she declared, 'How can anyone so desecrate an area of such beauty? The Scots have no soul. All this magnificent countryside is simply lost on them!'

To Magnus's surprise, Morag turned on the woman quite sharply, her face flushed an angry red.

'Things are not always what they seem,' she began, then modulated her tone as she continued, 'we need industry to stop the problem of depopulation in the Highlands. Without some form of manufacturing, towns like Inverlinnhe could not exist, and then there would be nowhere for the tourists to stay.'

The woman appeared suitably chastened but, nevertheless, Magnus was relieved when the ferry grounded on the far bank of the loch and the discussion had to be curtailed.

'You certainly put her in her place!' Magnus laughed when they were on their way again. He was full of admiration for his companion's spirited attack.

'Oh, I have listened to that sort of talk all my life,' Morag explained, ruefully. 'If it weren't for the slate quarrying that went on for two centuries and more on Eisdalsa, there would be nothing there to visit, yet visitors always complain of the heaps of waste slate and the rusty ironwork which is all that is left of a once great industry.'

She leaned back in her seat and allowed her long auburn hair to stream freely in the rush of air, glad that Magnus had thought to lower the hood of his hired car so that they could make the most of the fine day.

She caught his sidelong glance at her and was acutely aware of his heightened interest. Thus warned, she determined to back off from any closer relationship. There was only one person for whom she might be willing to sacrifice the career she had won with so much effort . . . and it was not Magnus Glendenning with his weakness for alcohol!

'Fraser has a finger in too many pies, if you ask me.' The reporter reverted suddenly to their former topic of conversation. 'He has power over the lives of thousands of people.' Morag was surprised by the bitterness of his tone.

'But surely his enterprises make him a great benefactor to the district?' she declared. 'He reminds me of the old clan chiefs . . .

like the Marquis of Stirling who owned all the lands of Lorn. My grandfather used to tell me how he took an interest in the welfare of his people, built schools and churches, supported the training of apprentices and provided medical care for the workers and their families . . .'

'Not all landlords are like that,' Magnus insisted, cynically. 'Fraser's primary consideration is profit. He's in a dominant position with interests in all the major enterprises in the town. He pays minimum wages because there's no competition for skilled workers, and if he were to find his income falling, he would close down the aluminium works without a thought for the men left unemployed.

'From what I have seen and heard of him, he is a very generous man,' Morag protested. 'Most of his work on behalf of the town is voluntary, and he's behind all the fund-raising enterprises at the hospital. I think you're being a little unfair.'

'For every penny he donates to charity he expects one hundredfold in return, believe me,' Magnus assured her. 'His sole purpose for being on the Municipal Council is for the concessions he receives in the form of contracts for his various undertakings. You have heard of Barr's Roads and Bridges, no doubt?' he suggested.

'Weren't they the contractors responsible for the upkeep of the road which collapsed?

'Fraser owns fifty-one per cent of the shares in that company. What do you know of Elsine and Keating?' he demanded.

'They're a large firm of building contractors,' she answered slowly. 'I seem to remember they were responsible for a considerable development of Corporation housing in Oban just after the war.'

'Exactly.' Magnus rammed the gear lever forward angrily as they entered a particularly tight bend. 'The same company has handled every new housing scheme in Inverlinnhe in the past ten years, on land bought up cheaply by Fraser when he first came to the area then sold by him to the Council at a handsome profit. His share of the deal included a fifteen per cent interest in Elsine and Keating! Profit is heaped upon profit.'

They drove in silence for some time, Morag discomfited by these revelations. The discussion had left a sour note which threatened to spoil the day.

'You seem to have a great deal of information on the enterprises of Graham Fraser,' she commented, with a hint of sarcasm. 'I wonder you have not exposed him in the pages of the *Gazette*.'

'Do you think I would not love to do just that?'

'What's stopping you then?'

'Who do you think owns the *Gazette*!'

She gave him a long hard stare and then answered her own question. 'Fraser?'

He nodded, and drove on in silence for a long time.

The road widened out as they approached the village of Benderloch where a ribbon development of housing, garages and shops indicated an attempt to provide some kind of support for the burgeoning tourist industry. Where the road skirted the shores of Loch Linnhe an area of flat grassland had been developed into a camping site where city dwellers, seeking the respite of the countryside, might spend their annual holidays.

'I doubt if our motor cycling friends would consider this to be an eyesore,' Morag observed acidly, remembering the bundles of camping gear strapped to their vehicles.

Magnus laughed heartily and suddenly the tension between them dispersed and their earlier mood of gaiety returned.

'You really should have invited your friend inside,' Millicent Beaton scolded her daughter. 'It was very kind of him to bring you all this way.'

'Actually he has to attend a conference in Oban this evening,' she explained, 'and will be staying the night at the Iona Hotel. You'll have a chance to inspect Magnus when he calls for me tomorrow afternoon!'

'Oh, don't be silly, girl, it's not a question of inspecting. It's just that your father and I always like to meet your friends.'

'I assure you, Mother, that that is all Magnus Glendenning is or will ever be . . . a friend. To begin with, he is nearer Pa's age than mine. He served in the war . . . in the Argylls.'

This explanation only served to worry her mother more. Millicent Beaton had been against her daughter's choice of profession from the outset. How could a girl with university degrees – a surgeon no less – expect to find herself a suitable husband? What man would wish to marry a woman probably better educated than he and who worked so intimately with the naked human body? Illogically, she was immensely proud of her two sons, both of whom were now working in hospitals – Ian at the Edinburgh Royal, and David in a hospital in Newcastle.

'Morag, my dear!' Hugh Beaton greeted his daughter with open arms. She had always been his favourite. There was something so spirited about her. He often thought that a little of the rebellious outlook must have rubbed off on Morag from her association with his sister-in-law, Annie Beaton, the family's famous suffragette.

'You got my letter, Pa?' asked Morag, anxiously. She hugged him, and tried not to notice the heavy scent of whisky on his breath.

'Yes . . .' He hesitated before smiling brightly, if unconvincingly, at her. 'Bit of a storm in a teacup, I should say.'

'Not from where I'm standing, it isn't, she replied.' After all, I have been suspended pending the outcome of the inquiry, and I haven't touched a patient for two weeks!'

'Your letter to me was very detailed. If you can corroborate what you say there, I cannot see that there is any case to answer.' Hugh placed a hand on her shoulder to guide her down the short corridor which led to his consulting room.

Struck by a familiar sense of loneliness, Millicent watched them go, feeling as she always did that her presence was unwanted when these two had professional matters to discuss.

'What was the outcome of the Procurator Fiscal's inquiry?' he demanded, making for the whisky decanter and offering his daughter a dram.

'No, thank you,' she responded. 'It's too early in the day for me.'

'Never too early for a drop of the *uisge-beatha*,' he retaliated and, sorrowfully, Morag watched him throw back the dram and pour himself another. She could not discard the notion that his optimism about her situation owed more to his inebriated condition than to any considered opinion.

'The verdict was that Mr Campbell died of heart failure,' she told her father, 'brought on either by the trauma of the accident, or the brain surgery which followed. The verdict given was accidental death, as with the other victims of the crash, but since there has been an accusation of medical negligence in Mr Campbell's case, the Hospital Board will make its own decision about how the blame, if any, is to be apportioned.'

Hugh Beaton was not so befuddled as Morag suspected. When he said that he needed a glass or two of spirits to get him through the day, he was not exaggerating. The drink really did sharpen his senses. He knew, for instance, that at this moment his daughter did not trust his judgement.

'According to your account, you dealt with a number of desperately injured people who would have died without immediate surgery. Is that the case?'

She nodded, miserably.

'You had experienced local practitioners and nursing staff keeping an eye on the remainder of the injured passengers?'

'Yes.'

'No one mentioned to you that Campbell was either in pain or distressed in any way?'

She was surprised by the incisiveness of these questions.

'Not at all,' she replied. 'In fact, Matron had to insist on his resting in the ward instead of going home, once all the other injured passengers had been dealt with.'

'Why did she do that?' Hugh demanded. 'Did she have some suspicion that he might be unwell?'

'I don't know. I assumed that because of his great age, she was naturally a little concerned.' Morag hesitated for a moment and then went on, thinking aloud, 'I suppose it's possible that she knew of his history of angina . . . Mr Maynard certainly did.'

'Did you speak to Matron before whisking Campbell off to the theatre?'

'No, she had already gone off duty.'

'When you first saw him he was already unconscious?' Hugh regarded her intently. She felt suddenly uncomfortable under her father's penetrating gaze.

'Yes,' she replied.

'You had no access to his previous records?'

'No. I did not know who his private physician was, and in any case it was the middle of the night and I could not have waited while the person was found. The hospital out-patient records, which might have told me something, were all locked up in the administrator's office.'

'Then they haven't a leg to stand on,' Hugh declared, his tone softening now that he had cleared up these important issues.

'I do hope you're right,' Morag replied, wishing that she could share his conviction.

'To make doubly certain that nothing is missed during this enquiry, I think we should call in our own advocate. I have already had a word with your Uncle Ewan. He will be happy to act on your behalf.' His wife's brother Ewan, following in his father's footsteps, was one of the most prominent criminal lawyers practising in Edinburgh. While Morag was flattered that he had agreed to support her case, she wondered if it was sensible to attend the hearing so heavily defended.

'Is it wise to have a lawyer acting for me, Pa?' she protested. 'Won't it look as if I actually do have something to hide?'

'Look, my dear, I have read your previous letters to your mother, and it is not difficult to see that there has been a concerted attempt by some of the staff with whom you work to oust you from the job. Whoever is behind that move has seized upon the circumstances of Campbell's death to get rid of you. A competent advocate will sift the evidence and present it in such a manner that there can be no doubt as to where the blame really lies. You are too close to the issues to be able to conduct your own defence impartially.' Hugh picked up the decanter to refill his glass, noted her worried look and replaced his empty glass and the whisky on the desk.

'Now then,' he said, as he stood up and made for the door, 'your mother will think I am keeping you all to myself . . . and you haven't told me yet who this mysterious fellow is who dropped you off in his magnificent automobile, and did not have the courtesy to come in and introduce himself!'

It was noon on the following day when Magnus's hired car turned into the drive of Tigh na Broch and drew to a halt beside the front door.

Morag ran out to greet him, anxious to speak privately before her mother appeared.

'I'm so glad you've arrived early,' she greeted him. 'Mother has prepared a light luncheon, and I wondered if there was time for me to show you the island before we leave?'

Magnus had listened to Morag's descriptions of the house below the cliffs where she had been born, and of the slate quarries on the Island of Eisdalsa where her grandfather and great-grandfather had acted as Medical Officer. Even so, nothing could have prepared him for the breathtaking view which greeted him when, having climbed the brae past the old ironclad building of the Free Church of Kilbrendan, he had rounded the corner and come to a halt on the crest of the hill.

The face of the sparkling ocean changed constantly as the shadows of the clouds above moved ceaselessly across its calm waters. A collection of islands, both small and large, stood black against the afternoon sun, pointing fingers of rock to the sky. Over to the right, a village of tiny, white, slate-roofed cottages nestled between the sheer cliffs of granite and an old wooden pier which stretched out across the narrow channel of sea towards one of the larger islands, a second village of white houses, clustered around a substantial harbour. Already intrigued by the view he had seen from the top of the brae, he was as anxious to see her island as she was to show it to him.

'There's no need to leave before six,' he agreed, 'but I do have to get back in time to file copy on last night's meeting before the presses run at midnight.'

He climbed down from the car and Morag grasped his arm as she led him towards the house.

'Look,' she said, trying to sound entirely casual, 'my parents aren't used to my bringing gentlemen to the house. They seem to think that we might be . . . well . . . romantically attached.'

He glanced at her anxious face and with a wicked grin queried: 'And aren't we?'

Exasperated, she released her hold on him and stepped back. 'No, we are not!' she almost shouted at him, then seeing the grin she laughed. 'Oh . . . you!'

'What you are trying to say, I believe, is that you do not wish me to tell your parents of my undying love for their daughter?'

'Something like that, anyway.' She took his arm again and led him into the house. 'Mother, this is Magnus Glendenning,' she introduced him, and Millicent smiled warmly.

'It was very good of you to give Morag a lift home, Mr Glendenning,' she said, glancing from one to the other, trying to see something in their expressions which would tell her what their real relationship was.

'Mrs Beaton, a pleasure to meet you, ma'am.' Magnus took her hand and smiled as he continued, 'Morag speaks so frequently of the attractions of her home, I thought she must be exaggerating until I drove around the bend up there on the brae. It was a magnificent sight, with the sun on the water and all the little islands so sharply silhouetted against the horizon.'

'That sounds like a poet speaking,' observed Hugh, emerging from his study and stuffing his empty pipe into his pocket as he extended his hand.

'He's very good at quoting other people's poetry,' said Morag, brightly, 'but I've never heard anything of his own! Pa, this is Magnus Glendenning of the *West Highland Gazette*.'

'A journalist? My sister is a writer . . . you may have come across some of her work? She writes under the name Margaret Beaton although she is married now, of course.'

Magnus seemed genuinely interested. 'Of course! Margaret Beaton. I have met her several times,' he responded, and then, turning to Morag, 'I never connected you with her . . . I should have known; there is a family resemblance. I remember you telling me you were related to Angus Beaton the historian . . . what a talented family you are!'

'Come along into the dining-room,' Millicent commanded. 'It's just a light luncheon, Mr Glendenning, cold, since we were not sure when you would arrive.'

'It's very kind of you to invite me, Mrs Beaton,' he replied, gallantly. Morag was dismayed to see the look which passed between her parents. Really, she did wish that they were not so anxious to see her married off!

It was one of those rare afternoons on the west coast when there was not a breath of wind and the sky was cloudless. They had decided to leave the car at the house and walk to the pier from where they would be able to hail a ferry boat to the tiny Island of Eisdalsa. The island lay just off the most westerly point of Seileach. Unlike Seileach itself, which was attached to the mainland of Argyll by an ancient bridge spanning a very narrow strait of the Atlantic Ocean, Eisdalsa lay about four hundred yards offshore. The channel between the two islands was deep enough for the passage of coastal steamers which, despite improved roads and an excellent train service, still carried large numbers of passengers back and forth to Glasgow, during the summer months.

From the windows of Tigh na Broch one could watch the tiny ferry boat plying its regular route between the islands.

'They used to call for help from my grandfather, using a coded system of flags flying from a mast over there,' Morag explained, pointing to where the ruins of an engine house marked the position of the sea wall of one of the old quarries. 'At night they raised lanterns on the same mast.'

Towards the centre of the island, a ridge of volcanic rock cut, serpent-like, across it from north to south. On the mainland side of this hill a village of whitewashed cottages, their slate roofs a dark bluish-grey in the bright sunlight, huddled close beside a deep harbour. Waste slate had been washed along the shoreline and threatened to close the entrance altogether.

'My goodness,' Morag remarked, startled by the obvious changes which had taken place since her last visit, 'it will soon be necessary for them to dredge a channel if the harbour is to remain open. The winter storms must have been very severe to have moved so much slate.'

They had reached the beginning of the village on the Seileach side of the deep water separating the two islands.

Magnus peered at the inscription over the door of the village hall.

'That's the old Volunteers' Drill Hall,' Morag told him. 'My grandfather was Company Surgeon with the honorary rank of Major.'

He glanced across at her, smiling.

'It seems to me that your grandfather was someone very special in your life,' he observed.

'When Pa went away to France in 1916, Dr David took charge of the whole family, and despite the fact that he was by then nearly seventy, held things together in the practice until my father could take up the reins again.'

She led the way along a narrow street lined with white-washed cottages, many of them crumbling into ruin through long disuse and neglect. On they walked along a grassy causeway at the end of which a large wooden pier still accommodated the passenger steamers plying their daily journey from the Caledonian Canal south to the Crinan Canal.

The tide was out, which meant that they must descend by steep steps to the lower landing stage beneath the main pier. Here they found a number of people already waiting to be ferried across to Eisdalsa Island.

'It's not often these days that there is a queue for the ferry,' Morag remarked, wryly. 'Many visitors are reluctant to risk the crossing except in the calmest weather.'

'You, on the other hand' he responded, grinning at her, 'are an old salt and ready to set sail whatever the conditions!' He measured the channel with his eye and concluded that it could be no more than four or five hundred yards.

'Don't be misled by the short distance,' she warned. 'The currents in this strait are very unpredictable, and in the middle it is deeper than you might think. Many experienced boatmen have paid dearly for treating it with less respect than it deserves.'

The ferry boat, a clinker-built dory some eighteen feet in length, was rowed by an ancient fellow who seemed almost too feeble for the task. Morag greeted him as an old friend.

'Hallo, Hector!' she said, handing over a handful of coppers for their fare. 'You look very busy . . . plenty of visitors about?'

'Oh, aye, Miss Morag,' he replied. 'Tis this fine spell of weather has brought them all out.'

He nodded in friendly fashion to Magnus and gave him a helping hand as the somewhat bulky figure made heavy weather of clambering aboard.

Morag, long practised in the art of handling small craft, put one foot on the gunwale and stepped lightly down into the boat. All the seats being taken, she settled on the thwart at Hector's side and took up an oar.

'Many people staying on the island just now?' she asked. The two of them pulled away steadily as he answered her query.

'There's a few up from Glasgow at number forty-two,' he said, 'and of course there's the English couple have taken your auntie's house for the season . . . some kind of a writer he is and the lady paints. They don't have much to say for themselves. The McPhersons have a party of their grandchildren up for the summer. That's them playing cricket on the green.' As though to confirm it, a huge roar was heard across the water as one of the children was caught out skying the ball.

Once across and inside the harbour, the ferry boat drew alongside the landing stage and the passengers prepared to disembark.

Morag led Magnus past an old school house, its tall windows boarded up and its door firmly barred.

'There were enough children living on the island to warrant a second school here, when my father was a boy,' she told him, and as they moved on towards a solid stone building with a curious roof shaped like a pyramid, she continued: 'This was the Drill Hall for the island's own Company of Volunteers.'

'Well, it's a pity someone doesn't do something to put it into better repair,' he observed dryly. 'It's a pretty unique structure to my way of thinking.'

'They say that the king-post is formed from the mast of a vessel which foundered over on Eileen nam Uan.' She related a little of the island's folklore and indicated a small island lying to the north west between Eisdalsa and the Island of Mull. 'I don't doubt that it's the truth,' she insisted, 'because the islanders made use of everything and anything which came ashore.'

Spotting a familiar figure over by the houses, she excused herself for a moment and ran across to greet some old friend amongst the cricketing McPhersons. Magnus watched her running back towards him, glowing with pleasure, and was made acutely aware of the enormous change in her whole demeanour in these much loved surroundings. She had shed all the starchiness of the professional woman and was behaving like a young girl let out of school.

Morag hurried back to him, waving as she ran. How good it was to be home! She watched Magnus walking along beside the harbour and thought how stooped and pale he looked. With a sudden insight she realised that the differences between them were immense, and whatever her parents thought she could never consider him as a suitor. She hoped he would not force her into a position in which she must refuse his attentions, because she really valued his friendship . . .

'We just have time to climb to the top of the hill,' she announced, when she reached him, breathless from running. Then, seeing him hesitate, 'You can't come to Eisdalsa and not admire the view from the top. It's compulsory for all visitors!'

Gaily she took his arm and together they hastened around the top of the harbour and started along the footpath beside a rusted railway track.

Magnus was feeling done in by the time he had followed his companion up the steep pathway to the highest point of the ridge.

Red-faced and gasping for breath, he flopped down on a carpet of thyme and heather at the cliffs edge. Morag glanced at him swiftly, and noticing a bluish tinge around his lips and beneath his eyes, chided herself for not taking the path more slowly. She had been so thrilled to be visiting her favourite place in all the world that she had quite forgotten that Magnus was not as fit as she.

She sat quiet for a while, allowing him time to recover. He lay staring up into the blue heavens while Morag surveyed the familiar scene. In her head she named all the islands which dotted the calm waters spread out before them – a game her grandfather had taught them, all those years ago. He seemed very close at this moment.

It was more than five years since David Beaton had died, quite suddenly, on an afternoon just such as this, in his garden at the Connel house. She had been in Edinburgh completing her training, and had regretted not having been home to see him for such a long time. It was to this place that she had come, following the funeral, to be reunited with him in spirit. To what better place could she bring her present troubles?

She thought about what her father had said . . . she had no case to answer . . . someone at the hospital was trying to get rid of her . . .

I did my best, she silently addressed the seabirds. What more could they expect of me?

Had it been a good idea to accept the help of her Uncle Ewan? It couldn't do any harm to take her own advocate along with her to the inquiry, she supposed. A disinterested viewpoint might be just what was required when she herself was torn between regret at the old man's death, and the need to defend her own position.

Magnus had been studying her face intently for some time when she suddenly became aware of his eyes upon her.

'Why so glum all of a sudden?' he demanded.

'I was going over in my mind the arguments I must use at the inquiry,' she answered frankly. 'I've been trying to avoid thinking about it, but up here, away from everything and everybody, it's possible to think more clearly.'

He nodded and sat up. Hugging his knees comfortably, he regarded the scene before him. It was so calm that there was only the slightest skirting of white foam around the base of the rocks, and the different shades of blue indicated clearly where shallows gave way to deeper waters. Black triangles of rock, some large enough to be called islands and others so small that they were submerged at high tide, marked the position of upended seams of slate, still untouched by man.

While he had lain there, watching Morag, some words had been forming in his head:-

> *Would that I could walk in your footprints*
> *And by some secret door*
> *Step into your mind.*
> *Then might I share the memories which linger there,*
> *The thoughts unspoken*
> *And the words unsaid.*

He had not realised he was actually speaking aloud.

'That's good,' said Morag. 'Who wrote it?'

'A no-good journalist called Magnus Glendenning.'

'Then you *are* a poet, after all!'

She scrambled to her feet and stood gazing down at him.

'Come on, it's time we were going.'

Reluctantly he put out his hand and she hauled him to his feet. For a moment they gazed at one another. Morag felt certain that if she stood there any longer, he would kiss her and spoil everything.

She pushed a lock of hair back from her forehead, exposing as she did so the cluster of freckles which had been a source of embarrassment to her since childhood.

'You look like a truly Scottish lassie,' he commented, lightly, and then, glancing over towards the north-west and shattering the mood abruptly, 'Is that the southern coast of Mull?'

'Yes. Do you see that inlet to the left where the cliff begins to dip down at the entrance to the loch?'

He strained his eyes and nodded.

'That is where my Great-uncle Angus lives.' She hesitated before continuing, 'If you are sincerely interested in meeting him, I might be able to arrange it.'

'Would you really?' Magnus demanded, eagerly. 'An interview

with him would make a terrific article in my series on notable local figures.'

'I'll talk to Pa about it,' she told him. 'Just to make sure Angus is well enough to receive visitors. He is well into his eighties and sometimes rather frail.'

They scrambled down the steep path to where the disused quarries, now filled with water, basked in the late-afternoon sunshine. Someone sounded the klaxon from the other side of the strait. If they hurried they would catch the ferry on its next journey back to the mainland.

# Chapter 8

❦

The hot weather which had so enhanced Morag's visit to Eisdalsa seemed set to last for a long time. Sunday morning dawned just as bright and clear as its predecessors, and it was with a light step that she set out for the eastern end of the town and the residence of Dr Gordon McDonald.

Feanagrogan had once been a village in its own right. Now the name, taken from the wind-ravaged alders which lined the banks of the many streams in the area, was the only thing about it which had survived the depredations of the years. As housing schemes and industrial developments radiated out from Inverlinnhe, the intervening countryside had been systematically swallowed up. Now a ribbon of miserable Corporation housing, unsightly warehouses, garages and scruffy shops lined either side of the road out of town, while small factory developments had been built, extending back as far as the lower slopes of the mountain.

Morag turned down a side road, at whose corner stood a small store – surprisingly open on the Sabbath. An untidy signboard gave a clue as to why there was a small queue of children waiting impatiently to be served.

*LUIGI'S GENUINE ITALIAN*

*HOKEY POKEY*

*Cornets ½d, 1d and 2d*

Morag wished she was eight years old again; the idea of an ice-cream cornet was suddenly very tempting on such a hot day.

A single row of Victorian villas indicated where once the village street had ended, and it was on the door of the last of these that she was thankful to find the brass plate she was seeking.

She rang the bell and heard the sound echoing through the large empty entrance hall. After a few minutes, there was a flurry of activity within. Some childish whispering and giggling was followed by a deeper voice which she guessed must be Gordon's own.

Suddenly the door flew open to reveal a huddle of children, ranging in age from a wee girl of three or four years to fifteen-year-old Andy whom she had met on the mountain.

Advancing along the hallway to join them came Gordon McDonald. Gently brushing aside his brood – Morag managed to count five in all – he took her coat and ushered her inside.

'I'm so glad you could come,' he said, leading the way through to a huge room at the back of the house. Painted entirely in white, its walls were almost bare, the only decoration being a single large painting of puffins nesting on a rocky coastline.

The room must have been at least twelve feet high. Enormous windows opened directly on to a leafy expanse of garden enclosed by a high stone wall. It was a magnificently light and airy space, made all the more inviting by the atmosphere of purposeful activity which filled it.

Along one wall stood an upright piano against which leaned an antique *clarsach*, the harp-like instrument of the Celts. Sheet music was scattered liberally over the piano's lid, which was weighted down by a concertina and a set of bagpipes.

The centre ground was occupied by a very large table covered in a cloth of green chenille. Upon this was spread an assortment of writing and drawing materials, some half-completed models and sketches and any number of books. Beside a comfortable armchair which had been drawn up to the open window, stood a solid wooden work box whose open lid revealed knitting wools, a half-finished garment of some kind and a heap of printed patterns.

Beneath the table, the largest dog basket Morag had ever seen was occupied by a pair of golden retrievers, their legs, ears and noses so intimately entwined it seemed they could never be unravelled. Here she was mistaken, however, because on the appearance of a stranger in their midst, both dogs shuffled to meet her, inspecting her thoroughly for tell-tale signs. Satisfied that she was acceptable company for their people, they both retreated to the basket, but this time the two noses were laid side by side over the edge and two pairs of limpid brown eyes regarded her fixedly.

Gordon, carrying the youngest child piggy-back, followed her into the room and called to his wife: 'Anna . . . our guest has arrived!

'Let me introduce the children,' he began. 'My eldest boy you already know.' Andy stepped forward to give her a warm handshake.

'It's good to see you again, Doctor.'

'This is Tim,' Gordon continued. A shy lad, whose dark skin and jet black hair were in sharp contrast to the fair-skinned, blond young McDonalds she had met up on the Ben, smiled shyly and had to be prompted to murmur, 'How do you do?'

'Mat and Melody are twins.' The two, neatly cropped red heads were almost identical, and despite their being boy and girl, dressed as they both were in blue shirts and beige shorts, it was difficult to tell one child from the other. 'And this little monster is our wee baby, Poppy.' He lifted the infant forward over his head and put her down gently at his feet. Poppy took hold of his trouser leg and, thrusting the thumb of the same puggy little hand into her pretty Cupid's bow mouth, gazed up at Morag with wide, startlingly blue eyes. 'What an unusual name,' said Morag stroking the velvety cheek. Gordon's eyes danced, 'It was Anna's idea. She was born on Armistice Day.'

Morag did her best to take in everyone at once as she exclaimed, 'You have a wonderful family, Doctor. I am quite overwhelmed!'

'Why so formal?' he demanded. 'I thought we were friends. Please call me Gordon . . . Morag.' His smile was as radiant and his glance as penetrating as that of his youngest child. Morag was startled by the similarity between Polly and her father. Gordon's hair was darker, although still abundant despite his forty years, but it curled behind his ears and at the temples in much the same way as his daughter's. What marked them both was the broad, intelligent forehead, wide-spaced eyes and square, determined chin.

'I thought we might all have a glass of lemonade,' he suggested, and Andy disappeared into the kitchen next door from which emanated the delicious smell of roasting beef. Morag suddenly realised just how hungry she was. The other children had slipped out into the garden, from whence there came shouts and a good deal of laughter. Only Poppy remained, intent upon monopolising her father's attention for as long as possible.

'Mother will be in directly,' Andy explained, returning with a tray of glasses and a glass jug in which swam a number of lemon halves. 'We had a little problem with the gravy, but everything's all right now.'

'Anna usually relies on Fran to help her with the Sunday meal,' Gordon explained. 'She is the only one in the household who can cook properly. I'm afraid Anna's mind is usually on a different plane.'

'Mother's an artist,' Andy announced, proudly, as if to explain why Mrs McDonald was not as other women when it came to household chores.

'During the week we have a daily help, who comes in to do the cooking and housework,' Gordon explained. 'Anna spends most of her time in her studio.'

Morag's glance went instantly to the huge picture on the wall behind them.

'That is one of her paintings,' he confirmed, obviously immensely proud of his wife's achievement.

Morag got to her feet and moved across to observe the puffin picture more thoroughly. The comical birds, which she knew as 'sea parrots' because of their large horny beaks, were gathered upon a rocky cliff above a restless ocean. Their perches were so precarious that it seemed they must be dislodged by the force of the gale, which ruffled feathers and flattened the few wispy grasses which had managed to root themselves in some pocket of loose soil. Morag felt that were she to reach out and touch those warm, pulsating bodies, the puffins would fly away.

'It's wonderful,' she breathed, overawed by the artistry of the work.

'I've had good enough offers for that one to pay for a new living-room carpet. Unfortunately Gordon won't allow me to sell it.'

Anna McDonald appeared wearing a flowery apron which she undid and cast aside as she advanced into the room. Her face was the colour of beetroot from working in a hot kitchen all morning.

'It was the picture she was working on the day I met her,' Gordon explained, coming up beside his wife and casually placing his arm around her waist. 'Besides which,' he grinned, 'I happen to like it!

'Gordon likes a picture to look like a photograph,' she explained, disparagingly, 'while my chief satisfaction comes from experimenting with other forms of expression.'

Well aware that this could lead to a discussion which might put luncheon back by forty minutes or so and ruin it, Gordon broke in hurriedly.

'Morag, this is my wife, Anna.'

The doctor's wife, stopped short as she launched into her favourite subject, looked surprised then mortified that she had been so rude to their guest. She now greeted Morag warmly. 'I am pleased to meet you at last, Dr Beaton,' she exclaimed. 'I can't tell you how much we appreciate what you did for our Fran ... She could have died if you had not been there.' She threw her arms around Morag's neck and kissed her enthusiastically.

Morag, embarrassed by this uninhibited outburst, asked, 'How is she getting on?'

Anna McDonald looked bewildered.

'I hoped you would be able to tell us?' she said.

'Unfortunately, no,' Morag replied, glancing at Gordon. Had he not told Anna of her personal troubles?

'I did mention that Morag has been suspended pending an

inquiry,' he interjected, embarrassed to think that his wife might have forgotten so important a matter.

'Oh, yes, of course,' she responded. 'I am so sorry for you, my dear. It must be very difficult having to wait to hear the outcome of the enquiry. Still, if we look at the matter in a more positive light, had you been working on the day the children went up the Ben, you would not have been able to help them. And then,' she added with a satisfied smile, 'we would not have had any reason to meet in this way.'

Morag could not dispute the logic. Anna McDonald appeared only to consider the bright side of any situation. One was unlikely to remain depressed for long in the company of this engaging woman.

'Fran seems to be mending nicely,' Gordon told Morag as he positioned a chair for his wife beside the table. Anna settled herself comfortably with her feet planted on one of the dogs, who stretched ecstatically as her probing heel found just the right spot to relieve an itch.

It was easy to see where Tim McDonald had acquired his dark gypsy-like features. Anna might easily have been cast as Carmen in the opera. Her long raven locks were tied back loosely with a bright scarlet ribbon which matched her sleeveless cotton gown with its plain bodice and full skirt falling in deep flounces almost to the floor. In these days of short, straight, tubular dresses, she looked both exotic and intensely feminine. Morag envied her ability to defy convention so outrageously.

They sat sipping the deliciously cool lemonade and discussing the relative merits of cubism, expressionism, and many other schools of modern art, which Morag found entertaining despite never previously having taken the slightest interest in the subject. Out of her depth in such matters, and ignorant of many of the names bandied about, she could only listen attentively while her hosts wrangled over the finer detail.

'Mother,' Adam called from the kitchen, 'something out here smells distinctly overdone!'

Anna shot to her feet. 'Oh, dear!' she cried. 'I forgot to turn down the gas.'

She ran into the kitchen and there followed loud banging, barked orders, and the occasional distinctly unfeminine expletive. Finally she emerged carrying a white table-cloth and a handful of cutlery.

'Do something with these, will you?' she demanded, thrusting everything into Gordon's hands.

He began clearing innumerable objects from the huge general-purpose table. Morag went to his aid.

'Are you sure you don't mind?' he asked, shaking out the spotless white cloth and inviting her to grab at it as he threw it over the green baize cover. 'I'm afraid it is always a trifle hectic at Sunday meal times . . . especially with Fran away. She's a splendid housewife.' He grinned as he added, 'Something she does not inherit from her mother!'

Morag, helping to set out the cutlery, felt herself completely at home in this enchantingly relaxed household which differed so greatly from the stolid, ordered regime in which she herself had grown up.

A sharp command from their mother brought the children scampering in from the garden.

'Hands!' came Anna's brisk reminder, and soon they could be heard splashing and arguing as they fought for space in the tiny downstairs cloakroom.

'For goodness' sake,' she bellowed, 'why don't some of you go upstairs?'

'They're all done now,' laughed Andrew as he reappeared carrying the toddler, Poppy, piggy-back.

Soon all five children and the adults were gathered around the table on which stood steaming dishes of vegetables and an enormous joint of roast beef. As he carved the meat which, blackened on the outside, was none the less pink and succulent within, Gordon glanced up at Morag and grinned. 'I feel I should hand over the tools in the presence of an expert.'

'Oh, I can't match that degree of skill with cooked meat,' she replied, laughing, as yet another neat slice of precise thickness fell away from the joint.

'Ugh!' It was Tim who caught their meaning first. 'How can

you be so crude, Dad?' he demanded. 'It's enough to put a fellow off his food!'

'You're too sensitive by half,' chided Andy, ruffling his younger brother's thick curly locks. 'It's a good job you don't intend to be a surgeon.'

'Does that mean that you do?' enquired Morag, happy to find that the conversation had turned to more familiar territory.

'I wasn't sure until that night on the mountain,' he told her. 'Now I know it's what I want to do.'

Recognising immediately that buzz of enthusiasm and excitement which she herself had known at his age, Morag smiled encouragingly. 'I hope you get your wish,' she said.

Despite Anna's assertion that she couldn't cook, the meal was excellent. She explained her success by saying she had taken lessons from Fran, when her daughter brought home various recipes from school. Morag felt that Anna's portrayal of herself as an artistic genius, incompetent in everyday affairs, was merely a pose. It was clearly a family joke which everyone enjoyed.

The last of the dishes were finally cleared and Anna announced that she was going to the hospital to visit Fran. Andy elected to accompany her, and Tim and the twins were set to wash the crockery. Even Poppy's help was enlisted to perform whatever tasks she could manage without damaging her mother's best china.

Satisfying himself that all was in good order in the kitchen, Gordon led the way into his consulting room.

'We'll not be disturbed here. There are certain things which I feel we must discuss before the enquiry next week.'

On her return from Eisdalsa the previous Saturday, Morag had found a note awaiting her. It had been a curt summons to attend an enquiry into the death of Mr Gregor Campbell in the early hours of 16 June 1932. The date appointed was Wednesday of the following week.

She had determined to put all thought of the impending investigation aside for the day, but realising that Gordon could prove a useful ally, was only too willing to accede to his suggestion.

'Oh, Tim!' he called out. 'Keep an eye on the little ones for a wee while will you? Dr Beaton and I have important matters to discuss.'

'All right, Dad,' came the reply.

Morag searched in her bag and brought out a handful of coppers. 'Would you mind if Tim bought the children ice-creams?' she asked. 'I passed an Italian parlour on my way here.'

'Not at all,' Gordon laughed, 'and I'm sure they will have no objection!

'Now then,' he said as he ushered her into his own private sanctum, a room filled with heavy Victorian furniture and smelling of a familiar mixture of wax polish and disinfectant, 'it seems to me that the main complaint concerning your handling of Mr Campbell's case is that you acted without knowing his previous history of heart trouble?'

'I believe that members of his own family were unaware he had consulted a heart specialist some years ago,' she confirmed. 'It was only after his death that I learned a policeman had found and administered an amyl nitrite tablet when Mr Campbell collapsed in the car bringing him to the hospital.'

'But this was not mentioned when he arrived?'

'No report at all was made out on Mr Campbell,' Morag answered. 'As far as I was aware, he was at the hospital only as a witness to events. He took it upon himself to look after distressed relatives as they began to arrive. His fellow passengers told me that he had taken charge immediately following the accident and until Adam Inglis and I arrived on the scene. It was a further hour before the rescuers appeared and during all that time he never complained of feeling unwell or gave any indication that he had been injured himself.'

They continued to talk over the events of that night, sifting and arranging their recollections of what had happened into some semblance of order.

'Thank you so much,' Morag declared as they at last came to an end. 'Tomorrow I have to go over everything with my lawyer. What we have discussed here will make that interview much easier.'

'I was going to ask whether you will be represented,' Gordon said. 'I think you are very wise to take professional advice. It's not easy for a doctor to stand up on his or her own, against the big wheels in the medical profession.'

'You don't suppose it will appear that I am protesting my innocence too loudly?' she demanded, anxiously. 'It was my father's idea to enlist the help of my mother's brother. He is quite highly thought of in Edinburgh . . .'

'I think your father is absolutely right!' declared McDonald. 'But I would like to see the faces of Sidney Maynard and his cohorts when you turn up with your own legal representative. They may get more than they bargain for!'

It was a very warm day. Sunlight penetrated the slats of the Venetian blind, only half-lowered to allow in sufficient air to prevent the room becoming stuffy. At least they had had the decency to assemble the witnesses in the superintendent's office on this occasion. It would have been highly embarrassing to have been asked to wait in that dingy little corridor in full view of the hospital staff.

All afternoon Morag had watched colleagues, friends many of them, and some such as Matron and her bosom pal Sister Dunwoodie, who might well be disposed to do her harm, pass through to be interviewed by the panel. They never emerged, and Morag supposed that, having said their piece, they exited by way of the corridor.

They had told her that the panel would hear all the evidence from witnesses first, before asking her to give her own account of what had occurred in the hours leading up to the death of Gregor Campbell. With her uncle, Ewan Menzies, she had gone carefully over the case. He had made it clear that he felt Gordon McDonald's testimony would be of vital importance, yet her colleague still had not arrived. It must be a matter of some urgency which had held him back until this late hour. Gordon had been so adamant that he would stand up for her!

Apart from him, Mary Neal was the only witness remaining now. They had sat alone and in silence for the last fifteen minutes, hardly daring to exchange even a smile.

Mary, uncomfortably aware of her immediate superior's determination to dispatch the female surgeon at the first opportunity, was torn between complying with Matron's wish that she show Morag in the worst possible light, and saying what she really felt about the way in which the doctor had acted throughout. The problem was that the bare facts would lead the panel inevitably to the conclusion that Morag had been careless, when Mary knew very well that Dr Beaton had done all in her power to save Gregor's life.

The sound of a buzzer broke the silence and Lucy McArdle lifted her gaze from the papers before her. 'You may go in now, Nurse Neal . . . perhaps you would be good enough to explain that Dr McDonald has not yet arrived?' The secretary looked sympathetically at Morag as she spoke. It was clear that Dr Beaton was relying heavily upon Gordon's testimony.

'I shouldn't worry,' she said kindly, as Mary closed the heavily panelled door behind her. 'Knowing Dr McDonald as I do, he will be here in time.'

Morag acknowledged the attempt to reassure her with a wan smile, and went to look out of the window yet again, hoping for a glimpse of her friend arriving.


'Miss Neal.' Graham Fraser directed Mary to the witness's chair and invited her to be seated. 'I must explain,' he began in a bored voice . . . it had been a long afternoon and he had said this same piece so many times . . . 'that the purpose of this inquiry is to ascertain the facts in the case of Mr Gregor Campbell, deceased. It is always distressing to find oneself in a position where there is a conflict between loyalty to one's colleagues and the need to establish the truth. You will not be placed on oath but I hope that you will answer the questions put to you, precisely and truthfully.'

Mary nodded nervously, while Fraser continued.

'The panel is made up of members of the Hospital Board whom you may already know: Mr McRae, Miss McKinnley, and of course Mr Sidney Maynard, the hospital's senior consultant surgeon. The gentleman on my right is Mr Ernest Lane of the British Medical

Council, and at the far end Mr Ewan Menzies, QC, representing the interests of Dr Beaton, the responsible surgeon in the case.'

Mary nodded in acknowledgement.

'Now, before we begin,' Fraser went on, 'I must emphasise that no one here is on trial. It is, however, the duty of this panel to decide whether the hospital staff were in any way negligent in their treatment of Mr Gregor Campbell and, if so, what action should be taken to prevent further tragedies of the kind.'

'Miss Neal,' Maynard took up the questioning,' I understand that you were not officially on duty at the time of the accident. Can you tell us how it was that you happened to be available when the rescue party arrived at the hospital?'

'I was off duty when word came through that there had been a serious accident,' she began, falteringly. 'I realised that the theatre would almost certainly be needed, and made my way there immediately.'

'Who was in charge of the situation when you arrived?'

'I don't know that anyone was in charge,' she replied. 'The police had rounded up all the available doctors and Matron was organising the distribution of linen and dressings for the emergency cubicles. People were mostly standing around until Dr Beaton arrived in a police car.'

'That was only minutes before the first of the ambulances arrived?' asked Duncan McRae.

'Yes.'

'There must have been some difficulty in assessing priorities,' observed McRae. 'How were the various tasks distributed?'

'Dr Beaton had already been able to assess the various degrees of trauma at the scene,' Mary explained. 'She ordered the worst cases to be prepared for theatre and allocated minor injuries to the other doctors. Dr Beaton then scrubbed up and went into the theatre. I later joined her there with Sister Dunwoodie and Dr Gordon McDonald.'

'Where did Mr Gregor Campbell come in Dr Beaton's list of priorities?' demanded Maynard.

Mary looked startled.

'He was not on the list at all,' she replied, hesitantly. 'No one suspected at that time that he had been injured.'

'He was not examined? Not even by one of the volunteer doctors?'

'No.'

'Did you not think it strange that an octogenarian, who had undergone a traumatic experience of this nature, should not have warranted even a cursory examination?' The question was put by the gentleman from the BMC.

'At the time, Mr Campbell was busy guiding distraught relatives to the injured, fetching cups of tea, and doing all manner of things to help out during the crisis. I don't think it occurred to anyone to ask him if he was injured. He seemed so full of energy.' Mary could not suppress a small sob. She had met Adam's uncle on only one occasion prior to the accident, but had so enjoyed his company . . . she could hardly believe even now that the lively old gentleman was gone forever.

'There was one person concerned for Mr Campbell's health, however,' Sidney Maynard observed. 'I gather that Matron . . . Miss Kemp . . . was sufficiently cautious as to have him admitted to a ward for the remainder of the night.'

'I cannot say who admitted Mr Campbell,' Mary insisted. 'I was in the operating theatre with Dr Beaton until after one o'clock in the morning. When we were finished, Dr Beaton dismissed the other staff and so far as I know everyone went to their room to try to get some rest. I accompanied her to the wards to have a last look at the casualties who had been admitted and was surprised to find Mr Campbell among them.'

'Did Dr Beaton examine Mr Campbell at that time?' Maynard demanded.

'It was clear, even to me, that Mr Campbell was in some distress,' Mary emphasised. 'Dr Beaton made a rapid examination of the patient and it was then that she showed me a large area of bruising behind his ear and across the back of his head.'

'Did Dr Beaton take temperature and blood pressure readings?' asked Mr Lane.

Mary thought carefully before replying. 'She consulted the chart and seemed satisfied to act on what was shown there.'

'Did she make a thoracic examination?'

'No, she only took Mr Campbell's pulse before deciding that an immediate operation was required. I was asked to recall the theatre staff and by the time I had roused them and prepared myself, Dr Beaton and the anaesthetist, Dr Strachan, were preparing Mr Campbell for surgery.'

'Would you say that there was panic in the manner in which Dr Beaton went about this emergency operation?' Maynard enquired.

Ewan Menzies, who until now had remained silent, looked up sharply. So that was it, he thought . . . they were going to try and say Morag panicked when she found Campbell's injury had been overlooked. They are going to pin his heart failure to her supposed negligence on the operating table.

'Dr Beaton was as calm and efficient as always when operating,' Mary replied, gallantly.

'Miss Neal, how many cranial operations have you assisted at during the course of your duties as a theatre nurse?' Miss McKinnley's question was so pat that Ewan felt sure the woman had been primed to ask it.

'This was the first,' Mary replied.

Her answer hung on the air in the silence which followed. It was Maynard who observed, 'Then you are hardly an expert in the procedures to be followed, nor are you in a position to judge the efficiency or otherwise of the surgeon.'

'No', she admitted, lamely.

'Thank you, Miss Neal, that will be all,' Fraser dismissed her, and signalled for the next witness.

It was Miss McArdle, Sidney Maynard's secretary, who appeared in the doorway.

'I'm afraid that there is still no sign of Dr McDonald,' she told them. 'Shall I send in Dr Beaton?'

The members of the panel conferred for a few moments. At last Fraser leaned forward and addressed Ewan Menzies.

'I'm sorry, old man,' he said, jovially, 'it seems that your witness has let you down. I fear we shall have to proceed without his testimony.'

Ewan could hardly protest. He had arrived unannounced, and to the discomfiture of all concerned had insisted upon being present for the entire proceedings. It was only when Ernest Lane had confirmed that Morag was entitled to be so represented that Maynard had given in, albeit ungraciously. Ewan had further disrupted proceedings by insisting that it was in his client's interest that the panel should hear the testimony of Dr McDonald. Now that Gordon had failed to appear, he could hardly risk antagonising the panel by requesting a recess.

'In the circumstances,' he replied, 'I cannot insist that we wait for Dr McDonald's testimony. I will however exercise my right to recall any of the witnesses we have already heard, once Miss Beaton has been questioned.'

'Dr Beaton,' Sidney Maynard began, 'the panel has been given to understand that Mr Gregor Campbell was not examined by any of the doctors in your team until you yourself examined him in the early hours of June the sixteenth and found him to be in a deeply unconscious state.'

'That is the case,' she agreed.

'Yet the man had been admitted to a ward . . . under whose authority?'

'In view of the urgent needs of patients requiring surgery, I had delegated responsibility for admissions to the senior of the volunteer GPs,' Morag consulted her notes, 'a Dr Russell Inglestone. I understand, however, that he had already left the premises when Matron, Miss Christine Kemp, decided Mr Campbell needed to be kept in for observation. Once I had delegated duties to the staff, I went to the theatre and remained working there until well after midnight.'

'Mr Campbell was not on your list of those requiring attention?' Maynard snapped at her.

'No.'

'How was it that an elderly man, who had undergone a severe shock, and who had already had some kind of a seizure while being transported to hospital in a police vehicle, should have been overlooked in this way?'

'Mr Campbell was at no time presented to me as one of the casualties,' Morag replied, calmly. 'I was too heavily engaged to find time to worry about a gentleman who for several hours had given every appearance of being uninjured and in full possession of all his faculties. Not once during the time we spent together at the scene of the accident did he complain of headache or injury of any kind.'

'Maybe, if you had summoned assistance from myself in the first instance, you would have had more time to examine *all* your patients thoroughly,' observed Maynard, dryly.

Fraser cast him a critical glance and urged Morag to continue.

'At no time did I consider Mr Campbell to be a patient,' she retorted angrily, then catching her uncle's eye, toned down her response. 'The first time that I became aware that Mr Campbell had suffered a seizure during the journey to the hospital,' she continued, 'was when I read the notes on his chart, in the ward, at approximately one o'clock in the morning.'

'What did you find when you examined Mr Campbell at that time?' asked Ernest Lane.

'I found the patient to be deeply unconscious, and on further examination discovered a large area of bruising over the left occipital area. His vital signs indicated a subdural haemorrhage. In view of the delay in discovering the injury, I decided that an immediate operation was indicated.'

'And so, despite the fact that your theatre staff had only just retired to their beds after a gruelling evening, you decided upon heroic surgery,' Sidney Maynard sneered. 'What were you trying to do, Miss Beaton . . . establish for all time your indispensability to the medical profession? Or were you perhaps attempting to cover up your earlier shortcomings in not diagnosing his condition when the patient first arrived at the hospital?

'I was trying to save a man's life!' she cried in response, mortified that her intentions should be so misinterpreted.

'Then perhaps you should have made a more thorough

examination before subjecting your patient to major surgery. Did you, for example, discover his heart abnormality?' Maynard demanded.

'The patient's reflexes were so weakened by the pressure on his brain that it was impossible to distinguish acute symptoms from any long-standing condition,' she answered, stoutly. 'The stertorous breathing, unequal pupils and a certain rigidity of the limbs, together with a lowered temperature over a period of time, suggested intracranial pressure.'

'Were you aware that Mr Campbell had been seeing a heart specialist over a period of some years and that he had a history of coronary disease?' Maynard persisted.

'I learned that that was the case on the following day,' she replied. 'At the time when I decided to operate, the patient was already unconscious, there were no members of his family present, and I did not have access to his medical records.'

'I wonder . . . may I ask a question of my client?' Ewan Menzies's modulated tones fell like oil upon troubled waters.

Graham Fraser, who had momentarily lost control of the proceedings, was relieved to hand over to the advocate.

'Dr Beaton,' Menzies began, 'do you believe that, given the same set of circumstances today, and in the light of experience, you would have acted differently in any way?'

'No, I am sure that I would not.'

'What do you believe would have been the outcome had you not operated upon Mr Campbell when you did?' Ewan asked.

'He would have been dead within a few hours,' she answered bluntly.

'Had you known of the patient's heart condition,' Menzies persisted, 'would that have deterred you from operating?'

Morag weighed her words carefully before replying.

'No, because while there was a chance that Mr Campbell's heart may have held out, there was no hope for him unless the pressure upon his brain was relieved.'

Satisfied with his client's answers, Ewan Menzies indicated to Fraser that he had finished his questioning. There was an audible sigh of relief from several quarters. It looked as though matters might now be drawn to a conclusion.

'There is, however, one question I would like to put to the matron . . .' Ewan perused his sheet of notes '. . . er . . . Miss Kemp.'

Wearily, Fraser pressed the buzzer and Maynard's secretary appeared.

'Will you please find Matron, Miss McArdle, and ask her to return to answer further questions?'

'Yes, sir,' Lucy replied. 'And Dr McDonald has now arrived. Will you see him?'

'We shall have to wait for Miss Kemp . . . we may as well hear what the good doctor has to say.' Fraser lifted his eyebrows questioningly. No one chose to disagree.

'Now that Miss Beaton has given her evidence,' he continued, 'I see no reason why she should not remain for the rest of the hearing.'

Duncan McRae, who had had very little to say throughout the proceedings, was the one to fetch an additional chair. This he positioned for Morag beside her counsellor. He smiled encouragingly at her as she murmured her thanks.

Gordon McDonald appeared worried. He was grey with fatigue and Morag was startled by the change which the past two days had wrought in him.

'I do apologise for arriving so late, Mr Chairman,' he murmured as he took his place. 'I fear we have a mild epidemic in the town . . . I was obliged to report my findings to the Medical Officer of Health before coming along here.'

'Thank you, Doctor, it's good of you to spare us a few minutes under the circumstances,' Fraser accepted the explanation graciously. 'We will not keep you longer than is necessary.' He glanced towards Maynard, but then allowed his gaze to fall upon the representative from the Medical Council.

'Do you have anything you wish to ask this witness, Mr Lane?'

'Dr McDonald, you assisted Dr Beaton in the theatre on the evening of June the fifteenth is that not so?'

'That is correct.'

'Was there at any moment a situation in which you felt that Dr Beaton might be overreaching her capabilities?'

'On the contrary, I have seen many operations carried out in emergency situations and have rarely witnessed such a display of competence and self-assurance in any surgeon. I would be happy to entrust my own children to the care of Dr Beaton at any time.' Weary as he was, Gordon raised a smile as he glanced in Morag's direction.

'Were you in the reception area when the casualties were being admitted, Dr McDonald?' Menzies now took up the questioning.

'Yes, I was,' he agreed.

'Were you acquainted with the late Mr Gregor Campbell?'

'Of course, he was a well-known figure in the town.'

'On the evening of June the fifteenth, did you happen to see Mr Campbell in the reception area?'

'It would have been difficult to miss him.'

'Can you describe for us his demeanour? Did you, for example, feel that he should perhaps be examined by one of your colleagues?'

'I hardly think he would have agreed to it,' Gordon replied, amused at the thought. 'Mr Campbell was far too busy getting everyone organised.'

'How do you mean, organised?' Maynard demanded.

'He was sorting out transport, contacting relatives . . . you know the sort of thing.'

'There was no reason to suppose that he had received the blow which subsequently led to the need for urgent surgery?' pressed Ewan Menzies.

'No reason at all,' Gordon replied. 'Furthermore the operation to relieve pressure in the cranium was completely successful. All the patient's vital signs were satisfactory when we left him to recover. His heart must have given out some minutes later.'

'Thank you, Doctor.' Graham Fraser rose to shake Gordon's hand before he left. 'It was good of you to come, considering the circumstances.'

Gordon's expression changed instantly. 'Yes,' he said, 'I'm afraid that we may have an epidemic of typhoid fever on our hands.'

There was a stunned silence as he left the room, passing Matron on his way out. Duncan McRae exchanged a few words with Miss McKinnley and looked as though he might go after McDonald for further information. An outbreak of fever in the town could be devastating for the tourist trade . . .

'Do come in, Miss Kemp,' Fraser called out, on catching sight of the new arrival through the open doorway. 'Mr Menzies has a question for you.'

Christine Kemp seemed a trifle disconcerted to find that Morag was to be present at this, her second interview of the day.

'I don't wish to keep you any longer than is absolutely necessary, Miss Kemp,' said Ewan Menzies, smoothly. 'But there is one matter which has been puzzling me.'

The woman looked alert and ready to be helpful.

'Why is it that you alone realised the need for Mr Campbell to be placed under observation. Had you perhaps noticed that he had sustained a blow to his head?'

'Oh, no,' she exclaimed. 'No, there was no sign of bruising at the time . . . I saw nothing when I put him to bed in the ward.'

'Did you carry out the routine procedures . . . pulse, temperature, blood pressure?'

'Oh, yes, they were all recorded on his chart, which Dr Beaton consulted on her rounds later in the night.'

'Were there any abnormalities at that time?'

'His temperature was a trifle below normal and he was perspiring rather freely . . . oh, and his blood pressure was rather high . . . but I assumed that was to do with all the activity. He had been running about like a two year old all evening.'

'Miss Kemp, as a nurse you are not expected to diagnose a patient's condition. You are, however, expected to bring to the attention of the doctors any irregularity, are you not?'

'Of course.'

'Then why did you not enlist the opinion of one of the doctors when you noticed these unusual symptoms?'

'The local GPs had all gone,' she stammered, 'and the medical resident had already retired. It seemed too trivial a matter for which to wake him.'

'So had not Dr Beaton made that last round of the wards after a long night in the operating theatre, Mr Campbell would have been left to die without attention?'

Christine Kemp was white-faced. Maynard hastened to intervene.

'It is to your credit, Matron, that you alone saw the necessity to keep Mr Campbell under observation,' he commented with a smile.

'That is my second question,' Ewan jumped in rapidly. 'When everyone else was so convinced that there was nothing wrong with Mr Campbell, how was it that you felt he should be kept in the hospital overnight?'

'Well . . . he was a very old gentleman, and there was a history of heart trouble . . .'

'You *knew* about his angina, Miss Kemp?'

'Well . . . yes.' She looked about her wildly for support. Maynard regarded her in stony silence.

'He attended for examination by our specialist consultant several times during the past few years,' she concluded.

'But you did not see fit to mention this to Dr Beaton, nor even to add a note concerning this condition to his chart?'

'No, sir, I did not.'

'Thank you, Miss Kemp, that will be all.'

She turned for support to Sidney Maynard. He was busily writing on his notepad and did not look up until she had left the room.

Fraser wound up the proceedings abruptly.

'Thank you, Dr Beaton . . . Mr Menzies. I believe we have heard all the relevant evidence in this matter. The panel will now have to spend some time sifting the information. We shall of course be advised by Mr Lane as to any further steps which should be taken. I will be in touch with you in a few days.'

Morag found herself trembling as she left the room. Out in

the corridor she leaned heavily against her uncle for a few moments.

'Don't worry, my dear,' he whispered, giving her a comforting hug. 'I think we won!'

# Chapter 9

'As I understand it,' Morag told Lucy McArdle, 'the terms of my suspension refer only to my employment as a surgeon in this hospital. There is nothing to prevent my practising in general medicine. Please tell Mr Maynard that I shall for the time being be acting under the direction of Dr Gordon McDonald . . . he has more work than he can reasonably cope with in the present circumstances.'

'I'll tell him,' Lucy responded hesitantly, 'but I don't think he will be very pleased.'

'Gordon already has twenty cases of typhoid on his hands,' Morag insisted, 'he needs my help.'

She did not wait for further protests.

At the hospital gate Charlie had parked his taxi and was waiting for her when she emerged. Surprised to see him, Morag approached the vehicle.

'Jump in, Doc,' he called to her. 'I canna hang about here all day!'

'How did you know I would be needing a lift?'

'Mr Glendenning sent me.'

Morag sank back against the leather upholstery, resting her medical bag on her knees.

She had received Gordon's urgent request for assistance not half an hour before. What Magnus Glendenning had to do with it she did not know . . . maybe he had been there with Gordon when he rang.

The taxi sped along the High Street and out on to the road to the industrial estate. It was a dull sultry afternoon, with low cloud blotting out the sun and keeping the hot moist air unmoving and close to the ground.

'Real midgy weather,' Morag remarked to Charlie, as she brushed away the tiny insects from her brow. 'Just right for spreading fevers of any kind.'

'It's surprising how quickly word gets around when something like this happens,' he observed, philosophically. 'All kinds of people suddenly find they have urgent business elsewhere.'

What he said appeared to have some foundation, for the steady flow of tourists through the town seemed to have come to an abrupt halt and the streets were almost empty.

'There is really no reason to suppose that any of the holiday accommodation will be affected,' Morag responded. 'The epidemic seems to be concentrated on the Corporation housing estate at Feanagrogan, but it's useless trying to convince people who are determined to believe the worst!'

As the cab drew up outside the McDonalds' house, Anna flung open the door and ran down the path, as though she had been waiting for the taxi to arrive.

'Thank goodness,' she blurted out, as Morag turned to pay the fare. 'Oh, don't dismiss the cab, you'll need it.'

Exchanging a quick word with Charlie, Morag secured his further services before turning to find that Anna had run back into the house.

'Gordon went out after his call to you,' she explained when Morag had joined her inside. 'He had requests to visit six patients, mostly in the area alongside the canal. Goodness knows when he will be back. All these have come in since he left.'

She handed Morag a fistful of paper slips, each with a separate name and address.

'There are supplies of serum in the surgery and bottles of the usual medicines: perchloride of mercury, creosote, lysol . . . oh, yes, and opiates for checking the diarrhoea. Gordon said to help yourself to whatever you needed.'

Anna pushed back her thick black hair, which was uncharacteristically dishevelled, and sat down abruptly on the nearest chair.

'I don't know how much longer we can go on like this,' she said wearily. 'It's like a field-dressing station at the height of the battle!'

Morag had had time the previous evening to revise her scant knowledge of the treatment of typhoid. She had studied the disease, of course, but there had been no epidemics in recent years and she had never seen an actual case of the fever. She glanced through the array of bottles before her and selected those she thought most appropriate, placing them carefully in the Gladstone bag which she had last used in earnest when on obstetrics duty, during the later stages of her residency at the Royal.

'I suppose these are all cases of typhoid?' she asked as an afterthought, before opening the front door.

'From the symptoms given over the telephone, yes,' Anna replied. 'Mind you, Gordon has been called out on more than one false errand in the last few days . . . people panicking . . . you know how it is!'

Morag hesitated for a moment before stepping back into the taxi. 'Goodness knows how I'm going to pay you, Charlie,' she said, anxiously.

'It's all right, miss, Mr Glendenning said I was to stick with you and take you wherever you needed to go.'

Morag wondered what would be the price of this public-spirited behaviour. Was it the *Gazette* which would foot the bill? If Magnus was after a story, it probably meant yet another conflict with Sidney Maynard, but at the moment she was more than grateful for Charlie's services.

She gave him the first address on her list and settled back once more. When they arrived at the house, she handed him the remaining scraps of paper.

'You know the area better than I,' she told him, 'will you arrange these in logical order for visiting? I'll be as quick as I can.'

She pushed open a rusty gate which looked surprisingly like an old iron bedstead, and made her way along a paved pathway, avoiding tufts of weed growing up through the cracks. The houses in this part of town were ugly, grey, two-storey buildings under slate tiles. Thrown up in their hundreds to accommodate men returning from the fighting at the end of the war, they were only ten years old and already showing signs of dilapidation. It was clear that poor quality construction was as much to blame for their condition as any neglect on the part of the householders.

Morag remembered Magnus's sour comments about Graham Fraser's part in the development of local housing schemes, and was forced to admit that his criticisms seemed well founded.

Her knock was answered by a spare, angular woman, probably in her late-twenties but looking a good ten years older. Her cheeks were hollow and there were dark shadows beneath her eyes. Loose strands of hair clung to her forehead, which was damp with perspiration. A thin wailing came from somewhere within the house and she turned to answer it before greeting Morag.

'Wul' ye get in yer bed this minute, Wully Prentice, or wul' I come in there and skelp ye?' she yelled. Then, turning abruptly to Morag: 'Yes?'

'I'm Dr Beaton . . . assisting Dr McDonald during the epidemic,' Morag introduced herself. When the woman hesitated, she continued, 'May I come in?'

'I don't know as my man would put up wi' a *woman* doctor,' she said, bluntly. 'McDonald's oor doctor . . . has been ever since the children was born.'

'Well,' replied Morag, equally blunt, 'it's me or no one today, I'm afraid, Mrs Prentice. Dr McDonald has many other cases to attend to in this part of town.'

'Ah, weel, you'd best come ben,' the woman capitulated, suddenly overwhelmed by weariness and unable to resist further.

Morag found her patients, two young boys aged six and four years old, their noses peeping over the top of a none-too-clean sheet, their heads resting on an uncovered bolster whose striped ticking had yellowed with age. William, the elder of the two, seemed bright-eyed and although a trifle flushed, probably because he had just jumped into bed in response to his mother's sharp warning, did not appear to be ailing at all. The younger child, however, seemed lethargic, was perspiring profusely, and she found his pulse to be weak and rapid.

'What is the wee boy's name?' Morag enquired.

'Rabbie . . . Robert,' his mother replied, fixing a steely eye upon

William who was wriggling uncomfortably, obviously resentful at having to be in his bed at this time of day.

Morag shone a torch into each of Rabbie's eyes and noticed the slow response in the pupils. She folded back the sheet and pulled up the child's nightshirt, searching for the tell-tale rosy spots. She found them, a small cluster on his abdomen and a few more in the small of his back.

'When I saw those,' the child's mother observed, 'I thought at first they were midgy bites, but then he started being sick an' all . . . and he was so hot!'

Morag placed a thermometer under the boy's armpit.

'Have you been taking his temperature?'

'Where would the likes of me get one of those things?' the woman demanded, indicating the thermometer. 'If it weren't for the HSA, I wouldn't be able to call you in at all, Doctor.'

The Hospital Savings Association was an organisation set up to insure working-class people against accident and illness. A small annual contribution ensured medical treatment for the member and his family whenever it was required.

'I shall need samples of blood and stools,' Morag stated, as she straightened up and noted the mercury reading on the thermometer, 'but I don't think there is any doubt that Rabbie has typhoid fever.'

Mrs Prentice gave a thin cry of alarm, which she stifled instantly by placing her hand over her mouth.

Morag continued, calmly, 'His temperature is one hundred and two degrees and I suspect will get higher. You will have to keep bathing him with tepid water to cool him, and see that he takes the medicine I am going to give you. Exactly as it says on the bottle, mind.'

As she spoke she took out a hypodermic needle and prepared an injection of serum for the child. While Rabbie remained unmoved at the sight of this activity, Wully looked extremely perturbed.

'Ye'll no stick ony needles in me, missus,' he wailed, plaintively.

'We'll see,' said Morag, smiling encouragingly at wee Rabbie

167

as she pushed the needle home. 'It depends if you need it.'

She dabbed at the site of the injection with a piece of cotton wool, and laid the thin little arm back beneath the covers. Only then did she walk around the bed to take a look at William.

A cursory examination of the child revealed none of the symptoms presented by his brother.

She found the boy's forehead to be quite cool, and his colour had returned to normal after his quick bout of exercise. Once again she searched for the tell-tale spots and, finding none, turned to the woman.

'William seems well enough for the present,' she pronounced, 'but the disease is highly infectious and I'm afraid it will be necessary to isolate Rabbie. We can't have the boys occupying the same bed . . . not until the wee one is clear of infection.'

'Where will I put Wullie?' the woman complained. 'His sisters have the small bedroom, and there's no space for another cot in our room . . .'

'I'm sure you'll think of something,' Morag replied. 'Besides, it may not be for long. As soon as arrangements can be made, we shall take Rabbie into hospital. In the meantime you must keep a close eye on all the children. If any of them show signs of fever – spots, vomiting or diarrhoea, call Dr McDonald immediately. You can help to prevent the spread of the disease by making sure that Rabbie's clothes and bedclothes are boiled in lysol and washed separately from the rest of the family's things, keeping aside his cup and plates, and being scrupulously clean in the kitchen and bathroom. The disease is passed on by contaminated water, so for the time being I would advise you to boil all drinking water used by everyone in the household.'

As she followed the woman down the stairs, she gave instructions for a light diet for the sick child, and tried to explain how regular recording of his temperature would give the doctors a better indication of how the disease was progressing.

'I will leave you this thermometer,' she said, washing it under the kitchen tap and replacing it in its metal case, 'You can give it back to Dr McDonald when Rabbie is better. Take the boy's

temperature every four hours and just write down what it is . . .'
She explained the reading and shaking down processes, but felt
it inappropriate to try to explain how the temperature could be
recorded on a graph. The raw figures should be enough for Dr
McDonald to assess the stage the disease had reached.

'Oh, and Mrs Prentice.' Morag turned back, her hand on the door
handle. 'I have no doubt that the Authorities will be conducting an
investigation to find the source of the disease. Since only Rabbie
has been affected in your household, maybe you could discover
what it was he had to eat or drink which the others did not . . .
it would have been about ten days ago.'

'I'd have to ask Mrs Locke . . . she stays two streets away,'
Mrs Prentice told her. 'With Rabbie the only one of the weans
not at school, I can earn a bit by working down at Fraser's for
a few hours every morning. I leave the wee one playing with
Mrs Locke's kids. She's a kindly woman and can do with a few
coppers.'

'Are any of her children ill?'

'I don't know,' the woman replied. 'I sent oor Katrina
along there before she went to school yesterday, to say Rab
wouldnae be coming. I havenae been outside the door mysel'
for three days!'

'The rest of your children are in school . . . now?' Alarm bells
were ringing in Morag's head.

'Aye, Katrina and Kirsty went off as usual this morning. Wullie
said he wasnae feeling well, and although he's never a one to
miss a chance of getting off the school, I let him stay hame just
in case he'd got the fever too.'

'It might be a good idea to keep him home for a day or
two,' Morag agreed, 'just in case he develops any symptoms.'
She hesitated to suggest that the whole family was at risk.
'Which school do the children go to?' she queried. She did
not want to start an unnecessary panic, but the school should
be informed and the premises examined for possible sources of
infection.

'King William Street Elementary,' the woman answered. 'Here,
you don't think it's coming from the school, do you?' she

demanded, anxiously. 'They've been talkin' for years about replacing those old stone lavvies.'

'Since Rabbie is the only one of your children who doesn't go there, it's very unlikely that the school is the source of the fever,' Morag replied, hastily squashing the idea.

She left Mrs Prentice staring after her. As she walked down the path towards Charlie's cab, a small figure, carelessly dressed in shorts and open-necked shirt, shot past her and ran off down the road towards the canal.

'Wullie Prentice, youse come back here this minute . . . do you hear me!' the child's mother shouted after him, ineffectually. Knowing her words would be disregarded, she turned and went inside, slamming the door behind her.

'How can we be expected to contain the disease when the parent's can't confine their own children?' Morag sighed, as she settled in the cab once more. 'Where next?' she demanded of Charlie.

'Not very far,' the cabbie replied. 'A Mrs Locke, number fifty-three Carmichael Terrace.'

'We have to find the common factor,' Gordon declared. 'So far, the cases have been youngsters under twenty and, more often than not, they are single cases from different households, which tends to rule out any particular set of drains, or the water supplies to specific housing schemes. The school gives us no clues . . . the victims occur haphazardly across the whole population.'

'I've had samples taken from water supplies to all public buildings in the Feanagrogan area, and from the mains supplies to each of the estates, but it will take ten days at least to see any results from the cultures,' the Assistant Borough Engineer explained, despondently

Morag noticed how tired Adam Inglis looked. He seemed to be taking the whole weight of the responsibility for the epidemic upon himself.

'There has to be something we're missing,' Gordon insisted 'Something unusual in the pattern of things. Why should the epidemic have come on so suddenly? Usually it's the kind of thing which starts off with one or two individuals and then spreads through a household, down a street, through a classroom ... This, on the other hand, appeared overnight. The first I knew about it I had ten patients, from different streets and all kinds of housing ... even family circumstances have no bearing. The fever has struck the reasonably well-to-do and the poor alike.'

Morag sipped gratefully at the glass of cool lemonade Anna had handed her the minute she had arrived. It seemed ages since she had asked for tea in mid-afternoon. The weather had been so unusually warm for more than a fortnight. It was a time for cold drinks and ice-creams ...

She had a sudden vision of children queuing outside the corner shop on that Sunday of her previous visit. She was about to speak out ... remembered that she herself had sent the young McDonalds off to buy ice-creams, and hesitated. If the ice-cream from Luigi's were to blame, Gordon's children could be expected to be presenting symptoms by now, and she knew they were perfectly healthy.

Adam Inglis, who had been sitting silently throughout this debate, regarded her quizzically and demanded, 'What were you going to say?'

Magnus Glendenning noticed how she coloured up the moment Adam acknowledged her contribution to the discussion.

'One factor resulting from the good weather,' Morag observed, hesitantly,' is the increased sales of ice-cream. The sudden appearance of typhoid does in fact tie in neatly with the dates for this fine spell.'

Morag could see Gordon and his other colleagues counting back to the day when the first calls had come in. An area of high pressure had settled over the Highlands in the first week of the month, and tourists and locals alike had enjoyed hot cloudless days for more than a fortnight.

'Are there many places which sell ice-cream in this part of town?' Morag enquired of Adam.

'Every small tobacconist and sweetie shop,' he replied. 'There must be dozens of outlets within a three-mile radius of this house.'

'How could ice-cream come to be contaminated?' Magnus asked.

'By the handlers . . . or it's possible that the water or milk used might carry the bacteria, but that's really most unlikely,' Adam assured him. 'Modern processing is designed to see that no contaminated fluids get into the product.'

'Besides,' observed Gordon, 'most of the ice-cream is factory produced, and sold ready-wrapped. I don't see how a local outbreak could be attributed to one of the major ice-cream companies.'

As a student, Morag had been in the habit of visiting a favourite Italian ice-cream parlour in Glasgow. She recalled how she had enjoyed watching the machine churning over the creamy mixture, while the proprietor added, by hand, flavouring and colours and all the special ingredients like chopped nuts and cherries which made his extensive variety of ice-cream the most popular on sale anywhere in the city. Was it just a coincidence that his name had been Luigi too?

'There is one parlour where I would lay a hundred to one on the ice-cream being made on the premises,' she said, suddenly. 'Luigi's . . . it's just down the road.'

Adam was on his feet in an instant.

'I'll go down there right away and collect some samples,' he declared. 'I think Morag may well be right.' He smiled across at her and she blushed with pleasure that he should take her suggestion so seriously. 'After all,' he added bluntly, rather spoiling the compliment, 'we have to start somewhere!'

'If you're going back to town, may I have a lift?' she asked. Glancing across at Magnus she added, almost apologetically, 'I thought it best to dismiss Charlie once I had finished the round. Please thank your proprietor for providing the transport. It was very thoughtful.'

Magnus had actually paid for Charlie out of his own pocket but her assumption that the *Gazette* was responsible did not bother him nearly so much as her apparent eagerness to accompany Adam Inglis.

'Perhaps we should pay a call on Luigi on the way?' Adam suggested.

'I think that might be a very good idea,' she agreed, beaming. Magnus considered her radiant smile quite inappropriate in the circumstances.

'Thank you so much for all your help,' Gordon told her, as he came hurrying after them along the path. 'I couldn't have managed without you.'

'I think I had better try to see Mr Maynard in the morning about opening the fever wing,' Morag said, her mind once more on the real problem. Remembering her encounter with the Prentice family that afternoon, she continued, 'Isolation seems to be the only way to contain the spread of infection.'

'Maynard will probably resist any suggestion of opening up the isolation ward, because of the cost,' Gordon warned. 'You will have to make him see how important it is to contain this outbreak before it goes any further. No matter how conscientious the people are around here, the facilities in their houses are poor for the most part. Washing clothes and boiling drinking water costs money, and once the adult population starts going down with the fever we shall begin to have a few deaths on our hands . . .'

Miserably, Magnus watched Morag step into Adam Inglis's car. Observing the two of them together these days, he was beginning to suspect something more between them than mere friendship.

Morag the Indomitable suddenly appeared to defer to Adam in all things. It may be that this recent censure had sapped her self-confidence, but Magnus thought there was more to it than that. She seemed consciously to take a back seat whenever Adam appeared. It was as though she wished to disguise her own superior intellect lest she should damage Adam's self-esteem.

She was behaving like a schoolgirl smitten with calf love at the appearance of a new curate in the parish. He told himself he was a fool to be so consumed with jealousy. What right had he to make any claim upon Morag's affections? Inglis was a strapping young fellow, sober, of good repute, and almost her age. How could a drunken reprobate like himself hope to compete?

He had hardly exchanged a word with her since she had come back to Gordon's house late that afternoon. Apart from thanking him for providing the taxi, her attention had centred upon the problems of the epidemic until Inglis had joined them.

He glanced down at the notes he had been making as they had discussed the situation, and wondered how best to write up the story. All his instincts were to put pressure on the Hospital Board and the Municipal authorities to do something about this mess. The trouble was that whatever he said was likely to involve Morag while at the same time showing Maynard in a bad light. He had no wish to endanger her position at the hospital still further while the board was still making up its mind about her continued employment.

To the rear of the West Highland Hospital stood a small group of wooden huts, typical of those used extensively by the Army. They had been erected to house the enormous increase in tuberculosis patients in the years immediately following the end of the war, and thus constituted Inverlinnhe's isolation hospital.

Fortunately, by the end of the previous decade the need for such a facility had disappeared, and the temporary wards had been closed down. The staff required to run them had either been dismissed or transferred to other duties, and the huts had been boarded up and forgotten by all except the caretaker, Harold Guthrie, who carried out essential repairs from time to time.

Before tackling Sidney Maynard on the subject of reopening the isolation wards, Morag decided to take a proper look at them for herself. She ran Guthrie to ground, taking his first tea-break of the day with Cook, in the hospital kitchen.

'Good morning, Dr Beaton,' Isa MacClachlan greeted her warmly. 'You're up and about early after the long day you had yesterday!'

Morag never ceased to wonder at the manner in which every

action she took was noted by the hospital staff. It was as though a super-efficient intelligence service had her under constant surveillance.

'I shall be away again very shortly, Isa,' she told Cook. 'There were ten new cases of typhoid yesterday, and goodness knows what has been happening overnight.'

'It'll be the drains,' Guthrie muttered, with the air of one fully conversant with such matters. 'I knew a man worked on that scheme at Feanagrogan . . . three pounds ten shillings per house is what they allowed for the plumbing. It's not surprising the pipes is beginning to leak after ten years!'

'We don't know that the plumbing is to blame,' Morag warned him. Loose talk of that kind, emanating from the hospital, would quickly be interpreted as fact by the newspapers.

'Well, what else could it be?' the man demanded in a surly manner. 'Everyone knows that typhoid is caused by bad drains.'

'No doubt the Public Health Department will discover the source of the disease in due course,' Morag replied, stoutly defending Adam and his colleagues, 'but in the meantime it will not help to jump to conclusions. All we can do is treat the victims . . . which brings me to the reason I have been looking for you Mr Guthrie. Is it possible for me to take a look at the old isolation wards?'

'I can let you in to have a look round,' he agreed, somewhat reluctantly, 'but if you're thinking about putting them back into use, I should forget it. It would take weeks of work to make them fit to take any patients.'

'I'd still like to see for myself, Harold, if it's not too much trouble.' She smiled disarmingly, and the caretaker was putty in her hands.

'I was going along in that direction, anyway,' he declared for the benefit of Isa MacClachlan, who was grinning at the way in which Morag had so easily persuaded Guthrie, a man who enjoyed a reputation for being a surly, uncooperative old tyrant.

\*     \*     \*

The huts were dirty, which was only to be expected. Cobwebs hung in festoons from the ceilings, and a layer of grime did its best to prevent any light at all from penetrating the row of windows along either side of each of the wooden buildings. Unusually for hospital accommodation of the period, the beds were arranged in small cubicles, each separated from the next by a thin partition wall which not only gave the patients privacy, but also provided a modicum of isolation. It was a crude attempt at preventing cross-infection, but with well-trained nursing staff it could prove effective.

The beds, although old, were quite adequate and were complete with mattresses and pillows. The utility room at the end of each ward appeared to hold a full set of equipment. Morag was thankful to see that everything had been put away in an orderly fashion and that apart from a general washing and cleaning, it would not be difficult to have the wards back in operation. She felt that Guthrie's estimate of weeks to restore the buildings to a usable condition was an exaggeration. She kept her conclusions to herself, however. If Guthrie thought that she might create a situation which was going to give him extra work, he would be down in Maynard's office, complaining, before she had time to formulate her own strategy.

'See what I mean,' the caretaker demanded, surveying the dilapidation with a certain degree of satisfaction. 'By the time we can get this back into use, the epidemic will be over.'

Morag nodded, thoughtfully, and Guthrie, taking her silence for agreement, locked the door behind them and sauntered off across the paved yard which separated the isolation block from the rest of the hospital complex. He was whistling as he went.

Careful to observe the recognised etiquette on this occasion, Morag approached Maynard's secretary for an appointment, only to find herself called into his office immediately he heard her speaking in the adjoining room.

'Ah, Dr Beaton, I was hoping to have a word with you before you went out this morning.'

She looked inquiringly at Lucy McArdle, who nodded her head, indicating she should go straight in.

'Sit down, sit down.' Maynard stood up and offered her a chair.

'I am pleased to be the bearer of good tidings,' he declared magnanimously. 'The investigating panel, having weighed all the evidence, has concluded that the hospital was not negligent in the matter of Gregor Campbell's death, and apart from making certain recommendations in order to avoid similar difficulties arising in the future, the report has exonerated all members of staff involved in the emergency.'

He leaned across his magnificent desk in order to hand her a copy of the findings.

'I can't express the great pleasure it gives me to be able to tell you that your suspension is lifted forthwith, and that you may return to your duties immediately.' While his words were ingratiating and a smile played about his lips, Morag noted the steely glint in Sidney Maynard's eyes.

He's lost, she thought, and now he has to make a semblance of accepting defeat . . . this time. It did not mean that she could lower her guard for one minute, but there was considerable satisfaction in having been proved to be in the right.

'Thank you,' she replied. She glanced through the document he had given her, before adding, 'Naturally I am relieved at the committee's findings, but I had not anticipated returning to surgical duties quite so quickly. As I informed Miss McArdle, I have been assisting the local doctors during the typhoid epidemic and would hope to continue to help Dr McDonald until such time as we can get the majority of his patients into hospital. He and his colleagues cannot continue to cope indefinitely with home visits for so many patients.'

'Unfortunately, we have no isolation unit at the West Highland,' Maynard replied, smoothly, 'so I really cannot envisage a situation in which any of McDonald's patients will be found hospital beds. If, however, you wish to continue assisting him until the end of this week, that will be quite in order. Our locum surgeon has been engaged on a weekly basis, and would have to be kept on until Sunday in any case.'

'What would it take to reopen the old isolation hospital?' Morag enquired.

'More money than the Hospital Committee would be able to find, I'm afraid,' came the curt reply.

'But the buildings are sound enough, and all the equipment is there, apart from linen. It would require staffing, of course, but much of the domestic work might be carried out by volunteers . . . I am sure that mothers of the sick children would willingly lend a hand, just to be sure that their little ones are being properly treated.'

'There is the question of the initial cleaning, and some rooms probably need redecoration before we could even consider admitting patients. How do you propose that this work should be done without incurring additional expenditure?'

'I would be willing to organise it myself,' she declared, stoutly, 'and I am sure that there are others in the hospital who would give up some of their free time to help.' Even as she spoke, she thought of Magnus's promise to assist in any way that he could . . . perhaps an appeal for funds, or even voluntary labour to get the isolation hospital operational?

'Well, Miss Beaton,' Maynard concluded, 'if, as you believe, you can find a group of volunteers to carry out the work, you have my permission to go ahead. But remember, no patients can be admitted without the approval of the Hospital Board. I will call an emergency meeting to put forward your proposal, but cannot guarantee that they will be prepared to meet the additional costs of staffing and supplying the unit.'

'Thank you, Mr Maynard, thank you so much!' Astonished by this unexpected capitulation, Morag decided to leave before he could change his mind.

'I shall keep you informed of every move,' she said, as she turned to open the door.

He acknowledged her assurance with a curt nod of the head.

'Kindly ask Miss McArdle to step in here, as you go out,' he replied.

\*   \*   \*

'Magnus . . . is that you?' She could hear a buzz of conversation, telephones ringing and typewriters clattering away in the background.

'Morag?' He sounded quite startled to hear her voice.

'Magnus, I have to see you most urgently. Could you meet me at the café . . . say about eleven-thirty?'

'I've an editorial meeting which should be over by then . . . will you wait if I can't get there exactly on time?'

'Yes, though I have promised to take over from Gordon at lunchtime,' she replied.

'I'll be there!' He put down the phone, wondering what could be important enough for Morag to call him at the office. Could she have heard the result of the inquiry already? He blanched at the possibility that she might have been dismissed. Hopeless as his devotion to Morag might appear to be, he could not bear to think that she might be leaving Inverlinnhe.

The café was nearly empty.

Morag sat by the window in the very same seat she had occupied on that bleak December day which now seemed so long ago. She toyed impatiently with her spoon, and glanced up expectantly every time the doorbell indicated an arrival or a departure.

It was well past noon when Magnus appeared. He looked hot and flustered as he dropped into the chair opposite.

'Thank goodness you've come at last!' she exclaimed. 'I was beginning to think I would have to go without seeing you.'

'What is it . . . what's happened?' he demanded, anxiously.

'I need your help, urgently,' she replied. 'I have to raise money quickly in order to get the isolation wing of the hospital opened. Sidney Maynard says I may go ahead with getting it cleaned up and ready to receive patients, but the work will have to be done by volunteer labour.'

'Hold on a minute . . . you're not talking about those scruffy old huts behind the main building, are you?' he asked, incredulously.

'Yes, they're not really in such bad condition,' she insisted. 'At least the wards are designed for barrier nursing, and although

179

the place needs a good cleaning and a lick of paint here and there, I can't see why we couldn't have it put to rights by the beginning of next week.'

'If you're hoping to get volunteers to do the work, where does the fund-raising come in?' he enquired, beginning to be swept along by her enthusiasm.

'It will cost money to provide the additional staff – isolation nursing requires experienced people. They'll have to be brought in from elsewhere.'

'Surely it is the board's responsibility to provide suitable accommodation in an emergency such as this?' he protested.

'Apparently not,' Morag replied. 'I was frankly amazed that Maynard was so ready to support the reopening of the old wing. He pointed out that the members of the board would have to agree before patients could be admitted, and of course he was insistent that additional money must be found to run it.'

'So where do I come in?' Magnus suspected he already knew what his role was to be.

'I wondered if your paper might launch an appeal . . . you were going to write a feature about the work of the doctors out at Feanagrogan and the latest news of the progress of the epidemic. Couldn't you include an appeal for money?'

'I suppose it's possible, but the decision would rest with the Editor, you understand. Perhaps you had better start from the beginning again and explain exactly what it is you have in mind?'

The waitress appeared, and took their order.

'Before you do that, however,' Magnus continued as though they had not been interrupted, 'can I assume from all this excitement that you are no longer expecting to leave the West Highland Hospital in the immediate future?'

'Oh, of course, you won't have heard,' she replied, suddenly reminded by his question. 'The inquiry found that the hospital staff had not been negligent in the case of Gregor Campbell, and that the medical team had done a splendid job in extremely difficult circumstances.

'Now then, as I see it we can start immediately on getting

the buildings put right . . . I shall try to get some of the hospital staff to help out, beginning this evening. If you can put out a general call for practical assistance . . . we could do with some expert painters and carpenters and probably a plumber and a glazier . . . they had better be told to contact me. I will give you a telephone number . . .'

Magnus was given no time to congratulate her or to tell her how relieved he was that she had weathered the storm without a blemish on her professional reputation. He was too busy scribbling down her requirements. She was right, he already had the bones of a first-class story. The hospital appeal would add another dimension which should get people thinking more positively about the situation:- what they could do to help, rather than whingeing about the epidemic at Feanagrogan causing them to lose holiday business.

# Chapter 10

'Now then, Mr Bernini,' Gordon said, picking up a large hypodermic syringe, 'I just need to take a small sample of your blood for analysis. This won't hurt a bit . . .'

The small, dark Italian gentleman who sat before him did not appear in the least convinced. He winced when he saw the size of the needle, and drew back.

'I not understand-a why you need my blood, *Dottore*,' he protested. 'As you can see, both I and my wife are quite-a well . . . our staff also.'

He was right, of course. The fat little man was in robust health, even if he was considerably overweight. He swore he had had no diarrhoea and certainly showed no signs of fever.

This was more than could be said for Luigi Bernini's two assistants who had followed Mrs Bernini into the surgery earlier that morning. One had been a thin, angular fellow who looked as though he could do with a good meal; the second, although less emaciated in appearance, had the grey complexion which Gordon had come to associate with the long-term unemployed. Both men had confessed that they had begun work only at the beginning of the hot spell, when Mr Bernini had found it necessary to increase his production of ice-cream in order to satisfy demand. No doubt both would soon begin to show signs of a more affluent life-style, provided their employment continued throughout the summer.

Acutely conscious that if he did find anything wrong with them, their employment would end abruptly, Gordon found himself torn between the desire to track down the source of the disease, and the hope that neither of these two was responsible!

'Just a matter of routine, Mr Bernini,' Gordon reassured him, grabbing the Italian's pudgy little arm and sinking the needle into his flesh. Luigi gazed, horrified at the deep red venous blood which flowed sluggishly into the tube of the syringe, but before he could either faint, or even summon the courage to complain, Gordon had deftly removed the instrument and swiftly transferred the blood to a labelled bottle.

'There, that wasn't so bad, was it?' he demanded. Luigi could only moan lightly as he pressed at the wound with the cotton which Gordon handed to him.

'A plaster on that to prevent any blood getting on your shirt . . . oh, and will you take this other bottle away with you? I shall require a sample of your stool. Perhaps you will bring it back to the surgery in the morning.'

Mr Bernini stared at him, uncomprehending, for a few seconds, and then light dawned. He thrust the bottle into his pocket and made for the door.

'I tell you, *Dottore*, you are-a wasting your time. Luigi's pure cream ices are known throughout-a Scotland.'

'Nevertheless, I have to eliminate every possibility . . . you understand?' Gordon bent his head to complete Luigi Bernini's record and did not look up as the man departed.

Despite his unceasing efforts to trace the source of the typhoid bacteria, Adam Inglis had had little success so far. The problem was that, no matter how suspicious a situation might be, before he could positively identify the source of infection he must have scientific evidence, and this could be obtained only by growing cultures of any suspect bacteria they discovered. It was an exercise which was irritatingly slow, taking several long and anxious days to complete.

Morag's instincts had told her that Luigi's ice-cream might be responsible for the epidemic. Adam, with Morag as his willing assistant, had given the premises a most thorough examination. Despite Luigi's protestations that his landlord would not allow it, he took samples from every piece of equipment, from ingredients used and the finished products made in the shop. Not content with concentrating upon this one possible source of infection, he had had his team take samples from sewer manholes and mains water pipes, as well as from the premises of other vendors of food situated in the area where the outbreak had occurred.

These investigations unearthed a number of cracked drainage pipes, and innumerable leakages of the mains water supply, due to earth movements in the unstable substrata of the alluvial plain at the mouth of the river. This damage was reported faithfully, but there was nothing to suggest that the leaks had any bearing upon the typhoid epidemic.

Morag, visiting Gordon's surgery daily to give her assistance with the growing number of fever cases, watched anxiously for any sign of the disease amongst the McDonald household. She was acutely aware that she had sent the children out to buy ice-cream on that Sunday afternoon. If she was right about Luigi's, they should present symptoms within ten days. Gordon, engrossed in the problems which the epidemic posed for his practice, seemed to have overlooked the incident, and Morag, not wishing to create unnecessary alarm, kept her fears to herself. There was nothing she could do but wait, and hope the McDonald children would not be affected.

'It's not definite, of course,' Adam announced, as he hurried into Gordon's consulting room on Friday morning. He handed the doctor a slip of paper.

'I persuaded the pathologist to take a look at some samples of ice-cream from Luigi's,' he explained 'He won't commit himself until he sees the results of the cultures, but he did find evidence of pathogenic bacteria being present. Unfortunately they were not in sufficient numbers for a positive identification.'

'Surely the very presence of a single dangerous bacillus in a food product is sufficient to condemn the source outright?' Gordon objected, testily.

'Regulations specify the level of contamination at which premises are deemed unfit and must be closed,' Adam explained. 'It would be unreasonable to shut down an operation because of the presence of any chance contaminant which might occur in only one sample. For one thing, it would be difficult to prove that the contamination was not secondary . . . even picked up in the pathology laboratory itself.'

'Can you not close down the ice-cream operation temporarily, until a conclusive result is obtained?' Gordon demanded, infuriated by what he regarded as petty bureaucracy.

'Unfortunately not,' Adam replied. 'Were we to close the premises, and it was subsequently found that we were mistaken, the proprietor might sue the Authority both for loss of reputation and interruption of trading. My boss won't take that kind of a risk.'

'Well then, there has to be some way we can warn people off eating ice-cream for the time being,' Gordon insisted. 'It would make things easier if we had some cooler weather,' he added, wiping perspiration from his deeply furrowed brow.

'We could put out a general warning against eating uncooked foods of any kind until the crisis is over,' suggested Morag. She appreciated Gordon's feeling of frustration, and the anger borne of his desperate weariness. On the other hand, she found herself championing Adam's position; a wrong decision now could easily cost him his job.

'If the notice mentioned such things as raw fruit and vegetables, coddled eggs and uncooked shellfish,' she suggested, tentatively, 'and also included ice-cream in the list, there might be a reduction in sales without the vendors being able to say we had pointed the finger at them directly.'

'I think Morag is right,' said Adam. 'There can be no cause for complaint against a general warning, suggesting people use their own common sense. I'll get word to the *Gazette* right away. May I use your telephone?'

Gordon had no option but to accept the common-sense approach of his colleagues. Gloomily, he nodded his assent.

It did not take long for news to travel around the hospital that Dr Beaton had borrowed cloths, brushes and buckets from the cleaners, and was busily scrubbing floors and washing down walls in the old isolation block.

Eddie Strachan peered in in disbelief before going on duty the following morning, only to find that what he had been told was true.

'Morag, what is this?' he asked.

'The epidemic is getting out of hand and it is no longer possible to treat the growing number of patients in their own homes,' she told him. 'I am making sure that Mr Maynard will have no grounds for refusing to open up the isolation wards because of the cost of cleaning and redecorating them.'

'Are you proposing to do it all by yourself?' he enquired with an amused grin.

'Not likely,' she replied. 'All volunteers will be made very welcome!'

He walked into the ward and studied the layout carefully.

'I reckon it will take about five gallons of distemper to cover the walls including the partitions,' he calculated, 'and I think I know where I can lay my hands on some cheap paint . . . If you like, I can get started this evening?'

She was joined during the morning by Mary Neal and Violet Dunwoodie, who each put in a couple of hours scrubbing after coming off night duty. They were forced to depart at noon, since both were due in theatre that evening and must have a few hours' sleep first. Anticipating a solitary afternoon spent scraping off the paint which was peeling from a pair of large double doors, Morag was startled to hear, from along the covered passageway which linked the two wards, the sound of scrubbing. Thinking she was mistaken, she rasped away at the woodwork for a few moments more and then paused to listen. Yes, it was definitely scrubbing. As though to confirm her suspicion, there came the clanging of a metal bucket, followed by a very loud expletive.

Curious to know what was going on in the next ward, she laid down her tools and walked towards the noise.

Balanced precariously on a rickety stool, attacking a grimy ceiling with concentrated vigour, she found Matron. Morag was so surprised to see her there that she let out an exclamation which startled Christine Kemp, who dropped her scrubbing brush and would have toppled backwards had not Morag leaped forward and caught her before she fell.

Christine, having steadied herself, gratefully accepted the brush which Morag had retrieved, and turned back to her task.

'Sister Dunwoodie told me to get on with this,' she explained. 'I hope that's all right?'

Morag, rendered speechless by the sight of Matron Kemp with her sleeves rolled up, found herself stammering, 'Oh . . . yes . . . of course. It's exactly what's wanted . . . thank you, Matron.'

Christine's hair was tied back, gypsy fashion, by a bright scarf. Her uniform dress had been replaced by the kind of flowery apron which Morag's mother wore to do her housework. Coming upon her in this situation, no stranger would ever suspect that this woman was in charge of the entire nursing operation in the hospital.

'Well,' demanded Matron, 'are you going to stand there all day gawping? If you have nothing better to do, you could change the water in that bucket!'

Sheepishly, Morag collected the heavy bucket and made for the sluice-room.

When she returned, Christine had descended from the step-ladder and was fixing her headgear.

'Thanks,' she said, dropping her scrubbing brush into the fresh suds. 'You know, I'm quite enjoying this. I haven't had to clean up in this way since we took over the old convent at Royaumont, in 1915.'

'Were you there?' Morag asked eagerly. 'My cousin drove an ambulance attached to the Scottish Women's Hospitals. She often speaks of the staff at Royaumont . . . Dr Ivens and my father were great friends.'

'It was a different world,' Christine mused. 'We lived each day under the threat of death. Our senses were sharpened, events etched permanently on our brains. People regarded the most casual acquaintance as a friend for life after sharing that experience.'

'I have met many men who were at the Front,' said Morag quietly, 'but you are the first woman other than my cousin Heather I have come across.'

'It's hardly surprising.' Christine's voice hardened suddenly. 'We thought that by taking such an active part in hostilities, we women would win the respect of the War Office and the Government. The women doctors, especially the surgeons, expected civilian hospitals to fling open their doors and welcome them in when the war ended. But, if anything, it was more difficult for a woman to get a hospital appointment in 1919 than it had been in 1913. Some of the best doctors I have ever met were forced to give up all hope of employment, and advised to return to the bosom of their families, as though the Scottish Women's Hospitals had never existed. Even men who owe their lives to Dr Ivens, Elsie Inglis and the rest, have forgotten all about them now.'

'I thought you disapproved of women doctors?' observed Morag, more puzzled than ever, remembering how Christine Kemp had resisted her own appointment.

'It makes me angry to see talent wasted, while those with influence are able to infiltrate a system which has destroyed so many of my friends. I must admit I had convinced myself the only reason that you were appointed was the Beaton family's reputation . . .'

'And you felt I had no right to occupy a post which had been closed to those other women?' Morag suggested.

'Precisely. I was wrong, of course!' Her tone changed as she continued, 'You have shown that you have the kind of spirit which took us into the war on equal terms with men. Sadly many of those others had already lost it when they returned to civilian life . . . maybe because they were simply worked out and dispirited by their experiences, who can say? There's something I have been wanting to say to you, even before you started on this extraordinary crusade of your . . .'

Morag waited patiently. The words did not come easily to this woman who was so used always to being right.

'I made a mistake. I wanted you out of here, and was prepared to do whatever it took to have you removed. When I heard

that the board was to take no action in the matter of Gregor
Campbell's death I was more relieved than I can say. If anything
I did, or implied, had any detrimental effect upon your case, I
am truly sorry.'

She held out her hand, which was red and swollen with
scrubbing. 'Can you ever forgive me?'

Grasping it warmly, Morag replied, 'There is nothing to
forgive.'

'Friends?' the older women asked, and Morag was touched by
the anxiety in her voice.

'Friends,' she replied, and shook the hand more firmly.

'Well then,' Matron reverted to her normal tone of command,
'let's get to it. We'll never have the place ready for Monday at
this rate!'


Not only did Eddie Strachan prove to be adept with a paintbrush
himself, he also showed he could motivate others. By the end of
the week, his team of willing slaves had given both wards and
service areas a coat of cream distemper.

The hospital's chief housekeeper appeared on Friday morning,
bearing a pile of colourful, freshly laundered chintz curtains.

'I remembered taking them down when we closed the
wards,' she explained, 'but it took me an hour or two to
unearth them.'

'Do you have enough linen?' Morag asked anxiously. 'We shall
need all forty beds to begin with.'

'Aye, we're all right there, Doctor,' the kindly woman assured
her. 'Mind you, Mr Maynard has already been around to work
out the cost of laundering for two additional wards.'

'What did you tell him?' Morag asked.

'That if we couldna afford to send the washing out, I would
do it myself!'

Morag threw her arms around the comfortable body.

'Oh, you are a dear, Mrs McCabe. I just don't know how to
thank you.'

Overjoyed at finding her project going so smoothly, Morag
was all the more disappointed when it was discovered that the

sluice did not function properly and that one of the main drains was blocked.

Despairing of ever being in a position to tell Maynard they would be ready in time for the Monday deadline, she sought out Harold Guthrie, whom she found deep in confrontation with a small, determined figure in moleskin trousers and flat cap, and carrying a heavy canvas tool bag.

'This chap reckons he has an appointment to see you, Doctor,' Guthrie muttered, disbelievingly.

The man touched his cap. 'Dr Beaton?' he enquired cheerfully, ignoring the sullen expression on Guthrie's face.

'Yes?' Morag replied, warily. She had never set eyes on him before.

'Mr Glendenning said I was to contact you personally, ma'am.'

When she did not immediately respond, he explained further.

'I'm a plumber, you see.'

How did Magnus do it? she wondered. He always seemed to pick the right moment to spring one of his surprises. She put out her hand, smiling.

'You don't know how glad I am to see you, Mr . . . ?' She hesitated.

'McQueen, miss. Ian McQueen.'

'You do realise the hospital cannot pay for your services?' she reminded him.

'That's all right, miss,' came the reply. 'I have more than once in my life had reason to be grateful to the West Highland. It will be a pleasure to make some contribution in return for having a fit and healthy family.'

'Then follow me.' She sighed thankfully. 'We have just the job for you to tackle . . .'

With Gordon's assurance that he could manage well enough, with some assistance from neighbouring GPs, Morag had spent all her time in the past few days supervising the preparation of the isolation hospital to receive patients. They had both agreed that it was vitally important to have the unit ready to go into action the moment the board agreed to open the wards to the victims of the epidemic.

'Until I can nail down all possible sources of infection,' Gordon reiterated, 'we shall never rid ourselves of this plague. The sooner we have all the patients where we can keep proper control of their recovery, the better!'

While it was essential that the primary source of infection be discovered as soon as possible, a further complication arose from the insanitary condition of the older and more rural houses in the area. Many had no running water, and most had only earth closets. In such circumstances, it became nearly impossible to avoid the transfer of the virulent bacteria from one household to the next.

The disease, which had begun among the low-income but relatively well-housed tenants of the Corporation's Victory Estate, gained a much firmer footing when it came to the poorest crofting families. In the rough stone cottages of canal workers, fishermen and scavengers, it began to take on a more sinister aspect.

Seven deaths had occurred by the end of the third week; four of the victims were elderly people, and three very young children.

Gordon was greatly perturbed to discover a case of typhoid in a family of tinkers. For the summer months, a group of these itinerant workers had set up their canvas village on the edge of town, in the hope of finding casual work on the margins of Inverlinnhe's successful tourist trade. Fearing that they might move on, taking his patient with them, Gordon made an impassioned plea to both Graham Fraser and Duncan McRae, over the telephone.

'I must have an isolation unit for the itinerants at least. Otherwise we shall have the fever spreading all over the countryside!'

'We're doing everything we can to get the isolation hospital open,' Fraser assured him smoothly, once he had been tracked down by his secretary on the tenth tee of Inverlinnhe's nine-hole golf course.

'As I understand it, the stumbling block is raising money to pay for extra staff,' observed Duncan McRae, when he was approached. 'I'll do my best to stir a few of those who can afford it, to dig a little deeper into their pockets. Other than that, I don't know how to help you. I don't think there will be any dissenters on the board, once the financial problems are solved.'

Gordon, forced to accept this rather disheartening assessment of the situation, went on about his work as best he could under the circumstances. Towards the end of the week, the local school closed for lack of pupils.

On Saturday morning Magnus telephoned Morag at the hospital.

'How's the work going?' he demanded.

'Absolutely splendidly,' she replied, but the flat tone of her voice did not suggest any kind of elation. 'A few finishing touches and we shall be ready to open for business by Monday.'

There was a long pause and he wondered if for some reason she had put down the phone.

'Hello . . . Morag?'

She continued dejectedly, 'Unfortunately, the Hospital Board has decided that unless we can guarantee a sum of two thousand pounds from the appeal, it will not be possible to engage the specialist staff we shall need.'

He gave a low whistle. 'That's a bit steep,' he observed. 'There has been a very encouraging response so far, but at the rate that money is coming in – it's mostly very small amounts from grateful ex-patients – we shall be nowhere near that target. Not next week, anyway.'

'I should hate to think that all this hard work had gone to waste, after all,' she sighed. 'I have been overwhelmed by the support given by my colleagues. Oh, thanks for Mr McQueen, by the way. He's an absolute treasure!'

'My pleasure!' Magnus chuckled

'And do you know,' she added, 'even Matron rolled up her sleeves and set to, cleaning the ceilings. I never anticipated such whole-hearted support.'

'It's because they admire your determination.'

'I would hope it is also because they can see the sense' of isolating the affected patients, to prevent any further secondary infection,' she retorted. 'There is still no positive identification of the source of the outbreak, I suppose?'

Morag knew that he had been shadowing the Borough's Sanitation Department, and keeping a watchful eye on Gordon and his colleagues. As soon as anything definite emerged, Magnus Glendenning would know.

'Nothing so far,' he told her now. 'Nothing, that is, which can be made public.'

'What then?' she demanded.

'I have done a little investigating on my own,' he explained. 'I've been talking to mums at the school gate, and dads in the pubs, and even to some of the children. There seems to be a common factor amongst the early cases . . . one which Gordon has been able to confirm: the initial cases all ate ice-cream from Luigi's Hokey Pokey parlour.'

Morag felt sick with apprehension. Glad as she was to know they were beginning to narrow down the possible source of the typhoid germs, she had prayed it was not Luigi's. The thought that she might have been responsible for an incidence of typhoid fever amongst the McDonald family was too much to bear.

'Look, Magnus, I must go now,' she declared. 'I have a few things to finish off here, and then I must get over to Gordon's surgery. I promised to relieve him this afternoon.'

'I'll send Charlie,' he said.

'Oh . . . there's no need,' she protested, but he had already put down the phone.

Morag was forced to ring the doorbell twice before she got a response. The McDonalds' villa seemed strangely quiet for a Saturday. Filled with foreboding, she watched a shadowy figure approach behind the frosted glass, and the door opened a slit.

'Yes?'

This must be the daily 'help' whom Gordon had mentioned.

'Is the doctor at home?' Morag asked, and realised immediately that it was the wrong question.

'No. Write down your address on this, and he'll get to you as soon as he can.' The woman held out a notepad and pencil.

'I'm sorry,' she stammered, 'I should have introduced myself properly. I am Dr Beaton. I have been helping Dr McDonald during the crisis. Is Mrs McDonald at home, perhaps?'

'She is.' The woman hesitated. 'But she's nae seein' anyone. The weans is sick.'

'Oh, no!' Morag's worst fears had been realised.

Forcing her way past the irresolute maid, she flew up the wide staircase, calling out as she went.

'Anna, Anna . . . it's Morag Beaton!'

She heard a door close softly on the floor above and hastened up the next, narrower flight, encountering Anna McDonald on the second landing.

'Why, Morag.' Anna looked tired, but there was no real sign of concern in her large dark eyes. 'Gordon has still not come in from his morning rounds. Were you looking for him?'

Morag glanced past her, regarding the closed bedroom door anxiously.

'Your maid said that the children were ill. I thought that . . .' She trailed off when she saw Anna's little smile.

'Look for yourself,' she said, and opened the door quietly. 'I put them in together for company. The twins are being quiet because wee Poppy is sleeping.'

It was a large airy room, with two fine dormer windows commanding a view across the flat plain which bordered the canal. Creamy lace curtains danced in the light breeze which had sprung up during the morning, dispersing the heavy humid air which had settled over the town for so long.

A pair of single beds were pushed up against two of the walls. Above each, a row of shelving housed a substantial collection of books, colourful children's annuals and encyclopedias, together with rather more sombre-looking volumes, among which Morag recognised some of her own favourite classics.

A third bed had been placed in a darkened corner beyond

the second window, in such a way that the sun could not fall directly upon the pillow. In it, Poppy, face ominously flushed, lay sleeping. Her light snoring was occasionally disturbed by a harsh dry cough.

Morag went over to the child and felt her forehead; she took note of the flush of rosy red, raised pustules on Poppy's cheeks and chest. There was no need to disturb the child further. Morag looked up at Anna.

'Measles,' she declared, breathing a sigh of relief. Anna nodded.

On one of the other two beds, Matthew and Melody were so absorbed in a game that they had not acknowledged the visitor at first.

On hearing her speak, they looked up and greeted her enthusiastically.

'Hello, Dr Beaton,' said Matt. 'Do you know how to play chess?'

'I used to play with my father,' she told them, 'but I'm not sure I can remember all the moves . . .'

She watched for a few minutes and as Melody went to lift her knight in a move which would surely sacrifice the piece, could not resist the urge to shake her head.

'That's not fair. You're helping her!' declared Matt, so loudly that Anna was obliged to quiet him. She put a finger to her lips and gestured towards the little cot in the corner, in an attempt to curb their excited chatter.

'The twins were the first to show symptoms,' she explained to Morag. 'It appears there were a few isolated cases at the school, but because they were overshadowed by the typhoid scare, no one thought to mention it until my little monsters started the fever. You can imagine that Gordon was rather perturbed at first.'

'I can't tell you how relieved I am to know it's only measles,' Murag told her. Then, noting Matt's disappointed expression, 'Not that measles is not a serious condition,' she added hastily, and made a show of taking the boy's pulse, just to mollify him.

Anna suddenly understood the reason for Morag's earlier anxiety.

'When you came rushing in just now, you thought they had typhoid!' she exclaimed. 'Oh, my dear, you must have had an awful shock. Elsie should have said . . . I'm so sorry.'

'I have been very worried because it was I who sent the children out to buy ice-cream from Luigi's parlour,' Morag confessed. Then, more positively, 'It's nearly two weeks since they had the ice-cream, so they should be safe now. Of course, we still don't know for sure that his shop *is* the source of the outbreak.'

'Don't like Luigi's,' muttered Melody. 'He's a nasty man. He only gives us tiny weeny dollops if we go into the shop on our own.'

'Stop me and buy one,' croaked Matt, his throat still painfully sore.

'What was that?' asked Morag, more sharply than she'd intended.

'Wall's ice-cream,' Melody explained. 'We bought Wall's fruit ices with the money you gave us, from the tricycle man . . . he always comes around on Sundays.'

'And I've been feeling guilty all this time, thinking I might have been responsible for them contracting typhoid fever!' Morag exclaimed.

A door banged down below, and they heard a noisy exchange in the hall.

'That will be Gordon,' said Anna, and held the door open for Morag. Turning to the children she said quietly, 'Now remember, no getting out of bed. And if wee Poppy wakes, ring the bell.'

'But I don't understand,' Adam was saying, as Morag opened the consulting-room door. 'How can the man have such a large infestation of the bacterium and not be showing any symptoms at all of typhoid fever?'

'He is what is known as a "carrier",' Gordon replied. 'Certain people are able to harbour such germs within their bodies – in this case the bowels – incubating them, and passing them on to others, without anyone suspecting they are responsible.'

'What's happened?' Morag demanded, glancing from one worried countenance to the other.

'All the samples from Luigi's ice-cream parlour were analysed,' explained Adam. 'The milk and other ingredients used were clear and, what's more, I made a number of unannounced visits to the shop and found nothing untoward in the preparation methods. The ice-cream itself, however, carried unacceptably large quantities of bacteria, including the typhoid bacillus. The specimens taken from the handlers were all clear, except in the case of the proprietor, Luigi Bernini.'

'And you are saying that this man is not himself unwell?'

'Far from it,' Gordon told her. 'He gives every appearance of being in robust health, and the fact that he consumes large quantities of his own product, daily, at first led me to believe you were both on the wrong track.'

'What will your next move be?' Morag demanded of Adam Inglis.

'Since the samples from the proprietor have proved positive, I can legitimately have the shop closed until the owners prove it is free from infection,' he reassured them.

'What will happen to Mr Bernini?' demanded Morag.

'His is a different problem altogether,' Gordon intervened. 'Unless he is willing to submit himself to a long stay in hospital, under the strictest medical supervision, there is no way of clearing his system of the disease. We cannot force him to take this course of action, but we can seek an injunction to prevent him from preparing or serving foodstuffs to the public, ever again.'

'One would think that under those circumstances he would not refuse treatment,' she observed.

'I wish I had your faith in human nature,' Gordon said, aware of the difficulties of enforcing such a measure.

'At any rate, Morag,' suggested Adam, disregarding Gordon's cynical remark, 'it looks as though one of your first patients in the fever hospital will be Mr Bernini himself. The sooner he is under proper supervision, the better.'

'Always supposing the isolation wards actually open next week,' she observed, rather despondently.

'I thought your preparations were nearing completion?' said Adam.

'They are,' she agreed, 'but the Hospital Board requires two thousand pounds to be raised by Monday, to cover the cost of specialist staffing.'

'And how much have they raised so far?' Gordon asked.

'A little over eight hundred.'

'What right has the board to deny anyone hospital care, who needs it?' asked Adam.

'It is a cottage hospital, run on voluntary contributions,' Gordon explained, patiently. 'The board has every right to put the care of its other patients before those suffering from an infectious disease which could prove fatal if it were allowed to contaminate wards where the sick are being treated. It costs a great deal to operate an isolation unit, believe me.'

'Magnus has promised to make another appeal in tomorrow's edition of the *Gazette*,' Morag added, 'but I cannot see him raising a further twelve hundred pounds.'

'Well, it's no good worrying at this stage,' said Gordon. We shall just have to hope that the Good Lord will provide.

'If you have come to lend a hand,' he addressed Morag, changing the subject abruptly, 'there are a number of new patients to be seen in Ross Terrace, and a couple of convalescents need checking, in Canal Row.'

Morag had begun replenishing her stocks of medicines as he spoke.

'Very well,' she replied. 'I'll be off right away.'

'Can I give you a lift somewhere?' Adam offered.

'That's very kind of you,' she replied eagerly, then scanning the list in her hand, added a trifle reluctantly, 'but these addresses are all nearby.'

'Thank you both for coming,' said Gordon, suddenly tired and needing a meal and a long rest. 'I think I'll go and have a scrub before I visit my measly children!'

'These came for you just after you went out, Dr Beaton.' The reception clerk called Morag over as she pushed open the doors to the main entrance hall. 'I had one of the nurses put them in water for you. Aren't they beautiful?'

Indeed they were. A dozen long-stemmed pink roses. Once before she had received a similar bouquet. Was it possible that these were from the same source?

'There was a note with them.' The woman stretched behind her and retrieved a large white envelope from Morag's pigeon-hole.

She recognised the crest immediately.

As she tore excitedly at the expensive-looking vellum, a slip of paper fell out and landed on the floor at her feet. She picked it up. It was a cheque made out to herself, for the sum of five hundred pounds.

She extracted the accompanying letter.

> *Laudale House*
> *Princes Street*
> *Edinburgh.*
> *31 July 1932*

*My Dear Dr Beaton,*

*I have been most remiss in not contacting you earlier to tell you of my progress following my unfortunate fall last winter. I am happy to say that due entirely to your excellent work, and the untiring efforts of my physiotherapist, I am again able to walk with scarcely any limp at all. So much improved am I that I have at last had the temerity to ask Miss Harriet McRae to be my wife. Our marriage will take place in September.*

*My fiancée has told me of the typhoid epidemic in Inverlinnhe, and of the efforts made by your colleagues and yourself to have the isolation wing of the hospital reinstated. I hope that this small contribution will prove useful in swinging the balance your way.*

*May I wish your enterprise every success, and express the hope that this troublesome disease will soon be eradicated.*

*Yours sincerely,*

*Richard Ashley Keynes*

Happily, Morag buried her face in the roses and inhaled their heady scent. The cheque would go a long way towards reaching their target. One or two more generous donations of this kind were all that was needed . . .

'Dr Beaton! The very lady I had hoped to see today.'

She looked up, startled, to find Duncan McRae advancing towards her from the direction of Sidney Maynard's office.

'First, let me say how pleased I was to see that the enquiry made such a sensible decision about the matter of Gregor Campbell's unfortunate demise.'

'Thank you,' she replied. She would have liked to say more, for she was sure that McRae had championed her cause.

'Those are magnificent,' he observed, admiring the flowers.

'They are from your future son-in-law,' she told him. 'They came with a handsome cheque, towards the cost of reopening the isolation ward.'

'It is the least young Richard could do,' replied McRae, dismissively. 'He has made a very fine recovery, thanks to you.'

'He tells me the wedding will be in September,' Morag said. 'Will it be held here, or in Edinburgh?'

'His Lordship insists that the wedding takes place at Kinloss Castle . . . the family seat. I'm not too happy about it myself, I would have preferred my girl to be married from her own home, but when one rubs shoulders with the aristocracy, I'm afraid one has little say in these matters.

'Anyway,' he continued, brushing aside these misgivings, 'that was not why I wanted to speak to you. Mr Maynard was good enough to show me around the isolation wing earlier on . . . I think you have done a remarkable job in restoring it.'

'I had a great deal of help,' she responded, modestly.

'I am not a practical sort of man,' he said, disarmingly, 'but I am able to help in the only way I know how.' He dug a hand into his inside pocket and extracted from his wallet five crisp white bank notes.

Morag had never held so much money in her hand before. Five one-hundred pound notes! With whatever Magnus had managed to amass during the weekend, they would surely have enough to open the ward the following week.

Overcome by this act of generosity, Morag threw all dignity to the wind. She flung her arms around Duncan's neck and kissed him.

'You darling, darling man!' she cried. Realising suddenly that half a dozen members of the hospital staff were watching this scene with the greatest interest, she blushed crimson and extended her hand to give her thanks more formally. McRae, momentarily overcome, took it and smiled.

'This hospital is lucky to have such a devoted servant,' he replied.

He bowed slightly, replaced his hat with a determined gesture, and strode out to his waiting limousine. His step was light and as he went he whistled a jaunty little tune. It was not every day that he was kissed in public by such a delightful young woman!

# Chapter 11

'I have had Mr Fraser in here, biting my head off about his ice-cream parlour out at Feanagrogan.'

Adam Inglis remained standing while Duncan McLeod, the Borough Engineer, continued to vent all his pent up rage upon his junior.

Luigi had not revealed the name of his landlord at the time of the investigation but it was no surprise to Adam to find Fraser associated with this unfortunate business.

'If you have traced the source of the disease, what purpose is to be served by closing down the premises?' McLeod demanded. 'Get the place cleaned up and let them open for business right away.'

'I'm afraid that's not possible,' Adam replied, patiently. 'The Sanitary Inspector cannot give the premises a clean bill of health until there have been three sets of swabs taken over a period of ten days. There will be a time lapse of a week apiece before the results of the three sets of cultures are known.'

'But I thought you said this Bernini fellow is the carrier?' observed McLeod, impatiently. 'Remove him and all should be well.'

'It's not that simple. He may have infected the processing plant,' Adam explained. 'There may still be infective material passing through the drainage system, and since the incubation period is ten days at least, there's still time for the other assistants in the shop to contract the disease. The inspector is not prepared to take the risk.'

'*He's* not prepared to take the risk . . . I like that!' Exasperated by the problems heaped upon him, McLeod let fly at the nearest person, who happened to be Adam. 'What about the risk *I* am having to take? Do you realise that if the tourist trade diminishes any further, half the small businesses in the town will go under? It's me who has to account for our actions to the committee . . . yours is the easy job. I am the one left to explain away *your* bloody inefficiency.'

'That's hardly fair, sir,' Adam protested, strongly. 'The Sanitary Inspector, and the rest of the men, have worked all the hours God sends investigating this problem. They have solved the mystery, and all I'm asking now is that we be given a free hand to ensure that the outbreak is dealt with once and for all.'

'And you think that closing down this one shop of Fraser's will do that?' asked the Borough Engineer, somewhat mollified.

'Well . . . no, since you mention it.' Adam hesitated to drive home his point. It was certain that his boss would not look kindly upon his estimate of the situation. 'We can eliminate the initial source of the disease by isolating Luigi's until the premises are clear, but the fever has been spread by way of the defective drainage arrangements in the low-lying areas to either side of the canal. Those old cottages along the waterfront should be demolished, and that section of the town requires an up-to-date sewage system.'

'And this is what you expect me to report to the committee is it, Mr Inglis?'

'Yes, sir, I am afraid it is.'

'Well, young man, I suggest you start looking around for some other form of employment, because I can assure you, if I am dismissed as a result of this mess, you will be going along with me!'

The Borough Engineer mopped his brow and waved Adam out of the room. As he reached the door, his boss called after him, using a more moderate tone. 'Let me have a full report in writing, and if you have any plans drawn up for those sewage improvements, I'd better have a look at those too.'

'Very good, sir,' Adam responded with greater enthusiasm. 'I'm sure that the members will see the sense of our proposals, once the facts are put to them.'

'How naïve you are,' sighed the older man. 'Another year or two in Local Government and you will learn to be as cynical as me.'

Morag's friends had arranged to gather in the Long John on Friday evening, to exchange progress reports.

The atmosphere had been hot and heavy all day. During the afternoon, black thunderclouds had been crowding in from the south-west and hung now, like a funeral pall, above the Ben. A late-evening breeze had helped to relieve the oppressiveness a little, but when Morag pushed open the door and looked around anxiously for her comrades, the distant rumblings of the threatened storm followed her into the bar.

They were gathered in Magnus's favourite corner beside the old stone fireplace, its grate filled by a huge vase of flowers on this summer's day. Gordon looked better than she had seen him for weeks. The burden of the epidemic had been lifted from him when the isolation unit had opened its doors the previous Wednesday.

He rose to greet her and made a show of offering her the best seat. Magnus, looking hot and uncomfortable, did his best to make her feel welcome while Adam seemed unusually restrained, a deep furrow across his brow indicating that they were by no means out of the wood yet.

'You look terrific,' Magnus told her. 'I like the new hairstyle.'

'Thank you,' she said, colouring just a little. 'It seemed more practical, during the epidemic . . . you know.'

'How does it feel to be a surgeon once again?' Magnus demanded, when Gordon had gone to the bar to order her drink.

'Exhausting,' replied Morag, pushing her fingers through her newly bobbed hair and tossing the red-gold curls out of her eyes.

'I have hardly had time to look in on the isolation unit since it opened . . . until today that is,' she told him. 'When I did manage to spare a few minutes this afternoon, I was warned off very firmly by the new sister, Ruth Irving. What a dragon!'

'A very efficient lady doing an excellent job,' observed Gordon as he placed Morag's glass before her. 'Water with your whisky, madam?'

She nodded brightly and then, noting the measure of spirit in the glass, remarked, 'I didn't ask for a double.'

'You're one or two behind us,' was Gordon's smooth reply. 'Besides it saves my having to make too many visits to the bar!'

'Did they have to bring in many additional staff for the new unit?' asked Magnus.

'We could only afford a small team, three nurses and a sister. It was all the board would agree to for the time being,' she replied. 'If the fund continues to grow, it may be possible to get a few more, but specialists in infectious disease are not easy to find.'

'It's not a job everyone would want,' observed Magnus, shuddering at the thought of being so intimately exposed to typhoid fever on a daily basis.

'This team seems to have been formed especially for emergencies such as this,' Morag explained. 'There are quite a number of nurses who gained their experience in the tropics during the war. I believe Miss Irving spent three years in Egypt and has since been stationed on the Gold Coast.'

'How many patients have been admitted so far?' asked Magnus, as always with pencil poised ready to take down the details.

'Ten males and fifteen females,' replied Gordon. 'They are mostly very young children and elderly people. The majority of the original patients are now out of the wood, and recovering at home.'

'Isn't that a large number of patients to be attended by such a small team of nurses?' he asked.

'There is a band of volunteers helping the laundry staff. Mothers, ex-VADs from the war and members of the local Church Women's Guild, are doing the menial tasks around the unit: cleaning, washing the linen, that sort of thing,' Morag explained. 'My impression when I called in this afternoon was that the whole operation was running very efficiently. No one comes or goes without receiving a thorough inspection by Miss Irving. Every precaution is taken to avoid cross-infection. I was very impressed, even if a little miffed, to be told I could not enter the premises I had been instrumental in having made ready! It was only when Gordon here turned up, and explained that I was a bona fide member of the hospital staff, that I was allowed to don a gown and take a walk round the wards!'

'Is it possible that there is anyone who has not heard of the West Highland's famous lady surgeon?' demanded Magnus, whose speech was already becoming more than a little slurred.

Laughing, Morag turned to Adam, but was dismayed to find him so solemn in such an otherwise convivial atmosphere.

'You hardly look as though you had solved a problem of such magnitude,' she observed, suddenly anxious for him.

'Finding the cause does not always solve the problem,' he responded, gloomily. 'The only way to ensure that there will be no further disasters of this kind is to tear down those old hovels along the canal, drain the marshy areas and put in a decent sewage system. It's a proposal so fraught with difficulties, and likely to raise so many hackles, that my boss is unlikely even to put it to the Council.'

'Which houses are you talking about, Inglis?' Magnus had sobered up remarkably during the last few moments. 'I'll have you know that I live in one of your hovels by the canal and I have no intention of removing myself!'

'There you are, you see,' moaned Adam, 'that is exactly the attitude I'm talking about.

'Surely it's not necessary to pull down the houses just to renovate the sewage system?' Gordon tried to channel the argument.

'Those old cottages have no space for bathrooms,' Adam persisted. 'To extend them and bring them up to standard would necessitate major rebuilding works. It would be cheaper to pull down the houses and start again.'

'My great-grandfather built that cottage,' Magnus protested, 'constructed it with his own two hands.'

Morag stifled a desire to comment. She was the only one among them who had actually visited his house, but she was not about to admit to that in the present company.

'He was a lock keeper,' Magnus continued, 'used timber and stone from the Laird's estate and built his own house. All the men did in those days.'

'Because he was a lock keeper, it doesn't make him any kind of builder,' Adam murmured. Recently qualified in Civil Engineering himself, he was very quick to defend the status of the professional builder. 'Anyway,' he added, 'you have simply emphasised my point. A hundred or more years ago there was no piped water, inside water closets, or official drainage arrangements. Anything which has been added since, has been makeshift and in many cases downright dangerous to public health. No, the only way to deal with the situation is to tear the lot down and start again.'

'I presume that the owners of those houses might be persuaded to have them brought up to an acceptable standard?' Gordon suggested.

'Rather than wait for a compulsory demolition order, I would certainly want to have my place done up myself,' declared Magnus.

'Unfortunately the remainder of that row is owned by Fraser,' observed Adam. 'You couldn't do anything about the mains drainage, unless he was willing to agree to do the same. It's all in my report to the Council,' he concluded, downing his beer and rising to buy the next round. 'So Fraser will be one of the first to know. Maybe you could sound him out, Magnus . . . see if he'd be willing to foot the bill for renovations to the cottages he owns? The Local Authority would of course have to find the money for the main drains and there would have to be a separate treatment works for the district. That in itself would doubtless be considered far too costly for such a small number of properties. The best thing that could happen would be a major new housing development in the area.'

'Heaven forbid!' exclaimed Magnus. 'I live there because I like the solitude.'

'There's a pressing need for more cheap housing,' Adam argued.

'And there you have it,' decided Magnus. 'Why do you suppose Fraser bought up those houses in the first place? He intends to sell the land on which they stand, for development . . . only he can't, while I continue to occupy my part of the property. Since I own my house, he can't do what he likes with the terrace, so he'll let the buildings he owns deteriorate until you serve a demolition order on them all.'

'There is one factor which may be to our advantage,' mused Gordon, who had been silent whilst the others had been engaged in this speculation. 'Fraser's term of office comes to an end next spring. He'll no doubt be standing again as Chairman of the Council. If there is a big enough campaign to clean up the older parts of town, he will want to jump on that band waggon. With luck we might bind him to some kind of action over the drainage. It could provide him with a useful pre-election promise.'

'That sounds like a job for Magnus,' suggested Morag, eager to change the tenor of the discussion. She had been listening to the argument, torn between a desire to support Adam and yet moved by Magnus's loyalty to his great-grandfather's work. She felt much the same way about her Aunt Margaret's cottage on Eisdalsa and could not imagine letting anyone demolish her family home, Tigh na Broch, to make way for a new housing estate.

The journalist shook his head. 'There are two problems with that proposition,' he responded. 'First there is my personal interest in the property under consideration, and secondly, as I have explained already, Fraser owns the *Gazette*. No, it will have to be something a little more subtle than an article by me.'

'How about a few letters to the Editor?' enquired Gordon. 'We could stir up quite a fuss if I was to get some of the parents of my young patients to write in, complaining about the drainage system.'

'If Fraser has so much say about what is printed in the newspaper, would such letters be published?' asked Morag.

'Oh, yes,' Magnus replied. 'Even he knows better than to try and muzzle the opinions of his precious voters.'

Adam returned from the bar with a fresh round of drinks. Morag felt that she had had enough and was convinced that Magnus had also. Not wishing to repeat the episode which had caused her to spend the night in his cottage on that previous occasion, she stood up.

'Look, I'm awfully sorry but I'll have to get back to the hospital,' she said. 'I have an early call tomorrow morning.'

'But I've just bought you another drink,' said Adam.

'Then I'm afraid you'll have to drink it yourself,' she replied. She wavered on seeing his petulant expression and was momentarily tempted to relent. With greater resolve than she had exhibited for a long time, she added, 'Sorry!' before getting to her feet and gathering up her coat.

They could hear the rain lashing down outside.

'Are you sure you don't want to wait until the storm's over?' suggested Gordon.

'Oh, no, really.' She shrugged on her lightweight mackintosh and shook out her umbrella. 'I came well prepared, as you can see.'

'Let me call you a cab.' Magnus began struggling to his feet.

'It's OK,' Gordon silenced the mumbled protestations. 'It's time I went anyway, and my car is just down the street. I'll run Morag back and then push off home.' He swallowed his own drink and picked up his hat.

Morag paused to say goodnight, and leaning over the back of Adam's chair, whispered, 'See Magnus gets home all right . . . he really shouldn't drink any more.' Then, to make amends for having been so abrupt with him, she laid a hand on his arm. 'Don't worry too much about the drains. I think Gordon's idea might work.'

Outside the gutters were awash. Storm drains, silted up by dirt and rubbish, the accumulated debris of weeks without rain, were unable to cope with the downpour, and the road was quickly becoming a fast-flowing river.

Gordon's car was parked some way down the street. With his arm around her shoulders, sharing the dainty umbrella, he steered Morag towards it and helped her inside.

She huddled up against the cold while Gordon started the engine and got the windscreen wipers working.

'By the way,' she said to him, 'I managed to have a look at your Fran at last. I don't think she remembered me.'

'She says she can't recall much about the accident,' said

Gordon. 'Only falling, and then being carried out of the valley on a stretcher. It's been a long job.'

'Yes,' Morag agreed. 'I know it seems a long time, but she really will have to be patient. If only we had an X-ray machine we could find out how things are going. I'd suggest we send her down to Oban, but if the leg is jarred at all we could undo all the good work so far.'

'I never really understood why Maynard decided against using a plaster cast. I've known patients sent home after a couple of weeks, still in the cast.'

'The collarbone has healed nicely but with the leg it seems the break was too close to the knee,' Morag told him. 'Mr Maynard felt that there was more chance of a mobile joint if he used plates and traction. She's young and should heal well. She'll just have to be patient.'

She had found no fault with Maynard's treatment of Gordon's daughter. He had taken the same measures with the leg she would have used herself. The only problem was that without an X-ray there was no way of knowing how the healing process was progressing.

'Has there ever been any suggestion that the hospital should get its own X-ray unit?' she asked, suddenly. 'Couldn't there be some fund-raising events to buy one?'

'Not content with successfully raising sufficient money to staff the isolation wards, young Dr Beaton launches out upon yet another campaign, this time to raise money for an X-ray machine!' But Gordon did not mean to mock. He understood her desire to see the hospital fulfilling its role properly.

'The trouble is,' he went on, sadly, 'people will only dig into their pockets when they can see the benefit of the project. Not too many people understand what an X-ray machine is, let alone what use it would be to the community.'

'Then we'll have to tell them!'

The car drew up under the canopy outside the emergencies entrance, and Morag prepared to alight.

'Incidentally, I have at last managed to persuade Mr Bernini to admit himself to the isolation unit,' Gordon told her. 'He was

211

very reluctant at first, but when I pointed out that he would not be allowed to run his ice-cream parlour until we were satisfied that he was free from the disease, he agreed, on the assumption that a stay in hospital would hurry up the process. I was reluctant to point out just how long a stay he might reasonably anticipate.'

'Won't it be horrifically expensive?' asked Morag. 'Are there any provisions made for long-term admissions of this kind?'

'Despite all the unpleasant talk we have heard this evening, I have to say I was extremely impressed with Graham Fraser's response to the situation. When he heard that Luigi might be forced to remain in hospital for a number of weeks, he offered to foot the bill himself.'

'One would like to think his motives were philanthropic but I can't help suspecting he is more concerned with getting a clean bill of health for his premises as soon as possible!'

Magnus was feeling very peculiar. All evening he had been fighting down waves of nausea, using his time-honoured expedient of swallowing one glass of whisky after another to combat the feeling. The remedy did not work on this occasion and now the excessive heat had got the better of him. He struggled to his feet and went to the window, throwing up the sash to let in the cool night air. There was an instant protest from those gathered around the bar.

'It's like the North Pole in here,' declared one.

'If I wanted to enjoy the gale, I'd not have come in in the first place,' said another.

With an apologetic gesture in Magnus's general direction, the landlord slammed the window shut.

'You know, it's really not that warm in here,' Adam told him. 'Are you feeling all right? You look very flushed.'

'To be honest with you, I feel pretty groggy,' Magnus admitted at last. 'Would you be kind enough to call me a cab, m'dear fellow? I don't think I can make it home on foot.'

'If you're going to be ill, you could have chosen a better moment,' observed Adam, dryly. 'Half an hour ago you had your choice of doctors. Now there's only me!'

'Oh, come on,' Magnus demanded, weakly, 'call me a cab and get me home. I'll be fine in the morning.' He fished in his pocket for the telephone number of Charlie's cab rank. 'Just ask for Charlie . . . he'll see I get home all right.'

Adam fought his way through the crush at the bar and found the public telephone. By the time he returned Magnus had fallen asleep, lying back uncomfortably in the hard Windsor chair and snoring loudly.

Adam waited with him until Charlie put his head around the door. Catching sight of the sleeping reporter, he negotiated a path towards them.

'Had a bit too much to drink, have we, Mr Glendenning?' the man asked, cheerfully, and put his arms beneath Magnus's shoulders to hoist him up.

'Actually, I don't think he's very well,' Adam explained. 'He's had a few jars of ale and a whisky or two, but I've seen him drink more with no ill effect.'

Charlie regarded his friend with a quizzical eye.

'He seems to be burning up,' he said. 'Look, sir, if you'll give me a hand to get him home and in bed, I'll go and fetch a doctor.'

Adam, none too pleased with the situation in which he found himself, wished that Morag and Gordon had not departed so abruptly or else that Magnus had admitted to feeling unwell sooner.

'Oh, very well,' he said to the cabbie, 'you grab his right side, I'll take the left.'

Magnus Glendenning was no lightweight. With a great deal of difficulty and some assistance from revellers at the bar, they at last managed to get him into the taxi.

Reluctantly, Adam agreed to accompany Magnus, and sat in the back of the cab beside him. All this activity had caused Magnus to stir slightly, but he was only half aware of what was going on. As the smooth tarmac of the main road gave way to the deeply rutted, unmade lane which led to the cottages in Canal Row, he came to rather suddenly.

'Water,' he croaked through parched lips. Perspiration stood out in beads on his forehead. 'Hot . . . too hot!' He made a grab

213

for the door handle and Adam, fearing he would open it and tumble out, restrained him. His companion's exceptionally high temperature filled him with alarm. Could he have contracted the fever?

'OK, old chap,' he said, with a calm he did not feel, 'We'll soon have you home now. Just hang on for a few more minutes.'

Charlie, glancing over his shoulder to see what was going on, noted the anxious expression on Adam's face.

'What's up?' he demanded.

'I think he's got typhoid.'

A few moments more and they had arrived.

Manhandling the semiconscious reporter into his house took their combined strength. By the time they had stripped off his sweat-soaked clothing and laid him on the bed, both the men were quite exhausted.

Charlie suggested he should go and fetch Dr McDonald. 'See what you can do to make him comfortable,' he said. 'I'll be right back.'

Adam looked about him, helplessly. He went into the kitchen in the hope of finding some source of hot water with which to sponge down the patient. He knew that it was necessary to cool him down, but cold water straight from the tap would be too much of a shock.

The fire was unlit. Although there was electric lighting in the cottage, it was clear that Magnus relied upon the elderly kitchen range to supply all heating, including water.

Taking the large black iron kettle from the hob, Adam filled it at the sink. He pumped away steadily for some seconds waiting for the water to flow. No mains water . . . Idly he considered what the source of supply might be. Surely not a holding reservoir in this part of town? No, it had to be a well.

Scarcely registering the significance of this discovery, he returned to the range and soon had the fire burning. He placed the kettle to heat on it and went in search of a bowl and towels. Having found everything he wanted, he returned to minister to the semiconscious Magnus, only to find the reporter tossing in a delirium and shivering uncontrollably.

Gently, Adam bathed his face, dabbing him dry with the towel he had found. He then began to sponge the remainder of his body, and as he did so his fingers traced the deep pits and ragged scars which criss-crossed the man's back and shoulders. Adam shuddered at the sight of these legacies of war.

'Poor devil,' he whispered, as he dabbed away with the towel. 'You certainly had your share, didn't you?'

He was nearly finished by the time he heard the taxi returning. He pulled the sheet up around Magnus's shoulders and covered him with blankets before going to the door to admit Gordon.

# Chapter 12

Passing through the main reception area on her way to the canteen, Morag was surprised to find Adam deep in conversation with Gordon.

'Hallo,' she greeted them. 'What's up?' She looked from one to the other, noting their serious expressions. 'What is it?' she demanded. 'What's happened?'

'I just called in to see how Magnus was . . .' Adam explained, tailing off lamely when he noted her look of surprise.

'Magnus . . . what about him?'

'I would have thought someone might have told you,' Gordon said. 'He was admitted to the isolation unit in the early hours. I'm afraid he has typhoid.'

She could feel herself reeling. Gordon caught hold of her and led her to a nearby bench.

In a few seconds Morag had regained her composure sufficiently to demand: 'How could he possibly have contracted the disease? Luigi's ice-cream isn't exactly his favourite tipple.'

'I've inspected his house,' Adam replied, 'and taken samples of well water for testing. As I have already pointed out to you, the sanitation in those old cottages leaves much to be desired . . . the drinking water might very well be affected.'

Gordon nodded sagely.

'There have already been two cases near the canal . . . both of them elderly people.' He did not elaborate. Both victims had been Magnus's immediate neighbours, and both had died before they could be removed to hospital.

He regarded Morag searchingly. She was pale, and although

she tried to disguise it by clasping her hands tightly together, she was trembling.

'Are you all right?' he asked, anxiously.

She nodded. 'It's the shock,' she told him, 'and the fact that I haven't eaten since last night. We were in theatre early this morning.'

Gordon covered her hands with his own and the warmth of his unspoken support suffused her whole body. After a few minutes, she recovered her composure.

'I don't know what came over me,' she gasped, smiling faintly.

'We might have been a little more tactful,' Adam remarked, glaring at his companion.

Gordon patted her hand and stood up. She glanced from one to the other of the two men.

'Tell me about Magnus,' she demanded. 'When was he taken ill?'

'He collapsed soon after you two left the Long John,' Adam explained. 'I managed to get him home in a taxi and while I put him to bed, the driver went to fetch Gordon.'

'How bad is it?' Morag asked, anxiously. She was already concerned that her friend had a weak constitution . . . a bout of typhoid might easily be sufficient to send him over the edge.

'Just about as bad as it could be.'

Gordon spared her nothing. There was no point in trying to disguise the fact that the reporter was at a very low ebb.

'He has obviously had the disease for some time and ignored the preliminary symptoms. His lungs are badly affected and even if he survives the fever itself, I'm afraid the pleurisy will put too much of a strain on his heart. I don't suppose he ever bothered to tell you that he received a dose of mustard gas in the trenches?'

'No,' she whispered, eyes wide with alarm, 'he never mentioned that.'

'I expect you'd like to see him?' Gordon suggested, gently.

With a guarded gesture to Adam, he steered Morag out into the courtyard and across the open space towards the isolation wards.

Mary Neal watched the two doctors as they disappeared around a turn in the corridor. She was disturbed to see the anguished expression on Morag's face.

'Whatever is the matter?' she asked. 'Morag was so cheerful just a few minutes ago ...'

'Her friend ... the reporter from the *Gazette* ... he's very ill ... typhoid,' Adam explained.

'How could he have got it?' she asked, alarmed. Magnus did not strike her as a likely victim.

'He lives in one of those houses alongside the canal ... bloody places should have been condemned years ago!' The young engineer made no apology for venting his anger in strong language.

Mary slipped her arm through his.

'You need a cup of tea,' she said, leading him into a side room where the nurses took their occasional breaks, 'and perhaps something just a little stronger?' She closed the door behind them, glancing up and down the corridor first to see if the coast was clear.

'Magnus ... it's me, Morag.' Masked and gowned as she was, she feared he would not recognise her.

The sound of her voice roused him from his stupor. His lips moved and she leaned over him to try to catch what he was saying.

The effort of speaking had caused him to collapse in a paroxysm of coughing. After a minute or two the spasm subsided and in a rather stronger voice, he recited:

> *Daughter of Galen, exceeding fair,*
> *Haloed in her red-gold hair,*
> *Oh, would that she might kindly care,*
> *For a sinner such as me.*

'Shouldn't that be *I*?' she chided gently.

'No, I don't think so,' he replied, a puzzled expression on his face. It was as though the effort of considering this point was too much for him. He closed his eyes and dozed.

Morag could not resist feeling for his pulse. His skin was burning to the touch and the pulse was rapid . . . much too rapid. She would have liked to listen to his heart but he was not her patient, and she hesitated to use her stethoscope. Instead she slipped her hand inside his pyjama jacket and felt for the rapid heart beat which accompanied his pyrexia.

He grabbed her hand and held it there.

'So cool . . .' he murmured.

'Usually people complain because my hands are too cold.'

'It's good to know you are here,' he said.

'Try to get some sleep,' she told him. 'I'll look in again later.'

She straightened the covers and tucked him in like a baby. He had closed his eyes again and she thought he had drifted off. She passed her fingers lightly across his forehead. At her touch, he opened one eye and smiled.

'I suspect you're not so ill as you're pretending to be,' Morag whispered, her voice filled with compassion.

At the opening to his cubicle she turned. With an enormous effort he lifted a hand in farewell.

'See you soon,' she promised.


For ten days Magnus remained in a state of high fever which was, for much of the time, accompanied by delirium. The congestion in his lungs gave the greatest cause for concern, and Gordon and Morag were obliged to look on while he suffered, powerless to do anything other than try to afford him some small relief from the more uncomfortable symptoms of the disease.

A light diet of milky drinks and thin broth helped to prevent any strain upon the alimentary tract but they watched anxiously for any signs of internal haemorrhage.

Early on, Morag had told Gordon of her fears that Magnus had been suffering from a gastric ulcer. The typhoid bacillus had an unfortunate habit of producing a weakness in the digestive system which might render the tissues liable to rupture. Coupled with the chronic weakness which she had already diagnosed, it seemed impossible that he could escape without severe blood loss at some point.

'If there is internal bleeding, he's going to need a transfusion,' Gordon warned, during the early days of Magnus's illness. 'It might be wise to be prepared.'

'Would you like me to find a compatible donor?' Morag suggested, anxious to make what contribution she could to her friend's recovery.

'Has he no family member upon whom we might call?'

'None that I know of. I can't remember his ever having spoken of any family. He grew up locally but I rather assumed his parents were dead. He's never mentioned brothers or sisters.'

'I'll take a sample of his blood down to the laboratory,' Gordon decided.' You will probably find some members of staff willing to offer themselves as donors. If you will collect blood samples from them, we can try cross-matching.'

Morag had had no difficulty assembling a group of people willing to act as blood donors. Magnus was a well-known figure in hospital circles and his recent efforts to raise money for the isolation wing had endeared him to many.

Mary Neal, Eddie Strachan and Archie Connolly, the cheerful theatre porter, had been the first to present themselves as potential donors. It was a simple matter for Morag to work her way along the line of volunteers, extracting from each a small sample of blood for testing.

Having added a few drops of sodium citrate to prevent coagulation, she labelled each of the glass phials carefully with the donor's number, before placing it in a rack beside the microscope.

When the last of her colleagues had gone, she took one further sample.

Wrapping a rubber tube tightly about her left upper arm, she flexed her hand to pump up the blood, then with a deft movement, inserted the needle into the brachial vein. It was not so easy to withdraw the plunger single-handed, but she managed to obtain sufficient blood for a sample, transferred it to a phial and labelled it, finally slipping it into the rack beside the others.

\*       \*       \*

Taking a sample of Magnus's blood on a slide, Gordon added a few drops from one of the labelled phials, and mixed the two bloods together. He placed the slide under the microscope and watched carefully for a few moments. Swearing quietly under his breath, he moved aside to allow Morag to take a look.

'Clumping again,' she sighed, after scanning the slide for a few moments.

As with all the other samples they had tried, this one would not do.

'How many more?' he asked despondently.

It had seemed a simple matter to identify one member of staff who would be able to provide Magnus with blood, should the need arise. Not so.

It had soon become clear that their friend had a type of blood which was not universally compatible. He needed a very special donor.

Morag reached for the one phial remaining and handed it to Gordon.

'That's the last,' she said.

Fearful that this one would react like all the others, he dropped a sample on to the slide, mixed the two bloods carefully and watched to see the result. He shifted the slide to another position, looked up at her with a triumphant expression and then returned for a further examination to make sure he was not mistaken. Finally, he stood up and motioned her to take his place.

She adjusted the focus, searched around the slide and looked up, smiling.

'It's all right,' she said, close to tears with the relief that she felt. 'There's no clumping!'

'Whose blood is that, anyway?' Gordon demanded, as he began to clear away the debris of their examination.

Morag glanced at the number on the label, and had no need to check it against the names on her list. The blood sample was her own.

Wordlessly, she passed Gordon the list and let him see the result for himself. When he read her name, he paled, dumped the used phials rather too heavily in the sink for washing, and stared out at the blank wall opposite.

Reluctantly, Gordon was forced to admit that she and Magnus possessed compatible blood.

Transfusions were never entirely safe, especially when made by the direct method, from donor to patient through a short length of tubing. He would have wished it was anyone other than Morag who was volunteering to donate blood to Magnus Glendenning.

'There is always a slight risk, you know,' he warned her, 'especially when the patient has an infectious disease. Are you sure you want to do this?'

'Of course. Don't look so gloomy,' she chided him. 'In any case, Magnus may never need a transfusion at all.'

It seemed that Morag's prediction was well-founded. Two weeks passed and Magnus's infection ran its course. The complication in his lungs, which had given such cause for concern, seemed to be improving and the daily pattern of higher and lower temperatures approached more normal levels.

The improvement in his general health was accompanied by mounting boredom, a condition which, under the circumstances, could not be relieved by his usual expedient, which was to turn to the whisky bottle. He soon wearied of exchanging the obligatory banter with the nursing staff. In any case, short-handed as they were, the girls were too busy to spend much time with him. His friends supplied him with books, but his concentration soon waned.

Finally the day came when Morag arrived with pencils and an exercise book and begged him to do some writing.

'It's the only thing to keep you quiet,' she declared. 'I expect Gordon will give me a trouncing for encouraging you to overtax your strength, but at least the nurses will get a bit of peace.'

Magnus opened the book at the first pristine page and caressed the paper reverently. In a few moments, he appeared to be about to make some profound announcement.

'I shall write about a strange world where the inhabitants are all exactly the same in outward appearance . . . covered from head to toe in uniform garb so that only their eyes and fingers show. And I shall find ways to distinguish one from another by their voices and eye movements. What shall I call it? I know . . . how about "Mummies I have Known", or "My Mummy Never Loved Me"?'

Morag grinned. He had seen only gowned and masked figures for weeks. Even though the most recent pathologist's report had declared him free from bacteria, the staff were still obliged to observe the rules of barrier nursing.

'If it weren't for the fact that there is a particular lock of hair which will not stay under your cap, I would have suspected you of being quite bald,' he teased her. Immediately Morag's hand went up to tuck away the offending curl, and he wished he had said nothing.

When she had gone, Magnus thought for a few moments, chewing at the end of the shiny new pencil. Then he began to write.

'Telephone message for you, Dr Beaton,' the porter called out to her as she passed through the main entrance hall. He handed her a scrap of paper and she read that Adam Inglis was anxious to speak with her. She could feel herself blushing but hoped the porter hadn't noticed.

'May I use the telephone?' she asked. Staff were not encouraged to use the hospital's only telephone, and despite continuous pleading from many quarters, the board had so far resisted attempts to have a public telephone installed.

On a non-visiting day, things were pretty slack in mid-afternoon. The porter glanced cautiously along both main corridors. There was no one of any significance approaching. He dialled the number which Adam had left and handed her the receiver.

'Council Offices.' The disembodied voice, using an exaggerated Oxford accent, sounded quite incongruous to Morag's ears.

'May I speak to Adam Inglis, please?'

'Engineer's Department,' the voice chipped in efficiently. 'Putting you through now!'

'Adam? It's Morag Beaton. You asked me to call.'

'Yes, indeed. What are you doing tomorrow?' he asked her.

Saturday was, he knew, a slack day for the surgical staff except when there was an emergency call-out.

'It's my day off,' she told him. 'Why?'

Morag found it difficult to disguise her mounting excitement.

'I wondered if you would care to come climbing with me tomorrow? I could take you through some of the basics . . . the weather forecast is good, it should be an ideal day.'

There was an expectant pause.

Since that one experience on the mountain when she had been instrumental in saving the life of Gordon's daughter, Morag had had little time to give any consideration to Adam's proposal that she should learn to climb properly.

She had not completely dismissed his suggestion that she should join the mountain rescue team, but feared that when it came to a really hazardous incident she might prove more of a liability than an asset to him. She was also uncertain how the Hospital Board would regard such an activity and was reluctant to make waves when things were just beginning to settle down nicely. She had hoped that Adam would not press her on the point for a while.

'Oh, I'm not sure . . .'

'Why don't you come along and find out if you like it? You can give up the minute you feel you've reached your limit . . . absolutely no obligation to get to the top, madam.'

'It's getting back to the bottom which worries me most!'

She had longed to have him invite her out . . . a quiet dinner or a drive in the country would have been nice . . . but she appreciated that he was having a very busy time, and of course mountaineering held a high priority in his leisure activities. If she didn't agree to this, he might never ask her out again.

'All right then,' she decided. 'What time shall I meet you?'

'Nine o'clock, at the foot of the track you took last time.'

She put down the phone, handed the set back to the porter and, humming softly to herself, made her way towards the operating theatre, smiling.

\*       \*       \*

The day was clear and bright when Charlie's taxi pulled up by the little wooden bridge which spanned the river at the foot of the path.

There were a lot of other vehicles, Morag noticed. Oh, well, it didn't matter. Adam would quickly leave the amateurs behind, she had no doubt.

They would soon be away by themselves high up on the mountain . . .

She turned to dismiss her driver.

'Don't worry about coming back for me, Charlie,' she said, 'I'll probably get a lift back with someone else. If not, I'll give you a ring from the box by the main road.'

He looked past her, greeting the familiar figure of Magnus Glendenning's friend with, 'Good morning, Mr Inglis, sir. It looks like a good day for an exercise!' He revved his engine, let in the gear and drove off steadily, negotiating the heavily rutted roadway like the professional that he was.

'Exercise?'

Morag turned to find Adam at her side, beyond him Finlay Anderson, Andy McDonald, and half a dozen other familiar faces. Her intimate day in the fresh air had suddenly turned into a public spectacle. She remembered the first time they had made her abseil down the cliff, and shuddered. Could she face that again?

She looked around her at a sea of smiling faces.

'I'm so pleased you decided to come,' said Adam. 'I had the feeling you weren't all that keen on joining us when I mentioned it before.'

She could see by the looks on some of their faces that there had been a fair amount of speculation about her willingness to come back for more. Well, she had accepted greater challenges than this in the past.

Annoyed at herself for having misinterpreted Adam's intentions, Morag took her place beside Andy McDonald and the two of them led the party up the lower slopes of the Ben.

Adam, quite unaware of having committed any form of deception, fell into step beside Finlay Anderson.

'Looks as though we might have found ourselves a doctor at last,' he said with some satisfaction.

# Chapter 13

There was an air of expectancy in the ward. Several of the patients admitted during the week of Magnus's collapse had already received three clear results from their tests and were about to be discharged. By the end of the day, only Magnus Glendenning and Luigi Bernini would be left.

Luigi had hardly been a model patient, and no one would be more thankful than Sister Ruth Irving to see the back of him. He had never once been really unwell during his six weeks' stay in the isolation unit, which was perhaps why he had proved so difficult to nurse. He complained constantly, was continuously bored, and when his wife was allowed to visit him, shouted abuse at her, venting his feelings where they would do the least harm to his situation.

'You know,' Magnus had observed, mildly, after one of these tirades, 'there are those among us who might blame you for our being here at all. It was, after all, your ice-cream which began this epidemic. If I were you, I'd try keeping a low profile while you remain here.'

'Nonsense,' Bernini had blustered. 'There was a-nothing wrong with the way I made-a my ice-a-cream. It was the drains that were to blame . . . why else-a would there be all this demand now to have the houses in Canal Row demolished?'

'Over my dead body!' Magnus had responded. 'They can improve the drainage and the water supply – no one would be more pleased than I if they did – but while I am here to fight against it, they shall not pull down my great-grandfather's cottage!' The strain of talking had made him cough so hard that Ruth had been obliged to pull the curtains across his cubicle to shut out the irate Italian, thus putting paid to their argument.

The effort of making even a mild verbal protest about the Council's proposals had left Magnus weak. He knew he should be expressing his opposition in the newspapers and putting his objections in writing to the Planning Committee, but could not raise the energy to do either. If he did not throw off this wretched lethargy soon, he would be leaving hospital without a home to go to.

The news that both patients had been waiting for arrived with the luncheon trolley.

Gordon McDonald strode into the ward, waving a letter in Magnus's direction and giving him the thumbs-up sign. He made for Bernini's cubicle first, however, leaving Magnus straining to hear what was said while he toyed with an unappetising plateful of steamed fish and watery boiled potatoes. He was looking forward to a decent meal at his favourite café, Maggie McKay's Kitchen . . . it would be the first place he would visit when he got out of hospital. He wondered if he might persuade Morag to join him.

'Mr Bernini, your last three test samples have been free from bacteria which means that we have no reason to detain you longer,' Gordon announced, cheerfully, expecting an equally enthusiastic response. 'There should be no further trouble,' he continued, 'but I cannot emphasise enough the importance of reporting even the slightest abnormalities in your physical condition, at least for the next year.'

Anxious that the doctor should not change his mind at this stage, Luigi Bernini nodded his head earnestly, 'Of course, *Dottore. Ciao.*'

He held out his hand and Gordon shook it, knowing in his heart that he would probably never see the man again. Rather than give up his family's traditional occupation, he would almost certainly move on to some other city where he was unknown, and Gordon was powerless to prevent it.

With sinking heart he came to his other patient.

Magnus lay propped against his pillows, his eyes bright and a tell-tale flush still lingering in his cheeks. His last three samples had been clear, but it was not so much the disease as its after-effects which concerned Gordon today.

'Well, what's the verdict, Doc?' Magnus demanded, hardly giving him time to draw up a chair.

'Good news on the typhoid at least,' Gordon replied, trying to be cheerful.

'No one would guess it, to look at you,' Magnus observed. He would have expected a greater show of enthusiasm from his friend. After all, they had expected him to die, hadn't they . . . and hadn't he defied all their gloomy predictions?

'I won't beat about the bush, Magnus,' Gordon began. 'You and I both know that you have been abusing your body systematically ever since the Germans began its destruction in 1916. Your lungs are badly affected from that time, and this most recent bout of pleurisy has left them congested and the major blood vessels considerably weakened. This, coupled with a gastric ulcer which has been aggravated over the years by your excessive drinking, has left your body without the normal mechanisms to fight off further attacks. You are going to have to take it very easy for some time to come.' Seeing that his patient was preparing to make a strong protest, he continued resolutely. Magnus might ignore his advice, but Gordon was determined he should be given all the facts.

'I don't think you should live alone for the time being,' he went on, 'particularly under the conditions that prevail down by the canal. Inglis has had the well that you have been using condemned, but he's still awaiting the go-ahead on the installation of piped water from the mains supply. Until something permanent has been done, I would suggest a long stay in a convalescent home, or at the very least a good residential hotel . . . just to ensure you get regular, nourishing meals and stay in a warm, well-ventilated atmosphere. Above all, you must give up the drinking and smoking.'

'How long?' Magnus demanded, suddenly very serious.

'How do you mean?' asked Gordon, avoiding the journalist's penetrating gaze.

'You know what I mean . . . how long have I got?'

'With care, avoiding alcohol, and providing you do not contract any other serious disease . . . I'd give you two or three years at least. If, on the other hand, you continue to live as you have been, you could go at any time.'

'Will I know anything about it?' demanded Magnus.

'The most likely scenario would be a sudden haemorrhage, either in the lungs or the alimentary tract. It would be very quick . . .'

Magnus nodded, appreciating fully what had been said. He made no further comment.

After a few moments of uncomfortable silence, Gordon got to his feet.

'We'll give it another couple of days,' he said, 'to allow you to make arrangements for somewhere to stay. How would Friday suit you?'

The question was rhetorical. Gordon had already been warned that with so few patients remaining in the unit, all of them convalescent, it was to be closed at the end of the week. Once the initial battle to open the isolation ward had been won the board had been generous in its provision of care, but there was a limit to all things, and Ruth Irving's specialist team was an expensive burden upon hospital funds.

At the other end of the ward, the Italian was clearing his locker noisily and delivering strident orders to his timid little wife. Magnus was left alone to contemplate his bleak future.

'While you have been languishing in the luxury of our exclusive isolation wing,' Morag observed lightly, 'I have been making a few arrangements.'

They were seated in Maggie McKay's Kitchen. Magnus, who had started out with an appetite, now found he could manage only a few bites of the delicious grilled steak before him. He was overcome by weakness but unwilling to admit to it.

'Tell me.' He tried to ignore his discomfort.

'There is a small guest-house on the outskirts of Feanagrogan, recommended by your friend Charlie. I have taken a room for you for a week, just to see how you get on with the landlady. She's a kindly soul and quite happy to take on a semi-invalid.' Morag hesitated, not knowing how he would respond to what she had to tell him. ' There is just one thing . . . it's a Temperance hotel!'

'Good God' he muttered. 'Has it really come to this?'

'Well, you know what both Gordon and I feel about your condition. The only way to keep you alive is to stop you from drinking.'

'Well, I've done without it for six weeks,' he reflected.

'Maybe it won't be too difficult to abstain now.'

'There's more,' she continued, relieved that he had taken her revelation so mildly.

'I haven't forgotten my promise to take you to see my Uncle Angus, so while you have been ill, I've been making arrangements for us to spend a few days at his home on Mull. It's a wonderful place to recuperate, and although Angus is well into his eighties now, on his better days he is still very alert. When I told him about you, and how much you wanted to meet him, he was absolutely delighted. I don't think he sees too many people these days . . . apart from my parents and other members of the family.'

'Won't that be a terrible imposition upon such an elderly gentleman?' Magnus protested, excited nevertheless by the prospect of meeting the eminent man of letters.

'Not really,' Morag responded. 'It's a big house and Uncle's housekeeper is a very friendly woman . . . almost one of the family. Her mother was housekeeper at the Manse before her.'

'Manse?' Magnus looked puzzled. 'I assumed that your uncle was a medical man like the rest of you?'

'Oh, he was, until he retired at the end of the war,' Morag explained. 'The house originally belonged to my grandmother's family. Her father was minister to the parish on the Ross of Mull but the population of the island had become so diminished by the time of his death that there was no longer any call for a local preacher. My uncle inherited the house and set up his medical practice there.'

'If there were so few people, I'm surprised he could make a living as a GP,' Magnus observed.

'I don't think he did,' she admitted. 'He made his living by writing. It was only when my grandfather needed help at Eisdalsa that he did any real medical work. It was different during the war, of course. Then he helped out at the hospital in Oban, and in a convalescent home on the Island of Seileach.'

'Well . . . if you're sure we'll not be an intolerable burden on your uncle, I shall be very happy to go,' Magnus consented. 'When will it be?'

'I have a few days' leave owing to me, so I thought we might go away at the end of next week.'

'That sounds perfect to me,' he agreed, finally surrendering his half-empty plate to a slightly miffed Maggie, who expected her customers to finish what they ordered.

The MacBrayne's paddle steamer, *Mountaineer*, blew her whistle proudly as she drew alongside the wooden pier at Appin, on Loch Linnhe. The wash from her two revolving paddle wheels produced a minor tidal wave which set the motley collection of small wooden sailing craft tied up along the beach dancing a jig – lively at first, but soon settling to a steady rocking as the waves receded.

Morag watched the trickle of passengers coming on board from the tiny village by the shore, and wondered where such a large number of people came from.

The country behind the village was low-lying and densely wooded, while beyond the Strath of Appin the wild crags and twin peaks, Beinn Donn and Bienn Churalain, glowered down upon the shimmering waters.

Apart from the huddle of white stone cottages beside the quay, the only sign of human habitation in that wild country was Castle Stalker, ancient fortress of the Stewart kings of Scotland, now lying derelict and starkly alone, surrounded by the shallow waters of Loch Laich.

She turned to say something to Magnus, only to find he had dozed off again. At her request, the steward had provided a long deck chair for the invalid on which he had most gratefully stretched out, still unable to last more than an hour or so upon his feet. Morag was relieved to see that the flush on his cheeks was a healthy one, caused only by the salt wind and strong sunlight. His rug had slipped to the floor. She spread it carefully, not wanting to disturb him, and wandered back to the rail.

There was talk of ending the steamer services such as this between Inverness and Oban. Steam trains and motor buses had taken much of their freight trade, and there were insufficient passengers to warrant a year-round service. But it would be a great pity if it became impossible to take this more leisurely means of transport.

With the new passengers safely on board and the remaining cargo secured, the steamer gathered way.

The island of Lismore slipped by on the starboard bow, a land of fertile farms and softly wooded slopes, so different from the sharp slate-rock crags and rough heath of her home on Seileach. St Fillan had named it Lismore, the garden island, when he landed there from Ireland eight hundred years ago. The rounded yellowing stooks of corn standing in rows across the fertile fields indicated just how apt the name had proved to be.

Soon they were passing the wide estuary at the entrance to Loch Etive. Excited passengers crowded to the rails to admire the Falls of Lora which, on the turn of the tide, emptied the waters of the loch in a wild, foaming cataract and swept them out to sea below the freshly painted steelwork of the Connel Bridge.

Morag's grandfather, David Beaton, had loved to sit in his garden just along the shore there, at Creag an Turich, and watch the sun setting behind the dark latticework of the bridge. He had considered the steel construction, built to carry a railway line which was never completed, one of the most beautiful of monuments to nineteenth-century ingenuity.

Even after all this time, Morag still missed her grandfather. Although she loved Hugh, her father, dearly, it had been David Beaton to whom she had gone with all her childish problems. How she wished she could talk to him now . . .

The troubles which had beset her early days at Inverlinnhe seemed to have been solved at last, but still there lingered a suspicion that the forces of opposition were acting against her.

She must watch every step she took, for the slightest breath of scandal would endanger her position.

She knew that her friendship with Magnus was regarded by Sidney Maynard, who harboured a certain degree of paranoia about the power of the press, as a form of disloyalty. Well, poor Magnus was pretty harmless now, and likely to remain so.

Although from the first time that she had met him Morag had felt drawn towards Adam Inglis, she was nevertheless uncertain of her true feelings towards him. She admired his frank, open approach to his work, and his skill on the mountainside had left her speechless with admiration. Adam was a natural leader among men. He could inspire, encourage, and galvanise his followers into action. She had often thought him misplaced in the Town Hall. he would have made an outstanding teacher. He was the one man of her own generation whom she had found to share all that was best in her grandfather's character. Perhaps it was this which most attracted her. Taking a long, cool look at the situation for the first time, Morag was forced to admit that Adam had never once indicated that her feelings were reciprocated. Had she been living in a fantasy world when she had imagined that his interest in her was something more than mere friendship between two professionals?

She sighed heavily and was startled out of her reverie by Magnus's hand on her arm.

'Why so pale and wan, fair damsel?' he demanded. Clearly his snooze had done him good. He seemed much more lively than he had been since they started out.

'Just thinking,' she replied. Then, seeing the other passengers preparing to disembark at Oban pier, she moved over to where their baggage was standing and lifted the two small cases.

'Hey, that's my job,' Magnus protested.

'Not today it's not,' she said, decisively, determined he should not over-tax his strength.

They disembarked at the North Pier, where Magnus hailed a taxi. Morag found it quite extraordinary to be driven the short distance from one pier to the other on the far side of the bay, but it was clear that he was in no fit state to make the journey on foot.

The taxi conveyed them to where the motor vessel *Lochfyne* awaited passengers for the Island of Mull. She was the newest member of the MacBrayne's fleet, and the first diesel electric ship to sail along the west coast.

'This is a treat in itself,' breathed Magnus, admiring the fine lines of the spanking steamer, which had only been launched in March the previous year. 'I'm told she has the most silent, electrically driven winches of any vessel on the western seaboard.'

'So long as she doesn't roll in choppy seas, I shall be happy,' laughed Morag, less concerned about the specifications of the ship than her own anxiety to avoid the indignity of being seasick.

'We're lucky to be taking the sea voyage on such a beautiful day,' she said, thrusting her qualms to the back of her mind. 'Have you ever seen the Island of Staffa?'

He admitted he had not.

'When we visited Uncle Angus as children, it was aboard my grandfather's sailing boat. He would take us straight across the Firth of Lorn and land us on the Ross of Mull, only a mile or two from the Manse. In fine weather it was a favourite picnic trip, to sail from there through Iona Sound and round to Staffa.'

Magnus regarded her with a certain longing. What an innocent she was, brought up within a loving family, protected from life's harsh realities . . . would that he could say the same!

His own father had died during the Relief of Mafeking, leaving his wife and young Magnus to fend for themselves on the meagre pension allotted to a soldier's widow. As a minister's daughter, she had been sufficiently well educated to offer herself for employment but this meant she was obliged to leave her little son in the care of his grandmother, a woman of high ideals but very little imagination. The minister's wife had had little understanding of the needs of a small boy. Her regime was harsh, demanding a standard of behaviour unattainable by one so young.

In self-defence, Magnus had buried himself in the books which were his father's only legacy to him, and it was from those early encounters with a catholic library, unmatched in most middle-class households of the day, that he had amassed the vast background of knowledge which was to stand him in such good stead in his career as a journalist.

In the absence of other children, his companions were the characters in the books he read. Arthurian knights and Greek warriors shared his adventures along with Gulliver and Jim Hawkins. He cried himself to sleep over the fate of David Copperfield and laughed himself sick at the antics of Mr Jingle and his friends. *Alice in Wonderland* held him in thrall; so much so that his first attempt at story writing was a fantasy about a boy lost on a mysterious island, where animals could talk and trees and flowers gathered together to protect him from the wicked wizard of the forest . . .

He smiled now at the recollection of his childish attempts at literature and Morag, seeing his changed expression, remarked, 'I do believe that the sea air is already doing its work, Magnus. You look so much better.'

On a calm, clear day the Treshnish Isles, which skirt the western shores of the Island of Mull, appear like giant flowers floating in a lily pond. Apart from the occasional intrusion of harder granite rock they are quite flat, lying only feet above the water at the highest tides. Fladda, Lunga and the Dutchman's Cap are home to countless sea birds and seals, while in the shallow waters surrounding the rocky shores lurk basking sharks, luxuriating in the warm waters of the Gulf Stream.

As the colonies of seals and shags which were gathered in their multitudes on every promontory disappeared from view, passengers aboard the *Lochfyne* turned away and began to pack their box Brownies and pocket Kodaks into leather cases. Suddenly there was a shout from another quarter and they ran back to the rails as the Island of Staffa appeared on the port side.

One hundred and fifty feet above the ocean swell, a stark cliff of columnar basalt rose out of the sea, its strange formation calling to the atavistic instincts of all on board. In Ireland they named a similar outcrop the Giant's Causeway. Ancient Celts had ascribed various mystical associations to this strange phenomenon, which had inspired artists and poets throughout the centuries. Training his binoculars on the cliff, Magnus strained to see every detail, marvelling at Nature's amazing symmetry.

'Just look at that wall of rock,' breathed a tall, burly figure who hung over the rail at his elbow. He turned to his equally imposing friend. 'What d'you say, Rudi? Fancy scaling that lot?'

'Sometime, maybe,' the other replied, contemplating the climb. 'It would take some careful planning,' he concluded. Morag thought she detected a European accent . . . German perhaps?

'The man's serious,' laughed the other, addressing his remarks to Morag and including her easily in their discussion. 'I was joking, Rudi. You don't imagine I'd risk taking a bath in there!'

As he spoke huge waves piled up against the sheer face of the cliff and broke in a deluge of spray. 'I mean . . . just look at it,' he stressed. 'And today the sea is relatively calm.'

'Are you here for the climbing?' Morag asked, in friendly fashion. From their casual dress, she had assumed they were holiday-makers.

'Oh, yes,' replied Rudi, 'we're contemplating an assault on Ben Buie, but Louis here insisted on visiting Iona also, so we have decided to get that over first!'

'Do I take it you're not the most serious of climbers then?' Morag enquired of the one called Louis. To her, they both appeared to be more suited to the rugby field than to dangling on the end of a rope, hundreds of feet above the ground. 'I must say I hope you never get into difficulties on the Nevis Range. I'd hate to be in the team that carried you down!'

'Are you a climber yourself?' Rudi viewed her with renewed interest.

'Not really,' she confessed. 'I'm a surgeon at the cottage hospital in Inverlinnhe. I've merely had to learn some of the basics of mountaineering so I can go out with the rescue team if someone is injured on the mountain.'

'Blessed lady!' Louis kissed her hand dramatically. 'Should I ever be so foolish as to break my leg climbing, let it be on the Nevis Range!'

Morag glanced over her shoulder at Magnus who had moved

away and now sat huddled on the passenger seating a few
yards off. He was frowning. Not with jealousy . . . surely not?
Old-fashioned enough to disapprove of her striking up a casual
conversation with complete strangers, perhaps. The thought
amused her, if only because that was precisely the manner in
which she and Magnus had met in the first place.

Smiling happily, she rejoined him in time to hear one of the
passengers forward call out, 'Look, there's Fingal's Cave.'

Morag knew better.

'Not yet,' she explained quietly to Magnus, 'that's only the Boat
Cave. Wait until we pass this next promontory.'

The sight that met his eyes then was to remain with him until
his end. The mouth of the cave was large enough to allow the
passage of a good-sized fishing boat. With its columned walls
and arched roof, it looked like the nave of a mighty cathedral.
He found it impossible to accept that this was Nature's work
alone. It was easy to see how the ancients had come to weave
so many magical tales about this place . . .

Over the loudspeaker a disembodied voice called for attention.
'Passengers wishing to visit Fingal's Cave should gather at the
starboard entry port on the lower deck. The ship will remain
hove-to while passengers go ashore aboard the lighter lying
alongside.'

Morag prayed that Magnus would not insist on leaving the ship.
It was a difficult walk, using the giant hexagonal columns, sawn
off by the tides, to serve as stepping stones around the base of
the cliff.

'Do you want to go ashore?' he asked eagerly.

'I have been, many times,' she replied. Then seeing his
disappointed expression, added, 'But I am happy to make the
effort if you feel you can manage it?'

'It's something I have wanted to do all my life,' he said. 'I
would like to try . . . there may never be another opportunity.'

The visitors moved carefully in single file, stepping with
great strides from rock to rock. Now that they were close
up, they could appreciate fully the extraordinary uniformity

of the hexagons of rock, formed from cooling magma so long ago.

Morag paused as they passed an outlier a few yards offshore and watched the waves breaking over its outer edge.

'See how the magma curves there.' She pointed out what appeared to be a wave drawn by the flow where the molten rock had met some immoveable object and been forced to go around it.

Magnus stopped, thankful for the opportunity to catch his breath. He was finding the going tougher than he had expected. As others of their party passed them by on either side, they each of them perched upon one of the truncated hexagonal columns.

'Perhaps it is telling us something,' he mused, his voice so low that she had to strain to hear him above the sound of the swirling tide. 'The rock which stood in the way of the lava flow must have been immoveable, but the magma was flexible . . . it changed course for a bit, overcame the obstacle and then went on its way. It was unwavering in its purpose even to the point of breaking up into its columns, just as before . . .'

Other members of their party were already returning from their visit to the cave.

'We must get along,' Morag insisted. 'The ship won't wait for us if we overstay the time.'

Without further comment, Magnus continued on his way, leaving her just a little disturbed by his philosophical mood.

When they arrived at the entrance to Fingal's Cave, the last of their party was departing.

'Just a quick look,' commanded Morag, as she took him by the hand and led him into the dark interior.

Ten feet below the cramped shelf on which they stood, the waves rushed through the narrow entrance, swirling and foaming as they reached the innermost corners of the cave and rebounded upon the waters which followed. The sounds of the sea echoed and re-echoed around the columns of basalt rock.

Morag raised her voice and sang out, 'Hallo, hallo,' and the shout reverberated from a thousand different surfaces.

'It's no wonder poets and musicians have been inspired to

produce some of their best work in this place,' Magnus observed, so quietly she might only have imagined she heard him. 'In fact,' he said, more brightly, 'I feel the muse coming upon me, now!'

'Oh, no!' Morag laughed. 'We don't have time for that . . . come on, there's the siren calling us to the embarkation point.'

Their return across the stepping stones, unhindered by any other visitors, was quicker, and Morag went on ahead, anxious to ensure that the lighter did not leave without them.

She thought she heard a cry on the wind, but dismissed it as a sea bird and continued towards the jetty, waving her arms frantically for the boatman to stand by.

Good, they had seen her at last. Satisfied that the little lighter would wait, she turned back to see how Magnus was managing.

He was nowhere to be seen.

Struck with horror at the thought that he might have slipped, she turned in her tracks and made her way swiftly across the wet and treacherous rocks to a point where she could see clearly right back to the mouth of the cave.

When she spotted him, seated upright on a rock and gazing out to sea, she was gripped by anger for a moment. What on earth was he playing at? He knew they would be left behind if he dallied.

As she approached, however, she realised that he had remained still because he dared not move. His clothes and the rock beneath his feet were red with blood. The haemorrhage they had feared had come upon him as suddenly as Gordon had predicted . . .

She crouched down at his side. Taking a handkerchief from the pocket of her waterproof jacket, she wiped his face clear of blood.

'It's all right,' she reassured him. 'From the look of this blood, it has been collecting quite slowly for some time. The bleeding may even have stopped altogether by now. Just stay still . . . I'll fetch someone to help us.'

A shout caused her to look up. Two men from the party of tourists were approaching across the rocks. It was the mountaineers, Rudi and Louis. They should be more than capable of lifting Magnus's poor wasted body.

'Oh, thank God,' she exclaimed when they reached her. 'My friend is ill, do you think you can carry him?'

'It's all right,' Magnus protested feebly, attempting to rise, 'give me an arm someone, I can walk.'

They helped him to his feet and half carrying, half dragging him across the uneven ground, the two young men supported him all the way back to the lighter.

Once aboard, Morag took charge.

'Please don't be alarmed,' she assured the passengers who crowded round in consternation at the sight of Magnus's blood-stained clothing. 'I'm a doctor. If you will please give us sufficient space on the deck to lay him down, my friend will be all right until we reach the ship.'

They made him as comfortable as they could with coats and blankets from the emergency box on board. In another ten minutes, with the small boat tossing uncomfortably on the ocean swell, the lighter drew alongside the steamer and the passengers were able to climb back on board.

A rapid exchange between the mountaineer, Louis, and one of the deck officers brought a couple of stewards hurrying to the scene carrying a lightweight stretcher which was handed down into the boat. The members of the crew would have taken charge from that point had not Rudi and Louis insisted on manhandling the stretcher themselves.

With Morag following behind, they were conducted to a small cabin and Magnus was transferred to the narrow bunk.

'Will you be returning to Oban, miss?' enquired the MacBrayne's officer.

'Our plan was to disembark at Fionnport,' she explained. 'I see no reason to change it. There will be someone to meet us at the pier.'

It seemed obvious to the sailor that although the young woman knew what she was doing, it would be wiser to take the gentleman back to Oban, where there was a hospital . . .

'My patient needs quiet and rest,' she said, 'and medical attention which I cannot give him here. I don't think he should remain on board any longer than is absolutely necessary. The additional hour's steaming time could mean the difference between life and death.' It sounded a little dramatic even to her, but the officer recoiled at the thought of a corpse on board. The thought of the inevitable pile of paperwork was sufficiently daunting for him to persuade his captain to comply with her request.

On seeing the officer waver, she continued, 'We are visiting my uncle, who is also a doctor. I can assure you, Mr Glendenning will be in the best of hands.'

It was a curious situation. Had the passenger succumbed to his infirmity while aboard the *Lochfyne*, the captain would have had the final say. In the circumstances, the ship had merely acted as an agent to assist an individual in distress. There could be no claim for negligence against the company if, as a result of permitting him to go ashore, Magnus should suffer greater deterioration or even die.

Morag solved the dilemma.

'Look, if your captain requires it, I will sign a disclaimer, exonerating the company from any responsibility in this matter.'

'I am not certain that that will satisfy him, Doctor,' said the young man, hesitating to dispute her authority. 'What right have you to make such a decision on behalf of the patient?'

Morag glanced quickly at Magnus. Although not unconscious he was apparently unaware of what was going on around him. She led the officer to the door and whispered.

'He is my fiancé,' she told him. 'We are to be married very soon.' This seemed to carry far greater weight than her claim to be his doctor.

'I will take your message to the captain, miss. A steward will be outside the door if you should need anything.'

'Some water and a towel would be useful to begin with,' she replied.

\*    \*    \*

'No one could accuse you of leading a dull life, my dear,' Angus Beaton remarked as he folded his arms around his great-niece and kissed her on the brow. 'How delightful to see you again. It has been far too long since you were last here.'

He looked past Morag to the figure remaining seated inside the car. He was clearly curious to see the man she had brought with her.

'Before I introduce you to Magnus, Uncle, I must explain what has happened,' she said. She led her uncle away to stand beside the low stone wall which edged a wide terrace fronting the building. Before them, the ground fell away to a neat stretch of lawn, and beyond to a wild *machair*, a narrow grassy plain separated from the sea by a ragged shoreline of sharply sculpted, low-lying rocks, black in the shadow cast by the setting sun.

Weakened by the loss of blood, Magnus could only wait and watch as they stood, deep in conversation. He noted, absently, the family resemblance which even so large an age-gap could not disguise.

Both Beatons were tall and willowy, and even in his eighty-fifth year Angus was only slightly stooped. His hair lacked the brightness of his great-niece's fiery halo, but still harboured unmistakable strands of red amongst the grey. The gestures of the two were so alike they might be puppets operated by the same strings: a toss of the head, a wave of an arm to emphasise a point . . . no, there was no mistaking the family connection between them.

'I'm so sorry to impose on you in this way,' Morag was saying. 'This was simply meant to be a period of convalescence for Magnus. He has been so depressed since his illness that I thought a little stimulating discussion with you might be just the thing to take him out of himself. He speaks so highly of your work, and has been looking forward to meeting you ever since I first disclosed we were related.'

Angus patted her arm, comfortingly. 'Nothing to apologise for, my dear,' he replied. 'You were not to know that your friend would take a turn for the worse. Anyway . . . he couldn't be in better hands now, could he? Let's get him into the house and make him comfortable. Then we will see what is to be done for the poor man.'

She flung her arms around his neck as she had done so often as a little girl, and kissed him on both cheeks.

'Thank you, Angus. I knew I could rely on you,' she said, and led him by the hand to be introduced to Magnus.

Without her two mountaineering friends, Morag had wondered how she and Angus's man, McPherson, were going to get her patient into the house. The problem was solved immediately by her uncle, who disappeared into the conservatory and re-emerged in a few minutes, pushing an ancient wooden bath chair.

This obsolete piece of furniture had, for many years, stood in the conservatory as a reminder of the time, long ago, when Angus was recovering from a serious injury incurred in a train crash.

Seeing it, Morag let out a cry of recognition. 'Oh, the old wheely chair . . . I'd quite forgotten. That will do splendidly!' She recalled the hours of fun that she and her brothers had had with in on wet days, charging around the ground floor of the house, the old housekeeper, the present Mrs McLean's mother, chasing after them, fearing for the safety of Angus's precious collection of porcelain.

As the years had taken their toll of his strength, Angus had had one of the downstairs rooms overlooking the terrace converted to a bedroom for himself. It was to this room that Magnus was taken.

With McPherson's assistance, Morag soon had her patient between freshly laundered sheets, all signs of his recent mishap quite removed.

'Now, old fellow, if it won't disturb you too much, I'd like to take a proper look at you.' Angus had managed to find his stethoscope in the drawer where he had placed it on his return from Oban, after the first Armistice Service in November 1919. Since that time he had left the doctoring to the younger generation . . . his nephew, Hugh, across the water at Eisdalsa, and some cocky young fellow with a fast car who had set up his practice on the far side of the island, in Pennygael.

The years had not diminished Angus's skills. He made a meticulous examination, moving across Magnus's abdomen, listening here, making a sharp tap with his fingers there, noting the hollow sounds and the dull ones – and all the time grunting away to himself, with an occasional satisfied nod of the head.

Morag looked on, admiring his technique and indulging in memories of other times when this dear man had been vigorous enough to sail with them, to fish the waters of the sea lochs or to stride across open moorland and over the hills in search of wild flowers, an eagle's eyrie or a badger's sett . . .

Soon he was finished. Without making any comment, he patted Magnus's hand encouragingly and replaced the covers. Indicating that Morag should follow him, Angus stepped out through the French door, into the conservatory beyond.

'The leakage is undoubtedly into the stomach,' he told her. 'That is to his advantage, of course, since the blood is confined to the alimentary tract and almost certainly is not causing havoc in the abdominal cavity.

'From the tension building up, I would say that he will be forced to vomit again soon, and there is nothing we can do to stop it. Without an operation for gastric resection, there is no way to put a stop to the bleeding.'

Angus had confirmed Morag's own diagnosis of the situation. In fact, she was already three steps ahead of him.

'We could set up your surgery as an operating theatre,' she suggested. 'I have never performed a gastric resection, but I have watched the operation. It's a simple enough procedure.'

'He has lost a great deal of blood already,' observed her uncle. 'He could not withstand the shock of major surgery now. If we leave him for the time necessary to make up the blood he has already lost, he will continue bleeding to death while we wait.'

'I can give him a transfusion,' she claimed, having already gone through the course of action in her mind. A transfusion, followed immediately by the necessary gastrectomy, and she might be able to staunch the bleeding and prevent Magnus from going into post-operative shock.

Angus was sceptical. Blood transfusion had been a technique in its infancy when he trained in the seventies. He had never used it himself and regarded the practice as something akin to voodoo. Wasn't there some problem about mixing different types of blood?

'That's the one thing in our favour,' she explained, quickly. 'Magnus has brought his spare blood supply with him!'

She explained how she and Gordon McDonald had cross-matched Magnus's blood, only to discover that Morag was the one person in the hospital suitable as a donor.

'But you can't perform the transfusion, yourself!' her uncle protested.

'No, but you can,' she responded, decisively.

He held out his hands to demonstrate how they trembled.

'You can hardly expect me to risk your life performing such a delicate operation,' he protested.

'It's a simple procedure, Uncle, believe me,' she insisted. 'I'll get everything ready . . . all you will have to do is insert the canula into my artery at the last minute.'

'How do you avoid introducing an air bubble?' he demanded, not at all convinced by her optimism.

'I'll think of something,' she promised. 'Now, come along, Uncle Angus . . . you get Mrs McLean on to scrubbing down the surgery, and I'll instruct McPherson about moving furniture and so on. While they are busy, we will carry out the transfusion.'

# Chapter 14

Morag was relieved to find that despite her great-uncle's apparent
lack of enthusiasm for practising medicine again, he nevertheless
held a collection of instruments which might have found a use
in any operating theatre in the country. She searched around
for forceps and clamps and threw these into the steriliser. The
canula she needed might be rather more difficult to unearth.

A small drawer in the white-painted cabinet which held his
surgical instruments, revealed a collection of fine metal tubes of
the kind she sought. She found a pair, each about three inches
in length, one slightly larger in internal diameter than the other,
and slid the smaller into the open end of the larger. They fitted
perfectly. A smear of Vaseline would ensure a leak-proof joint.

It would be a simple enough matter to expose a peripheral
vein in Magnus's arm, insert the canula and clamp it in place.
The trickier moment would come when the same operation was
performed on her own arm and into an artery. Should the wound
which Angus made be too large, and should there be any damage
to surrounding tissues, her competence in the surgery to follow
might be impaired.

Morag took the covered dish containing the transfusion
instruments into the bedroom, and closed the door firmly.
The next half-hour would be crucial to their plans and she
had no wish to be disturbed.

Magnus was still very pale, but the rest and quiet which he
had enjoyed since his arrival at the Manse had cleared his mind
somewhat, and she felt able to convey their intentions to him.

'Magnus, you have lost a great deal of blood,' she began,
cautiously, not wishing to alarm him unduly, 'so Angus is going

to perform a transfusion of my blood into you . . . it is a perfectly standard procedure and one which will hurt neither of us. It will, however, provide you with sufficient strength to undergo an operation to seal off the gastric ulcer which is causing the bleeding. Do you understand?'

His face clouded.

'Are you certain you will do no harm to yourself?' he murmured weakly.

'Do you really believe I would risk my own life for an old reprobate like you?' she replied, lightly.

Too feeble to say anything more, he nodded briefly. Angus wondered if he was giving his consent to the transfusion, or indicating that he thought she might, indeed, be so foolish.

Morag chose to assume the former.

'Right then.' She turned to her uncle. 'First, a Novocaine injection into Magnus's forearm . . .' she turned back to the patient '. . . just so that you won't feel anything.'

She prepared the syringe and injected the localised anaesthetic. While she waited for the drug to take effect, Angus gave *her* a similar injection.

'Now, Uncle, I am going to expose about an inch of the radial vein . . .' She took up a scalpel and made the shallow incision about four inches from the base of Magnus's thumb. Having exposed the vein, she tied a silk thread around the vessel and a short distance nearer to the elbow she clamped it, leaving a section of vein just long enough to take a V-shaped incision. Through this she thrust the end of one of the fine metal tubes she had prepared, and clamped it in position.

'Now, Angus,' she climbed on to the bed beside the patient, 'I want you to carry out exactly the same procedure using my radial artery.'

He would have made one final plea for common sense, but it was obvious that she was quite determined. Without further protest, he proceeded to follow her instructions to the letter.

She lay back and relaxed. There was nothing more she could do for the moment, only wait while her life-giving blood surged into Magnus's vein and circulated around his body.

'Twenty minutes is as much as I will allow,' Angus decided, firmly. 'There is no point in weakening you so that you're incapable of performing the operation.'

Morag grinned happily at him. Now that the transfusion was successfully underway, she felt sure that twenty minutes would be sufficient. She could always donate more blood later, if they thought it necessary.

Angus had been sufficiently overawed by the prospect of carrying out this procedure to refrain from arguing with her about the method she had chosen. His concern was that she needed both her hands in good working order to perform a gastrectomy, and her arm was going to be sore while she worked. Himself new to the whole concept of transfusion, he hoped above all that she had not endangered herself by this procedure.

It was Magnus, gaining strength by the second, who broke the tense silence as they waited for the requisite time to pass.

'I've often dreamed of this moment,' he grinned, 'but I never expected us to share a bed quite so soon . . . then again, since we are betrothed, I suppose it hardly matters.'

'You were not supposed to hear that.' She grinned at him. 'I'm sure the captain would have insisted on us going on to Oban if I hadn't told him that little white lie.' She enlightened Angus as to what had passed between herself and the MacBrayne's officer.

To tell the truth, Morag had been a little shocked by Magnus's remark, and regarded her uncle guardedly for any sign of disapproval on his part.

To her relief, he laughed heartily at Magnus's declaration, but otherwise made no comment. Unobserved, he looked searchingly from one to the other of his visitors. His niece might regard the suggestion of an engagement as a joke, but the journalist most assuredly did not!

The twenty minutes were up. Angus proceeded to remove the cannulae and suture both incisions. A tight wad of cotton, held down by sticking plaster, prevented bleeding from either wound. Magnus stopped bleeding immediately but Morag's artery had been penetrated and she continued to bleed long after the canula was removed. Angus applied a pressure bandage to the site and insisted that she rest for a short while before beginning the operation. She would be forced to stand for a long time, once they had begun.

When Angus had cleared away the paraphernalia of the transfusion, Magnus asked, 'Might I have a few words with you, Dr Beaton?' He glanced apologetically at Morag. 'In private?'

She regarded Magnus quizzically, then seeing that her presence was definitely no longer required, excused herself on the grounds that she needed a cup of tea.

Once they had Magnus lying on the examination couch in Angus's surgery, swathed in sterile sheets and snoring under the anaesthetic, Morag was able to disregard the fact that she was working in less than ideal conditions. All she had to do now was concentrate on the task confronting her.

At the moment when Angus lifted his head to give her the signal to begin, she experienced a sudden wave of nausea.

It was almost certainly weakness from the loss of blood during the transfusion. Mrs McLean's cup of sweet tea would take effect, shortly. Dismissing the feeling, she reached for a scalpel.

Concerned at the patient's generally debilitated condition, they had kept him at a shallow level of unconsciousness. To Morag's relief, Angus was still capable of using the old-fashioned Schimmelbusch frame for administering the chloroform. She admired the skill he had developed in the course of fifty years or more, performing his kitchen-table surgery in the most remote corners of the island.

As luck would have it, the ulcer was located on the anterior aspect of the stomach. With each inspiration a sour-smelling liquid, thin, with flakes of half-digested food and flecks of blood in it, oozed from the perforation. At the site, tell-tale fibrinous lymph lingered, and there was evidence of adherence to the wall of the peritoneum. The ulcer gave every sign of having existed for a very long time.

Morag mopped up the fluids, thankful that the serious bleeding had stopped. She had feared that the increased blood-pressure brought about by the transfusion might start another haemorrhage, but in this respect Magnus had been fortunate.

The wall of the stomach surrounding the ulcer had deteriorated so badly, that when Morag tried to make the normal purse-string suture to draw the opening together, the silk tore into the weakened tissue.

'I shall have to cut away a portion of the omentum wall,' she told Angus. 'Do you think he can stand another few minutes?'

'His blood pressure is steady,' came the reply, 'but his pulse is very fast and thready . . .' The old man glanced up at her. There was pain in his eyes as he noted her worried expression. 'Carry on, my dear, you have no alternative.'

Mrs McLean, who had long served as Angus's theatre assistant in the past and had stood guard over the instrument tray today, ready to hand out each item as Morag called for it, looked up sharply. She could tell by the tone of his voice that they were losing the battle.

Morag cleared away the diseased tissue and tried again to draw the edges of the enlarged hole together. This time the suture held, and the tissues were gathered up to resemble a badly mended sock.

She reinforced the single suture with a line of tiny stitches, inserting between them a Keith's glass draining tube before swabbing out the peritoneal cavity.

Up till now Morag had been concentrating so hard that she had paid no heed to the warning signs given by her own body. Suddenly, as she was closing the abdominal wall, one layer at a time, she was overcome by a wave of nausea. She staggered a little, and dropped the needle she was using. As she fumbled to retrieve it, Angus's hand closed over hers.

'All right,' he said firmly, 'I can finish it. You go and have a lie down.'

Gratefully, she left the patient in his care, and went out into the conservatory, where a well-padded wicker garden chair beckoned invitingly. Exhausted as she was by the events of the day, the loss of her own blood and the strain of the operation, she thought she might sleep immediately.

As it was, she lay in a twilight state on the edge of consciousness, only vaguely aware of what was going on around her.

She heard Angus calling out for Mrs McLean and McPherson to lend a hand.

There was a shifting of furniture, a rattling of glassware and then the unmistakable sound of the old bath-chair being trundled across the hall to Magnus's bedroom. She sighed contentedly . . . they were putting him back in his own bed. Everything must be all right. She turned over, and slept.

'Morag, Morag . . .' The hand shook her shoulder relentlessly. She tried to shrug it off, but Angus persisted until she was fully awake.

'I think you should come, my dear,' he said. 'There is not much time.'

His face was grey with fatigue.

What could she be thinking of to leave this poor frail old gentleman to do her work for her while she slept? She started up suddenly. What was that he had said?

'What is it?' she demanded. 'What has happened?'

'You have nothing for which to blame yourself,' he said, firmly. 'The case was hopeless from the outset. In your heart, you knew it yourself.'

Realisation dawning, she stared at her uncle in dismay.

'I must go to him,' she said more calmly, and moving to the far end of the conservatory, stepped over the threshold into Magnus's room.

He was propped against the pillows, shoulders only slightly elevated to ease his breathing. His flesh appeared to have shrunk away from the bones in the few hours since she had last seen him. His skin was like parchment, grey against the whiteness of the linen. He might have been taken for a corpse already, had it not been for the feverish sparkle in his eyes, which seemed all the more alive in their sunken sockets.

As she approached the bed he raised a smile, and made a feeble gesture with one skeletal hand.

'Too bad you wasted your precious blood after all,' he whispered, his face a drawn mask. 'It was pleasant to be so intimately connected, if only for a short while . . .'

She squeezed his hand, comfortingly. 'Don't try to talk,' she said.

'Why not?' he demanded, voice weakening, 'I shall be a long time silent.'

Tears sprang to her eyes. She leaned over, and kissed him on the forehead.

He raised a hand and made a feeble attempt to wipe away her tears with the tips of his fingers.

'What a pity we had to wait until it was almost too late for our first kiss,' he murmured.

'Oh, don't say that,' she cried.

'At least we were betrothed, if only for a few short hours,' he whispered, his gaze penetrating, demanding . . .

Unable to deny him the comfort of believing that she might have married him, she remained silent while she rubbed the back of his hand, very gently.

'You remember . . . in the hospital . . . you wanted me to start writing again,' he said, his breathing had worsened and his words were interrupted by painful gasps. 'I tried . . . would you read what I have written?'

She nodded in reply.

'I was working on this . . . on the boat . . . while you were talking . . . with those two young fellows . . .'

He fumbled beneath the pillow and she leaned across to help him, withdrawing a small notebook, lying open at a page covered in his scrawling handwriting.

'You read it,' he sighed, exhausted by the effort.

She scanned the writing. There were crossings out and insertions in a wavering hand, quite unlike the original. Could he have been trying to finish it while she slept? She puzzled momentarily over some of the words, and then began to read in a faltering voice:

> *Look kindly now*
> *Upon this fading spirit,*
> *And send it on its way rejoicing.*
> *Forget its failings, many though they be,*
> *Recalling only laughter;*
> *A secret shared; fond dreams in harmony.*
> *Waste no time in lamentations,*
> *Have no regret for words which went unsaid.*

> *Samaritan, upon life's rocky road,*
> *You offered comfort to an impoverished soul.*
> *I'm thankful for it.*

Her tears blinded her, so that she missed the moment of his passing. At one instant he had been gazing at her and smiling . . . but when she wiped her eyes and looked at him again, he was already gone.

He seemed so peaceful once the strain of staying alive was over. That last smile still lingered on his lips, and his eyes, sightless now, stared out upon the garden and the distant seascape.

She did not hear Angus enter the room, and was only vaguely aware of Mrs McLean putting her arms around her and leading her away.

Morag brought his remains home to Inverlinnhe by boat . . . the way Magnus would have wished to travel.

When she had disembarked, she waited while a group of seamen carried the plain oak casket down a plank reserved for freight, and smiled a little, wondering how Magnus would have described this modest arrival.

She was relieved to find Charlie waiting to drive her, behind the undertaker's hearse, to the funeral parlour of Lawson and McConnel, joiners and undertakers. Together, they followed the coffin into the funeral parlour and silently bade their friend farewell.

'If you will call again in, shall we say, two days' time, the departed will be ready for viewing.' The sombrely clad, unctuous Mr Lawson intruded upon this quiet moment. Bowing obsequiously and wringing his hands in time-honoured fashion, he steered them out of the cell-like room in which the coffin had been laid.

'I am not sure who is to make the arrangements,' Morag began, hesitantly. She had no knowledge of family or friends who might take it upon themselves to see to everything. The only contact she had was Magnus's solicitor, whose name and address he had given to Angus before the operation.

'Everything has been taken care of by Mr Glendenning's solicitors,' Lawson explained. 'They will be making the arrangements at the request of the family.'

Being quite unaware of his family ties, Morag was forced to accept that, having delivered Magnus's body into Mr Lawson's charge, her own responsibilities in the matter were at an end. She looked about her helplessly, not knowing quite what to do. Charlie placed a hand under her arm to steady her. She looked up into his face and the pain she saw there was almost reassuring, for she found that she was not alone in her grief. Somewhat comforted by this, she allowed him to conduct her out into the busy street.

It was a miserable wet day when they laid Magnus Glendenning to rest in the town's new cemetery, a bleak meadow on the slopes below the Ben.

Morag thought it a sadly isolated resting place; no more than half a dozen graves bore proper headstones as yet. On several others, the freshly turned earth was still covered with wreaths of decaying flowers.

A grave which was smaller than the rest bore the name of one of Gordon's young patients whom she herself had visited at the height of the typhoid epidemic. Recognising it, she shuddered, and her father placed his arm around her to keep her warm.

She stood in the rain between her parents . . . Angus had asked them to represent him, but she knew that her mother would have insisted on being there anyway. Millicent Beaton had found it impossible to accept that the two of them were not planning to marry when they had visited Eisdalsa earlier in the year.

Morag smiled faintly at the recollection. Perhaps now her mother would stop nagging her to find a suitable husband. For a while, at least, she might be expected to accept that Morag was in mourning, and would leave her alone. Around this story of a tragic betrothal, Millicent would be able to weave a plausible excuse to explain why, at the age of twenty-eight, her daughter remained unmarried.

Morag was still uncertain as to her motives in declaring to the

MacBrayne's officer that Magnus was her fiancé. Was it merely an expedient to get him off the boat, or had she wished, subconsciously at least, that he was to be her husband?

It was of no importance now. Her declaration had done no harm to anyone, and it had given him a few hours of happiness.

There were not many people present to witness his interment.

The chief mourners appeared to be three women, heavily veiled and dressed from head to toe in black. They had made no attempt to introduce themselves as the congregation filed out of the church, but Morag thought that the older woman, red-eyed, and grasping a small square of damp cambric in her left hand as she shook with her right, might well have been Magnus's mother. She had felt moved to give the poor soul a hug of comfort, but there was a coldness about the woman which resisted any such spontaneous demonstration of affection.

Magnus had never mentioned any member of his family, other than a father of whom he had only the vaguest recollection. On the subject of parents he had always appeared very cynical and Morag wondered why.

The Editor of the *Gazette* and some of Magnus's colleagues from the paper were there, as one might have expected. She recognised the photographer from the *Glasgow Evening Chronicle* and some of those other reporters from the national 'dailies' who had appeared on the night when McRae's daughter and her boyfriend were brought into the hospital. The presence of Duncan McRae at the graveside did not surprise Morag. He appeared to take an interest in every facet of the town and its people.

She caught a fleeting glimpse of Charlie at one point, but when she looked again, he was gone.

She was aware of Gordon McDonald's presence, too, in company with Adam Inglis and two of Ruth Irving's staff. During the service they had occupied a pew at the rear of the church, and even here at the graveside they kept in the background. Gordon cast a sympathetic glance in her direction but, intimidated perhaps by the presence of her parents, kept his distance. Before she had a chance to speak with him, he'd slipped away.

At last it was all over. The reception, held in the lounge of the Highland Hotel, close by the cemetery, had been a chilling affair from which most people made a retreat as soon as decently possible. Morag watched enviously as the newspaper fraternity departed in the direction of the Long John, and suspecting that that was where Gordon and the others had also gone, she wished she might join them. She felt the need to be close to those who had known Magnus, but her parents had driven a long way to be with her and she felt obliged to remain with them until they were ready to leave. Left to her own devices at last, she decided to walk back to the hospital, but on leaving the grounds of the hotel she turned away from the town and took a path which led her in the direction of the glen.

The rain had stopped and her mackintosh dried on the outside, becoming damp with perspiration within. She took it off and folded it over her arm.

For a while she wandered along beside the burn, its watery harmonies drowning out her troubled thoughts, but soon the midges drove her out on to the hillside, away from the trees.

Too weary to go any further she sank down upon a patch of soft turf with her back against a boulder, and watched the August sun descend behind Druim Fada. The mountain cast its shadow on the waters of the loch and made it suddenly black and menacing. Overcome by loneliness and aching with grief, she threw herself face down in the heather and wept. After a time, exhausted by her crying, she drifted off into a dreamless slumber.

She must have been asleep for some time because the daylight had almost gone when she awoke, shivering in the evening breeze.

'Mor . . . ag, Mor . . . ag!'

She looked up, startled by the shouting, and saw a familiar figure striding towards her across the heather.

'Thank God I've found you,' gasped Gordon as he sank to the ground beside her. 'I went up to the hospital, looking for you . . . I thought you might need . . . well . . . a shoulder to cry on. When they told me you hadn't returned since the funeral, I wondered where you could have got to.'

He was breathing heavily, not merely from his exertions. When he had found that she was missing, he had feared for her safety . . . people did strange things when they were shocked and grieving.

'I just needed to be alone for a while,' she told him. 'I should have told someone where I was going . . . forgive me.'

'I don't know why I thought of this place,' he said, brushing aside her apology.' I remembered you once saying that when you were homesick, this was the view which made you feel nearest to home.'

He stretched out beside her and for a time they hardly spoke. There seemed to be no need for words. Then, unable to look at her, he summoned up the courage to ask: 'You loved him, didn't you?'

'Yes,' she admitted to herself.

'He was my friend,' Gordon said, and before she could respond he went on, 'Oh not just over the last few months. We go back further than that. The war you know. I was there when he was wounded. I attended to him when they brought him in . . . My God, what a mess!'

He was trembling as the memories flooded back. She took his hand; the comforter suddenly, no longer the comforted.

'Tell me about Magnus,' she whispered.

'He was a sergeant in the same Company in which I was the MO. We were stationed on the Belgian border at the time. Magnus and I had become pretty friendly, coming as we both did from Inverlinnhe. Anyway, Magnus was with a night patrol which got itself caught up in an enemy ambush. The officer was wounded, which left Magnus in charge and he decided that they must make a run for it, or be taken prisoner. The officer couldn't walk, so they did what they could to patch up his wounds and then Magnus got the men to heave him onto his shoulders. They ran hell for leather, right through the enemy lines. There was a little firing, but the enemy snipers must have lost sight of them because it soon stopped. It must have been ten or fifteen minutes later when they dropped down into one of our own trenches.

It was I who examined them, on arrival. The officer was dead and Magnus had taken several bullets in his back. It seemed that the officer's body had shielded his spine, otherwise he would have been a goner too.'

'I saw the scars,' she said. 'He wouldn't talk about them.'

'He might have made a full recovery if it hadn't been for the gas attack which caught us before we could evacuate the dressing station.'

She shivered at the horror of the scene his description had conjured up.

'I always felt there must be a good reason for his alcoholism,' she murmured. 'He was too strong willed to allow himself to become addicted without good cause.'

Gordon regarded her with interest. She never ceased to surprise him. Few women would sympathise with a man who took to drinking as heavily as Magnus had done. Far from shunning him on that account, Morag had not only accepted his affliction but had actually helped him, according to Magnus himself, on more than one occasion.

'My own life has been clouded by similar circumstances,' she explained. 'My father still finds it difficult to face the day without a couple of whiskies inside him. He was the superintendent of a Field Hospital in Flanders . . .'

They both fell silent.

Out on the loch the surface was absolutely still, the waters dark in the shadow of the Ardgour Mountains. Behind the blackened hills, the sun had begun to set in a triumphant burst of red and orange. The rain which had fallen earlier in the day, had left the air fresh and sweet with the scent of heather and damp bracken.

Morag breathed in deeply and as she did so a tiny breath of warm wind brushed her hair.

'Do you believe in ghosts?' she asked him.

As though reading her thoughts, Gordon replied, 'If Magnus is out there, you can be sure he will be happy.'

'His was such a restless spirit,' she mused, 'always tackling a dozen problems at once. It was as though he knew there was not enough time in which to get everything finished.'

Gordon nodded, remembering their many heated discussions in the Long John.

'He was really a poet,' she said. 'Did you know that?'

'No.' He regarded her with some concern. She was beginning to get morbid. Perhaps it was time to go.

'He was so busy writing about one crusade of his after another that he never stopped to say what was really in his heart. It was only in the last few weeks, following his illness, that he began to put down his innermost thoughts.'

'Was his poetry any good?' Gordon asked.

'I'm afraid I'm no judge,' she replied, 'I liked what I saw.'

She shivered as the breeze blew a little more strongly.

'Come on,' he said, 'it's time we were getting back. Inglis will be sending out a search party.'

She started, wondering why he had introduced Adam's name. Then realising that he had meant no more than that they would be missed and feared lost, she gave him her hand and he pulled her to her feet.

It was nearly dark as they made their way down towards the little bridge over the burn.

The chambers of Brown, Laurie and Spalding, Solicitors, were two doors down from the Borough Council Offices, just off the High Street.

Morag climbed the narrow stairs to the second floor where, at the invitation of the rather prim, bird-like receptionist, she sank gratefully on to an antiquated horsehair sofa. The woman was dressed severely in a tailored suit of navy blue serge, her hair was pulled back tightly into an unattractive bun and her spectacles secured by a light chain.

After a few moments of sorting fussily amongst the piles of bulging folders, each neatly labelled and tied with the ubiquitous pink tape of the legal profession, she selected one and came from behind the massive mahogany counter, inviting Morag to follow her.

'If you will kindly wait in here with the other beneficiaries, Mr Laurie will be with you shortly.'

With that she closed the door, leaving Morag to find a seat amongst the assembled company, each of whom, apart from the familiar figure of Charlie the taxi driver, wore deepest mourning. Morag recognised immediately the grim trio who had attended Magnus's funeral. She half smiled, and was rewarded with three hostile glares. Charlie, however, leaped to his feet and offered her the last remaining seat. She accepted gratefully.

'This is a sad occasion, Dr Beaton, and no mistake,' said her friend. 'I can't tell you how much I've missed seeing the gentleman home these past few weeks. And then, to go like this . . . just when he seemed to be recovering so well . . .'

She nodded, still unable to speak of Magnus's death.

There was a sound, something between a sniff and a snort, from the over-large elderly woman in black bombazine who sat upright in her straight-backed chair, hands folded firmly over her immense leather handbag as though to guard it with her life.

Morag smiled and nodded. Much to her annoyance she found herself reddening with embarrassment when the trio deliberately ignored her. Then she stared at them quite openly. If the older woman was Magnus's mother, who were the others . . . his sisters perhaps? He had never mentioned any siblings. The women had been strangely aloof at the funeral and clearly had no intention of striking up an acquaintance now.

'Good morning, ladies and gentlemen.' William Laurie advanced into the room, rubbing his hands together to show his satisfaction that they had all appeared on time.

The portly little man was followed by his receptionist, who carried in her hand another of those files which Morag had noticed on her arrival. This one, however, was very slim. When the woman placed it on the desk in front of her employer and released the tie, it was seen to contain only one sheet of flimsy paper.

'As you can see,' Laurie said, his tone light in a feeble attempt to relieve the tension which had built up within the room, 'this is not going to take very long.'

His nervous chuckle dissipated into a stony silence.

Glancing in Morag's direction apologetically, he began to read from the document.

' "This is the last will and testament of me, Magnus Tourmaddy Glendenning, of number one Canal Row, Feanagrogan by Inverlinnhe." '

There was another snort of disapproval from the elder of the women; clearly some aspect of Magnus's home address annoyed her.

' "To my friend Charles Edward Stewart, driver for the Inverlinnhe Taxi and Hackney Carriage Company, I leave the sum of £500 for the purchase of his own taxicab . . ." '

Morag regarded Charlie with fresh interest. Could that really be his name? she wondered. He deserved his good fortune . . . Charlie had looked after Magnus like a nanny throughout the time she had known them both.

' "To my mother, Mrs Fiona Buller, née Glendenning, and to my two half-sisters, Alice Buller and Marjorie Buller . . .' Mr Laurie shuffled uncomfortably on his seat and glanced nervously at the three poker-faced women in black ' ". . . I bequeath my heartfelt thanks for leaving me to my own devices for the past twelve years, since my return from Flanders." '

The two younger females glanced at each other in dismay, whilst their mother appeared about to explode. Ignoring them, Laurie continued, ' "The remainder of my estate, including my property in Canal Row, Inverlinnhe, I leave to my fiancée, Dr Morag Beaton, of the West Highland Hospital, Inverlinnhe, and Tigh na Broch, Eisdalsa, by Oban, Argyll." '

While the other women gasped out their indignation, Morag sat, stunned. She only barely registered the significance of the solicitor's final comment.

' "Signed this twelfth day of September 1932, in the presence of Angus Beaton MD, ChB, and Emily Agnes McLean, housekeeper, both of The Old Manse, Alasgaig, by Bunessan, Isle of Mull." '

Magnus had dictated his last will and testament on his death bed. That must have been why he had asked her to leave him alone with Angus, prior to the operation . . .

Mrs Buller was speaking loudly. Her harsh tones penetrated Morag's thoughts.

'How dare he . . . the ungrateful boy!' she demanded. Then

she advanced across the room towards Morag, shaking her umbrella.

'As for you, you hussy . . . I suppose you think you are going to get away with this? Well, let me tell you, I shall contest this will, even with the last breath in my body!'

That would be rather pointless, thought Charlie, as he half rose to the defence of *his* young lady.

'Let us view this dispassionately, if we can, madam.' Mr Laurie waved the irate woman to her seat.

When she had resettled herself to his satisfaction, he continued. 'Mr Glendenning has been my client since he first took up his post with the *Gazette* some ten years ago. I have acted for him on many occasions but, so far as I am aware, he has never produced any form of Will other than this which I hold in my hand. The document is quite legal and, although composed when *in extremis*, I have it on the best authority that Mr Glendenning was entirely rational and in his right mind when he dictated its contents. I can see no grounds for anyone to dispute that these are the last wishes of my client.

Now, ladies, if you will excuse us, I have matters to discuss with Miss Beaton and Mr Stewart.'

The solicitor ushered the three protesting women outside as though clearing a farmyard of a flock of cackling hens. Having delivered them safely into the hands of his female assistant, he returned, smiling.

'I can't tell you what immense pleasure it gave me to do that,' he exclaimed, rubbing his hands together in satisfaction. 'That woman has given Mr Glendenning so much pain in years past, you wouldn't believe it. Why, she fought a battle in the courts with him over the ownership of his great-grandfather's house, which continued even after the war had begun . . . she was sending him solicitor's letters in the trenches.'

'But I don't understand,' responded Morag. 'Surely Magnus's mother had every right to her late husband's property?'

'Not at all,' Laurie replied. 'By the terms of her former husband's will, on her remarriage she gave up all claim to his estate, in favour of her son.'

'I feel very uncomfortable about accepting this bequest,' Morag said. It had been a long and tedious week since Magnus was buried, and she felt exhausted. For two pins, she thought, I could walk out of here and not look back . . .

'No need to feel badly, miss,' Charlie assured her. 'Mr Glendenning was aye fond of you, that I can tell you. He would sit there in the back of my cab, goin' on about ye all the time . . . I'd say that he decided to leave you his house just as soon as he suspected his time might be up. He didn't make up his mind about that at the last minute even if he drew up the Will then.'

She smiled at him gratefully.

'It will be a while yet before I can arrange probate,' Laurie explained. 'Neither of you will receive any money for some time. If, however, you wish to proceed with the sale of the house, Miss Beaton, there is nothing to stop us from beginning the arrangements right away. It takes a considerable time to reach the point where property can be transferred . . .'

'I don't understand.' Morag looked quite bewildered now. 'If I have inherited Magnus's cottage, surely I am entitled to occupy it if I wish?'

'Of course,' he blustered in response. 'It was just that . . . well . . . in view of the condition of the property, I assumed you would not want to keep it?'

'I'm afraid that you presumed wrong then,' she replied.

'But I already have a firm offer for the house,' he protested, 'One which you would be ill advised to reject.'

'Am I to understand that before disclosing the contents of my fiancé's will to the beneficiaries, you had already entered into negotiations with a third party?' Morag was surprised and irritated. 'Surely that is somewhat dubious behaviour for one of your standing, Mr Laurie?'

Without giving him an opportunity to explain further, she rose to leave. Gathering her bag and umbrella, she turned to Charlie.

'Are you available to take me back to the hospital, Mr Stewart?' she asked, ignoring the fact that Laurie had come around the desk to try to detain her.

Charlie leaped to his feet.

'Of course, miss,' he responded directly.

'Then I shall say good day to you, Mr Laurie,' she said, politely but firmly. 'I shall look forward to hearing from you in due course.' As she reached the door she turned, adding, 'Have no doubt that I intend to live in Mr Glendenning's house, since that was his wish, and that I shall use the money in the bequest to help pay for whatever improvements are necessary.'

The solicitor, flustered because things had not gone at all as he had planned, scuttled after her, reaching the door just in time. In a conciliatory manner, he offered her his hand. There was no point in antagonising a potential client. She took it, condescendingly, with the tips of her gloved fingers.

As Morag and Charlie descended to the ground floor, they heard the lower door slam shut and the sound of someone climbing up towards them. When Charlie stood aside to allow the gentleman to pass, Morag was somewhat startled to recognise Graham Fraser, Chairman of the Hospital Board.

'Ah, I hoped I might catch you before you left, Dr Beaton,' he gasped.

Morag thought absently, He should lose a little weight . . . climbing stairs quickly does not seem to agree with him!

Without waiting for any response from her, Fraser continued, 'There is a matter I would like to discuss with you. Look . . .' He hesitated, recognising belatedly that she and Charlie were together. 'If your friend will forgive us, I would like to take you to tea.'

Charlie knew when he was not wanted.

'I'll be on my way then, miss,' he said, quickly. 'Just give a ring – any time you need a cab.'

Morag, more than a little put out by Fraser's assumption that she was free to go with him, stayed the taxi driver's departure for a moment.

'I wanted to congratulate you, Charlie, on your good fortune. I know how highly Mr Glendenning thought of you . . .' She smiled, near to tears again, and held out her hand.

He shook it as though it were made of fine china.

'Thank you, miss,' came his reply. 'Mr Glendenning was a very fine gentleman. There's those in this town will rue the loss of such a good man.' The remark seemed to be directed at Graham Fraser.

Charlie replaced his driver's cap and saluted them both before slowly descending the stairs.

'I fear that I intruded,' Fraser began, in a weak attempt at apology.

'Mr Stewart and I did have matters to discuss, yes,' Morag replied primly. 'I am sure there will another opportunity, soon.'

Having put Fraser in his place, she was prepared to go along with his suggestion of tea, partly because she was parched from the long wait in Laurie's stuffy room, and partly because she was intrigued to know what the man wanted, and how it was that he had known she was going to be there.

The lounge of the Prince's Hotel was a far cry from Maggie McKay's in the High Street. Morag's feet sank into the thick pile of the carpet, and the overall hush was almost tangible.

Chandeliers hung from a high, vaulted ceiling, richly decorated with the rag-and-stick work so highly thought of in the previous century. Wallpaper and furnishing fabrics were all in the red Royal Stewart tartan. Scattered upon low tables about the room, brass oil lamps, wired for electricity, were intended to give a hint of an earlier age.

The walls were hung with heavily framed portraits of unprepossessing burghers, pictures of gun dogs with realistically bloodied dead hares hanging from their jaws, and a pair of glass cases, one of which held an enormous stuffed salmon, while in the other a fearsome-looking pike lurked in a dusty-looking, dried up reed bed.

To Morag's eyes it was all both vulgar and tasteless. She could just imagine Magnus voicing his opinion on the subject, and found herself smiling, unwittingly.

Fraser busied himself with ordering tea, and until the tray arrived made trivial conversation about the weather, the disastrous tourist season and the splendid work of the town's medical officers in their fight against the scourge of typhoid fever.

'I have never found an opportunity to congratulate you on your determination to get the isolation unit opened,' he told her. 'That really was a most splendid effort. I'm glad to say that although, naturally, it will be necessary to place the wards in mothballs now that the crisis is past, we shall leave it in a state of readiness in case a similar problem should arise in the future.'

'I think that is very wise,' Morag replied, coolly. 'Unless something is done soon about the drainage and the water supply to the poorer areas of the town, another outbreak of infectious disease is almost inevitable.'

Fraser handed her a cup and fussed over the plate of rich-looking pastries. She took the tea gratefully, but refused a cake.

He stirred his tea thoughtfully for a few moments before replying to her remark.

'You are referring, of course, to the housing in the Lochy valley, alongside the canal. Well, the surveyors inform me that the only solution to that problem is to tear down the whole lot and rebuild on the site using modern housing techniques.' He sipped his tea slowly, regarding her warily over the rim of his cup.

'Alternatively, drains and water could be run to the houses and structural repairs could be made,' Morag suggested. 'I believe that the cost would not be so very great, and certainly the existing stone cottages are sturdier than any of the modern housing built by the Corporation.' She was glad now of those tedious hours during which she had been forced to listen, while Adam and Magnus had argued out the pros and cons of redevelopment.

She had taken the councillor by surprise. Fraser had not expected quite such a well-informed assessment of the situation. He rapidly decided to come at the problem from another angle.

'Mr Laurie tells me that you are a very fortunate young lady,' he said, disarmingly. 'I understand you have come into a considerable legacy.'

'Mr Laurie should be more careful with his clients' confidentiality,' she replied, angrily. So Fraser had been appraised in advance of the contents of Magnus's will. She might have known it!

She suspected that in his eagerness to buy number one Canal Row, Fraser had put pressure on Laurie to reveal the name of the new owner of Magnus's house and had rushed along to Laurie's chambers expecting to encounter her, apparently by chance. No doubt he was supposed to enter the office just as she was leaving, and have the information about her good fortune related to him in her presence, by Laurie.

Fraser had no option now but to come clean. He leaned towards her in an ingratiating manner, even to the extent of placing his hand upon hers as it lay upon the table. She withdrew it, hastily.

'You can hardly be considering living in the place which has been left to you,' he said. 'It is not exactly the kind of house that you are used to.'

'You must understand that I was brought up in a quarrying community,' Morag replied, haughtily. 'I have visited and indeed occupied several houses of the kind. Mr Glendenning's is an old building, certainly, but it is constructed of local stone and has lasted the best part of a hundred and fifty years. I see no reason to demolish it now. In fact, I will go so far as to say that I intend to use what money has been left to me for the purpose of restoring the cottage and, if the Council will not make the provision, upgrading the septic tank and laying in a clean water supply myself!'

To say that Graham Fraser was stunned would be to underestimate the matter. He must have anticipated opposition of some kind, if only of a sentimental nature . . . a desire, perhaps, to keep the house as a memorial to Magnus. He had not expected so reasoned an argument as Morag had put forth. It was time to lay his cards on the table.

'You may not realise,' he began, 'that apart from Glendenning's house, all the cottages in Canal Row are my property.'

'Judging from their outward appearance, that is hardly something to be proud of,' she responded.

'I bought them with the intention of pulling down the entire row and redeveloping the site,' he continued. 'There seemed no point in spending money to renovate houses due for demolition.'

'Meanwhile, their occupants must live in squalor.' Morag was getting angry. 'Well, at least you have fewer tenants to rehouse now. I understand there were four deaths from typhoid in your houses in Canal Row!'

He paled, but remained calm.

'There has been no proof that the water supply to the houses had anything to do with the epidemic,' he stated, firmly.

'I think if you read the report of the County pathologist, you will find you are mistaken,' she replied, coldly.

He coloured now. His secretary had placed a number of reports on his desk earlier in the week . . . none of which he had found time to study. No doubt Morag was right.

'Look, Miss Beaton . . .' His tone was almost ingratiating. Morag recoiled from the honeyed voice he now adopted.

'. . . I need to buy the Glendenning property. I am willing to make you a handsome offer for the house, and will even go so far as to lease you, at a peppercorn rent, a plot of ground in a pleasant area of the town on which you can build another house. Now, what do you say to that?'

He beamed at her, certain that his final offer was irresistible.

'I thought I had made myself clear, Mr Fraser,' she answered him. 'I have no intention of selling the cottage until I have investigated the situation fully. It was Mr Glendenning's wish that his great-grandfather's house, built I understand with his own hands, should be preserved. If I find that I can afford to carry out the necessary work, I shall comply with his wishes.' She noted the disappointment which Fraser made no attempt to hide. Striking while the enemy was at a low ebb, she added, 'Magnus also considered that the whole row of cottages was worthy of restoration, as a monument to those men who constructed and operated the Caledonian Canal in the early days. It might be considered a generous gesture towards the town, were you to restore the houses you already own.'

She decided to leave him with that thought. Gathering her things, she stood up.

'Now, if you will excuse me, I must be getting back to the hospital. Thank you for the tea.'

Allowing him no chance to delay her further, she swept out of the lounge, nearly colliding with the waiter who had reappeared, ready to replenish their teapot. At her hurried, 'Excuse me!' he stood aside and stared after her in surprise.

# Chapter 15

Morag drew up outside the house in Canal Row and switched off the engine of her new, dark green Morris 8. To avoid the puddles, she stepped down cautiously on to the muddy track and crossed the wide grass verge which separated number one from the waterside.

A confused jungle of weeds dominated what must once have been a carefully planted cottage garden. One overgrown bush of autumn-flowering Viburnum blocked her path. As she thrust aside the branches, its late blooms filled the air with their heady scent. Torn between excitement and apprehension, she stepped up to the porch and searched in her pocket for the key Mr Laurie had given her.

The lawyers had taken fully three months to obtain probate for Magnus's will.

They had had considerable difficulty in persuading Mrs Buller and her daughters that there was no case to answer on the grounds of Magnus's diminished responsibility, and that his mother and half-sisters would simply be throwing good money after bad were they to dispute the matter in the courts. Morag was well aware that she had accumulated a wealth of bad feeling in the Bullers' quarter of the town, and felt helpless to do anything about it.

Apart from the house in Canal Row, her legacy had amounted to a sum in excess of a thousand pounds – more than enough, she believed, to cover the cost of refurbishment, and the replacement of substandard sanitation. She had felt that the expenditure of a little over one hundred pounds on a new car was justified, since this would enable her to live outside the hospital while still being available in an emergency. There had been nothing in her contract to suggest that she must live in during off-duty periods.

The question of a decent water supply to the cottages in Canal Row had yet to be resolved. Ever since the typhoid epidemic, the authorities had continued to carry water to the houses in the area in large containers. It was a costly business, and there had been some agitation within Council circles about doing something more permanent, as a matter of urgency. Graham Fraser, still clinging to the belief that he could force Morag to give up her property if the prospect of ownership were made as uninviting as possible, had tried every trick in the book to stall any decision on the extension of the public water supply to the houses by the canal, but even *he* was running out of reasons to delay action.

Morag had nothing to lose by refusing Fraser's various proposals. She still had her accommodation at the hospital, and although determined to occupy the property at some time, was in no hurry to move into her new home.

The door was stuck. She had to shove hard with her shoulder to force it open. The house smelled a little musty, and she noted patches of damp on the ceiling in the entrance lobby.

There was scarcely any light in the living room. Fumbling with unfamiliar objects, and stumbling blindly over the heavy pieces of furniture, she edged her way to the window and pulled aside the curtains, allowing in what little daylight remained on this gloomy November day.

The room was much as she remembered it from her first visit, except that the books had been returned to their places on the shelves, and the papers which had formerly littered every flat surface were stacked in a tidy pile on the open roll-top desk which occupied much of one wall.

She cast a glance over the document on the top of the pile, noting the date. It was a rough draft of one of Magnus's last articles to appear in the *Gazette*. He must have been preparing it only hours before he fell ill.

She fingered the paper, and was suddenly acutely aware of his closeness.

Replacing it on the pile, she reached for a small leather-bound dictionary which, from its well-used appearance, must have been his constant companion.

It fell open at the flyleaf.

*To my son Magnus on his sixth birthday, 26 January 1902*
*Robert Glendenning*

Morag felt the breath catch in her throat. She had not even known the date of his birthday . . .

They had never spoken of their respective ages. She was surprised to discover that he had been only eight years older than herself . . . why had she always assumed he was so much nearer her father's generation than her own?

The war of course . . . that was it. Those years in the trenches had forced all manner of men into the same mould, creating relationships which would have been impossible in former times and other circumstances. That was why he had numbered amongst his closest friends both Charlie Stewart and Gordon McDonald, two people from widely different backgrounds who, prior to 1914, would have had nothing in common.

A photograph caught her eye. She picked it up and carried it to the window to examine it more closely. It was of a group of soldiers in shirt-sleeves and braces, taken during their off-duty activities. They were smiling into the camera. A very young Magnus, he could have been no more than eighteen or nineteen at the time, had been caught in the act of shaving. The figure holding the mirror seemed familiar also . . . she stared at it for several moments, before deciding that it was indeed Gordon who held up the shiny piece of steel for Magnus to see what he was doing. To one side of the group, a soldier wearing the kilt appeared to be playing a tune on his pipes . . . it was a Scottish regiment, then . . . while another was making a mocking attempt at dancing a highland fling. She looked closely at this figure and thought she recognised him. Smiling in an oddly understanding manner, she set the photograph back on the shelf and made her way into the tiny kitchen.

From the condition of the scullery, it was quite clear that someone had been into the house since Magnus's departure on the day when he was whisked into hospital.

She had half expected to see the remains of food rotting on the pantry shelves, and had even been prepared for a heap of dirty dishes such as that which had greeted her on that earlier occasion. She was pleasantly surprised to find none of these things.

Every cup, saucer and plate had been washed and returned to its place on the old pine dresser in the living room. The pans arranged around the iron range were burnished, reflecting what light there was.

Steeling herself to enter the privacy of Magnus's bedroom, she found that here also a kindly hand had been at work, for the bedcovers were straight. The linen, freshly washed and ironed, was stacked in tidy piles upon the patchwork counterpane while, inside an over-large Victorian wardrobe, Magnus's shirts and suits were arranged in a neat row.

As her hand wandered idly over a collection of faded family photographs arranged upon the mahogany tallboy, Morag heard a slight noise from the living-room and went to find out who the intruder might be.

She found there a stout lady who could have been any age, with the clear, newly scrubbed complexion of many highland women, her cheeks flushed pink and the corners of her eyes screwed up from a lifetime of exposure to the blustery north-east wind. Her full bosom was exaggerated by a flower-patterned overall, which was pulled in tightly at the waist and only partially concealed a skirt of black woollen material which fell to just above her ankles, exposing a pair of workman's heavy leather boots.

'You'll be Miss Morag,' the newcomer said firmly. Hands placed on hips, she viewed the doctor critically from every angle.

'He said you were beautiful,' she remarked, then sniffed as though in disagreement with what she had been told.

'I am sorry to disappoint you,' replied Morag. 'Mr Glendenning was prone to slight exaggeration on occasion.'

She took no offence . . . the woman was clearly another of Magnus's curious collection of acquaintances.

'Always looked after the gentleman, I did,' she explained, 'ever since he come back from the war. McWorter was against it . . . Mr Glendenning being a bit strange, and all . . . but I says to him, I says, "He's a poor soul with no woman to care for him and a man needs a bit of cosseting." Came in every day after he'd gone to work, so I did . . . cleaned the house and did his washing. He said he would do his own cooking, though a sorry mess he made of things when he tried! Most times he ate out in the town . . .'

Suddenly overcome by the full impact of Magnus's death and how it had affected her own life, the woman slumped down upon the sofa and buried her head in her hands. To Morag's distress, her visitor began to weep, sobbing and wailing as though her heart would break.

After a few moments she stopped crying as suddenly as she had begun. Wiping her eyes on her pinafore, she murmured, 'Such a kind gentleman he was. He used to pay me five shillings every week on the dot of a Friday evening. It's been hard to manage since he's been gone.'

Her voice trailed off as she regarded Morag sorrowfully. She had become genuinely fond of Magnus Glendenning, even if she hadn't understood half of what he said.

'Well, Mrs . . . McWorter?' Morag hesitated.

'Ellen. You c'n call me Nellie if you want . . . just like he used to,' the woman suggested, in hopeful anticipation.

'It must have been you who came in and cleaned the house after . . .' Even now Morag found it difficult to speak of that terrible time, and the miserable weeks which had followed Magnus's death.

Mrs McWorter nodded.

'When Dr McDonald told me that Mr Glendenning was in the hospital, I popped in to see there was nothing left lying about to go bad, you understand. Once I had finished, the doctor locked up the house and took away the key.

'When Mr Glendenning died . . .' she gulped back further tears '. . . that Mr Laurie, the solicitor, came down here to see me . . . asked me to be a witness as he went through the personal things, in case there was anything valuable . . .' Her voice trailed off and an embarrassed silence followed.

'You have made a splendid job of everything,' Morag assured her. 'Thank you.'

'It was a pleasure, ma'am,' she answered, again near to tears.

'Nellie . . .' After a few moments' deliberation, Morag made up her mind. 'I suppose you wouldn't care to continue keeping house for me, once I come to live here permanently? I will still be working at the hospital, of course, so there will be very little time for me to do my own housework.'

When Mrs McWorter did not respond immediately, Morag enquired, 'Do you live far away?'

'At number six, miss, just along the lane,' came the hesitant reply. Then, 'The man from the Council says we have to move out soon . . . they're going to pull the houses down.'

'They'll not be pulling down this one, I can assure you,' Morag declared. 'And if they offer you one of the new houses they are going to build, you will still be very near. Will you work for me?'

'Yes, miss,' she blurted out, after a moment's hesitation.

Morag was not too sure what she was getting herself into. The house was undoubtedly clean and tidy now, so presumably Nellie was reasonably able to cope with normal household duties. Nevertheless, Magnus's house had not seemed so well cared for on that previous occasion. Why was that? Morag wondered.

As though reading her thoughts, Nellie continued, 'I don't know what McWorter will say. He used to get very upset when Mr Glendenning was having one of his drinking spells. He got a bit rowdy you see, ma'am . . . threw things about and that. McWorter always made me stay away until the gentleman was back to normal.'

'Well, Mrs McWorter . . . Nellie . . . I can assure you that *I* do not indulge in drunken orgies, so your husband need have no apprehensions on that score.' Before the woman could protest that she had not meant to imply anything of the kind, Morag went on, 'If you would like to carry on as before, I shall be happy to give you the same wages as Mr Glendenning paid. Five shillings a week, I think you said?'

'Five shillings will do nicely, ma'am, thank you,' Nellie replied hurriedly, lest Morag should change her mind.

'For some time there will be workmen in here, repairing the roof and replacing some of the windows,' Morag explained. 'There will also be some plumbing work done during the next fortnight, so shall we say that you will begin in my employment two weeks from now?'

Mrs McWorter looked disappointed. The few shillings which she contributed to the family coffers from her domestic work, made the difference between poverty and a decent living wage for her family. She had hoped to begin working straight away.

Morag was not insensitive to the problems of the working classes, who lived from hand to mouth with nothing put by to tide them over in difficult times. She felt it would be imprudent for her, however, to begin their working partnership by paying the woman when there was nothing for her to do. What, she wondered, could she do to help without offending Nellie by offering her charity?

As Mrs McWorter turned to go, Morag called her back.

'Mr Glendenning's clothes . . . I notice that you have washed and ironed everything very carefully. Thank you. Unfortunately I have no use for them as you may well imagine . . . would they fit Mr McWorter, do you think?'

The woman's eyes lit up.

'Why, yes, miss, I'm sure that they would,' she replied. 'A very kindly thought if I might say so.'

There was tinker blood in Ellen McWorter. She knew any number of ways to make money from discarded clothing. What was in Magnus's wardrobe would more than cover the loss of wages she had suffered these past few weeks.

'Well, why don't you take the things now?' Morag suggested, generously. 'Take the bedding too, if you can make use of it.'

She would be buying new linen and blankets for her own use, there was no point in keeping what was in the house. 'It will only get dirty again if we leave it here while the workmen are in,' she added, making it seem as though it was Mrs McWorter who would be doing *her* the favour.

Nellie needed no second bidding. Hastily she gathered up the things and tied them into a bundle. With a promise to return in two weeks, she departed.

Left to her own devices, Morag collected the photographs and various ornaments which, no doubt, had belonged to an earlier generation of Glendennings. Magnus may not have wanted his mother to benefit from his own endeavours, but that did not mean that family heirlooms were necessarily his to dispose of. She found an old wicker hamper and wrapped each item carefully in newspaper, before laying it inside.

There were one or two things which were clearly of Magnus's own choosing. A delightful water-colour attracted her attention. It was a landscape of the ruined abbey of Iona . . . a mystical piece, reminiscent of one of the English School of Impressionists, but vibrant colour distinguished it from some of those more delicate images of an earlier decade. She turned the painting over to find that the label confirmed her suspicions: FCB Cadell, 1920. The dealer's name, Alexander Reid, confirmed that the picture was by one of the Glasgow Boys, and the date suggested it had either been purchased by Magnus himself, or given to him by a friend. She felt no remorse over deciding to keep it for herself, together with a chiming clock which bore on the dial an inscription showing it to have been a gift from the staff of the Glasgow newspaper for which Magnus had worked before returning to Inverlinnhe.

She knew from what he had told her that many of the books in the house had belonged to his father and that they had been left specifically to Magnus. In any case, Morag suspected that Mrs Buller would have very little interest in literature and, given the opportunity, would most likely confine the books to the bonfire. She decided to retain them all.

Reaching for the first of the family photographs, she began to wrap it . . .

Her hand finally came to rest once again upon the photograph of the soldiers, taken at the Front. After a few moments' contemplation, she decided to return it to the shelf above the desk . . . this one she would keep.

With the last of the items safely disposed of, Morag sat down at the desk and selected a piece of paper on which to write.

> 1, Canal Row
> Feanagrogan
> by Inverlinnhe
> 8 November 1932

*Dear Mrs Buller,*

*I very much regret that we parted on unfriendly terms at our first meeting. Magnus had made no mention to me of his Will, or indeed of his family either, and I was as surprised as you and your daughters were to hear of my good fortune.*

*I hope that it will please you to know that I intend to use the bulk of the money to restore his great-grandfather's house, just as Magnus would have wanted . . . indeed it is my conviction that he left the cottage to me, knowing that I would fulfil his wishes in the matter.*

*I shall place this hamper, containing items of family interest, in the care of Mr Laurie, in the hope that you will find some comfort in having them in your charge. Should there be pieces of furniture in the house which you value particularly, I will be pleased to consider any reasonable request for their transfer to your safekeeping.*

*Yours sincerely,*
*Morag Beaton*

She sealed the envelope and wrote Mrs Buller's name on it, then dropping it into the hamper, she closed the lid and adjusted the straps.

At barely three o'clock in the afternoon, it was already nearly dusk. The wicker basket was heavy, and its bulk prevented Morag from seeing clearly where she was stepping. She collided first of all with the door-post, and then nearly fell over an iron boot-scraper which stood to one side of the garden path. Finally, she stumbled on the crumbling flagstones and in saving the contents of the hamper from certain destruction, fell heavily on to both knees.

As she hauled herself up by placing her full weight on the wicker basket which had miraculously survived the jolting, the expletives which issued from Morag's lips were less than ladylike.

She heard the click of the catch on the gate and looked up to find a tall young man advancing towards her down the garden path. Chuckling at her curses, the stranger took the hamper from her and swung it up on to his shoulder.

'Oh, do be careful,' she cried, 'it has china and glass . .'

'Let's hope it survived the battering you have just given it then,' he laughed. 'Is that your car?'

She followed his swiftly moving figure as far as her vehicle and opened the boot to allow him to place the hamper inside. He closed it with a decisive gesture and stood back, rubbing the circulation back into his arms.

'Roomy little job, for a cheap runabout,' he remarked, condescendingly.

Even after a whole year, that voice was unmistakable. It was as a result of their altercation in the High Street that she had first met Magnus Glendenning. She supposed she should be grateful to this arrogant stranger but felt only extreme irritation.

'You'll be Morag Beaton,' he said, casually, opening the car door for her to step in.

She eyed him critically. Who was this brash young man, five years her junior at least, to be so impertinent as to call her by her Christian name when they had not even been introduced?

Over his shoulder she glimpsed the shiny grey roadster which she remembered as a murderous weapon in his hands.

She replied, coldly.

'You have the advantage of me, sir?'

'Fraser . . . Edward Fraser . . . Teddy to my friends.'

He thrust out a hand.

As she took it, Morag thought it unlikely he would ever be 'Teddy' to her.

So this was Graham Fraser's son. That would explain Magnus's outburst in the café, when she was repairing the damage done by this same young man's dangerous driving. What was he doing down here by the canal ... hardly his usual stamping ground, surely?

'Moving house?' he asked, casually.

'Not at all,' she replied. 'Quite the opposite in fact. I shall be moving in, in a couple of weeks ... once the builders have finished what they have to do.'

'You're not wasting money fixing the place up, surely?' He seemed genuinely surprised by her reply. 'These houses are all due for demolition.'

'Not this one.' Morag indicated her own cottage. 'It has just come into my possession, and I have every intention of living in it.'

'But ...' He tailed off, uncertain what to say. He had been instructed to tell his father's tenants that the site was to be cleared before the beginning of April, in order that the new building work might take place during the summer months. What Graham Fraser had failed to mention, it seemed, was that there was one house in the row which was not his to demolish.

'I've just been visiting all the tenants with proposals for alternative accommodation,' he insisted. 'Yours was the last house on the list. Most people have agreed to move out at the end of the year ...' He realised, too late, that this was the wrong approach in the circumstances.

'I am afraid that your instructions should not have included number one,' she replied. 'The house was privately owned by Magnus Glendenning. It is now mine.'

Morag showed no sign of the anguish she was feeling. She had known of Fraser's intentions, of course, but had hoped that he might have had second thoughts by now. 'The rest of the cottages may be pulled down,' she declared, 'but mine stays!'

'Oh, no, that can't be right,' Teddy Fraser persisted, adamantly. 'The plan is to demolish all of these buildings and to move the building line back from the canal bank by fifty yards, in order to make room for the road.'

'What road?' she exclaimed. Nothing had been mentioned about a new road.

'It will be necessary to make a proper metalled road to carry the lorries,' he explained.

'Lorries . . . what lorries?'

'The vehicles going to and from the new works, further on along the canal bank. See . . . here. I thought everyone knew about my father's intention to expand his aluminium smelting business?'

'No,' she barked at him, thoroughly angered by now, 'no one mentioned anything of the kind.'

What was that solicitor, Laurie, up to? Had he known about the new smelting works planned for construction almost in her garden? It was true that she had been preoccupied of late and had not read a copy of the *Gazette* since before Magnus's death, but surely Mr Laurie should have warned her of this additional threat to her newly acquired property?

'If you don't believe me, look at the plans. I have shown them to all the other . . . householders, this afternoon.'

Relieved that he had managed not to compound his error by calling her a tenant a second time, Teddy spread a large blueprint out over the bonnet of the Morris, holding on to the edges of the linen sheet to prevent the breeze from tearing it out of his hands. Morag, anxious to see the plans, obligingly took hold of one edge and struggled to understand what she was looking at.

'Here you are,' he showed her. 'This is the site of Canal Row. As you can see, the new road runs a few feet from the canal and by-passes the housing estate, running behind the rear gardens. The occupants of the houses will neither see nor hear the traffic passing.'

'Nor will they look out across the canal to the wooded valley on the further bank,' she murmured. 'Even their view of the Ben will be obstructed by the mounds of waste material generated by the smelting works.' She recalled the trip she had taken with Magnus when they had driven the length of Loch Linnhe, and along the coast of Lorn to Eisdalsa. Morag knew just what to expect from a new smelting works!

Leaving him to struggle with the unwieldy sheet, she turned to look again at her new home . . . Magnus's home.

The sun had all but set on the chilly autumnal scene. A ruddy glow suffused the whole countryside around, changing the mountains in the east into an artist's palette of purples, blues, oranges and reds, while to the west, the peaks of Ardnamurchan stood out black against the fiery sky. Canal Row, whose buildings had worn an air of dereliction in the harsher light of noonday, glowed pink, transformed suddenly into a row of fairy-tale cottages in a pantomime setting. As if on cue, a flock of wild geese flew in from the west, black spots moving against the darkening sky, and with a cacophonous babel of sound, settled for the night on the salt marshes at the eastern end of the loch.

'Look at it,' she demanded. 'Just look at it, and tell me that you will have no regrets about the destruction of this area?'

'You can't stand in the way of progress,' Teddy pointed out. 'Scenery doesn't put bread into the mouths of starving children.'

'Any more than it puts profit into the pockets of men like your father,' she retorted, sharply, 'but that is no reason to destroy our natural heritage so wantonly.'

She climbed into her car and started the engine. Winding down the side window, she said, 'If Graham Fraser wants me out of that house he will have to obtain a compulsory purchase order, and even if he manages to do that, I shall fight him every step of the way.'

Morag was still shaking with rage when she pulled up outside the offices of Brown, Laurie and Spalding, Solicitors, in the High Street.

As she struggled with the wicker hamper, she was relieved to be greeted by the familiar voice of Gordon McDonald.

'Morag!' he called. 'Here . . . wait a minute, I'll help you!'

She watched him dart between parked vehicles as he crossed over from the other pavement and came up beside her.

Lifting the heavy container easily, he demanded, 'Where to?'

'You could be sorry.' She smiled despite herself. 'I was taking it up to the solicitor's offices on the second floor.'

'OK,' he said, 'you lead the way, I'll follow.'

She climbed the stairs quickly, anxious to get her interview with Laurie over as soon as possible. At each turn she waited to see if Gordon was still following her, and then hurried on.

'This really is very good of you,' she said, when they reached the glass-panelled door to the solicitor's chambers. 'I don't know how I would have managed without your help.'

'Always ready to oblige, ma'am,' Gordon replied, as he edged past her and set the hamper down just inside the door. Red in the face from his exertions, he paused to catch his breath and mop the perspiration from his brow.

'I wondered if I might have a word with Mr Laurie, on a matter of some urgency?' Morag asked the receptionist.

'I'm sorry, Dr Beaton,' she replied, 'Mr Laurie is in court today and tomorrow. I can make an appointment for you on Thursday, if that is convenient?'

'No, I'm afraid that will not do,' said Morag, her frustration at not being able to vent her wrath on Laurie causing her to become annoyed once again. 'I shall be working on Thursday . . .'

As the two women discussed the earliest possible date for an appointment, Gordon lingered. If Morag were free for the next half-hour, he would take her to tea.

They had reached the door of the office when she remembered the hamper.

'Oh, yes,' she called out, as the receptionist was about to exit by the other door. 'There are some household items here, most probably family heirlooms, which I think should be passed on to Mrs Buller. Will you ask Mr Laurie to deal with them, please?'

Without waiting for a reply, she thrust her hand under Gordon's arm and, together, they descended to the ground floor.

Maggie McKay's was unusually full for a Wednesday afternoon in late November and the doctors were obliged to wait beside the counter until a table could be cleared for them.

Morag shivered despite the exceptionally mild afternoon and the stuffy atmosphere in the café. Was she ill? enquired Gordon.

'It's nothing, . . . reaction, I expect. I have just had some very disturbing news.'

They were ushered to a table which was tucked away conveniently in a corner, well shielded from prying eyes and ears.

The waitress took their order and departed. Gordon stretched out a hand to Morag and caught her wrist.

'Your pulse is racing,' he said, 'are you sure you are not ill?'

'No, not ill,' she answered, 'only very angry.'

She told him of her encounter with Fraser's son, and his revelation about the aluminium plant.

'Have you heard anything about it?' she demanded, wondering if, in trying to cope with the problems of the past weeks, she had somehow missed the announcement.

'I can't say that I have,' said Gordon, 'although I must confess that I have been too busy to take any interest in local politics, myself.'

'That's just it,' said Morag. 'Fraser has gone ahead with this plan despite the town's being preoccupied with the epidemic. He was probably banking on the fact that people would be too busy with their own problems to bother about his activities.'

'We knew that he had hoped to pull down the old houses and sell off the land by the canal for Corporation housing,' Gordon remembered. 'It was the reason Magnus got so upset that evening in the Long John.'

'But nothing was said about any industrial development on the site,' Morag insisted. 'Can you imagine how Magnus would have reacted to any such suggestion? Fraser must have been keeping the whole thing very quiet, anticipating strong objections from local residents when the matter was brought before the Planning Committee.'

'He would, of course, argue that we are not able to halt the march of progress,' Gordon suggested, gently, reluctant to provoke any further resentment. 'By setting up a second, larger extraction plant close to the town, he would provide much needed employment.'

'But it won't stop there, will it?' Morag insisted. 'As I understand it, the reason for importing bauxite from Spain and carrying out the extraction process here on the west coast, is that hydro-electricity is the cheapest form of power. Where is the power source for such a plant at Inverlinnhe?'

Gordon was at a loss to reply.

'I believe that an additional hydro-electric plant must be planned as well,' she told him, adding, 'and there is only one place where such a plant could be built . . . on the west face of the Ben. If it is anything like the unsightly development at Inverleven, it will destroy some of the most attractive aspects of the town. How do you suppose such a development will affect the only other important industry here . . . tourism?'

'We don't know yet whether the Council has given consent to the development,' said Gordon, attempting to calm her. 'You have only young Fraser's word for it. I suggest we try to get hold of Adam and see what he knows about it.'

Gordon paid the bill and they emerged on to High Street to find that a sharp breeze had got up, and there had been a distinct fall in the temperature. The shops and offices were closing and both customers and workers were pouring out on to the streets, scurrying away in all directions, anxious to get home to a warm meal and a cosy fireside.

'Come on.' Gordon took her by the hand and hurried across to the Municipal Offices. 'We may be lucky enough to catch Adam before he leaves.'

The door to the Borough Engineer's department swung open at Gordon's touch. The room was in semi-darkness, lit only by a single, angle-poise lamp. Adam was poring over his drawing board with such sustained concentration that he scarcely noticed their arrival.

Morag was surprised to find herself looking at a copy of the plans which Teddy Fraser had shown her that afternoon.

'So you do know about it?' she said accusingly, pointing to the drawing of the housing scheme and the road running beside the canal. 'You know all about this . . . and this as well, I suppose!' She tapped so sharply on the position of the proposed aluminium works that Adam was forced to hold the blueprint to the board, to prevent it from slipping to the floor.

'Hold on a minute,' he gasped, startled by her abrupt behaviour. 'I've only just managed to get sight of this myself . . . that's why I'm still here, when everyone else has gone!'

'Look here,' Gordon sought to calm things down a little, 'why don't we make a proper assessment of this proposal, calmly and sensibly, and then get on over to the Long John to discuss strategy?'

'How d'you mean, strategy?' asked Adam.

'Well, we don't want another aluminium works there, do we?' Gordon demanded. 'It will ruin the whole valley.'

Morag glanced at him, gratefully. Earlier on she had thought he might support Fraser's viewpoint. Now it seemed he was prepared to fight alongside her in the interest of preserving the doomed area.

They studied the drawing carefully for some time, with Adam jotting down notes on a pad, and taking the occasional measurement. At last he leaned back in his chair and stretched his arms over his head.

'That's enough for now,' he decided. 'Let's go and discuss it over a pint.'

The bar of the Long John was crowded with office workers and late shoppers, happy to be released from the daily grind. The noise at the bar was deafening. While Gordon went to order their drinks, Morag and Adam made for Magnus's favourite place beside the inglenook. Adam took the chair which the reporter had always occupied, and Morag would have voiced an objection had she not remembered, belatedly, that Magnus was no longer there to claim his accustomed seat.

Quite unaware of the thoughts which were occupying her, Adam began talking again about the housing project. Only when he mentioned Canal Row did Morag pay him any attention.

'I've thought quite a lot about Magnus's idea of preserving those old cottages,' Adam was saying. 'It might be a feasible proposition, given a good water supply and electricity and gas services. If a smaller Corporation development were approved, which left the old cottages standing by the canal, it might be possible to upgrade them without enormous additional expenditure . . .'

'According to Magnus,' Morag suggested, 'Fraser bought that land and most of the cottages, in order to sell the whole lot to the Council at an inflated price, as soon as provision of new Corporation housing became essential. Would he not be expected to pull down the old places before selling?'

'Possibly not,' Adam responded. 'Fraser may believe that he can only sell the land if it is free from buildings of any kind, but what I am suggesting is that the Council buys the site with the houses left standing. Those old places could be restored and sold to private owners, providing additional funds for the development of Corporation housing on another part of the site. The cottages are small, but the setting is sufficiently attractive for people to buy them as holiday accommodation, if not for permanent homes.'

He had Morag's full attention now.

'You're suggesting preserving the entire row of old cottages in their original form?' she asked, hardly able to contain her excitement. 'This is wonderful,' she exclaimed, excitedly. 'It's exactly what Magnus wanted. He said that pleasure boats travelling along the canal should see only the original historic buildings which were put there for the canal workers. Anything new should be set back and hidden behind trees to preserve the atmosphere of the old days.'

'Like a living museum,' added Gordon, pleased to see Morag happy at last.

As they spoke, Adam had been sketching in a notebook which he had drawn from his pocket.

'From the plan that we have been looking at, it would mean removing just one row of the new houses envisaged. See . . . here.'

Morag admired the neat reproduction of Fraser's blueprint.

'That would leave the Canal Row gardens untouched.'

'And the road by the canal?' she asked.

'It need only be a narrow access road to the cottages,' Adam replied decisively. 'No more than a few feet would have to be taken off the front gardens to allow for a footpath.'

'But what about the aluminium smelting plant?' demanded Gordon.

'Fraser doesn't have much hope of getting that past the Council,' Adam declared, 'not once I have got together a package of objections.'

'If there is any way in which I can help,' said Gordon, 'you can count on me.'

'And I have a few strings to my bow too,' said Morag, mysteriously. She was remembering that third soldier whom she had recognised in the photograph. Surely he would support their efforts to carry out Magnus's last wishes?

# Chapter 16

In the dreary weeks which followed Magnus's funeral, Morag had found solace only in her work. While she was concentrating on what she was doing with her hands, she was able to blot out her grief for Magnus and the worry over the fate of his cottage which troubled her all the time, waking or sleeping.

She glanced at her watch and realised that Mr Maynard would be waiting for her in theatre. Thrusting aside her preoccupations, she hurried along the corridor and, in so doing, nearly collided with Violet Dunwoodie.

'I hear you're moving out at the end of the week,' said the theatre sister, as she fell into step beside Morag.

'Yes, I can't tell you how I'm longing to be able to sit by my own fireside,' Morag replied. 'Oh, to be able to get up and make a cup of tea for myself whenever I feel like it, and above all to be warm . . . all the time!' She shuddered at the recollection of that icy, uncarpeted linoleum which met her feet every morning, and the chill draught which whistled around her shoulders as she tried to prepare her notes for the next day's operations. She would not be sorry to vacate the room which she had occupied since January.

'I wondered,' Violet ventured timidly, aware that Morag was still raw around the edges after a summer which had brought her so much unhappiness, 'whether you have been able to give any further consideration to the campaign to raise money for an X-ray machine?'

'To be honest with you . . . I had forgotten all about it,' Morag confessed.

'Well . . . the thing is . . . this is the time of year when fund-raising can be most successful,' Sister Dunwoodie explained. 'People are more ready to give generously during the festivities, particularly when they have a few drams taken!'

'Had you anything particular in mind?' Morag asked, warming to the idea of any project which would occupy her free time now that the house was ready for occupation.

'A Hogmanay Ball,' said Violet, decisively. 'I happen to know that nothing has yet been arranged at the Assembly Rooms. If we get in our bid for the hall immediately, we should be able to hire it.'

She did not mention that she had made a booking weeks before, anticipating that just such an event might provide a suitable opportunity to launch the fund-raising. Morag's preoccupation with her own affairs had made Violet hold back. Only four clear weeks now remained before the end of the year. They would have a great deal to do if they were to be ready for the event.

'I think that's a splendid idea,' said Morag. 'Let's collect together a few useful people and get things started.'

'All right,' said Violet, very much relieved. 'You can leave the hall booking to me if you like . . . I know the fellow in charge.'

The events of the summer had shown Morag which members of the hospital staff could be relied upon to give useful assistance in organising an event such as the Hogmanay Ball. A small committee was assembled that same day, and over tea in the canteen plans began to take shape.

Making sure that the right people attended, and brought with them their wealthy friends, was quite another matter. Morag decided that members of the Hospital Board should be approached, and who better to muster their support than Duncan McRae?

Although barely four o'clock in the afternoon, it was nearly dark when she drew up before an imposing wrought-iron gateway which was guarded by a pair of heraldic gryphons in red sandstone.

In seeking an interview with Duncan, she had anticipated that she would be visiting one of the usual Victorian villas occupied by the better-off members of the middle-class population of Inverlinnhe. This gateway, which sported its own lodge house, suggested something far more grand.

As she pulled on the handbrake a figure emerged from the lodge and shuffled painfully towards her.

'Is it Dr Beaton?' he asked, his highland brogue evoking memories of her island upbringing.

'Good afternoon,' she ventured. 'I believe that Mr McRae is expecting me.'

'Indeed he is, madam,' said the venerable retainer, and doffed his bonnet as he pulled open the gate and waved her on.

The driveway took her through ancient oak woods, the road climbing steadily in a series of zigzags up the steep hillside.

As she rounded yet another blind bend, suddenly there was the house, a magnificent grey edifice of towers and turrets, slate roofs and tall arched windows. It might have been transported straight from the banks of the river Rhine!

At the sound of her car wheels on the gravel, the great studded oak door was flung open and Duncan McRae came striding down the stone steps. She could not help but compare his lean good looks and healthy physique with that of his contemporaries, Gordon McDonald and the portly Graham Fraser.

'Dr Beaton, how delightful!' he cried, pulling open the door and handing her out. 'Don't worry about the car, my man will park it for you. Do come along inside, out of the cold.'

He fussed over her, removing her coat and scarf and finally tossing them to a manservant who, in impeccable morning dress, stood by to take his orders.

'Tea, McGregor . . . thank you,' McRae called over his shoulder. The servant was already on his way to the butler's pantry.

It was a large room, with lofty ceilings and huge windows affording a breathtaking view across the loch towards the town. Beyond the rooftops of Inverlinnhe crouched the Ben, its snowy peaks shrouded in clouds.

In a wrought-iron fire basket a heap of hardwood logs burned merrily, bathing the grey stone hearth in a ruddy glow which was reflected off the gleaming brass of the firedogs. The furnishings were heavy brocades in Paisley designs incorporating rich jewel colours, reds, blues and purples, while across the polished hardwood flooring were scattered costly Turkish and Afghan rugs. Before the fire was stretched a magnificent tiger-skin, the animal's expression so benign, its eyes so bright in the firelight, that Morag was tempted to get down on her knees and hug it.

'Go on,' said Duncan McRae, watching her closely and smiling broadly, 'everyone does . . . sooner or later.'

She took him at his word and sank down beside the beast's head, fondling its ears and allowing her hands to wander over the elaborately patterned silky fur.

'More beautiful alive than dead,' he observed, apologetically. 'I'm afraid that our ancestors thought only of killing and bringing home their trophies. Personally, I would prefer to see a creature like that still roaming in the wild.'

'Towards the end of his life, my grandfather became quite fanatical about preserving the wild life of the district,' Morag told him, 'although that was in Argyll, of course . . . nothing so exotic and magnificent as this poor beast.'

She went on stroking the tiger-skin thoughtfully, then continued, 'My teacher, Elizabeth Whylie, told me that when she first knew him, Grandfather was always keen to take pot shots at the chuffs and golden eagles, but over the course of twenty years or so she talked him out of it! Before he died, he was writing to the papers about saving the otters and badgers.'

Morag had no idea why she should be rattling on like this with reminiscences which could not be of the slightest interest to her host. She had no reason to be nervous, yet here she was prattling like a silly schoolgirl . . .

The tea arrived on a silver tray. McGregor placed it upon a side table and stood back, raising one eyebrow at his employer.

In response, McRae waved him away.

'We'll take care of it for ourselves, thank you,' he said, giving Morag a half smile. 'It's not often that we entertain a lady in this bachelor-ridden establishment. McGregor usually has to play mother.'

'Oh, I didn't realise . . .' She blushed unaccountably. It

had never occurred to her that there might not be a Mrs McRae.

'Sadly, my wife died many years ago,' he told her, his glance shifting automatically to a painting which hung above the mantelshelf.

Following the direction of his gaze, Morag saw the portrait of a young woman in her early-twenties, dressed in the white ball gown and plaid which was the court dress of Scottish gentlewomen.

'It was the outfit she wore when she was presented to King George and Queen Mary, soon after their coronation. The brooch was a gift from the Queen. She gave one to every lady present who was also named Mary. A charming gesture, don't you think?'

As Morag stood up to view the picture more closely, he went on, 'We were married a year later, and my daughter Harriet was born in April 1914. She was a healthy babe but, sadly, her mother did not survive the birth.' There was a long pause while he steeled himself to continue. 'Had it not been for the war, I think I would have gone out of my mind. As it was, I joined the army at the first possible opportunity and threw myself into the fray – hoping, I suppose, that the Almighty in His great wisdom would choose to take me also. It was not to be, however. Perhaps because I didn't care what happened to me, I came through the whole thing without a scratch.'

'I'm sure that your daughter is very glad that you did,' observed Morag gently.

'Poor wee scrap, I was a complete stranger to her when I came home in 1918.' For a moment he remained silent. Suddenly, brushing the back of his hand lightly across his cheek, he added in brighter tones, 'We made up for it later. No man could have had a sweeter, more gentle companion while she was growing up. I miss her.'

Morag remembered the letter from Richard Ashley Keynes. He and Harriet McRae must be married by now.

Duncan lapsed into silence again.

'Shall I do the honours?' asked Morag, moving towards the tea tray. The painful moment had passed. Soon she felt that she could introduce the subject which she had come to discuss.

'Having had so much success in raising funds to open the isolation wing during the summer,' she began, tentatively, 'my colleagues and I thought that we should keep up the momentum and continue to raise money, this time for an X-ray machine.'

'I think that is a splendid idea,' he agreed enthusiastically, and reached inside his jacket.

'Oh . . . I'm sorry . . . I haven't explained myself very well. I didn't come here to collect a contribution from you,' she insisted, awkwardly. Then with a little grin she added, 'Although that might well come later. No, I am seeking help of a different kind.

'We are planning to hold a Hogmanay Ball in the Assembly Rooms. The tickets will be modestly priced in order not to deter anyone at all who wishes to be present, but there will be several fund-raising events during the evening which will be aimed unashamedly at those with plenty of money.'

'And you want me to ensure that a few people with gold-lined pockets turn up at your party, is that it?' His eyes were twinkling.

'Yes, please' She found his directness very refreshing.

She poured a second cup of tea for them both and took her place opposite him.

'It was only after Magnus Glendenning died that I realised that he and Gordon McDonald had served with you in Flanders,' she commented. At these words he looked up, taken by surprise.

'There was a photograph of the three of you amongst his things,' she explained. 'Although you were *en déshabillé* . . . Magnus was shaving and you seemed to be doing a highland fling . . . you were all quite recognisable.'

'Fancy Magnus keeping that old photograph,' he pondered. 'They were so very young . . . I was an old man by comparison. They used to call me Pop even though I was only twenty-four or twenty-five at the time . . . little more than a boy myself really. We spent two years together in those filthy trenches.'

'Did you ever visit Magnus in the cottage he inherited from

his great-grandfather?' she asked, suddenly. 'It's one of the old canal worker's houses at Feanagrogan.'

'As I remember, it was in a pretty delapidated state. Isn't it one of those scheduled for demolition?'

'You must have seen it when Magnus was having a bad day.' She laughed. 'Really it's a very sound little house . . . anyway, it's mine now. He left it to me in his Will.'

Duncan looked up sharply. He had known that the two of them had been friendly, but had never guessed that their relationship had progressed so far.

Morag hastened to explain.

'Magnus wanted all the houses in the row preserved as a monument to those old canal people. He chose me to carry on the fight to retain them . . . after . . .' She tried to disguise the catch in her voice but it did not escape him.

'I realised from the very first that he felt great respect for you,' he said quietly. 'Magnus was a different man after you came on the scene, you know. He even tried to curb his drinking on those occasions when he thought he might be meeting you.'

No, Morag hadn't known. It saddened her to think that his efforts should have been overlooked by her.

'And what about you?' Duncan asked gently. 'Were you in love with him?'

'I believe I was . . . a little,' she answered. 'Towards the end.' She could feel her eyes brimming with tears and fumbled in her bag, searching for a handkerchief.

'I'm sorry,' she said. 'I don't know why I'm doing this . . . I haven't . . . not since the day of the funeral.'

Reproaching himself for his clumsiness, he took a seat beside her on the sofa, and removing the white handkerchief from his breast pocket, leaned forward and dabbed at her cheek. She took the cambric square from him and blew her nose loudly, smiling through her tears.

He sat back, watching as she took a small powder compact from her bag and repaired the damage.

'Did you know that Fraser plans to demolish those old houses so he can gain access to the new aluminium smelting plant he intends to set up beside the canal?' she demanded, anxious now to change the subject. She snapped shut the shiny metal compact.

When Duncan did not respond immediately she added, 'Gordon McDonald agrees with me that an aluminium works, built so close to a populated area, could be a serious risk to health.'

After a few moments he said, 'There are those who will claim that the proposed new smelting operation would bring much needed employment to the area.' Then, seeing her crestfallen expression, he added hastily, 'Although I must admit that such a development would seriously impair the natural beauty of the wetlands by the canal.'

'Adam Inglis was all for the project originally,' she told him, 'but I think Magnus convinced him that there was an alternative . . . he's working on the plans now. Meanwhile, we must find a voice to speak against Fraser's proposal at the planning meeting. I rather hoped that you might be able to suggest someone?'

McRae stood up and went over to the window. For some minutes he gazed out at the dark November sky, trying to sort out his priorities. He turned to her abruptly, his mind made up.

'You're right, of course,' he declared, 'Fraser must be stopped. I'll have a word with Ewan McEwan . . . see what he makes of it. He's a man to be relied upon to give an unbiased opinion.

'Now then,' he said, offering her his hand, 'that's enough of other people's problems. Before you leave, I want you to see the rest of the house. We have some very fine water-colours in the tower gallery.'

They wandered through a bewildering assembly of corridors and spacious rooms, coming at last to a small oak door which gave access to the tower room.

He gave her his hand again to guide her steps as they mounted the spiral staircase which disappeared into the gloom above their heads. An occasional electric light fitting, which jutted from the wall like a medieval torch, provided the only source of light.

'This was an old fortified house,' Duncan explained, 'sixteenth-century, I believe. Some wealthy coal baron bought the estate in the 1850s and incorporated the tower into the building which you see today.'

'What a pity he did not simply build nearby,' commented Morag. 'It's sad to see any fine old building spoilt by modernisation.'

'Yes, I suppose it was a pretty dreadful thing to do, but it makes an interesting feature in an otherwise rather mediocre house.'

'Mediocre' was the last word that she would have used to describe his home!

At the head of the stairs they emerged into a large room some eighteen feet wide.

In daylight, the room clearly received its illumination from above, where the centre of the ceiling was occupied by a great dome of leaded glass. Deliberately, Duncan waited for a few moments before turning on the lights. The earlier clouds had been dispersed by a strong breeze, and now the whole panoply of the heavens was displayed against the deep blue of the night sky.

Morag gazed up at the stars, enchanted.

'Were I to own this house, I think I would live in this room all the time,' she declared.

Duncan watched her covertly. The dull ache he had carried in his heart for so long seemed to evaporate in her presence. Her delighted exclamations warmed the chill atmosphere which permeated his life.

This had been Mary's room . . . her 'studio' she had laughingly called it, and indeed she had spent many hours here, sketching and painting. She was no artist, but one or two of her paintings hung here amongst the masterpieces.

'Let me show you the collection,' he said to Morag, switching on the lights to reveal the contents of the room. It was simply furnished with a pair of comfortable armchairs and a low table between them. A glass-fronted bookcase covered one wall and on the three remaining walls hung a collection of water-colours.

Reluctantly she turned her back on the panorama and allowed him to conduct her around the little exhibition of paintings.

They clearly meant a great deal to him . . . he spoke of them lovingly, devoting a few moments to each artist and explaining the subjects in detail.

A small group of three exquisitely executed highland scenes took her eye.

'Those are lovely.'

He paused, wondering if he should tell her that they were Mary's work. Not trusting himself to speak of his dead wife again, he made no comment and passed on to the next pictures.

'You know this artist,' he told her. 'These were painted by Anna McDonald.'

He had stopped in front of a pair of pictures of sea birds at the water's edge. Oyster catchers and terns, tiny ringed plovers and long-billed greenshanks busily searched among rocks at low tide. Morag recalled the huge picture on the McDonald's living-room wall and wondered if it had been Duncan who had offered to buy that one too.

'A truly magnificent artist,' said he, 'and such a fine woman.'

Morag was startled by this clear expression of his admiration for Gordon's wife. She turned to him for an explanation.

'Few people have any idea what a struggle she had when Gordon returned from Flanders. For a time we were all of us mental cases and probably very difficult to live with. Gordon was only an assistant in the practice in those days so they had very little to live on . . . his small salary and what she could earn from her painting.'

*So you did your best to help, by buying her pictures,* Morag thought to herself, reminded once again of the generous nature of this sad, lonely man.

Duncan was continuing their tour of the gallery, unaware that her concentration was no longer upon the paintings.

'. . . don't you think so?' he demanded suddenly.

'What? Sorry, I'm afraid my mind was wandering,' she apologised.

'You are tired,' he said, 'how thoughtless of me. We can look at the rest another time. I'm afraid that when it comes to art, I allow my own enthusiasm to outweigh all other considerations.'

He led her back to the main entrance where McGregor,

anticipating her departure, had her car waiting with the engine already ticking over. She wondered what he had thought about having to drive such an insignificant vehicle . . . Rolls-Royces and Bentleys were more his mark.

'I'll do what I can about that planning meeting,' Duncan called to her as she drew away. 'Oh, and by the way, don't forget that I shall be expecting to buy some tickets for the ball!'

The ball! Morag wondered if she would have time to participate in any of it. These days her life seemed to be taken up entirely with organising things for others to enjoy. She wondered wistfully if anyone would ask to escort her. Probably not – they would all imagine that she had no need of a partner. It would be nice if Adam were to ask her, of course, but she had no idea if he ever attended such functions. Smiling wryly at the thought of him appearing at the dance in his climbing boots, she waited for a farm lorry to pass by her in the lane before turning left on to the road and heading towards the lights of the town.

The Inverlinnhe District Council had reached the final item on its agenda for the meeting. Chairman Graham Fraser began collecting his papers together as he exchanged a few words with his deputy, Martin Strong. There were a number of bantering remarks passed between friends, and not a few derogatory asides from members of the opposition when Fraser vacated his chair and made for the door.

Adam Inglis noted the confidence expressed in the glances exchanged between the Chairman and the Borough Engineer. It was not going to be easy. His own job could be in jeopardy, but he was determined to make his stand no matter what obstacles were put in his way.

'Gentlemen.' Martin Strong took pleasure in wielding the gavel to gain control of the meeting. It was a rare event when Graham Fraser was obliged to leave Council business in his hands. 'Our Chairman has expressed an interest in the next item and begs to be excused from the discussion.'

There was a roar of laughter. No one in the room was unaware of Fraser's interest.

'Mr McLeod?'

The Borough Engineer rose ponderously to his feet. Already past his sixtieth birthday, he was anticipating his retirement with a great deal of pleasure. He looked forward to the time when he could spend *every* day on the golf course, no longer restricted to those Thursday afternoon rounds which he regarded as an essential part of his duties. It was on these occasions that the really important business of the Council was discussed and those decisions arrived at which must later be steered through the democratic process without too much interference from the opposition.

McLeod was a stout man, impeccably dressed. His thinning hair had been allowed to grow long enough to be swept across from ear to ear in an attempt to disguise his baldness. A heavy gold watch chain decorated the flamboyant waistcoat which contained, with obvious difficulty, an enormous abdomen, a monument to Mrs McLeod's baking. With a somewhat nervous gesture, he patted the swathe of hair against his scalp. He was an engineer, not a politician.

'Mr Chairman, the next item on your agenda is the proposal to purchase a parcel of land alongside the canal, amounting to some fifteen acres, with a view to developing the site for Corporation housing. I hardly need stress the importance of such a project to the town. The recent tragic events, which have led to the deaths of several of our citizens from typhoid fever, have served to emphasise the need for modern accommodation with proper water and sewage services.'

There was no dispute on this score. The opposition had been advocating just such a development for several years.

McLeod continued, gaining in confidence in the absence of any dissent.

'Graham Fraser Associates has agreed to sell the required land at a very favourable price.' Many heads nodded appreciatively.

'There is, however, one small proviso, with which I hope the Council will feel able to comply.' There was some shuffling in their seats by members of the opposition. Here it came, the inevitable quid pro quo . . .

'Fraser Associates request that an access road, capable of carrying heavy lorries and large-scale industrial plant, be built at the Authority's expense, to link their adjacent site with the main trunk road to Inverness.'

The murmurs were louder now and there was a very different, almost hostile, atmosphere developing.

'Mr Chairman . . .' A lean, thin-faced individual whose tweed jacket and Fair Isle pullover marked him out as a member of the Socialist Group, jumped to his feet. 'There have been rumours flying around for weeks that Fraser intends to open up another aluminium smelting plant right here in the town. Can this proposal have anything to do with that development?'

Martin Strong invited McLeod to answer the question.

'At the present time, Mr Chairman,' he responded smoothly, 'there is no planning application on the table for such a project, although it is unlikely that Fraser Associates would want an access road of this quality built were they not anticipating some sort of industrial development on that site at some time in the future.'

'May we know the position of this access road, Mr Chairman?' demanded the Labour member, his suspicions aroused by McLeod's noncommittal answer.

'I will ask my assistant, Mr Inglis, to explain the plans, Mr Chairman.' With this, McLeod sat down, mopping his brow and obviously relieved to be off the hook.

Adam brought forward an easel on which was displayed a plan showing the area by the canal and the existing buildings.

'As you can see,' the younger man began, allowing the members time to get their bearings, 'the land which Fraser Associates have offered us for purchase lies alongside the canal and constitutes approximately half the area at present owned by the company. You will notice that included in it is this row of old properties, originally built to house canal workers some one hundred and fifty years ago. In the original plan for development which was submitted by Fraser's, these cottages would have to be demolished and replaced by the access road which Mr McLeod has already mentioned.'

Adam covered the plan with the one which had so incensed Morag.

'Here you can see that the old cottages have been demolished. The new estate has the houses facing away from the canal, in four terraces of twenty houses, serviced by two roads. The large access road required by the company passes behind the houses, separating their gardens from the canal.'

There were some murmurs of approval from the seats occupied by the main party . . . the provision seemed more than adequate for housing eighty working-class families.

Adam allowed time for the members to absorb the information before continuing.

'The scheme, as it stands, would certainly provide much-needed housing but it has, to my mind, a number of serious failings.' He saw McLeod lean forward as though to interrupt and hurried on with his statement. 'The plan lacks imagination, and completely ignores certain criteria which have been laid down by the Scottish Office with regard to new housing developments of this kind.'

'Such as?' It was a pompous, arrogant voice which could only belong to one of Fraser's acolytes.

'There are no public amenities envisaged. Developments of this nature should include such facilities as a village shop and post office, a school, easy access to medical attention . . . even a church. There should be adequate land set aside for a playing field for the children and for adult sports, and some form of community centre.'

'Good God,' exclaimed the previous speaker, 'whatever next! What's wrong with these people using the shops in town and sending their children to the existing schools?'

'The distance from the nearest school is three miles and from the shops and post office it is more like four. There is no public transport available, and we are not speaking here of families who are able to afford their own vehicles. It would be courting disaster to move large numbers of people out to occupy these houses and leave them stranded, miles from anywhere.

'But for eighty families . . . ?' Even the Socialist representative was dubious about Adam's suggestion.

'Precisely,' he agreed. The intervention could not have been better timed had he arranged it prior to the meeting. 'That is why I am proposing that the Council purchases *all* the land held by Fraser Associates, an area of nearly thirty acres in total, upon which it would be possible to build sufficient houses to warrant the amenities I have described.'

'But what about . . .' McLeod stuck his fist into his mouth. He had nearly disclosed his knowledge of Fraser's other plans, and he had come to the meeting ostensibly as an impartial official of the Council.

'Supposing Fraser's won't sell the rest of the land?' asked one cynical voice.

'Oh, I think they will,' replied Adam, 'when they find that their request for an enlarged service road has been denied.'

'And why should this Council deny Mr Fraser the benefit of an adequate access road into his holding?' queried Martin Strong. This young fellow had an almighty cheek, he reflected, though one had to admire his gall.

'The road envisaged by Fraser's is so wide that it would cut right through the row of old cottages by the canal,' Adam explained.

'But I thought they were coming down anyway?' observed Strong.

'I hope not, Mr Chairman,' he replied. 'To begin with, not all the cottages are owned by Fraser Associates. One of them is privately owned, and the occupier flatly refuses to relinquish her property for the purpose of development.'

'This person could be persuaded, surely?' suggested Strong, voicing the opinion of half the members.

'The lady is determined to put up a strong fight,' Adam replied. 'I think it fair to warn you that she would be willing to make a legal battle of it if needs be . . . and could very well win her case.'

There was more than one member at the meeting who had experienced the process of the law to his detriment, and they were all aware that the Council would be collectively responsible for any costs involved if the case were lost. Most would prefer not to get involved in that kind of wrangling.

During this exchange, McLeod was becoming more and more frustrated. He had underestimated the strength of character of his junior. He supposed he should have let the boy in on the deal with Fraser. Now, he had drifted too far from the original plan. If they were to retract at this stage, someone would be bound to smell a rat. Fearing for his pension, as well as the comfortable little bonus he had anticipated from this particular deal, McLeod decided to hold his tongue. He even managed a smile of encouragement when Adam continued with, 'If the members will allow me, I would like to put forward a proposal of my own, based on the idea of taking all the Fraser Associates land holdings into consideration.'

At Strong's nod of approval, he produced a third plan which he stretched out on the easel and pinned into place.

As the members around the table registered this new proposition there were one or two expressions of disdain, but more exclamations of interest and even admiration.

'As you can see,' Adam began, using a ruler to point out the features as he reeled them off one by one, 'the scheme is based on two concentric circles of housing, with connecting roads radiating from this central green. I have even made use of a natural feature here to create a village duck pond.' There was a titter of laughter, but members were straining forward, greatly interested in seeing Adam's plan.

'Facing on to the green we have a group of amenity buildings,' he continued, 'the church and school here, together with a community meeting hall ... village shop and post office ... doctor's surgery and a site for a petrol filling station.'

'I thought you said that people wouldn't have cars?' came a voice from somewhere at the back of the room.

'In my scheme, not all the houses would be for rent,' he explained. 'My proposal includes a certain amount of property for private sale, so that this new village will attract all manner of people, professional as well as artisans. There would be different types of housing, some suitable for larger families, and other more compact accommodation, for newly-weds and elderly couples. What I want to avoid is the kind of housing development which gets a bad reputation because it caters only for one section of the community and lacks the balance which puts restraints upon the more disruptive elements.'

'Well said, young man,' commented a composed, elderly gentleman who had sat silent throughout the meeting. It was clear that he commanded considerable respect because as he put his pipe carefully in the ashtray before him, the room fell silent.

'Councillor McEwan?' Martin Strong invited the elder statesman to continue.

'I have listened to what you have to say, Mr Inglis, and it makes a lot of sense to me,' McEwan began. 'Unfortunately, however, we already have a serious problem with unemployment in the town. It seems an ill-conceived plan to gather together a large number of people in an area where there is no work. How are your villagers going to find a means of making a living, way out there in the country? You have said yourself that many of the working-class folk, and no doubt the owner-occupiers too, will be without transport . . . what are they going to do for employment?'

Adam lifted his pointer to the plan once again. 'You will notice an area of undeveloped land in this corner of the site which fronts the main road. Here I propose to erect a group of industrial units to house small businesses which would employ just a few workers apiece. These would be leased from the Council at a modest rent, at least for the setting-up period.'

'Very laudable,' McEwan agreed, 'but hardly sufficient to satisfy the needs of the numbers of workers you are proposing to bring to the site.'

'I think it is no secret,' Adam continued boldly, aware that he was about to lay his future on the line, 'that Fraser Associates were planning to build a new aluminium smelting plant on the land we have been discussing.'

There was an anxious murmur from some of Fraser's supporters. The opposition remained quiet, but grim-faced.

'While I am opposed to the Fraser plan,' Adam continued,

'because of the serious risk to health of siting a housing scheme within a few yards of a large industrial development of this nature, I am not opposed to the idea of bringing much-needed employment to the area.' He drew out yet another map.

'Two miles from the proposed housing scheme,' he explained, 'is this gully where the Eas an Briosaid drops into the valley, here . . . The Authority acquired this land just before the war. A hydro-electric scheme was proposed which was never built. Any aluminium smelting plant would require more power than Inverlinnhe is able to provide at present, so even if Fraser's were to receive consent to build their plant, they would still need a supply of electricity from somewhere. I propose, therefore, that we initiate a scheme to build a hydro-electric plant in this valley, which incidentally is well out of sight of the surrounding area and will not create a nuisance so far as tourism is concerned. In addition, I propose that we sell off a part of the adjacent land to Fraser's, for their smelting plant. The initial construction work, and subsequent jobs at the factory, should provide a suitable range of employment for the people who come to live in the new village.'

There were now expressions of agreement from all quarters. Even McLeod seemed to be approving Adam's suggestion. If the original idea were rejected, he would at least be able to approach Graham Fraser with a viable alternative . . .

'There's just one thing,' McEwan interrupted once again. 'I notice that in your drawing,' Adam slipped his own blueprint back on to the board, 'the old cottages by the canal are still standing.'

'Well . . . yes.' Adam hesitated momentarily. Would it be asking too much to get their agreement on this too? 'These cottages were built by the men who constructed and operated the canal late in the eighteenth century. They are, in a sense, a monument to their original occupants. I believe that for a small outlay, they could be modernised without detracting from their outward appearance. I therefore propose that we retain those buildings currently owned by Fraser's, and restore them incorporating every modern facility. From their sale to private owners, we can not only recover the cost of modernisation but also contribute to some other parts of the project . . . the public amenity buildings, for example.'

'Thank you, Mr Inglis . . . Mr McLeod,' Martin Strong dismissed the officers. They had heard the opinion of the experts, it was now time for Council members to decide upon the proposals.

As Adam and McLeod departed, the last words they overheard were Martin Strong's. 'You have heard the arguments against the proposal outlined by Fraser Associates, gentlemen. Is there anyone who wishes to speak in support of the proposal?'

There were a few glances exchanged between those members of the main party who had come to the meeting ready to vote unquestioningly for their leader's plans. They were not insensitive, however, to the logic of young Inglis's arguments. If word got out that any of them had voted against a scheme which promised to be so beneficial to the ordinary citizens of the town, there was bound to be a sharp fall in voting figures at the next election.

'There are several alternatives to consider,' said Strong, relishing his moment of power, 'I shall take them in the order in which they were presented to us.

'May I first of all have your opinion upon the initial proposition laid down by Fraser Associates, that we purchase fifteen acres of land from them for the erection of eighty houses, and construct a wide access road to Fraser's remaining property . . . all those in favour?' Two hands were half-raised, wavered slightly as their owners realised suddenly that they were alone, and were then withdrawn.

'The Council is unanimously opposed to Fraser Associates' proposal,' Strong declared, and paused dramatically while the Minute Secretary made her entry.

'The second proposal before you is that made by Mr Adam Inglis – that the Authority should seek to purchase the whole site, with a view to constructing a much larger housing scheme with public amenities as outlined.'

Every hand in the room went up.

'Carried unanimously,' declared Strong, and the entire company broke into spontaneous applause.

\*      \*      \*

Morag was thankful for the lightweight pale green shift which she had chosen to wear for the Hogmanay Ball. It reached barely to her calf and was made of some form of rayon which had the appearance of silk, but was not nearly so warm to wear. Never one for frills and ribbons, she had avoided the elaborate fringes worn by so many of her contemporaries. In her one concession to fashion, she had allowed the dressmaker to add some darker green braiding at the hem of the dress and around the scooped neck and capped sleeves.

She had been taught to dance at school, of course, along with all those other ladylike activities considered essential for the girl intent upon finding a suitable husband. She could waltz and she was very familiar with the set dances so favoured by an earlier generation, but as for the post-war innovations such as the Black Bottom and the Charleston . . . their advent and subsequent demise had passed by without her realising it. Now the foxtrot and quickstep were all the rage, together with a collection of Latin American dances which she had seen performed only on the cinema screen.

The years of Morag's training had passed by on a nightmarish treadmill of endless days on the wards, followed by long nights, reading. On the rare occasions when she had ventured out to sample the night-life of Edinburgh, it had been in company with clod-hopping fellow students with no more idea of modern dance steps than she.

Tonight she had had some accomplished partners, among them Duncan McRae and Andy McDonald, both of whom seemed to consider that her entertainment was their responsibility. She was glad of their attention, for she had seen little enough of her other friends.

Morag had been disappointed to see Adam Inglis arrive with Mary Neal on his arm and would have begun to speculate on his motives had he not sought her out in a little while to give what she took to be an explanation for choosing to bring her friend.

'You seem to be so busy with all the organisation,' he said. 'I hope you're going to find time to have a little fun yourself.'

'Maybe . . . a little later, perhaps,' she replied hoping he would take the hint and ask her to dance.

'I'll tell you what I have been thinking about,' he told her. 'We are coming up to the busiest season in the mountaineer's calendar and you've never had any experience on ice. What do you say to a day's climbing? The first good day we get, when you're free.'

'I'd like that,' she answered, glowing with anticipation.

'Good . . . oh dear,' as the music began again, 'I promised Mary I'd struggle round the floor with her to a Slow Foxtrot. Do forgive me.'

He mingled with the dancers already on the floor and in a moment, he was gone.

She looked around for a friendly face and spotted Gordon McDonald seated at a corner table with his wife and daughter. The McDonalds made a handsome couple. Morag had never seen Gordon in full highland dress before. He certainly cut a very impressive figure.

Always in advance of fashion trends and happy to be bordering on the outrageous, Anna had shocked more than one Inverlinnhe matron that evening with her scarlet silk evening pyjamas worn under a loose-fitting tunic of gold lamé. Tiny gold slippers peeped out from beneath the chiffon trousers and a turban of gold-coloured satin completely enveloped her thick black tresses.

The effect was quite striking, but Morag could see that Gordon looked slightly ill at ease with his partner's exotic appearance. Perhaps that was why they appeared to be hiding in the corner.

'How nice to see you all here,' she exclaimed as she approached their table.

Gordon got to his feet.

'It's a splendid affair, Morag . . . well done!' Seeing an old acquaintance across the room, he said, 'you girls must have plenty to say to one another. Will you excuse me for a few minutes?' Morag took a seat beside Frances and enquired after her progress.

Unlike her mother, the girl had chosen to be as inconspicuous as possible in a short simple dress of embroidered white organdie. She looked sweet.

'Frances,' Morag exclaimed, with genuine admiration, 'how well you are looking. You're not dancing . . . does your leg still bother you?'

'I'm walking better now, Dr Beaton,' the girl replied, 'but I haven't the courage to try dancing, not yet at any rate.'

'Never mind,' Morag tried to reassure her. 'A few more months of physiotherapy, and lots of swimming, and this time next year you'll be dancing with the rest.'

Fran tried hard to smile, but could not disguise her frustration at seeing her friends being whirled around the ballroom on the arms of all the most interesting young men.

'There will be an interval quite soon,' Morag went on, 'in which we hope to have some fun and raise a lot of money. You'll enjoy that, I'm sure.' Then, turning to Anna, 'I have to rush away,' she excused herself. 'We must get ready for the next part of the proceedings.'

Anna placed a restraining hand on her arm.

'Do you know, Fran,' she addressed her daughter, 'I would kill for a long cold drink.' She handed her daughter a small gold satin purse and sent her off to fetch it.

'It's been such a long time since you came to see us', said Anna, settling into the chair vacated by her daughter. 'Only the other day Poppy was complaining at your long absence.'

'It's been a very busy time.' Morag's excuses sounded lame, she knew. 'I haven't been very good company for anyone what with the business of my suspension and then the epidemic . . . and Magnus . . .'

'My dear, I know you've had a bad time.'

Anna placed a hand over Morag's as it lay on the table. The warmth of her compassion appeared to flow from her in a most extraordinary way and Morag felt her eyes brimming with tears.

Quick to sense the change of mood, Anna said brightly, 'How is the little house which Magnus left you? He must have thought a great deal of you, to leave it in your charge. He was quite sentimental about it you know.'

'Yes,' Morag felt herself smiling at the memory, 'his great-grandfather built it with his own hands.'

'You're happy living there?' Anna asked.

'It's wonderful to have a place of my own, if only to sleep there which seems to be the case most of the time.'

'That Maynard is an old slave driver,' Anna declared, 'everyone tells me so.'

Morag was reminded how small was the circle in which they all moved. Like her husband, Anna had many friends amongst the hospital staff. No doubt she was up to date with all the gossip.

'Once the good weather comes,' Morag told her, 'I intend to do something about the garden. I dream of a velvet green lawn running down to the canal with neat flower beds glowing with colour all summer. The reality is thistles and dandelions a mile high and a scraggy privet hedge with a colony of nasty wee green caterpillars which seem to inhabit it all year, in one form or another!'

'Perhaps I could give you some help there,' Anna suggested. 'I'll come and have a look at it if you like.'

Recalling the delightful garden at the McDonalds' house, Morag was overjoyed at the suggestion.

'Would you really?' she asked. 'That would be absolutely marvellous!'

'What would be marvellous?' asked Fran, setting before them a tray carrying three tall glasses of sparkling lemonade.

'Mr McRae insisted upon paying for them,' Fran explained. To Morag she said, 'he asked me to give you a message. He will be waiting for you in front of the platform when it's time for the competitions.'

Anna clapped her hands in delight.

'Oooh . . .' she cried, 'a tryst . . . how exciting! Morag has an admirer.' When she saw her blush Anna regretted her outburst, but Morag was clearly under considerable strain and the best thing for her would be a little pampering from a male companion.

'Go along and enjoy yourself, my dear,' she said patting the hand she had been holding all the while. 'Duncan McRae is one of the nicest people I know.'

'He has been a good friend to me ever since the day I was appointed to the hospital staff,' Morag replied.

Anna watched closely as she moved across the floor to where Duncan McRae stood, conversing with Gordon. At her approach, Duncan turned to her, all smiles. Anna nodded wisely when she saw the way he looked at Morag, but she determined to keep her observations to herself.

Morag had been amazed at the ingenuity of her colleagues in dreaming up ways of raising money. There were feats of skill to be attempted, remarkable races on which to lay wagers, and most spectacular of all, Eddie Strachan had been wheeled about all evening, bandaged from head to toe, with one arm and one leg arranged at crazy angles in splints. For a small sum, guests were invited to guess the length of his bandages. As midnight approached, a roar went up when Matron, wielding an oversized pair of scissors, prepared to remove his dressings and ceremonially unwound the bandages for measuring. When the winning estimate had been announced and the prize duly presented, Sidney Maynard, who had rather surprisingly offered his services as Master of Ceremonies, announced the grand total of the monies raised.

On the last stroke of midnight, balloons cascaded from the ceiling and paper horns and whistles added to the tumult of cheering and laughter. As they all linked hands and sang, the band played *Auld Lang Syne*. Above the noise in the hall, they could hear the church bells from all around the town ringing in the new year.

Adam Inglis swept his partner into his arms and kissed her soundly on the mouth. Morag would have been envious had she seen it, but she was too preoccupied with Duncan's gentlemanly peck on her cheek. Gordon McDonald kissed his wife with a passion equal to any he had shown at their first Hogmanay together, twenty years before. Fran looked on, wishing that she could be a part of it all. Seeing her looking forlorn and unpartnered, her brother Andy came over to their table and persuaded his sister to come and join his pals in the other room.

Soon all the greetings were over, the toasts made, and the

music began again. To the notes of fiddle, flute and accordion, the dancers whirled in and out following the time-honoured figures of the eightsome reel.

'Here, take this, you'll need it when we begin climbing the chimney.'

Adam handed her a woollen balaclava helmet. It smelt musty and she suspected it had lain damp in the bottom of his rucksack since the last time he had had anyone out alone on the mountains with him.

She looked around her at the clear blue sky and the bright sunshine and would have declined his offer.

'No go on, really. You'll be glad of it,' he assured her.

Reluctantly she pulled the offensive garment over her head, tucking her curls under the ribbing. Now only her eyes, nose and mouth were exposed. She thought she must look something like a seal in the featureless headgear.

As they stepped into the shadow of the sheer rock face which towered above them, she felt the sudden change of temperature and began to realise why he had insisted on the balaclava.

In front of them, rising steeply to a height of three hundred feet above their heads, was a gully or couloir which in summer would have carried a raging torrent of falling water after every downpour. In midwinter, it was filled with ice and looked like a ten foot wide vein of quartz, bisecting the cliff almost vertically.

Adam checked her rope, made sure that her ice axe was secure and turned his attention to the ice wall.

'I shall have to go up first,' he explained, 'to cut footsteps for you to follow.' He noticed her look of alarm and added hastily, 'no, really, it's much easier than it looks.'

He gave her last minute instructions and returned to the business of climbing. Soon splinters of ice were cascading all around her as Adam made his way laboriously upwards.

She shivered as the wind blew suddenly chill. While they had been talking, the sun had disappeared behind a bank of darkening clouds and the day had taken on an altogether more unpleasant aspect.

It was nearly an hour before he let out a shout and she looked up to see him signalling for her to follow. She felt the rope go taut as he reeled it in, and then she had no recourse but to follow in his footsteps. She banged her arms against her sides to get the blood flowing in them more freely and experienced the unpleasant sensation of pins and needles in her finger tips.

Digging the point of her ice axe in a little to the right and at her shoulder level, she placed one foot in the first step he had made, and heaved herself upwards. Soon her other toe engaged with the next foothold and again she was able to use the axe to pull herself upwards.

One thing was certain, she was no longer cold. A combination of adrenalin and effort had raised her temperature to normal and beyond in a matter of minutes. She began to perspire freely and the ripe smell of the balaclava was almost unbearable. She must knit herself one of her own, she decided. It would be the only way to avoid upsetting Adam on another occasion by refusing his.

With surprising ease she reached the ledge on which Adam waited to begin the next stage of the climb.

'Well done,' he said, examining her ropes and tightening them for the next phase. 'You're doing marvellously well for a beginner.'

Morag glowed with pleasure.

If the first hundred feet had seemed sheer, Morag now realised that the angle had been nothing to what faced them now. The wall of rock was vertical.

'Perhaps it's an optical illusion,' she said, gazing upwards, 'but I would swear the rock is actually leaning outwards.'

Adam grinned.

'Well spotted,' he said. 'I believe the angle is about ninety-two degrees in actual fact.'

She paled.

'Don't worry, you won't even notice once you get started.'

She watched him go, chipping steadily at the ice while stopping from time to time to fix a piton where he could find solid rock grinning through. Threading an additional rope through these iron rings took extra time and once more she began to feel the cold seeping into her bones.

At last he shouted for her and she started up. Once again laboriously, hand over hand, step by step, she negotiated the seemingly impossible wall of rock. This time she was comforted by the presence of a rope travelling across the face alongside her, for by taking a hold on it she was able to climb several steps at a time without having to use her ice axe at every move. She accomplished the ascent quite quickly and it was with a glow of immense satisfaction that she sank down beside Adam on the narrow ledge on which he had made his stand.

She looked back the way she had come and was astonished to find that their world was now confined to a circle no more than ten yards across, whose inner edge was formed by the cliff they had scaled. Behind her was a grey formless void which she knew disguised a drop of over two hundred feet to the bottom of the corrie from which they had started.

It was like being cocooned inside a bundle of cotton wool . . . she felt herself beginning to panic.

'It's come down rather more quickly than I anticipated.'

His unruffled observation did much to steady her.

'What now?' she asked, sure that he would find them a way out.

'We'll have to find a bit of shelter and bed down until it blows over,' he decided.

She frowned: there seemed little chance of bedding down, as he put it, on this goat track or deer path or whatever it was.

'Just above our heads, no more than twenty feet, I assure you, there's a narrow cleft in the rock which opens out after a few yards into a space just wide enough to put up a tent. I've done it before, so I know . . .'

'We've got sleeping bags, a stove, plenty to eat . . . we'll be fine 'till morning or when the mist clears.'

How could she argue? There was no alternative. She understood now why he had insisted that they came prepared for a night on the mountain. 'Never go out on a climb without sufficient gear to ensure that you can survive if the weather changes for the worse.

Always carry extra lightweight clothing – lots of thin layers are far better than one eskimo's sealskin coat,' he had told her. 'Food's important too, of course. I always have chocolate and soup cubes which can be dissolved in hot water, sweet biscuits and condensed milk. A pressure stove will work at altitude although you can rarely get the water to boil properly.'

She picked up the rucksack she had dropped with such relief a few moments before.

'Best get going, then?' she asked, not looking forward to a further climb.

'Its easier than before,' he assured her, checking her ropes once again. 'Give me a few feet to get clear and then follow closely in the footholds you see me taking, OK?'

She nodded.

For what seemed like an hour, but could only have been ten minutes at the most, she gazed up at his disembodied boots to which crampons had been strapped to give him extra grip. She was deterred from forging ahead too fast by the thought that he might inadvertently step down on to her hand with those metal spikes.

At last the moment came when instead of the boot, it was his hand which reached to her from out of the mist. She grabbed hold and was pulled to safety.

He led the way between a rock portal in the side of the cliff and they found themselves in what appeared to be a cave without a roof. At some prehistoric time, the roof must have been carried away . . . by ice perhaps? Now the floor was littered with large pieces of rock and a thin layer of soil in which a bed of alpine plants had taken root, making a soft springy turf on which to pitch their tent.

Replete at last, Adam lay back on his sleeping bag which he had spread out for a groundsheet, while Morag crept outside to wash their dishes under a trickle of water which coursed down the rock at the head of the gully.

When she returned, ready to bed down for the night, she found he had opened out both bags and pinned them together to make one large double.

He caught her look of disapproval and grinned.

'It will get much colder if the wind gets up,' he explained. 'We need to share our body warmth.'

When she continued to look doubtful he pointed out his six layers of clothing and her four or five . . . she hadn't disclosed how many.

'If you're thinking of it as a nuptial bed,' he teased, 'it's a pretty chaste one.'

Unprotesting she slipped in beside him. It was cosy as he had said. The climb had sapped more of her strength than she had realised. Warm, her stomach full of high energy food, she turned her face to the wall of the tent and slept.

The wind had dropped an hour before dawn, the sudden silence bringing Morag instantly awake. She went outside to find that the mist had lifted, leaving the moon high and bright in the heavens. She would have crept back in beside Adam and slept some more, but as she did so, her movements disturbed him and he woke with a start.

'What's it like?' he demanded, throwing back the covers.

'Bright moonlight, almost as clear as day.'

'Good,' he decided, and to her astonishment, lit the pressure stove and put some water on to boil.

'A cup of tea,' he suggested, 'then we must be on our way. I've got work to do this morning . . . I dare say you have too.'

She had, of course. It was just that she had lost track of time.

They had set out early on Sunday. It was now half past five on Monday and by rights, she should be reporting for duty at nine o'clock. Well, there was no way they were going to make it in the time. She resigned herself to thinking up some good excuse for her lateness as she began the difficult task of repacking her rucksack.

Adam's associates in the mountain rescue team had been prepared to go out in search of their leader when he did not return at the estimated hour the previous evening, but when they found that visibility had fallen almost to nothing, they decided they must wait until morning. After all, Adam should be able to survive a night out on the mountain in any kind of weather.

Before they could load up Finlay Anderson's old Ford truck the following day, the two wanderers returned, safe and sound. It did not occur to any of these hardened climbers that there might be some impropriety about the events of the previous twenty four hours.

Now that Morag resided outwith the hospital, it was no longer possible for the staff to keep track of her activities. Her night out alone with Adam on the bare mountain passed without comment. In the team's diary the incident was recorded as: *Mr Inglis and trainee stranded overnight on Stob Ghabhar. No assistance required.*

# Chapter 17

For the most part, 1933 did turn out to be a good year for the citizens of Inverlinnhe. Half a dozen further events were staged to raise money for the hospital's X-ray machine. These culminated in a revival of the ancient tradition of holding a Highland Gathering, where entrants paid for the privilege of pitting their strength and skills against their neighbours upon the sports field, while pipers and highland dancers competed in the ring for their prizes.

Tourists began to flood back to the town which the previous summer they had shunned, and the builders got to work on the new housing scheme out beyond Feanagrogan.

The development of the village created a great many new jobs, which meant that there was more money in everybody's pocket. It began to look as though the long years of depression in the aftermath of the Great War were coming to an end.

In the euphoria which was generated by this extraordinary improvement in Inverlinnhe's prospects, it was difficult for people to feel concerned about what was happening abroad. Politics might be holding the attention of barrack-room lawyers in the city pubs, and speakers on their soap-boxes in London's Hyde Park or St Georges Cross in Glasgow, but in Inverlinnhe minds were concentrated upon more parochial matters.

In the *Gazette*, an account of a fire in the German Reichstag, in which volumes containing the wisdom and philosophy of centuries had been committed to the flames, consisted of two paragraphs sandwiched between the results of the Local Government elections, and a report on the increasing numbers of well-known mountaineers who were coming to try their skills out on the Ben.

In March, on a wave of good feeling generated by tangible evidence that the Councillors were at long last doing something about the appalling state of Municipal housing, Fraser and his party were returned to office with a thumping majority. A promise of further long-term employment offered by Fraser's new aluminium smelting works, ensured that Graham Fraser himself would be elected Chairman of the Council for a further term.

During the summer months, the rescue service was called out six times to fetch unfortunate, if often foolhardy, adventurers down from the mountain. On those occasions when she was free to do so, Morag had joined the team, and in more than one case her presence early at the scene had resulted in a life being saved. The time had come for her to obtain official permission to attend rescue missions where the need for a doctor's presence was indicated.

The date chosen for her submission to the Hospital Board happened to coincide with the official hand-over to the hospital of the new X-ray apparatus.

Morag, waiting anxiously to hear the outcome of the debate on her own proposal, was obliged to sit through the presentation ceremony before hearing the committee's decision.

'Ladies and gentlemen!' Graham Fraser called for silence. 'It gives me great pleasure to welcome you here today to witness the presentation to our hospital of some valuable new equipment which has been purchased with money raised through public subscription . . .

Eddie Strachan gave Morag a congratulatory pat on the back, and Mary Neal coloured when she heard Graham Fraser read out her name amongst the list of those involved in the fund raising.

'. . . This hospital strives, at all times, to serve the needs of the entire community, both the residents and the growing number of visitors to the area . . .'

Fraser, once launched upon his prepared speech, lapsed into that accomplished style of delivery which had brought him to the forefront of the political scene. Morag wondered how long it would be before he stood for Parliament.

'The fact that this is a place where people engage in dangerous pursuits, whether on the water or in the mountains, coupled with the growing volume of traffic on our roads, has brought to the West Highland Hospital a greater than average number of those kinds of casualties which require the use of an X-ray machine. I can assure you that this magnificent example of scientific advancement in the twentieth century will be used to the full, and I am sure that successive generations of patients will give thanks for the generosity of the people of Inverlinnhe in contributing towards its purchase.'

The company broke into spontaneous applause.

'I shall now call upon Mrs Ashley Keynes to make the formal presentation of the X-ray unit to the hospital, by unveiling a plaque commemorating the event.

'I need hardly tell you that our guest of honour is no stranger to the town. As the daughter of one of our most distinguished citizens, Harriet McRae grew up in Inverlinnhe and attended school here until she went away to college in Edinburgh.'

Fraser turned to Duncan's daughter, and offered her the golden cord which was attached to a small blue velvet curtain.

'Mrs Ashley Keynes?'

Harriet took the cord from him and turned to face the audience.

'As one who, in my younger days, was more than grateful for the ministrations of doctors and nurses in the West Highland . . . I was forever falling off horses or capsizing my boat . . .' there was a murmur of polite laughter from the older members of staff '. . . it gives me great pleasure to present this X-ray machine to the hospital on behalf of the citizens of Inverlinnhe.'

She pulled the cord and to Christine Kemp's enormous relief, the tiny blue curtain flew back easily to reveal a small brass plaque. Matron and Guthrie had been fiddling with that wretched mechanism for half the morning!

The applause died down and the meeting began to break up as people milled about in the overcrowded foyer. Wine glasses were replenished and the chatter became noisier.

Duncan McRae, with his daughter in tow, made a bee-line to where Morag was standing, surrounded by her colleagues.

'Morag, I believe you may remember having met my daughter Harriet?' he introduced them.

'Under rather stressful circumstances.' Morag smiled as she took Harriet's hand. 'I cannot believe that Mrs Ashley Keynes remembers me . . .'

'Indeed I do, Dr Beaton,' she protested. 'My husband never ceases to sing your praises for what you did for him. And without any X-ray machine to help her, I might add,' she explained to all those about her.

'I trust he is now fully mobile?' Morag enquired.

'There is a slight limp,' Harriet told her, 'but I am so used to it I hardly notice it. It gives him a rather distinguished bearing actually,' she added. 'Makes him sort of interesting . . . you know?' She blushed a little as she found herself revealing this rather charming picture of a youthful bride still basking in the rosy glow of her recent marriage.

'Since Harriet is staying at Achnafraoch for a few days, I thought of having a little garden party on Saturday,' said Duncan. 'I wonder if you would like to come along . . . bring some of your friends?' He included those standing around them in the invitation, and several heads nodded enthusiastically. Duncan McRae's hospitality was well-known in the district and very much appreciated by the townsfolk.

'That's very kind of you, sir.' Eddie Strachan spoke for them all. 'I am sure we would be pleased to take you up on your invitation.'

Duncan acknowledged their acceptance with a smile but it was to Morag that he directed his next words, insisting, 'You will come, won't you? It seems so long since we last met.'

'Well . . . yes, I'd love to.' Flattered to be singled out in this way, she felt the blood rush to her face.

'Oh, good,' Harriet joined in, 'I shall look forward to seeing you again.' She turned to her father with an air which suggested it was time for them to leave.

'I just want one moment in private with Dr Beaton, my dear,' he told her. Then, drawing Morag to one side, he said, 'Your report was excellent.'

'And?' She could hardly bear to hear the outcome of the debate.

'The hospital has agreed that a doctor shall be assigned to the rescue service whenever there is a call-out demanding medical assistance.'

He noted her puzzled frown, and found that he was rather enjoying holding her on tenterhooks in this way.

'But . . .'

He interrupted her protest, smiling broadly.

'Since there is only one doctor on the staff at present who is fully trained in mountain rescue techniques, yours will be the first name on the list for call-out.'

'Oh . . . that's wonderful!' she cried. Without thinking, and before all that gathering of important officials, she threw her arms around Duncan McRae's neck and kissed him on the cheek.

Startled, but relishing the moment, he released himself from her grasp, laughing.

'That was worth all the argument,' he said as he shook her hand, more formally now and then bent forwards and returned her kiss, on the lips this time. 'My congratulations, Morag. I trust you will still be just as delighted the next time you find yourself suspended from a rope, dangling over some bottomless ravine in the pouring rain!'

With mixed emotions, she watched Duncan and his daughter take their leave of Graham Fraser. Christine Kemp and Sidney Maynard had lined up alongside the Chairman to thank the departing guests, and now escorted the couple deferentially towards their limousine as it glided forward and stopped opposite the main door.

Was she imagining it, or was Duncan's response to her kiss just a little more than merely congratulatory? Immediately she put the thought out if her mind. Duncan McRae was an important personage. His daughter was married to the son of a Marquis; one day she would carry a title herself. All three of them moved in circles to which Morag could never hope to be admitted. She felt it foolish even to imagine that he might ever regard her as anything other than a friend.

\* \* \*

It had been a particularly busy morning at the hospital. The Friday list had been longer than usual and Morag's ward round was consequently protracted. By the time she had driven home and changed into a suitable dress for the garden party, she knew that she was going to arrive very late.

She passed the gryphon-guarded gates, waved on by the same ancient retainer she had met in the winter, but now as each turn of the road revealed a different aspect of the loch and the hills beyond, she realised just why Duncan McRae's predecessors had chosen to call their house Achnafroach – the field of heather.

The dull scrubland of November had been obliterated by swathes of ling in full bloom. It painted the acres of open hillside in every shade from pale pink to deepest purple.

She pulled on to the grass verge, beside a collection of vehicles which ranged from a great green Bentley to a little Austin Ruby which sheltered in the shade provided by Gordon McDonald's old Argyll tourer.

As she alighted and shook out the full skirts of her pale green cotton dress, she looked up to see Duncan McRae hurrying towards her.

'I was beginning to think you were not coming,' he said, greeting her warmly with a friendly peck on the cheek.

'I'm sorry, I had a busy morning.'

'Never mind, you're here now and that's what counts.'

He took her by the elbow and led her past groups of gaily dressed women and casually attired men in shirt-sleeves or brightly striped blazers. McRae himself, and several others, wore the kilt.

Those she knew greeted them both cheerfully, while others observed with interest McRae's striking-looking partner, her fiery red hair and pale skin so elegantly set off by the simple green dress.

They wended their way between white-painted wrought-iron furniture scattered about the lawn and up on to the terrace where a gramophone had been set outside to provide music for dancing. A number of young people, oblivious to the rough stonework underfoot, expended a great deal of energy in their wild gyrations. Morag viewed their activities with admiration and not a little regret. She was probably ten years older than most of the dancers, and had to accept that she was past taking such exercise in this heat.

'What a delightful setting for a party,' she observed to Duncan as they approached a particular group situated to one side of the terrace, beside the stone balustrade.

Harriet and her husband, Richard, were surrounded by guests, most of whom were strangers to Morag. She was surprised to see Adam Inglis in this company, and all the more startled to recognise the tall dark figure who was waving his arms animatedly, demonstrating some point that he was making to Adam.

'Dr Beaton, how marvellous to see you again.' Richard Ashley Keynes came forward to greet her. He, like his father-in-law, wore the kilt.

He certainly seemed to Morag to have recovered well. As Harriet had suggested, the slight limp did nothing to detract from his attractive appearance.

Distracted by this encounter with her distinguished patient, Morag failed to notice how Adam's companion had stiffened at the sound of her voice and halted his speech in mid-sentence. Unable to believe his own ears, the gentleman turned so abruptly towards her that he jogged Adam's arm, sending a teacup flying through the air to land with a crash on the stone paving, splattering several people with hot tea.

In the confusion that followed, their eyes met.

'The mountaineering doctor,' he said, smiling broadly. 'We meet again.'

Morag's emotions were mixed. This unexpected encounter conjured up all the circumstances of that day aboard the *Lochfyne* when she had first spoken with the two mountaineers and later been compelled to call upon their assistance . . .

Richard intervened.

'Do you two know each other?' he enquired in surprised tones.

'We have met,' Morag replied, her gaze still locked upon the mountaineer, 'but we have not been properly introduced.'

'Then allow me to do the honours,' said Richard, easily, apparently unaware of the strange tension between them.

'Dr Morag Beaton, this is Rudolf Braun . . . Rudi to his friends.'

'Dr Beaton.' He drew his heels together smartly and bowed stiffly, then to her surprise and embarrassment, as she put out her hand he took it, and kissed it.

She withdrew it quickly, and immediately he was all contrition.

'Oh, excuse me,' he said, 'it is an old-fashioned custom which we have in my country . . .' He shrugged and smiled, beseeching her forgiveness.

'Germany?' she asked.

'Austria.'

'Rudi and I used to climb together in the Alps before . . .' Richard tapped his leg. 'We were planning another expedition to the Himalayas, but I'm afraid we had to call it off after the accident.'

'Did you manage to reach the top of Ben Buie?' she asked Rudi, remembering their conversation aboard ship.

'It was a leisurely afternoon's walk,' he said with a grin, 'but unfortunately, by the time we had reached the top, the mist had come down and we saw nothing.'

'As is so often the way with mountains,' observed Harriet, who had never been able to understand her husband's fascination with climbing.

Because Richard was such an enthusiast, she had agreed to learn to climb herself, but had never been comfortable with the sport. If his accident had done nothing else, it had brought to an end that dangerous aspect of their life.

'And you . . . are you still climbing?' Rudi asked Morag.

'When I can find the time,' she replied, and then, remembering the main topic of the board meeting, turned to Adam.

'By the way, you will be pleased to learn that the Mountain Rescue Service now has an honorary surgeon . . . it's official.'

'Yes, I know,' he said, smiling at her. 'Mr McRae has just been telling us about Wednesday's meeting. It seems that the board was so impressed by your report that they are prepared to supply a certain amount of equipment, together with your services.'

Morag could not have been more pleased.

'I'm almost looking forward to a real call-out,' she said excitedly, and then realising what this implied, looked a trifle embarrassed. 'Not that I would want anyone to get into trouble on the mountain just to give me the opportunity to show off,' she emphasised.

'Maybe I can oblige,' said Rudi, teasing her. 'Adam has promised to join me in an attempt on some of the Cuillins.'

'That's far too far away.' Morag joined in the laughter. 'They must have their own rescue team.'

'In fact, they don't have any official service on Skye,' Adam explained. 'When people go missing in the mountains up there it's often the next Spring before they're brought down.'

Morag shuddered at the thought. It would have been good to have gone with them, all the same. If only she could get the time off work. She pictured a cosy mountain bothy, winds howling outside and rain beating against the window. Snug before a roaring stove, just the two of them. Rudi would have to be there too of course . . .

She shrugged off the thought.

When Mary had been introduced to everyone, she sidled over to where Rudi and Morag stood at the fringe of the crowd.

'Have you heard the good news?' she demanded excitedly. 'McLeod has resigned, and Adam has been offered the post of Borough Engineer . . . isn't it marvellous? He must be one of the youngest people in the country to hold such a post.'

'I'm sure he deserves it,' Morag responded, noting her friend's extraordinary radiance which could hardly be attributed solely to this news of Adam's good fortune.

'Congratulations, Adam,' she called over to him.

He looked bewildered for a moment, raising an eyebrow in query as Mary approached him once more.

'Your promotion,' she explained.

'Oh, right . . . yes . . . thanks. It was quite a surprise,' he called back.

She watched Duncan move across to join the little group surrounding Adam and turned her attentions to Rudi.

On the far side of the terrace, Duncan drew Adam aside, 'Now then young Inglis, this lady is waiting for you to claim her and I am ready to make the announcement.'

Standing at his side, Mary looked particularly demure in a dress of white piqué cotton, almost as severe in cut as her uniform overalls. Despite this she also looked astonishingly beautiful.

Duncan McRae, having checked carefully to see that the waiters had provided everyone with a glass of champagne, now climbed on to a table to make his announcement.

'Ladies and gentlemen . . .' His voice competed unsuccessfully with the noise from the gramophone and someone hurriedly turned off the music.

They were all gathering round and straining to hear him now.

'Ladies and gentlemen, this is a particularly happy occasion for me. I cannot express adequately, the enormous pleasure that it gives me to have so many good friends here today, to celebrate with me the return of my daughter and her husband from their extensive travels abroad.

'Today is special in another respect as well, because I have been asked to perform a particularly pleasant duty on behalf of an old friend who, sadly, is no longer with us.'

He turned to where Adam and Mary were standing, hand in hand, beside the balustrade.

'I only wish that Gregor Campbell were here himself to make this particular speech.' McRae paused, while a number of older guests murmured their agreement. 'But since that cannot be, I take great delight in announcing the engagement of my old friend's nephew, Adam, to this lovely lady here . . . Miss Mary Neal. I give you a toast my friends . . . to Adam and Mary. We wish them a long and happy life together.'

Morag paled.

'Is the young lady a friend of yours?' asked Rudi.

He had noticed her sudden change of expression at Duncan's announcement and gripped her arm firmly, fearing she might faint.

'They both are,' Morag replied in a low voice.

'They did not tell you they were going to announce their betrothal today?'

'No . . . it has come as rather a shock.'

That slight hesitation in giving her reply had not escaped Rudi's notice. 'You feel a little put out that they have kept it from you until now?' he suggested.

How extraordinarily perceptive he is, Morag thought.

'I can only assume that the announcement is in some way connected with the news of Adam's promotion,' she said. Anyway, it's of no importance how I feel. They will make a perfect couple. I am very happy for them.'

He admired her resilience.

'It looks as though you may have to wait a while to offer your congratulations,' he said, pointing out the crowd of people gathered around the couple.

'Are you familiar with the gardens? Will you perhaps show me around while we wait for the crowds to disperse?'

Morag was happy to grab at any excuse for absenting herself from the scene at this moment.

'I have only been here once before myself, and that was in the winter,' she replied, 'but I shall be pleased to explore the grounds with you, if that is what you want.'

She took hold of his arm and he responded by clamping her fingers against his side so that she could feel his muscles moving inside the thin stuff of his shirt. The musky, masculine smell of him was rather disturbing.

In complete silence they wandered from one enclosed garden to the next, indifferent to the careful horticulture and the astonishing array of scents and colours.

While Rudi enjoyed the sensation of having this intriguing woman at his side, Morag was tracing in her mind the series of clues which should have prepared her for today's announcement.

In her fantasies about her own relationship with Adam she had chosen to ignore every sign which might have led her to the truth. Incidents she had witnessed, words spoken, moments when she had observed Adam and Mary together, now came clearly in focus. Never suspecting anything other than friendship between the two, she had always found some reasoned explanation for their closeness. What a fool she had been.

At the stile which marked the edge of the formal gardens and the beginning of the oak wood, she released her hold upon Rudi and stepped over effortlessly. Angry with herself and with Mary who as her friend, had surely owed it to her to give some indication of their intentions, she strode out, unaware that Rudi had fallen behind.

He was quite out of breath by the time he had caught up with her.

Through the gnarled branches, festooned with silvery epiphytic plants, they glimpsed the purple heather in the distance and continued along the path together – no longer touching.

Beyond the edge of the wood they came upon a clearing in amongst the gorse and bracken. Here Morag sank down, burying her nose in the cushions of thyme which carpeted the ground.

Rudi sprawled beside her on the turf watching as idly, she examined one dainty alpine flower after another, breathing the names of each so that he had to strain forward to catch what she said.

'A surgeon, a mountaineer and a botanist,' he teased. 'Is there no end to your accomplishments?

Startled out of her reverie, remembering the times which she had spent alone with Adam, she answered tonelessly, 'Grandfather taught me the names of all the flowers before I could read.' She described the memory games which David Beaton had played with Morag and her brothers on Eisdalsa Island.

'I too had a grandfather whom I loved,' Rudi said, suddenly serious. 'He was more like a father to me.'

'Were you an orphan then?' she asked.

'My mother lives still in our home town of Brenner, but my father was killed on the Somme in 1916.'

'I'm so sorry,' she felt somehow compelled to apologise for the loss her countrymen had inflicted upon him. By way of mitigation she added, 'My father was running a field dressing station in Northern France. He was never in the firing line, but the experience scarred him for life.'

For some reason she felt able to unburden herself to this comparative stranger, anxieties which had gone unspoken for the past fifteen years.

'War is terrible,' she concluded. 'We must never let it happen again.'

He did not reply.

It was as though there had risen between them an invisible barrier through which she must struggle to make further contact.

'We hear so little of what is happening in Germany,' she said, trying to reach him. 'Is Mr Churchill right to warn us against this man Hitler?'

'Oh, yes,' Rudi answered, and there was an edge of steel in his tone. 'It is a pity that none of your other politicians will listen to him.'

'But they say that the National Socialist Party has done so much for the German people,' she protested. 'What about the wonderful roads and all the new building which is going on there? They came out of recession much more quickly than we did.'

'One has to look deeper than efficient railway systems and new schools and hospitals,' he replied. 'One has to listen to what is being said . . . what is being done . . . in the name of German Nationalism.'

'But all those stories about the Jews – surely that's simply newspaper sensationalism? Our Prince of Wales is a frequent visitor there. He seems to consider we have a great deal to learn from the new German order.'

'The ordinary German people themselves have no idea what is going on,' Rudi said, bitterly. 'Or, if they do, they close their eyes to it. In Austria the Nazis are everywhere . . . taking over businesses and local government. Chancellor Dolfuss is their pawn. He has suspended the democratically elected government. Mark my words, there will be an uprising there very soon. My people will not put up with German domination for long.'

'If you feel so strongly about it,' she observed, 'I wonder that you are not at home now, helping to resist the take-over.'

She had not meant it as a reprimand, but it was clear that in his sensitive state Rudi regarded her words as such.

He rose abruptly to his feet.

'It's getting late,' he said. 'I am sure you will want to speak to your friends before they leave.'

He did not offer her his arm this time.

They walked shoulder to shoulder, carefully not coming into closer contact. Morag shivered. The whole afternoon suddenly felt cold.

After a long silence, he spoke again.

'Your friend . . . the one who was so ill on the boat. How is he?'

She took so long to answer that he stopped and turned her to face him.

'He died,' Morag said, quietly.

'Oh, my dear lady . . . I am so sorry. I have been a selfish boor,' Rudi declared, and tucked her hand under his arm once more to lead her back through the wood.

As they emerged on to the sunlit lawn, they caught sight of their host, alone now with his daughter and son-in-law. When Duncan saw them approaching, arm in arm, his face clouded a little, but shrugging off a momentary and inexplicable sense of annoyance, he strode towards them.

'Dr Beaton has been showing me your wonderful gardens,' Rudi greeted him suavely. Then, with an air of studied surprise, 'Oh, dear, has everybody else gone?'

'Thankfully, yes,' Duncan replied. 'It means I can invite you both to stay for dinner . . .'

It had been his intention all along to detain Morag. He had a keen desire to have her spend an evening with his daughter and her husband . . . wanting them to get to know each other, better. This Austrian friend of Richard's had not figured in his scheming. All afternoon he had been agonising over the fact that he and Morag appeared to know one another from some previous encounter. It was obvious that she had been pleased to renew their acquaintance.

Hoping to disguise the strength of his antagonism towards the poor fellow, Duncan casually linked arms and strolled back with them towards the house.

# Chapter 18

Whatever plans Adam and Mary may have had for an early wedding, events during the year which followed combined to prevent their marriage.

In a new wave of prosperity for the region, the Inverlinnhe councillors drew up elaborate plans for developing the local economy and to this end sent their officers on fact-finding tours to both Germany and America. Adam was required to make a number of such trips, while Mary, anticipating that a hospital nursing career would prove incompatible with married life, undertook a six-months' training to become a District Nurse, an occupation with regular hours, and no shift system.

It was late in the summer of 1934 before invitations went out to the marriage of Adam Inglis and Mary McLean, in the village church of Airdmaol on the banks of Loch Lochar.

From occasional casual meetings Morag and Duncan had slipped into an easy relationship which quickly developed into a firm friendship. Duncan now took it for granted that for any local event, he would be Morag's escort. She in turn had come to expect him to collect her beforehand and return her to her cottage at the end of the evening.

Her heavy workload occasionally impinged upon these meetings and she would be forced to call off at the last minute. Duncan never complained, and usually made up for the disappointment with little gifts of flowers or chocolates which she would find waiting on her doorstep at the end of a gruelling evening in theatre.

Morag never questioned his motives in maintaining their friendship on these terms.

From as far back as she could remember she had disregarded any thought of following the conventional role of a woman as wife and mother, and the few romantic adventures she'd allowed herself had never reached a point where she must choose between her lover and her work. She found it difficult to imagine anything taking priority over that.

Even in these enlightened days, married women who continued to follow their profession were the exception rather than the rule. Morag had resigned herself to spinsterhood.

The companionable relationship which she enjoyed with Duncan made few demands upon her emotions. It was, therefore, an acceptable solution to the problems of being a single female moving within a society which still required its women to be accompanied by a respectable male companion, if not a husband.

While Morag took the situation for granted however, Duncan most certainly did not.

Since the day when he had conducted her around his home and taken the unprecedented step of showing her his most treasured possessions, he had hoped ultimately to persuade her to become his wife. That was why, when she had suggested that he accompany her to her friend Mary's wedding, he had been tempted to refuse. He did not think he could bear to attend any wedding ceremony in Morag's company, unless it was their own.

'Miss Neal is your colleague,' he had insisted, 'I hardly know her.'

'But Adam is the nephew of your old friend,' Morag replied. 'Why, it was you who announced their betrothal.'

Only her obvious disappointment that he might not be coming with her, had caused him to relent, for the truth was that he could deny her nothing.

They were early.

Duncan had called for Morag at number one Canal Row with ample time to spare for the drive along the canal and north-east towards Loch Lochar.

There had been little sign of wedding festivities as they drove into the village of Airdmaol, a single row of slate-roofed cottages which crouched beside the loch on the lower slopes of Binneach Dubh. There were a few private cars parked haphazardly along both sides of the street, almost certainly more than usual, but the houses were silent in the morning sunshine.

Duncan drove past the tiny post office and pulled in to park on a wide grassy verge in front of the gates to the village school which Mary had once attended.

'We might as well go on to the church,' he suggested, helping Morag to alight. 'It looks as though it might be quite a step.'

Built at the time of the Disruption by the breakaway section which was to become known as the Wee Frees, Airdmaol's sole place of worship stood on a grassy promontory which jutted out into the loch. It was approached by a narrow stony path where mechanised forms of transport had no place. Coffins for burial and babies for christening must be carried up from the road. By tradition, bride and groom walked to the church in company with their families and friends.

A rickety sign indicated the direction they should take and they set off, ambling slowly, enjoying the sights and scents of the countryside.

Morag, uncomfortable in her high-heeled shoes, bought new for the occasion, tottered along uncertainly until Duncan took pity on her and grasped her hand to steady her.

'It's a very romantic setting for a wedding,' he remarked as they passed through an old, wrought-iron kissing gate which gave access to a spinney of gnarled oaks and alders.

Under the trees the ground was still soft despite the recent spell of dry weather. Morag was obliged to hop from one dry patch to another to avoid muddying her shoes.

'Mary said it was an unmade path . . . she didn't suggest it might be a muddy one!' she laughed, holding on to her large floppy hat to prevent it from being brushed off by the lowest branches.

She seemed so young and full of spirit. Duncan feasted his eyes upon her . . . and wished.

Pausing beside the burn, they watched young mallards testing their strength against their fledgling brothers. There was much squawking and flashing of new-grown coloured wing feathers.

'How like young males everywhere,' she observed. 'They always have to resort to fighting for their territory ... surely there must be a less aggressive solution to the problem?'

'The survival of the fittest,' he replied. 'You of all people must uphold the Darwinian theory.'

'It's a solution for animals in the wild, perhaps,' she agreed, 'but human beings have been given minds with which to reason. Surely we are meant to solve our problems without shooting one another?'

'You'd think people of our generation would have had enough of fighting, wouldn't you?' he said. 'But the way things look at present, another war seems almost inevitable.'

They had been following newspaper reports of events in Austria following the assassination of Chancellor Dolfuss. Just as Rudi Braun had predicted, the Nazi Party had begun to infiltrate every facet of local and national government. Even more disturbing had been the newsreel reports showing rallies of uniformed young men, even women and children, parading arrogantly through the streets, while crowded assemblies were harangued by blustering politicians.

'Have you heard anything more of Rudi Braun?' she asked him, suddenly, remembering the intense hatred the Austrian climber had shown for the Germans. 'It must be nearly a year since he was over here.'

'No, not a word,' replied Duncan. Then, tentatively, he asked,

'You have not kept in touch with him yourself?'

'No, why should I? I hardly know him.'

Duncan struggled to disguise his relief. Many times during the past months he had wondered about her association with the Austrian. He was a rugged, adventurous fellow, just about her own age, the kind of man that a woman like Morag might well find attractive. They had seemed to have a great deal to say to each other that afternoon at Achnafraoch . . . But obviously Duncan need not have worried.

'It's quite possible that Rudi's not even in the country,' Duncan suggested. 'There was some talk of an expedition to Everest you may remember. Perhaps he found someone else to take Richard's place.'

For Rudi's sake he hoped that this was true, but from what his son-in-law had told him, it was more than likely that the ebullient young man was in conflict with the authorities in his homeland.

As though reading Duncan's thoughts, Morag said suddenly, 'I hope that he hasn't got himself into any trouble . . . with the new regime, I mean. He struck me as being patriotic to the point of fanaticism.'

'How did the two of you come to know one another?'

Before this, Duncan had not wanted to hear the truth about their friendship. Now that it was clear that there was nothing for him to worry about, he was curious to know how they had met.

'He was with an English friend, travelling on the steamer to Iona, the day that Magnus was taken ill on Staffa. The two of them helped me to carry him back to the boat. Meeting Rudi again at your house brought it all back . . .'

The thought of Magnus still brought tears to her eyes, he noticed. Well, that was understandable. He himself was easily moved by any reference to his wife, even after all these years . . .

Anxious to change the mood he said, 'Anyway, we should be talking of more agreeable things than what is happening in Europe, on a day like this.'

'I suppose so,' she agreed. 'It's just that you are the only person I *can* talk to about these things, without being branded a scaremonger. No one else seems to want to discuss what is going on under their noses. It's almost as if they believe that by ignoring it, they will make it go away.'

He had always considered himself privileged to be allowed

to share her confidences. It was one aspect of their friendship that he had come to value above all else.

She trusts me, he told himself, but is it as friend . . . a father figure perhaps? Or . . . is it possible . . . could it ever be . . . as a lover?

'It is so good to have a real friend,' she told him enthusiastically, giving his hand a little squeeze. 'There were times when I first came here to work that I felt the whole world was against me. It hasn't been easy, you know. Even now I feel all the time that I am under a microscope. I don't think I could have stuck it out had it not been for you . . . and Magnus and Gordon too, of course,' she added hastily.

Is this the moment? he wondered.

Despite their growing intimacy in recent months, Duncan had never found a suitable opportunity to reveal the truth about his feelings for Morag. Perhaps he was a trifle intimidated by her.

He admired so much about her. She was such a strong character, always so determined, so persistent . . . and yet she managed to balance her toughness with such charm and good humour. It was difficult to believe that anyone could resist her when she was bent on one of her crusades.

He admired her knowledge and skill as a surgeon. He had often found himself envying Gordon McDonald his ability to discuss the topics which interested her most profoundly and he was intrigued by her dedication to her work, knowing in his heart that not even marriage to a man she truly loved would persuade her to give it up.

He loved her with an extraordinary devotion, yet he feared that were he to express the strength of feeling which the very mention of her name stirred within him, he might frighten her off for good.

How can I ever tell her how much I love her? he demanded of himself. Why should such a handsome and gifted young woman have any romantic interest in a widower, so much older than herself?

While he pondered this in an agony of indecision, Duncan steered her along the path in silence.

Morag gave her attention to the wild flowers scattered in the long grass and the occasional flash of a bird's wing in the dense undergrowth. If she noticed his silence at all, it was to suppose that he, like her, was totally absorbed in the beauty of their surroundings.

Soon they emerged into the sunlight and were confronted by their first proper view of Kilcladach, the kirk by the shore.

In the still air, there was not even a ripple on the water. The glorious reds, yellows and browns of autumn, the tall peaks of the surrounding mountains and the clear blue September sky, were all reflected faithfully in the mirror-like surface of the loch.

The grim little church had been softened over the years by honeysuckle and ivy which, clinging to the walls of corrugated iron, crept out between window frames and from underneath the eaves. It was as though Nature, having taken the steel and timber framework to her bosom, had encouraged the old building to take root here, uniting with the bracken, gorse and heather which encroached on every side.

Duncan would have gone straight up to the door, but Morag held back.

'Do we have to go straight in?' she asked. 'It is so beautiful out here.'

Without waiting for his reply, she pulled her hand free from his and continued on down to the shore of the loch. There she began to seek for flat pebbles which she could skim across the surface.

She made a masterly shot. The stone bounced three times before slithering across the water and sinking.

Not to be outdone, he too stooped down and gathered up a stone. He flung it well out into the loch. It skipped once and sank. Even in this she could outclass him.

She threw again, tripped, lost her balance and would have tumbled into the water had he not grabbed her, laughing.

'Look out ... you can hardly go into church dripping wet!'

He retained his hold on her arm rather longer than necessary.

Sensing the tension in him, Morag did not pull away immediately but turned towards him. Then, disturbed by the intensity of his gaze, she drew back.

He took her hand, led her over to a fallen log and gently pulled her down beside him. He had spent hours rehearsing the words he would use when this moment arrived, but now all he could find to say was, 'I love you, Morag.'

'Duncan . . . I . . .' Taken completely off guard, she searched desperately for the right words.

'Oh, I have taken unfair advantage of you,' he declared miserably, assuming that her silence meant refusal. 'It was stupid of me to choose a time when you are thinking only about your friends and their future happiness. Forgive me, it was just that I couldn't wait any longer to tell you how I feel about you . . .'

She placed her fingers over his lips to stop the flow of words.

'Hush, my dear,' she said, her voice low and tremulous, 'there is no need to apologise for telling me that you love me.'

She withdrew her fingers, placing her hands in her lap and absently fiddling with the thin gold ring she always wore on her right hand.

'I have been trying to find the courage to speak, ever since the day you came to Achnafraoch about the Hogmanay ball. Do you remember?'

'I course.' She smiled. Could she ever forget?

'I have always regarded you as a good friend,' she began, hesitantly. 'You have been my knight in shining armour. I suspect you were even responsible for my appointment to the hospital, and when there was all that trouble about poor Mr Campbell, you were the one who stood up for me.'

She knew now that all those small attentions, his many kindnesses, had been not because he felt sorry for her, but because he loved her. How could she have been so stupid as not to have realised that? All this time she had been living from one moment to the next, enjoying the time that they spent together but too preoccupied with her work to give him a moment's thought when they were apart. How selfish and inconsiderate she must have seemed at times; how careless of his feelings on those occasions when for quite trivial reasons she had turned down some treat which he had planned for her entertainment. If only he had given her a clue, some small indication of how he felt about things.

'Look,' he said, 'I can see that this has come as a surprise. Don't give me your answer yet. Take time to think about it . . . please.'

He kissed her lightly on the lips and drew away.

The desire to return his kiss was strong in her. She put out her hand to bring him back, but at that moment the notes of *Bonnets of Blue*, played on the bagpipes, heralded the approach of the wedding party.

The spell was broken.

'We might as well go along in,' Duncan said, getting to his feet and offering her his hand. 'In such a little church it will probably be quite difficult to find a seat.'

Hand in hand, they climbed the grassy knoll to the iron-studded, wooden door then, standing to one side, Duncan allowed Morag to precede him into the dim interior.


On this perfect autumnal day, bride and groom, parents, family and friends, marched along gaily to the drone of the pipes.

Pipe-major Laughlan was resplendent in the dress uniform of the Highland Light Infantry. As his kilt swung to the rhythm of the tune he played, the occasional whiff of mustiness and naphtha mingled with the heavy scent of gorse and heather. He had long ago put away his uniform, to be brought out only on the most important of occasions.

Laughlan had set a punishing pace to get them marching along the village street, but by the time that the church came into view over the crest of the hillock, he was forced to rest. He leaned heavily on the parapet of a tiny stone bridge and allowed the guests to pass on to the church ahead of him.

The day was warm it was true, but his shortness of breath

owed more to the mustard gas he had inhaled nearly twenty years before, at a place called Ypres in Northern France.

Mary stopped when she saw him resting on the wall, and slipped her hand from beneath Adam's arm.

'Are you all right, Dad?' she demanded anxiously, running to his side.

She had tried to dissuade him from playing his pipes, but he had insisted.

'My wee 'un shall be piped to her wedding,' he had insisted. 'I have waited far too long for this day!'

'Och, leave the piping now, you stupit wee mon!' Mary's mother cried, as she too left the main cortège and came to see what was amiss.

'Ye'll be needing all y'strength to stand up in the kirk beside our girl. Here, gie me the pipes an' I'll leave them by the door.'

She wrested the instrument from his grasp and shuffled into the church behind the guests, pausing in the porch to rid herself of the bagpipes.

Mary hovered anxiously over her father until he had recovered himself.

'If ye'll just give me a wee hand . . . aye, that's it.' Laughlan rose unsteadily to his feet, then leaned heavily on Mary's arm. Father and daughter moved slowly towards the church.

It was a highland wedding in the truest sense, similar in every respect to those which Morag had witnessed so often in the church of Kilbrendan, over the hill from her home at Tigh na Broch.

In general the ladies wore short, full-skirted summer dresses in pastel shades, and the wide-brimmed straw hats which were the current fashion.

Mary's outfit was a smart suit in cream silk, of a cut as severe as one of her uniform dresses. Morag had often wondered why she always chose to wear such tailored clothes and concluded that this was how Adam liked to see her.

The bride's wide-brimmed, cream straw hat was decorated with silk ribbons of palest yellow, and a posy of roses which matched those in her small bouquet.

Adam, in the dark green tartan of the Campbell clan, and Mary's father in his splendid uniform, provided the perfect foil to this vision of elegant simplicity.

Most of the men wore the kilt. Gordon McDonald, looking as always at his best in his clan tartan, had swept past them with an unusually demure Anna upon his arm. Her simply-cut dress in light green silk was relieved only by a large, floppy hat in black straw which covered her dark locks completely, placing half her face in deep shadow. As usual she had managed to achieve an alluring air of mystery.

The doctor and his wife seated themselves a few rows in front, and Gordon turned in his pew to acknowledge Morag and Duncan's presence. She nodded to him in response, then stared, unseeing, towards the altar. It was clear that her thoughts were elsewhere . . .

A gentle nudge from Duncan caused Morag to look up as Eddie Strachan, surrounded, it seemed, by the entire nursing staff of the West Highland Hospital, tried to attract her attention.

'They must have hired a coach,' she muttered as she gave a little wave of acknowledgement.

A disapproving sniff from behind them made her turn around. She turned back swiftly on seeing the offended expressions of two of the village matrons, and did her best not to laugh. She was reminded of the women in the church at home. They too had been strict disciplinarians, frowning upon any sign of frivolity in the congregation.

Duncan raised a questioning eyebrow, wondering what was causing her to smile, and Morag shook her head. She would save her explanation until later . . .

As the ceremony unfolded before them, she could feel Duncan's eyes upon her. Each part of the service seemed to have a powerful significance for their own situation.

*If anyone can show just cause . . .*

There was so much against a marriage to Duncan. He came from such a different background. His daughter was married to a Marquis' son. One day she would be a Marchioness. What would she think of her father's marriage to the daughter of a humble general practitioner? How would she react to a step-mother who had been obliged to work for her living? Then there was the house itself. How could Morag hope to manage such a mansion? The only experience she had had of servants was the maid of all work who had been her mother's helper and friend for a quarter of a century.

*Do you, Adam, take Mary?*

Did Duncan want to take Morag? Yes, she was sure of it. Oh, yes, he would love, honour and keep her.

*Do you Mary, take Adam?*

Did Morag want to take Duncan? Could she love, honour . . . and obey? After all these years of making decisions for herself, was she prepared to let him take her over, body and soul? Was she ready to give up the freedom she had won so arduously?

She sneaked a glance in his direction.

He was a handsome man, always immaculate in his appearance, a person whom any woman would be proud to partner. At all times he was solicitous for her comfort. They shared a quirky sense of humour which often left their companions wondering what the joke was. They both loved fine things – porcelain, paintings, furniture – and both were able to speak the language of the Gaels which they had inherited from their ancestors. Often in their quiet moments together they conversed in the melodic language of the Highlands.

Feeling her eyes upon him, and guessing perhaps at the thoughts tumbling through her mind at this moment, he took hold of her hand, gripping it so firmly that their knuckles scraped the hard wooden pew between them. This was how they remained until the last strains of the harmonium had died away and the rest of the congregation had filed out.

In the confusion outside the church, as family and friends gathered for the inevitable photographs, they managed to slip away unseen and took a path which led back towards the village along the shore.

Once out of sight of the wedding guests, Duncan stopped and turned away from her, facing out across the water.

'I am just as you find me,' he blurted out, 'fifteen years older than you and no way near so intelligent. I know how much your work means to you . . . I wouldn't expect you to give up, you know, not unless you wanted to, of course.' He threw his arms wide in despair. 'There is absolutely no reason why you should want to marry me . . .'

Morag could not believe that this tongue-tied creature was the forceful person she had come to know and respect. Was this what love did to a man?

'Perhaps you should try asking me?' she suggested, smiling at his confusion.

'Morag . . . Morag, *will* you marry me?'

She spoke so softly that he thought he might have misheard her.

'Say that again,' he demanded.

'Oh, Duncan, of course I'll marry you.'

'My dearest love!' He drew her into his arms.

In all the time they had known each other, never once had he said or done anything to indicate the strength of his feelings for her. Now it all came tumbling out . . . a mixture of disjointed phrases, interrupted by the flurry of little kisses which were rained upon her hands, her cheeks, her neck, her ears . . . teasing, caressing, thrilling.

At last their lips met in one long passionate kiss which left them both breathless.

They separated for a moment, too amazed by their own reactions to speak at all.

'When shall we have the wedding?' he demanded at last. The great weight of indecision had been lifted. He felt as carefree as a schoolboy.

'Hold on a minute,' she said, laughing with him, 'we shall have to tell people . . . my parents.' She giggled.

'What?'

'Suppose they don't approve of you?'

He frowned, taking her seriously for a minute.

'You don't think . . . ?'

'No, of course not. They will love you as I do.' There, she had said it and she meant it with all her heart.

He hugged her again.

'You make me so happy,' he said.

Talk of her family reminded her of the one matter which did concern her still.

'What will Harriet and Richard think?' she asked, suddenly serious. Duncan was devoted to his daughter . . . she had no wish to cause any kind of friction between them.

'Harriet will love you as I do,' he answered, 'and Richard is already your devoted slave. We'll invite the two of them to dinner very soon, and make an official announcement.'

He gathered her in his arms once more and kissed her tenderly. 'My own darling, darling Morag.'

# *Chapter 19*

⤛

'Morag . . . sorry to wake you so early . . .'

'Adam?' Morag turned over in bed so that she could prop herself against the headboard to speak into the phone. 'What is it?'

'An emergency . . . I can't really discuss it now. Can you meet me at the hospital in half an hour?'

Adam was not given to exaggeration; the urgency of his tone was enough to bring her fully awake.

'OK,' she replied. 'I presume we're talking about major surgery?'

'I'm afraid so,' he replied laconically.

'Then I'd better alert the theatre staff.'

'There's no need,' he answered mysteriously, 'Gordon says he can assist.'

'What about Eddie Strachan?'

'Don't bother him. Gordon says *he* will administer the anaesthetic too if necessary.'

'All right . . . thirty minutes.' She replaced the handset in its cradle and slipped out of bed.

She always slept with her window slightly open and the curtain drawn back. It was still pitch-black outside. Whatever time was it?

She pulled the curtains to, and switched on the light. She glanced at the clock . . . three-twenty. With a groan she pulled on her clothes and hurried into the kitchen.

The cottage still had only one bedroom and a large living room on the ground floor. The builders had adapted the old closet and the box-bed behind it to form a passage through to the neat extension at the rear which now provided a small

349

kitchen and a bathroom large enough to house a full-length slipper bath.

Morag turned on the gas and half filled a kettle before slipping into the bathroom and dashing cold water on her face. That was better . . . she felt more awake, now.

She ran a comb through her hair and then, alerted by the whistling kettle, hurried back into the kitchen and made the tea. Emergency it might be, but it would be no use her arriving at the hospital still only half awake and weak from hunger. She cut a thick slice of bread and spread it liberally with butter.

Precious minutes were passing. She crammed the last of the bread in and swallowed the tea while it was still too hot. The liquid scalded her throat as it went down, but at least she felt prepared to meet the world again. Closing the front door quietly so as not to disturb her elderly neighbours, she hurried down the path and climbed into her car.

The sky was beginning to lighten now.

In the grey light of an early dawn, the houses in Canal Row appeared quite unchanged from that day, nearly eighteen months ago, when she had taken possession of Magnus's bequest to her. In daylight she knew that things looked very different. Rotten windows and ill-fitting doors had been replaced, chimney stacks had been rebuilt, and in many cases the tiles had been removed and the whole roof reslated. The provision of a good supply of fresh water and a proper sewage system had made it feasible to add bathroom and kitchen extensions to all the houses.

Adam's plan for a new village had worked out well on the whole, she reflected, slipping the Morris into top gear as she approached the green. Even if some of the buildings were still under construction. After the first flush of enthusiasm, when houses had shot up almost overnight, things had slowed down considerably. When it came to the special facilities which had been promised, the Municipal coffers had suddenly become strangely empty once again, and several essential buildings had been deferred.

On the far side of the pond, the school and church still had scaffolding around them, but nevertheless the school had opened in time for the new academic year.

The village shop and the garage had been two of the earlier buildings to be completed, together with the first circle of Corporation houses. The doctor's tiny surgery next door to the garage had remained empty for nearly a year, until Gordon had agreed to take it over. Now he held a surgery there on two mornings and one evening each week.

As had been anticipated, there was no shortage of employment.

The construction of Fraser's new aluminium plant and the Authority's anticipated hydro-electric station had got underway during the first months of the development of the new village, and many of the incoming residents on the estate were well placed to seek employment at the works.

Morag's Morris 8 groaned alarmingly as she reduced speed and changed gear before turning out on to the main road into town. She had been thinking about buying another car for some time. She rather fancied one of the latest Morgans . . . there had been several of them about Inverlinnhe this summer. Earlier on, the thought of spending two hundred pounds on a car had seemed out of the question. It was strange to think that in such a short time financial worries of that kind would all be behind her.

Would she ever get used to the idea of being wealthy? she wondered. Sometimes she felt quite frightened at the thought of the enormous responsibility she was about to take on. She was not just marrying Duncan, but the whole Achnafraoch Estate and goodness knows what business interests that helped to maintain it. Duncan had scarcely touched upon the source of his wealth during their discussions about their future together. She supposed that he took such matters so much for granted that he had not thought to mention them.

Little had been said so far about her work at the hospital. He had been adamant that she should continue there for as long as she wanted, but she was not so foolish as to believe that their marriage could have any sound basis were she to continue working the long hours she was obliged to under her present contract.

The elderly engine coughed, cleared and sped smoothly along the recently relaid tarmac into the town centre. As though it were trying to justify a stay of execution, it made no further protest even when Morag made a left-hand turn up the steep hill on the approach to the hospital.

Gordon's car was parked outside the emergency exit alongside a plain khaki truck ... some kind of military vehicle, she supposed.

She hurried inside to find Adam waiting by the night porter's desk and a worried-looking army officer impatiently pacing the floor of the reception area.

Seeing Morag approach, Adam held open the swing door and led her to the officer who had stopped his perambulations at her appearance and now stood transfixed, staring rudely at her through the monocle which was screwed firmly into his right eye.

'Major Prendergast, this is Dr Beaton.'

The officer glared at them both.

'You said nothing about your precious surgeon being a ...' he cleared his throat noisily '... well, a female, Inglis. I hardly think this is a job for a lady.'

'Dr Beaton is the best there is, Major,' Adam replied hastily, seeing Morag colour in annoyance.

Ignoring the soldier, she demanded of Adam, 'I imagine I shall find the patient already in theatre?'

He nodded, sheepishly.

'Gordon is with him.'

She turned on her heel and disappeared into the accident wing. As the swing door closed behind her she distinctly heard the Major's gruff voice saying, 'God knows what the world is coming to. No gel of mine would be allowed to do a job like that!'

It was unbelievable. The year was 1934 and there were still men who regarded their women as decorative chattels. Seething with rage, she burst into the theatre's ante-room.

Gordon, already gowned, was busy with the patient who lay on a narrow trolley. A light sheet covering his naked body left only his head exposed. A wad of gauze covered one side of his face and from the appearance of the exposed skin she guessed he had been severely burned.

Gordon looked up sharply at her entrance.

'He's a bit of a mess, Morag . . .'

'So I see.' She lifted the corner of the wadding. It came away with a layer of charred skin adhering to it. The facial tissues were red and raw, the features barely distinguishable.

She pulled back the sheet.

Gordon had done his best to remove the man's clothing but a large area down one side of the body was so badly burned that the remaining scraps of clothing were firmly stuck to the scorched tissues.

'I thought perhaps a boracic acid bath?' Gordon suggested. He adjusted the oxygen mask which he was obliged to hold a few millimetres above the scorched mouth and nose for fear of touching the raw tissues.

'Yes,' she said as she went through the stages of a routine examination. One thing which the Gregor Campbell episode had taught her was that no matter how urgent the case, as complete a history as possible should be obtained before proceeding with any treatment.

'What do we know about the subject? Apart from the burns, that is.'

'He is an exceptionally healthy young man . . . classed A1 by the Military,' Gordon emphasised.

She noted the rapid pulse and slow heart rate, and assessed the probability of the patient going into shock. It was no good hanging about . . . Gordon was quite right. First they must get the burned areas clean or septicaemia would undoubtedly set in.

'How long since the accident?' she asked abruptly.

Gordon examined his watch.

'Approximately six hours,' he estimated.

'What took so long to get him here?'

'He had to be located, then carried down from the north face of Meall Breac.'

'How on earth . . . ?' Morag thought she had witnessed every kind of injury which might be incurred on the mountains. Burning was a new one and quite incomprehensible to her.

'It was a plane crash.' Gordon, having had the need for extreme secrecy impressed upon him by the Major, was unsure just how much he should tell Morag.

'What on earth was the fool doing in an aircraft, in the mountains, in the middle of the night?'

As she spoke Morag had moved into the sluice room where a large slipper bath occupied a central position. She turned on the taps, tested their temperature and added a liberal amount of boracic acid.

'All right, wheel him in here,' she called.

The patient was a heavily built young man, weighing thirteen stones at least. 'I'll take the oxygen mask,' she said brusquely, 'go and fetch Adam to help you lift him.' As an afterthought she shouted after him, 'Not that obnoxious creature that's with him . . . I've seen just about enough of him for one night!'

Mystified by her vehemence as Morag was not usually given to taking an instant dislike to people, Gordon hurried away, to return minutes later with Adam.

With some difficulty the three of them lifted the patient and lowered him gently into the bath of lukewarm water.

The sudden change in environment revived him and he screamed out in agony. Gordon grabbed for the oxygen mask once again while Morag took up a substantial pair of tweezers and began to peel away an indistinguishable mess of charred clothing and flesh. As the man sank into unconsciousness once more, Adam and Gordon struggled to keep his head above the water while she worked.

At last they were ready to lift him back on to the trolley. Morag dried the areas of unaffected skin and covered him with a clean sheet.

'Layers of gauze soaked in picric acid?' She put the question to Gordon. He had far more experience of this kind of accident than she.

He nodded, concentrating once again on ensuring that the patient had sufficient oxygen. A sudden collapse at this stage and he might die, or at the very least suffer brain damage.

She covered the affected areas with the bright yellow gauze, holding it firmly in place with bandages. Now only the face remained. Uncontaminated by clothing as were the other wounds, the charred skin could be removed with comparative ease. More layers of gauze completed the dressing.

'We used to use saline injections,' observed Gordon, remembering long-forgotten techniques carried out on the battlefield. 'It's to compensate for the loss of fluids over the burned area.'

'Of course!' She prepared the equipment rapidly and pumped the life-giving fluid into the patient's undamaged left arm.

'We'll leave him here to recover,' Morag decided, giving a morphine injection to dull the inevitable pain. 'I'll have him taken up to the ward when the day staff come on duty.'

She looked to Gordon for confirmation. He turned to Adam who shuffled uncomfortably and murmured, 'I'll go and see what he wants done,' before hurrying from the room.

'What's going on?' Morag demanded, bewildered.

'It's a bit awkward,' Gordon attempted to explain. 'The fact is they don't want anyone to know about this . . . it's all a bit hush-hush.'

'This man requires expert nursing over a long period of time,' she insisted. 'How does your precious Major hope to keep that a secret?'

Gordon shrugged. 'He's not my Major,' he told her. 'I just happened to be around when Adam was called out to act as guide in the search for the crashed plane. They thought I might be useful so I went along too.'

'If the mountain rescue team was called out, why was I not included?' Everyone knew she was deemed to be the best doctor to attend climbing accidents.

'They weren't,' he explained patiently. 'Only Adam. The rest were Military personnel.'

Adam returned with Major Prendergast. The officer approached the trolley upon which the patient was sleeping as a result of the drug he had been given. He sniffed, cleared his throat loudly and turned to Morag.

'Looks as though you've done a reasonable job, young woman,' he said, grudgingly. 'You can leave him to us now.' He called out to a pair of uniformed soldiers hovering in the corridor.

'Right, Corporal, wheel him out to the ambulance, at the double.'

'Just a moment!' Morag protested, holding fast to the trolley. 'When you delivered this man into my hands, he became my patient. I decide whether he is fit to be moved, and I am telling you now that he is not!'

'Madam, you have no say whatsoever in the matter. This is Ministry of Defence business and no concern of yours.'

His condescending manner was more than she could stand.

'Then I require a written statement that you have, against my advice, removed this patient from the hospital. You will also exonerate the Hospital Authorities from responsibility for any deterioration in the patient's condition resulting from this interference.'

Predergast looked at her with a certain admiration. Damn me if she isn't a spirited little filly, he thought, and wished himself a few years younger.

'Very well,' he blustered, 'give me a sheet of paper . . .'

If Morag noticed the grins which were exchanged by Adam and Gordon, she chose to ignore them. She returned to her patient, checking him over thoroughly before allowing the soldiers to wheel him away.


'I wanted you to know the position as soon as you arrived.'

Wearily, Morag placed the Major's statement in front of Sydney Maynard. She had been looking out for his arrival anxiously since early morning. It was unusual for him to arrive so late in the day.

'I managed to get the officer in charge to sign a waiver,' she explained. 'In my opinion the patient was too ill to be moved, but it seemed that National Security was more important than a man's life.'

'You appear to have managed the affair with your usual efficiency, Dr Beaton.' Although Maynard had never softened in his attitude towards her, during the years in which they had worked together he had formed a grudging respect for her abilities.

'I suspect we will hear no more of the affair,' she continued. 'As long as the Press don't get hold of it. I just hope there will be no more night flights into the mountains. What the Military think they're up to, heaven knows. I have never seen such horrific injuries . . .'

'If things continue as they are going,' Maynard murmured with unusual vehemence, 'you will be seeing plenty more . . . and worse. Thank heaven I shall be out of it, myself.'

She looked up, inquiringly.

'The news will be out officially soon enough,' he explained. 'I think you should hear it straight from the horse's mouth, as it were.'

He got up from his chair and moved over to the window. His glance took in the activity in the forecourt of the hospital. Nurses in their blue-and-white uniforms and white-coated doctors hurried back and forth between the buildings, anxious to get inside out of the strong November wind which, as it did every year at this time, had veered to the north-east and blew down the Great Glen at almost hurricane force.

No patients outside in wheelchairs today, Maynard thought, as he watched visitors, laden with paper bags and bunches of flowers, hurrying from the bus stop to the main entrance, heads down, battling against the elements.

It had been a long time . . . nearly twenty years . . . since he was invalided out of the RAMC just as the war ended. He had got in ahead of the rush for appointments. Inverlinnhe was a backwater, hardly a place to be sought after by the most go-ahead young surgeons. It had suited him, however. The work was not arduous on the whole – especially since this young woman, here, had come to lift much of the burden from his shoulders. He had managed to disregard his disability . . . until recently.

The pains had become intolerable lately. So much so that he

357

had made a couple of visits to an old college chum at the Royal . . . a specialist in brain surgery. It seemed that the blow he had received during the fighting in the closing stages of the war had been the initial cause. According to old Dougie Dewer, the tumour was now inoperable.

Morag waited. It was clear that her boss was having difficulty finding the words to tell her . . . whatever it was. He staggered slightly as he turned to face her.

She half rose from her seat. 'Are you ill?' she asked, startled by his appearance.

The change in him, which must have been happening steadily during the past few weeks, had been so subtle as to go unnoticed until this moment. Now, as if seeing him properly for the first time, she observed the sunken eyes and cheeks, the deep shadows which threw his normally round and rosy features into sharp relief. He had lost a great deal of weight. Why had she not seen this coming? Wrapped up in her own exciting new life, she had been blind to what was taking place under her nose.

'I am forced to retire, it seems,' he told her bluntly. 'Some trouble arising from an old wound.'

'But surely . . . an operation? You're a relatively young man. You'd soon pick up afterwards.' She might have been talking to a lay person. Of course, if he said he must retire, then he must know best.

'It's a tumour . . . inoperable they tell me.'

'How long?'

'A few months at the most.'

'I am so sorry.' What more could she say? They had not been the best of friends, but she would not wish for such an end to befall anyone.

'The fact remains that the West Highland will soon be without its consultant in surgery,' he went on.

She was sorry that it had to end this way. So the hospital would be having a new consultant as well as a new registrar in surgery. She had intended to give Maynard notice today of her own departure at the end of the year.

Her news could wait for a while . . . there was no need to burden him with additional problems just at present.

'Of course, consultancy carries no salary.' He seemed to be thinking aloud. 'One has to rely upon private practice to pay the bills, with the occasional windfall from some grateful private patient who is willing to pay an astronomical fee. Still, *you* won't have to worry about where the next meal's coming from.'

He laughed with just a hint of that old derision with which he had addressed her in the early days. 'One advantage of being a *woman* surgeon, I suppose,' he concluded.

Morag found the conversation confusing. Was the poor man wandering . . . had his mind already begun to deteriorate?

'Well, when do you want to take over? So far as I am concerned, it can't be too soon. I'll hang around if you really want me, but I have to confess that my eyesight is beginning to fail. I've had a few little turns recently while operating. Sister Dunwoodie is too polite to say anything but I know she has been a bit concerned . . .'

'Are you saying you want me to stand in for you until a new consultant can be appointed?' she demanded.

'I'm suggesting that you take on the job permanently,' he replied. 'Who better?'

'But the board . . . won't they have something to say about it?'

'Of course they will. Don't you realise that they are one hundred percent behind everything you do these days? Besides, you won't be able to carry on as registrar once you marry McRae. It seems to me an ideal solution . . . two days a week here and as little or as much as you want to do elsewhere.'

Morag didn't ask how he came to know about her forthcoming marriage. There were few secrets inside a hospital and only a blind man would have missed the subtle change in Duncan's behaviour towards her since Mary and Adam's wedding. The following week Eddie Strachan had demanded to know when the happy day was to be, and was he going to get an invitation to the next wedding?

'It's a very tempting idea,' Morag said, 'but I think I must discuss it with my fiancé before making any decision.'

'Of course,' replied Maynard with that old dismissive attitude, 'but I think you'll find he's all for it.'

So, they had already discussed it behind her back! How dare they? Was this how it was always going to be she wondered? Was she never to be allowed any decision without her husband's intervention, even in medical matters?

So angry was Morag that she stood up abruptly.

'I presume that some move has already been made to obtain a replacement for the post of registrar?' Here she had been, concerned not to cause him additional worry by announcing her forthcoming marriage, and he had known already! She assumed now that it was Duncan who had told him.

Maynard nodded, not understanding her sudden change of attitude. 'Miss McArdle is preparing an advertisement at this very minute.'

'You can rely on me to look after your workload until other arrangements can be made,' Morag said bluntly.

'The superintendent's role will, of course, be undertaken by the senior medical consultant,' he added hastily.

With a curt nod, she walked out, closed the door with extreme care to prevent herself from slamming it as she wanted to, and stamped out of the office. Lucy McArdle looked up, surprised. It wasn't like Morag to pass her by without a word.

The secretary sighed deeply. What a pity the two surgeons did not get on better. They were really so alike . . . one might have expected them to make an excellent team.

She put the final touches to the letter she had been typing and carried it in to her employer for signature.

They watched McGregor poke at the embers and add another couple of logs to the fire. He fussed over the ashes in the hearth until Duncan, irritated by the delay, barked, 'That will be all, John . . . thank you!'

All evening there had been an atmosphere between them. Morag had only played with her food, and had drunk more wine than she was accustomed to do. He had watched her growing red in the face and had gallantly got up to open a window, suggesting the room was a trifle warm.

After a few moments in which the heavy brocade curtains had gusted into the room, threatening to scatter valuable ornaments in all directions, Morag had leaped up and slammed the window closed.

'For goodness' sake, you know it's only the wine,' she had shouted at him. Then, taking her place at table once again, murmured, ashamed of her outburst, 'I'm sorry.'

With the servants hovering around them, it had been impossible to ask her what was troubling her. The remainder of the meal was conducted politely through the butler and maid. Duncan and Morag did not exchange a single word directly.

Now Duncan waited until McGregor had departed.

'A brandy . . . or a whisky perhaps?' he asked, moving to the side table and pouring himself a glass of Napoleon.

'A whisky, please,' Morag replied stiffly. 'And a little water.'

She sipped at the drink, staring absently into the fire.

'All right,' he said at last, 'are you going to tell me what I've done, or are we doomed to live like Trappists for the remainder of our lives?'

'I thought we had agreed that *I* would be the one to tell Mr Maynard about our engagement . . . when *I* considered the time was right?'

'Well?'

'So how is it that today, he not only alluded to our marriage but also indicated that you and he had been discussing *my* future career?'

'Oh, now I begin to understand.' Duncan's relieved expression did nothing to cool her temper.

'Well?' she demanded.

'My dear girl, you may or may not recall that for a very long time – years before you graced the corridors of the West Highland Hospital, I might add – I have been a member of the Hospital Board.'

'Well, yes, of course, but . . .'

'In this capacity, I was summoned to an emergency meeting last evening, to be told of the tragic circumstances of Sydney Maynard's retirement.'

'Go on.' She was cooling down rapidly and beginning to feel just a trifle stupid.

'Naturally, the question of his successor was raised. I have to tell you that there was only one nomination which met with the unanimous approval of the board, your own.

'To do him justice,' Duncan continued, 'Maynard made no objection to the proposal, but he did warn that an appointee without alternative financial resources might find the absence of a regular salary a serious drawback. It was also the case that while the surgery consultancy was in the gift of the committee, the superintendent's role was traditionally passed on to the next most senior member of staff. The additional gratuity which Maynard himself receives in respect of this area of his work will, therefore, be paid to the senior medical consultant in future. Now, what was I to do? Should I have allowed him to talk the committee out of offering you the post, or explain to them why your financial circumstances are about to take a dramatic turn for the better?'

'Oh, Duncan . . . I'm sorry,' Morag apologised. 'I think I must be supersensitive on this issue of my independence. It comes of having to fight my corner for as long as I can remember . . . ever since the first of my brothers was born, in fact.

My mother was forever talking about when the boys would go away to school, and speculating about what careers they would follow. She would argue endlessly that one of them should be a lawyer like her father, but Dad wouldn't hear of them being anything but medical men. It never occurred to my parents that I might want to train for a profession also . . . not until I was ten years old, anyway. That was when I got my father to take me out on his rounds for the first time.

'He and I had a sort of conspiracy from then on. I persuaded him to send me to a school where the sciences formed an important element of the curriculum and when I was eighteen, we sprang it on my mother that I had enrolled in Medical School.'

'What a terrible little schemer you must have been.'

She slipped down on to the tiger-skin rug and took up her favourite position, leaning back against his legs. He fondled her hair, watching the tresses glow and sparkle in the firelight.

'I hate it when we don't see eye to eye,' Duncan said. 'Dinner was awful.'

'I was beastly,' she admitted.

'Well, there won't be any similar problems in the future,' he declared. 'Once I had announced my personal interest in the new appointment, I withdrew from the board. They will receive my official resignation in the morning.'

'Oh, Duncan, that's a pity.' Morag turned round, searching his face anxiously. She knew how much pleasure his association with the hospital had always given him. 'Won't you miss being a member of the board?'

'I don't think so,' he replied, a little smile hovering about his lips. 'I shall have my own ways of influencing events.'

He slid down beside her and gathered her into his arms. As she cuddled up to him, her cheek brushing the lace front of his dress shirt, she whispered, 'What about McGregor? He could come in at any minute.'

'Oh, damn McGregor,' came Duncan's muffled reply as he slipped a hand beneath her red-gold locks, drawing them back so that he could rain kisses on her slender white neck.

They were to be married on New year's Day, in the little church at Kilbrendan.

In deference to Hugh Beaton's failing health, Duncan had suggested that the wedding be held at Achnafraoch, but Morag's mother, Millicent, had been quite adamant.

'Beaton daughters are married from Tigh na Broch,' she declared. 'It has always been so, and I hope the tradition will be upheld for many generations to come.'

Morag was secretly pleased that her parents had been so insistent. It meant that the wedding would be a modest affair, the guests confined to members of their immediate families and a few close friends.

She worried a little about how her future step-daughter would view the Beaton house, but wished Richard and Harriet to have no false illusions about her antecedents.

The two of them had seemed very pleased when told of the engagement. Harriet had indicated that she simply wanted her father to be happy. If life with Morag was what he had chosen, she was only too pleased to go along with that.

'I have never known a mother,' she had confided, during a quiet moment together. 'I always longed for some older woman to advise me. Father has never been anything but kind and thoughtful, of course, but men don't understand everything, do they?'

Morag was a little overwhelmed by the suggestion that she should play the part of mother to this sophisticated young woman who was only a few years her junior.

'I don't know what kind of a step-mother I will make,' she had replied, 'but I hope that we will be good friends, always. I wouldn't want you to feel that I am replacing you in your father's affections . . . I am sure that there is room in his heart for us both.'

In the event, her worries proved to be groundless.

On the night before the wedding the two families gathered at Tigh na Broch in order to get to know one another at an informal Hogmanay celebration. It was arranged that Harriet and Richard should stay at the doctor's house, while Duncan had been found a room in the Temperance hotel on the quay. It would never do for the bride and groom to sleep under the same roof on the eve of their wedding.

He and Hugh had discovered an instant rapport. They were able to share many memories of wartime experiences, and like old soldiers everywhere, revelled in well-rehearsed tales which had them both laughing heartily.

Harriet took instantly to Millicent, finding her a comfortable person to be with, possessing that concern for everyday matters which she had always imagined to be the hallmark of a real mother.

They sat long over the evening meal, and it was well past eleven o'clock when at last the company repaired to the drawing-room.

As they gathered about the blazing fire, Hugh poured out the drams while Richard distributed the glasses to the ladies.

Morag savoured the moment. It was the first time in her life that she had sat before her parents' hearth in company with a man who was her lover. Duncan seemed to have gained the approval of all the family and tomorrow he was to be her husband.

She sat on the rug at his feet, leaning against his bare knees. She loved to see her menfolk in the kilt and they had all promised to be similarly attired tomorrow. He stroked her neck. Her mother most probably disapproved of this public demonstration of affection, but Morag didn't care. A feeling of deep contentment filled her.

She looked across at her brothers, and smiled to see they had taken up the same positions they had as children, one on either side of their mother on the deep couch which was drawn across in front of the window.

Ian had travelled home for the holiday from his post across the border, as medical registrar in an English hospital. David, in his twenty-fourth year the image of his namesake, their grandfather, would complete his training at the end of the year. Hugh hoped that he would want to take over the family practice, but suspected that the young man had a more ambitious project in view. Like his sister, David's sights had long been set on higher things than a small country practice. He was just waiting for a suitable opportunity to tell his father that he had been offered a residency in London, to work for his Fellowship in Surgery.

Watching them, Morag was carried back through the years . . . little had changed, except that now Duncan occupied the chair that would have been her father's.

As the thought brought home to her the significance of this little gathering, her heart gave a lurch.

She watched Hugh take up a position before the fireplace and felt compelled to go and join him. She had half risen to her feet when her father began to speak.

'I know that it is usual to reserve speeches of this kind for the wedding breakfast,' he began, 'but it seems that now is the more appropriate moment. Tomorrow's party in the Drill Hall will be a village affair, for the benefit of *our* friends . . . those who have watched Morag grow up here. Many of them will be strangers to Duncan and his family. In the intimacy of a family gathering, it is perhaps possible to speak a little more freely.'

Ian and David exchanged glances with raised eyebrows. What was the old man blethering about, for goodness' sake?

Millicent shifted uncomfortably. Hugh's excessive drinking had been brought under control in recent months. He had been told in no uncertain terms that his liver would not stand any further abuse. She had watched him carefully all evening and had not noticed anything untoward . . .

Morag, long removed from the daily drama surrounding her parents' relentless struggle against the aftermath of war, had disregarded her father's problem until now. She got to her feet and held his hand as he continued to speak.

'Every father must have doubts about giving responsibility for his daughter's well-being into the hands of another man. Morag assures me, however, that Duncan is a decent enough fellow, and as I have had no reason to disagree with her judgement in the past, I do not doubt what she says.'

There were a few chortles, but Millicent continued to look a trifle strained as her husband went on speaking.

'Duncan, on the other hand, has had no one to acquaint him with first-hand knowledge of the youthful Morag. He has no idea what problems he may be storing up for himself. You see,' he turned now to Duncan, with just the suggestion of a twinkle in his eye, 'my daughter comes from a very extraordinary background. Her tutors were feminists who believed that women are easily the equal of their male counterparts . . . Elizabeth Whylie, her teacher, my sister-in law, Annie Beaton, who was both a lawyer and a suffragette and who served a prison sentence for her beliefs; her cousin, my sister Margaret's stepdaughter, Heather Brown, who drove an ambulance in France; and Margaret herself who has maintained her independence of thought throughout twenty years of marriage and has established herself as a Scottish author of great renown.'

He raised his glass to Morag's Aunt Margaret, who shared an

old horsehair sofa with her husband Dr Michael Brown. She smiled her acknowledgement of his compliment and turned to say something to the elderly gentleman in the wheelchair on her other side.

Morag had been shocked to see the change in her Great-uncle Angus since the visit to Mull which had culminated in Magnus's death. He was now very frail indeed, but not too weak, it seemed, to have himself transported by boat across the Sound to be present at her wedding.

Her thoughts had been wandering. She tried harder to concentrate upon what her father was saying . . .

'All of these women had some hand in shaping my daughter's character, but if we are to believe what we are told by Herr Gregor Mendel, many of our characteristics are inherited from our forebears. From what I remember, and what I learned from my parents, my grandmother, after whom Morag was named, was the most formidable lady of them all. I suspect that it is from her that my daughter acquired her stubbornness and determination. When my grandmother was adamant about anything, it was more than my grandfather's life was worth to deny her!'

Amidst the laughter which followed, Morag complained, 'Oh, Dad, how could you? And I thought that you were my greatest champion.'

'I am, my dear, I am,' he confirmed in mock terror, shielding his head from her threatened attack.

'Anyway,' he continued once they had settled down again, 'despite all that has been said, I want you to know how proud it makes me to be able to propose a toast to my daughter and her fiancé.' He lifted his glass. 'To Morag and Duncan: may their lives be filled with happiness.'

'And all their troubles be little ones,' added David, smirking.

What a baby he still is, Morag thought, disdainfully, but she laughed at the old joke with the rest and waited for Duncan to reply.

'Since we have reached the moment when the hoary old remarks are appropriate,' he said, happily, 'may I add another? Dr Beaton . . . Hugh . . . and Millicent, you have made me so welcome that already I feel a part of the family. Truly I can tell you that you have not lost a daughter, but gained a son.' He grinned before continuing, 'Though, please, don't ask *me* to remove anybody's gallstones!'

They all roared at the joke. Apart from Morag, there were five doctors in the room.

Millicent then declared that it was time for the bride's mother to get some sleep, even if the rest of them were prepared to sit up all night, and the party broke up.

Hugh offered to accompany Duncan along the road to his hotel and the two set off in such high spirits that Millicent wondered if her future son-in-law would not be turned away by Mrs McCaulay, the innkeeper, for whom the word *temperance* meant exactly that.

Her fears proved groundless, however. The cold night air quickly cleared their heads, and by the time the two men had passed the last white cottage and paused to watch the waves beating against the harbour wall, they were quite sober.

Duncan was intrigued by the tiny Island of Eisdalsa which they could see across the water, a dark shadow lit from behind the hill by a waning moon. As they watched, a small rowing boat shot out from beneath the old wooden pier, no doubt carrying late-night revellers home to their beds.

The MacBrayne's jetty, seemingly far too large for so small a village, indicated the past importance of this place on the sea route from Glasgow to the Isles. At the far end of the planking, a tall crane which had been used to lift cargo on and off the ships for more than fifty years, stood sentinel, silhouetted against the night sky. The last rusty remnant of a bygone age of travel.

'When I was a boy, before the railway came to Oban and long before the roads were metalled, we travelled everywhere by sea,' Hugh explained. 'It was a sad day when the *Lochfyne* called here on her last journey to the Clyde.'

Duncan recalled a number of sailings which he had been obliged to make as a boy on his way to school in Edinburgh. Although he must have been on board when the steamer picked up its passengers from here, the significance of the place had eluded him then.

'Morag talks with such affection of her childhood here,' he said. 'I used to think she was exaggerating its appeal. I remembered it only as an industrial port where everything was dominated by the grey slates stacked on the quay, and by the heaps of waste stone which seemed to cover the whole area. Now that I have seen it under the stars, I can appreciate more easily what a pull it must have upon her.'

'The place has changed dramatically during my lifetime,' Hugh told him. 'My father attended seventy families on that island alone, and in my grandfather's day five hundred people lived over there, men, women and children . . .'

'With such a narrow channel, one would have thought they might have built a bridge, or even filled in the space linking the two islands?' Duncan suggested.

Hugh was appalled.

'I wouldn't mention such a thing to any of the locals,' he warned. 'And if you are interested in marital harmony, I wouldn't propose it to Morag either. The islanders consider themselves to be quite exclusive. Eisdalsa and Seileach are two different worlds . . . nothing on earth would induce the folks over there to become a part of the *mainland*. In the old days, my father used to tell us, if an Eisdalsa girl married a Seileach man and came to live in the village over here, it was as though she was departing for another continent. Such a weeping and wailing among the womenfolk you wouldn't believe.'

Duncan shivered a little as the breeze strengthened and Hugh suggested they should proceed.

'It wouldn't do for you to arrive at the altar sneezing your head off,' he exclaimed. 'Morag would never forgive me.'

'Before we go in, sir . . .' Duncan hesitated. All evening he had addressed Hugh as a friend, a comrade in arms. Now, speaking to him as his future father-in-law, he felt as though the few years which separated them constituted an entire generation. 'I wondered how you felt about our marriage? I am a lot older than Morag . . .'

'She was bound to choose an older man,' Hugh replied. 'My sister Margaret did the same. Her husband was seventeen years her senior, but the marriage has been a huge success. Morag is an intelligent young woman, not a simpering débutante. She has a very forceful personality, as I was at pains to illustrate earlier this evening. A younger fellow, someone nearer her own age, wouldn't survive for five minutes married to her!'

'I am so relieved to have your approval.' Duncan grinned. 'Morag is devoted to you both. I wouldn't wish to be the cause of friction in such a happy relationship.'

'My dear fellow, Millicent and I are delighted that she has made such a sensible choice. I know her mother was beginning to fear that Morag would remain a spinster always.

'Poor Millicent, she has never come to terms with the idea that her only daughter should have chosen a profession in preference to a dancing partner. I must thank you for relieving me of the burden of my wife's endless speculation about Morag's personal life. Something to which I have been subjected since the day our daughter left school!'

They had reached the hotel now and stood for a moment in the shelter of the stone porch. A spluttering storm lantern was the only indication that the household was still awake.

Hugh turned to his companion and shook his hand. It was an emotional moment for them both.

'Take good care of her,' he exhorted, a catch in his voice.

Before Duncan could make any reply, Hugh Beaton turned on his heel and swung away, his boots ringing on the cobbled roadway as he disappeared into the night.

# Chapter 20

Morag slipped into her new role more easily than she could possibly have imagined.

So well-oiled was the management of the house at Achnafraoch, that she could happily leave the day-to-day organisation to McGregor and his well-trained band of footmen, cooks, house-maids and scullery maids.

She had declined the offer of a personal maid, declaring that she had managed to take care of herself all her life and proposed to go on doing so. One of the housemaids was promoted to look after Morag's wardrobe. She had never cared for washing and ironing her own clothes, and in this one respect was only too pleased to be served.

With a new registrar installed at the West Highland in her place, Morag was able to confine her visits there to the two days a week set aside for surgery. She revelled in her new-found freedom and as the warmer spring days brought the magnificent grounds of Achnafraoch to life, found herself spending more and more time with the head gardener, Joseph.

A honeymoon in Madeira had given her many exotic notions for new plantings. These at first mystified and then enthused the old fellow, who went scurrying off to his nursery catalogues in search of the plants she had suggested.

Duncan watched her now from the library window, amused to see the belligerent old gardener, for years the terror of anyone who attempted anything other than admiring appreciation of his domain, hanging upon Morag's every word. He saw Joseph nod his head in agreement, and stand by as she snipped at a shrub. As they strolled on, she plucked a dead flower head from the scattering of spring bulbs and then paused to turn over the soil using the special light spade which the old retainer had found for her.

Unable to resist the temptation to join them, Duncan hurried down the broad staircase and was about to make his way out via the conservatory, when the doorbell rang. He waited while McGregor went to answer the call, and was surprised to see that the visitor was his son-in-law, Richard.

Seeing him across the hall, Richard hurried towards him, his obvious agitation emphasising the limp which in normal circumstances was almost undetectable.

'Thank goodness you're here, sir.'

'Richard, it's good to see you! Morag and I were only this morning wondering whether you had gone down to London for the festivities.'

'Festivities?' Richard looked baffled.

'The Silver Jubilee Celebrations,' Duncan reminded him.

'Oh that. No . . . I leave that sort of thing to the old man. I'm afraid I have more urgent matters to deal with.

'And how is Harriet?' Duncan persisted. 'She's well . . . fine. Look . . . can we talk?' He watched McGregor approaching, and added, 'In private?'

Concerned at his son-in-law's agitation, Duncan halted McGregor in his tracks.

'Tell Mrs McRae that Mr Ashley Keynes is here, and ask her to join us in the Long Room for coffee in half an hour. Until then, we shall be in my study . . . I don't wish to be disturbed there.'

Richard followed Duncan back upstairs and waited until the panelled oak door had closed behind them before he spoke again.

'Duncan, I've had word from Rudi Braun.'

'At last!'

'The situation is bad and likely to get worse. Since the election of von Schuschnigg, the Nazis have infiltrated every office of the Austrian Government. Those intellectuals who spoke out against the election of the puppet Chancellor, mainly Jewish doctors, lawyers and bankers, have been arrested and are awaiting trial on a host of trumped up charges. There is every possibility that if . . . when . . . they are found guilty, their families will also be in danger. Rudi has a plan to get some of them out . . .'

'You're not going to get mixed up in it, are you?' Duncan demanded. 'For Harriet's sake, don't do anything foolish.'

'Mine will be a very minor part. I shan't even step over the border into Austria. The fact is,' continued Richard, coming to the point of his visit, 'we need your help.'

Duncan frowned.

'Once we get the refugees out of the country there will be no time for formalities . . . passports and so on. The French and German Governments have all manner of treaties between them which could mean our people being sent back to Austria, and you know how the Swiss hate to get themselves involved in the problems of other countries.'

'In other words you intend to smuggle them into England?'

'No, Scotland actually . . . and that's where you come in.'

Before Duncan could protest, Richard hurried on.

'We need a safe haven, somewhere where we can rest up for a few days until things can be sorted out with the authorities. Even our own people are reluctant to accept that these refugees won't get fair treatment in their own country. We have to persuade them otherwise. It might take a little time . . .'

'You want me to offer them sanctuary?'

'Exactly.'

'I shall have to consult Morag. She would have to know what was going on.'

'Naturally. Her presence here will be a bonus.'

'You're not expecting that sort of trouble, are you? You don't imagine anyone is going to be injured?'

'No, nothing like that,' Richard assured him. 'It's just that there may be young children or elderly people. It's still spring, there's a lot of snow in the high passes . . . they may have a long trek through the mountains. Who knows what condition they'll be in when we arrive?'

'How will you get them here? It seems a very long way to bring refugees before finding sanctuary.'

'I shall be using the *Dalriada*. We will sail through the canal from the east coast. The customs boys are so used to seeing her plying between Inverness and Oban, they'll probably not even bother to search her.'

It was a terrible risk to take. No matter what individuals in the British Government thought about the situation on the Continent, the current attitude towards Germany, and the Nazi Party in particular, was one of appeasement. The authorities would not appreciate any kind of scandal endangering diplomatic agreements.

Duncan wondered if he should be drawn into this affair. I must talk it over with Morag . . . it wouldn't be fair to involve her unwittingly, he told himself.

Unable to wait longer for an answer, Richard demanded, 'Well, can we rely on your co-operation or not?'

'I suppose so . . . yes,' his father-in-law concluded. 'Say nothing to Morag now. I will explain it all to her in my own time.'

'Look, I won't wait for coffee,' Richard said. 'Give my love to Morag . . . tell her Harriet will be calling on her very soon.'

Before Duncan could protest, he opened the window on to the terrace and slipped away, down the steps and across the garden.

'Morag came into the room, glancing about her.

'I came in and washed my hands when McGregor told me,' she protested. 'I've been sitting in the Long Room for ages, presiding over a tray of coffee cups . . .' She looked about her.

'Where's Richard?'

'He couldn't stay after all.'

'Where is he off to in such a hurry? We haven't seen anything of him since the wedding.' She was struck by another thought. 'Nothing wrong with Harriet, is there?'

'Harriet? No . . . no, of course not.' How could he tell her? Wouldn't it be better to keep her in the dark after all?

Saying nothing of the reason for Richard's visit, Duncan placed an arm round her shoulders and led her outside to where cane

'*Gute Nacht, Fräulein Arzte.*'

Gordon wheeled him away as Morag stripped off her gloves and strode into the adjoining room.

'How is the boy?' asked Richard, anxiously.

'He'll do,' she replied, rather shortly. They had still to explain to her exactly what they were playing at, dragging a ten-year-old child . . . and others . . . over an Alpine pass, even in late spring.

Rudi lay on his side. As she turned him over to try to examine him, he groaned. She felt the board-like material of his jacket, stiffened with dried blood, and looked up in alarm.

'What has happened here?' she demanded.

'He's been shot,' Richard replied simply. 'Rudi insisted that it was a flesh wound only, and should not hold us up. Had we attempted to get medical aid, the matter would have been reported to the police and that could have caused all kinds of problems.'

'I'm not sure I want to hear all this,' Morag stopped him, abruptly. 'I'll do what I can to patch him up, but after that I too am obliged to report a shooting to the police; you must know that.'

'Of course,' Richard agreed. 'I'm sure that our own local constabulary will be more understanding . . .'

More understanding than whom? she wondered, but for the moment the patient needed all her attention.

She handed Richard a pair of scissors.

'Remove his clothes . . . cut away anything you cannot pull off without disturbing him. I'll go and get ready.'

She returned to the theatre, hurriedly cleared up after the previous operation, and laid out what she thought she might need by way of instruments.

She had never before seen a gunshot wound, let alone removed a bullet.

When she was ready, she called out to Richard, 'Wheel him in here, will you? I'll be with you in just a minute.'

By the time she had returned, scrubbed and gowned in fresh clothing, Gordon had taken over from Richard.

'There's a lot of debris in this wound,' he observed, lifting off the wadding with which he had replaced the rough bandage applied at the time of the shooting. 'It's going to take some time to clear everything away before you go looking for the bullet. How about a general anaesthetic?'

The bullet had entered Rudi's shoulder just below the right clavicle. Morag turned him gently to see if there was an exit site. There was none, but the skin covering the upper part of his rib cage was purple with bruising. With the tips of her fingers she explored the bruised area and felt a hard lump lying approximately halfway between sternum and oxter.

Allowing herself a small sigh of relief, she said, 'It looks as though we may be able to get the bullet out without too much probing.'

She examined Rudi's vital signs, then looked more closely at the entry wound. She had expected to be confronted by putrefaction and had anticipated that familiar smell which she associated with a neglected, suppurating wound. She was surprised, therefore, to find that although there was, as Gordon had said, debris of different kinds lodged in the tissues, the surrounding flesh seemed to be relatively healthy and the stench of sepsis was absent.

'This must be several days old,' she said, looking at Richard accusingly.

'It happened on Sunday night,' he responded. 'We have been travelling for three days.'

'Then it's no wonder he has a fever,' she observed, laconically. 'I'm surprised he hasn't already died from septicaemia.'

With tweezers, she searched the wound, lifting out small pieces of detritus. After a moment she came across something unexpected and held it to the light to examine it more carefully.

'I anticipated fragments of cloth and bone,' she commented, 'but how do you account for sphagnum moss?'

'It was a little trick we learned in the Himalayas on one of our expeditions,' Richard volunteered, looking sheepishly at Gordon. 'The Sherpas used moss to pack their wounds. It stopped the bleeding remarkably well . . .' he tailed off, reacting to the look of disbelief in Morag's eyes.

Swallowing a flood of questions, she resorted to verbal chastisement.

'You should have known better than to have neglected a gunshot wound for so long.'

'I'm sorry, Morag.' Richard looked genuinely contrite as he attempted to explain. 'Rudi had his reasons for pressing on through France and getting back here. I was merely the navigator . . . he wouldn't listen to me.'

'Can we leave the recriminations until later?' Gordon demanded, anxious to get on.

'Of course.' Morag managed to thrust all remaining questions to the back of her mind and concentrated on the job in hand.

'I'm not happy about his breathing,' she told Gordon, 'it might be risky to use a general anaesthetic . . . we'll try Novocaine.'

As the injection Gordon had given began to take effect, she swabbed the site where the bullet had entered, removing as best she could dried blood and pus which had begun to form a scab over the opening. Once exposed, it was clear that despite the moss the deeper tissues were infected. Even now, she might be too late . . .

Once Gordon had applied the Novocaine, she felt she could work with greater speed and less concern about hurting Rudi who, while aware of what was happening, appeared to take very little interest. From time to time she looked up, to find him apparently semi-comatose and gazing into space.

She returned to her task with greater urgency.

Strands of cloth had been forced deep into the wound and must be removed, together with the splinters of bone which had been torn from the edge of the shoulder blade. He must have been in terrible pain all that time, she thought. No wonder he seemed so exhausted.

'I think we'll irrigate this now with carbolic solution,' she decided, 'then I'll have another go using the magnifying glass . . . just to make sure.'

Gordon washed the wound scrupulously, while Morag selected

further instruments then returned to the task. When they were both satisfied that the site was clear, she applied a dressing and taped it in place.

They turned Rudi on to his back with the greatest care, but as the bandaged area came in contact with the table, he groaned. The effects of the Novocaine must be wearing off.

Gordon applied more of the local anaesthetic to the chest muscles.

Morag took up a scalpel and made a small incision above the position of the bullet. To her immense relief, as she pressed down on either side of the wound she had made, the bullet popped out through the opening. Here, at least, the healing should be quick and uncomplicated.

She slipped the bullet into Rudi's good hand, smiling.

'Souvenir,' she said, lightly, and was relieved to see him attempt a grin.

'I knew I would be all right if I could just get back to you,' he murmured, so quietly that only she could hear him.

In minutes, Morag and Gordon had completed their task and had Rudi sitting up, his arm in a sling and the remains of his mutilated jacket lying across his shoulders.

'By rights, you should stay here in the hospital until the infection clears up,' Morag told him.

Richard disagreed.

'It would be better for all concerned if the hospital were not involved in this matter,' he said. 'Duncan has the remainder of the party up at Achnafraoch . . .'

Morag looked at him, dumbfounded.

'Duncan? What has he to do with all this?'

She didn't know about it! Duncan must have decided not to let her in on the secret after all.

'I asked for his help . . . after you had spoken to Gordon,' he improvised.

Duncan had been put on the spot, she realised. What else could he have done?

'So far as reporting the gunshot wound is concerned,' Richard said now, relieved that she appeared to have accepted his explanation, 'I will have to inform the Chief Constable of the arrival, without passports, of a number of foreign nationals. I promise to mention the bullet wound at the same time. Trust me, please? After all, it's not as though the shooting took place on British soil.'

'Oh, very well,' she agreed. 'I'll have to stay here for a while to check on the boy. Tell Duncan I'll be home as soon as possible.'

'I'll go back with them,' suggested Gordon. 'Just to see Rudi settled in.'

She eyed her colleague suspiciously. Why did she have the impression that Gordon had been a part of this conspiracy from the outset?

They moved Rudi into a wheelchair and took him out to Gordon's car.

As Morag stood with Richard beside his green Bentley, watching Gordon drive away with uncharacteristic caution, he turned to thank her.

'About the wee boy . . .' he said as he climbed in behind the wheel of his magnificent vehicle. 'Would it be possible to list him as a boating accident?'

'Leave it to me,' replied Morag. Whatever their motives for such secrecy, there was no harm in explaining the amputation this way. Any sign of the frostbite which had necessitated the operation had been removed.

Morag waited until the day staff came on duty before handing over responsibility for Johannes.

No awkward questions had arisen about the Austrian child who had been brought in off a pleasure cruiser at some time in the early hours. None of the nursing staff spoke any German, but they managed to communicate with the boy through sign language, and it seemed that, young as he was, he had already mastered quite a few English words himself.

As the morning wore on, the staff became very attached to the little fellow and made every effort to cheer him up, so that when Morag called in before leaving for home, she found him propped up on his pillows and smiling, despite the obvious pain which his wounds caused him.

When he saw her approaching, he began to talk excitedly in his own language. Morag, needing to keep him calm, but also having difficulty translating the child's gabble, put a finger to her lips to quiet him, and then began to talk softly to him in her schoolgirl German.

Avoiding the subject of the journey across the mountains, she asked him about his home and school.

'I won a scholarship to the Boys' Academy in Vienna,' he told her, somewhat petulantly, 'but they said I could not go because I was a Jew.'

Shocked, and unable to respond in any helpful way to this, Morag suggested that perhaps he would be happier in his own village school anyway.

'They took away the schoolmaster,' he told her, laconically.

She began to feel very uncomfortable in this conversation and decided to steer it to more immediate matters.

'Would you like some of the other children to visit you?' she asked. 'Did you have a particular friend on the journey ... brothers and sisters perhaps?'

'They are all such babies,' he replied, haughtily. He thought for a moment and then said, 'Maria can come, she is nearly as old as me.'

'I'm going to meet the rest of your party now,' Morag told him. 'I'll see if I can arrange for Maria to come tomorrow.'

'Is Uncle Rudi all right?' he asked anxiously.

The familiarity of his term of address amused her; Rudi had never struck her as an 'uncle' figure. 'Oh, yes,' she replied. 'After I had dressed his wound, we sent him away with Mr Ashley Keynes.' She avoided going into details.

'He saved my life,' said the boy. 'When the soldiers started firing, he threw me to the ground and the bullet caught him instead.'

'He will be fine,' she reassured him, 'but it would not be a good idea to mention the soldiers while you are here ... or Rudi's wound. Do you understand?'

He was communicating with the nurses so readily that he might well be able to convey to them the substance of his adventures, even if they could not understand him fully.

The boy's smiling countenance changed suddenly as that fearful look, which she had noticed the previous night, returned.

His gaze traversed the ward. 'Are there people here who will talk?' he demanded. 'Will the police come?'

'Even if they do,' she attempted to comfort him, 'they will not bother you, Johannes. Rudi would not let them.'

Apparently satisfied with that, he turned to his other major concern.

His legs were covered by a wire cradle which not only protected them from the weight of the bedcovers, but also prevented him from seeing his feet.

All morning he had suffered a dull pain in either leg without fuss, but now his right foot itched mercilessly, while his left felt strangely numb. Sister had given him some tablets to take away the pain but he was nevertheless aware that something was very wrong.

'What did you do to my legs, Doctor?' he demanded, gripping her hand tenaciously, lest she try to escape telling him.

'You know that you were seriously injured?' Morag asked, tentatively. He seemed strong, but would he be able to bear the terrible news that she must give him?

'I know what frostbite can do to people,' he answered. 'We live half the year surrounded by snow and ice, you know.'

'Then you will understand that it is sometimes necessary to cut away that part of a limb which is so badly affected that, if left, it would go rotten?'

He tried to remove his hands from hers as though to evade the truth she must tell him, but she held on to him.

'I have had to take away part of your left leg, Johannes. It is cut off below the knee.' Continuing without pause, allowing him no time for speculation, she added, 'You will soon be able to walk quite comfortably using a false leg.' She watched his expression closely as she continued, 'I am pleased to say that on your right foot it was only necessary to take off two of the small toes. You will soon learn to balance on those remaining.'

For a moment he remained silent and then, amazing her with the maturity of his response, he murmured, 'Thank you for telling me, Fräulein.'

Realising that the child needed time to adjust to what she had said, Morag stood up, patting his hand comfortingly.

'I think that it is time for you to have a little nap,' she observed. 'I will get Sister to give you something to take away the pain.'

'My mother always kissed me before I went to sleep,' Johannes recalled, eyes brimming with tears.

Morag cradled the little waif in her arms and hugged him to her. She kissed him on the forehead and whispered, 'Say a little prayer for your mother, Johannes . . . I am sure that she is doing the same for you. Perhaps your thoughts will meet somewhere out there, in the ether.'

He tried hard to smile as Morag turned at the door and waved. Only when he was sure that she was gone, did he allow himself to cry.

# Chapter 21

When she arrived home, Morag found Donald and Richard holed up in the library with Duncan, taking a dram before dinner. The rest of the vast house seemed to have been given over to an army of small children who were using the long galleries and wide entrance hall as an indoor playground.

Two of the servants appeared to have been assigned to their supervision and it seemed they had the situation well under control. The tight lips and heavy frowns of the remainder, however, indicated that not everyone approved of the invasion. Morag wondered for how much longer they would tolerate this interruption to their ordered way of life.

'Where's Rudi?' she enquired, half expecting him to be already up and about.

'I had to order him back to bed,' Gordon explained. 'He insisted on remaining with the children most of the morning . . . no one else in the household can speak their language. By early-afternoon he was becoming feverish so I insisted that he lay down to rest.'

Leaving Richard and Duncan to their whisky, the two doctors mounted the stairs to the first floor, assailed on all sides by cries of excitement, squabbling and tearful arguments carried out in the same Austrian dialect in which Morag had been struggling to communicate with Johannes.

A little boy hurtled down the shallow flight of stairs and fell into her arms.

'*Entschuldigung!*' he gasped.

'*Bitte,*' she replied automatically.

The child ran on and Gordon took her arm to help her up the last flight.

'I meant to tell you how impressed I was to hear you speaking with Johannes last night.'

'I must admit I rather astonished myself.' She laughed. 'Mrs Whylie's Academy for Young Ladies furnished me with a smattering of both French and German, but I have to admit that this is the first time I have found any use for either!'

'I wondered if you had picked up the language from our Austrian mountaineering friend? You and he seemed well acquainted the afternoon of Duncan's garden party.'

'That was nearly two years ago,' she replied. 'I've heard nothing from Rudi since. How much do you know about this exploit?' she demanded.

'I had hoped you would be able to tell me about it,' Gordon answered, 'I had a call from Richard in Inverness the night before last, asking me to meet the *Dalriada* at Corpach dock. He was waiting for me when I arrived. As soon as I saw the condition of our two patients, I telephoned you and after we had spoken, Richard asked Duncan to collect the rest of the children.'

'I can't imagine how he managed at such short notice,' Morag began, but Gordon put his finger to his lips to silence her. 'Later,' he mouthed, as he opened a door at the far end of the corridor.

'Rudi's in here,' he said more normally, as he pushed it open to reveal the patient, comfortably settled amongst the pillows. Duncan had placed their guest in his own dressing-room.

'He wanted to be close by should Rudi need anything in the night,' Gordon explained.

The dressing-room had a communicating door to the master bedroom. A little too close for comfort, thought Morag, making a mental note to have Rudi removed to an ordinary guest room as soon as possible.

She crossed to the narrow bed.

He looked flushed, and his eyes held that same feverish sparkle she had noticed the previous day.

'Ah . . . the Fräulein Doctor who is also a mountaineer!' he greeted her with false heartiness.

'Gordon tells me you are not feeling so well,' she said, adding by way of remonstrance, 'trying to do too much, too soon, I daresay.'

'I daresay,' he agreed, savouring the unfamiliar expression.

'I would have expected you to have more sense,' she told him. 'It was a very nasty wound and you lost a lot of blood . . .'

Rudi looked suitably ashamed.

'The poor little ones are missing their parents,' he said by way of explanation. 'I thought I should cheer them up . . . there are no adults in this household who can speak even a smattering of their language.'

'Hush now,' said Morag, popping a thermometer under his tongue. She took his pulse and then reached for her stethoscope. Unhappy with the results of these tests, she glanced up at Gordon with a worried frown.

'I think we had better have a look, don't you?' she queried.

He nodded glumly and began to peel off the patient's pyjama jacket so that she could get at the bandages.

The wound, which had looked so clean the night before, was now puckered at the edges and the blood had congealed into an unhealthy-looking scab. When Morag squeezed this gently, slimy yellow pus oozed from beneath the crust. The whole area was obviously badly infected and it could not be long before the poison began to invade his entire system.

'Perhaps you should have gathered some more moss,' suggested Rudi. Gordon smiled, but Morag merely threw him a withering glance.

'I hope we can manage something a little more clinical than that,' she replied as she replaced the bandages and prepared a dose of quinine which, with some difficulty, she persuaded him to swallow. Really, men could be such babies when it came to taking unpleasant medicine.

'I'll have the maid bring you up more lemon barley water,' she said, observing with some satisfaction that Gordon had already been administering plenty of fluids. 'You are to stay where you are until *I* tell you that you can get up,' she ordered Rudi, severely. From the look of him, he would have little desire to leave his bed for some time. She settled him in as comfortable a position as possible and indicated to Gordon that it was time to leave.

'Nothing we can do now but wait,' he remarked as they took the corridor to the main landing. 'Rudi is a strong and otherwise healthy man. Maybe he will be able to fight it.' His worried frown belied his optimistic words.

'I think there might be something more we can do,' Morag replied, thoughtfully, and went on to ask, 'Have you heard about these new Sulphonamide drugs which are used to control septicaemia?'

'Well, yes,' he replied doubtfully. 'I did follow the discussion a year or two back, but after the first flush of excitement it seemed there were problematic side-effects. The BMA has not recommended them for general use so far as I'm aware.'

Morag had read everything she could lay her hands on about the new development, which had been shown to be useful in the treatment of certain types of bacterial infection. Gerhard Domagk, the German biochemist, had first developed the drug and used it successfully on a patient with a severe streptococcal infection. Under normal circumstances the case would have been deemed hopeless. The patient made a miraculous recovery, and Domagk was applauded for his services to medical science.

The Sulphonamides had been heralded as the wonder drugs of the age; they were going to eliminate forever all those diseases caused by bacteria. The British Medical Association, however, always sceptical of any miracle-drug claims which had not been tested to the limit, had not given *carte blanche* for the use of Domagk's drug. Sulphanilamide, as he had named it, had been given to certain British university hospitals for a limited number of trials to be carried out in strictly controlled conditions. Morag's father, Hugh Beaton, had mentioned that an old colleague of his, a friend of the family whom she had known all her life, was engaged in such experiments at the Edinburgh Royal Infirmary . . .

In the library, the gentlemen were preparing to go in to dinner.

'Can I get you a drink, Morag?' asked Duncan, rising to his feet as she entered.

'I need to make a phone call,' she replied, distractedly. 'Do you mind?'

Sensing her urgency, he rallied the others. 'Of course not. We will go in to dinner and give you some privacy. Join us when you're ready.'

It took Morag fully twenty minutes to track down Professor George Murray at the Royal. Reluctant at first even to consider her request, he listened carefully to her assessment of the patient's condition and was forced to conclude that the young man was not going to survive unless drastic action was taken.

'All right, my dear,' he agreed. 'I'll have the package placed in the hands of the guard on the first train out tomorrow. Can you arrange to have someone pick it up?'

'Of course, Uncle George,' she exclaimed excitedly. 'I'm so grateful to you . . . how can I ever thank you?'

'Write up the case with all the details and let me have a complete record of the results. That will be reward enough. It can be added to our other experiments.'

She put down the phone, thought for a few minutes and then dialled Charlie's home number.

'It's Morag Beaton, Mrs Stewart,' she said, hearing Charlie's wife answer. 'Would you be kind enough to ask him to carry out a special mission for me tomorrow morning? It means meeting the first train from Glasgow . . .'

She listened while Mrs Stewart repeated the instructions carefully, then put down the phone. Short of being flown here, the drug could not reach them any sooner. She smiled at such a ridiculous thought, and went through to the dining-room.

The others were halfway through their main course when she sat down.

'Oh, no, thank you, John, I'll skip the soup,' she said, as the three men settled themselves once more to their game pie.

Morag realised suddenly just how famished she was. She had eaten very little since breakfast.

The others carried on their conversation above her head until, satisfied at last that she could not swallow another morsel, she placed her knife and fork carefully on the plate and dabbed at her lips with her table napkin.

This was Duncan's signal. He leaned towards her. 'I believe you are very concerned about our friend upstairs?'

'Very,' she replied, shortly, and turned on Richard, her weariness and anxiety making her belligerent.

'You do realise, don't you, that had that wound received proper medical attention immediately, Rudi would be well on the way to recovery by now?'

He looked at Duncan in appeal before answering, 'You don't understand, Morag. It wasn't that simple . . .'

'Oh, you are so right,' she barked at him. 'I *don't* understand, and it appears that no one in this room is willing to enlighten me!'

'It's just that we were concerned not to involve you . . . knowing about it could land you in serious trouble,' Duncan pleaded.

'But I *am* involved now,' she complained.

Richard looked helplessly at Duncan and shrugged his shoulders. 'She had better know it all. As Morag says, she is already implicated.'

Duncan nodded unhappily and Richard turned to her.

'You have been keeping abreast of what's been happening in Europe?'

'I've been reading the newspapers, if that's what you mean.'

'Then you will be aware that the Germans have marched into Austria and the Nazis have taken power?'

'I have read something of it,' she replied. 'But I can't say I understand what's been happening.'

'The German Army is implementing a regime of martial law at the invitation of the Austrian Nazi Government.'

'But isn't it up to the Austrian people themselves to vote the Nazis out of office?' Morag suggested, naïvely.

'Not if they are five years old and Jewish,' replied Duncan, quietly.

Morag looked at him, aghast.

'The children you have met are Jewish refugees from Rudi's

home town of Brenner. A short while ago, the Austrian under-ground movement heard that the Nazi governor of the province was about to round up members of the Jewish community and pack them off to labour camps in Germany. In order to encourage people to behave in a sensible and controlled manner, he first of all arrested the local schoolmaster and the rabbi and had them hanged.'

Morag gasped.

'When some of the younger men decided to resist arrest, they were shot. The remainder went quietly, their only consolation the knowledge that Rudi Braun was going to escort their children to a place of safety.' Duncan, visibly moved, could not continue. Richard took up the story.

'Rudi had to plan a route which would avoid the borders with both Germany and Italy. To reach the Swiss border, his party would have to walk more than thirty miles through the mountains. There were sufficient men with him – mountain guides like Rudi himself – to carry the smaller children, but the bigger ones, like Johannes, walked all the way.'

Morag understood now. Poor, brave little Johannes . . . She had a vision of the child struggling through the snow, trying to keep up with the men.

'But how did Rudi get shot?' she asked, remembering the boy's description of what had happened.

'The children had been spirited away at night,' Richard explained, 'before the police came to arrest their parents. Someone in the village must have talked . . .'

Morag shuddered at the thought of what dreadful things must have been done to those poor people to force any of them to tell where their precious children had gone.

'. . . anyway, the soldiers were pretty soon on the trail of the children. Fortunately, they didn't catch up until they were close to the Swiss border. Ordering one of the guides to lead the party across the frontier, Rudi and the rest of the men hung back to hold a narrow pass by which the soldiers must approach.'

'That was when he was shot?' Morag asked.

Richard nodded.

'But Johannes said that Rudi saved his life in the shooting?'

'That is true,' said Richard. 'The boy had formed a particular attachment to him on the journey. When they stopped at the pass, Johannes remained behind with the men, insisting he could be useful as a messenger or something. As they retreated down the pass, firing began. Rudi pulled Johannes in front of him to shield him and took the bullet in his shoulder. When the boy realised that Rudi had been hit, he managed to pull him into a thicket until the Germans had gone. It was then that he suffered the frostbite . . . while both of them were lying low for a couple of hours, for fear of being spotted.'

'I still don't see why they could not have got medical help once they had crossed the Swiss border,' Morag protested.

'The Swiss aren't too bothered about refugees so long as they are just passing through,' Richard explained, 'but the French might well have returned the children to Austria. That was why we had to smuggle them across France and on to my boat. I suggested we should stop at a doctor's surgery, but Rudi insisted we must get the children away before the whole country was overrun by the Germans. Maybe he was already delirious, I don't know. I wasn't inclined to argue.'

'Even if Rudi was unhappy about stopping in France, did you really have to come the long way home?'

'There was always a risk that the immigration officials would send the children back if we landed at Dover,' he explained. 'By coming here and announcing our arrival to the local constabulary, we thought we could buy time for the children. Every day the situation in Germany and Austria is getting worse. Our Government cannot remain blind to what is going on forever.'

'And have you . . . announced your arrival to the local constabulary?' she asked.

'This afternoon,' Duncan assured her. 'I asked the Chief Constable to come to the house, introduced him to the children, and explained Rudi's gunshot wound to his satisfaction. He never enquired who it was who had rendered medical assistance, so there is no reason for either you, or Gordon, to be implicated.'

'You make it sound as though we are frightened for our own

skins,' said Gordon. 'Morag is only concerned for the reputation of the hospital, you do know that?'

'I must take some of the blame for not preparing you for this,' Duncan confessed. 'The day Richard appeared so unexpectedly, it was to tell us both what Rudi intended, and to ask our permission to bring the refugees here. Stupidly, I decided there was no point in upsetting you over something which might never happen . . . I'm sorry.'

'Nothing has really changed, has it?' Morag demanded bitterly. 'You men play your little games in secret, knowing full well that somewhere along the line you are going to need the help of some poor unsuspecting female. On the pretence of protecting the *weaker sex* from the truth, you keep us in the dark until the last possible moment. You have no idea how galling that can be.'

She recalled the occasion when she had been obliged to attend the burned airman with no details given of how he had been injured.

'Let me tell you this, all of you . . . if there are to be any more mysterious casualties dragged from burning aeroplanes, or refugees with gunshot wounds appearing in the dead of night, I want to be informed about it just as soon as you know yourselves!'

Suddenly weary and deflated, Morag sipped at her brandy. After a few minutes she began to recover her good humour.

'I'm sorry,' she said, by way of explanation for her outburst. 'I am really very worried about Rudi's condition. He'll have to be watched over throughout the night.'

She rapidly excused herself and made her way back to his room.

He was tossing on his pillows, perspiration streaming down his face. She folded back the blankets, finding the sheets soaked with sweat.

She pressed a buzzer by the bedside table and in seconds McGregor appeared.

'Is there something I can do to help, Doctor?' he enquired. Morag noticed that, even after her marriage, McGregor still did not address her as Mrs McRae. He seemed more comfortable with *Doctor* and she never questioned it.

'Yes, John,' she replied. 'I need a change of bed linen, a bowl of lukewarm water, sponges and towels. As quickly as possible, please.'

The butler disappeared, returning shortly with a small army of servants carrying a number of burdens. Having checked that they had brought all Morag's requirements, McGregor dismissed them while he himself remained.

'Just tell me what you want me to do, madam,' he said, when she looked up inquiringly.

Rudi's strong constitution was helping him to fight the bacteria in his blood, but the battle had sent his temperature soaring to a life-threatening level.

'You will have to help me to cool him down,' Morag briefly instructed the manservant.

Together they worked on Rudi for an hour or more, sponging his body with the cool water, and placing ice packs on his head and feet. It was all that they could do at this stage.

From time to time Morag stopped to test his vital signs. Although his temperature was falling, Rudi's pulse remained rapid and his heart seemed to be working overtime. She administered a cocktail of strychnine and digitalis by injection and saw with satisfaction that the heart rate had slowed to near normal.

Morag woke with a start.

She must have dropped off to sleep sometime in the early hours. She remembered giving Rudi another dose of quinine and sponging him down about three o'clock . . . She snuggled under the thick woolly blanket then realised that someone had come in while she slept and covered her. Dear Duncan, she thought, he must have been awake all night himself.

She heard the scrunch of tyres on the gravel and, throwing off the blanket, went to the window and drew up the blind.

The familiar sight of Charlie Stewart's taxi had her out of the door and charging down the staircase before McGregor, who had also had a sleepless night, could answer the bell.

'Oh, Charlie!' she cried, taking the small parcel from his hands, very carefully. 'Thank you so much . . . you cannot imagine how important this is. A matter of life and death.'

'It usually is, Miss . . . Dr McRae,' her friend corrected himself. 'You know I'm always glad to be of assistance.'

Morag ran back to Rudi's room. She tore away the packaging and came upon a brief set of instructions from Professor Murray and a dozen small phials of a colourless liquid.

She turned to where Rudi lay, tossing in a state of delirium. His pulse and heart rate had risen again. She would administer the first dose of Sulphanilamide before embarking once more upon her efforts to get his temperature down. She slid the needle into his vein and rubbed the spot vigorously to ensure rapid distribution of the drug. While she held a piece of cotton wool to the site to prevent bleeding, she watched her patient's face intently.

He woke suddenly and stared at her, uncomprehending, for a few moments.

'Hallo, Rudi,' she said softly. 'How are you feeling?'

'Terrible.' He tried to smile. 'But I'll be better now that you're here.'

He seemed to have no memory of what had taken place in the past twelve hours, but disorientated though he was, he had not forgotten her. 'My lovely mountaineering doctor,' he murmured, before falling into a troubled doze.

She checked him again. More digitalis to slow the heart; another dose of quinine in case the other drug didn't work . . . should she use it, now that the Sulphanilamide was doing its stuff? Couldn't do any harm . . . She lifted Rudi's head and forced the bitter liquid down his throat.

Every four hours had been the professor's instruction. How was she going to pass four hours?

Her gaze rested upon a notepad lying on the dainty Chippendale desk set before the great stone-mullioned window. Of course, Uncle George would be expecting her report . . . She would start it right away.

Pausing only to enjoy the steaming hot coffee and buttered toast which McGregor brought her, Morag wrote steadily for a couple of hours. From time to time she examined her patient for any changes and was pleased to see that, although his temperature was still far too high, it had not risen further since the last sponging, and his pulse rate, although abnormally rapid, was now steady on eighty-six beats per minute. It was too soon to say that the Sulphanilamide was working but the signs were encouraging.

Throughout the day Morag administered the drug every four hours as instructed. By evening, Rudi was showing definite signs of recovery and when she inspected the wound before settling him down for the night, she found that it was looking less inflamed and much healthier.

After dinner, Duncan insisted that she should go to bed and rest properly.

'I will watch Rudi for the first spell,' he assured her, 'and McGregor insists on taking the graveyard watch. One of the children's nurses has also volunteered, so there is no need for you to be up for a second night.'

Morag had been so engrossed in her treatment of Rudi that she had quite forgotten the children. It occurred to her that they had been inordinately quiet during the day.

'I have managed to track down a couple of German-speaking nursemaids,' Duncan told her. 'They arrived from Glasgow by the noon train. The larger rooms in the west wing have been converted into dormitories and there are a number of smaller rooms for the women, so once we have made a few necessary alterations, they should not impinge too much on our privacy.'

Morag never ceased to be amazed at how simple such major readjustments could be when there was sufficient money to pay for them. The additional staff sounded a good idea . . . she felt sure the servants would be relieved.

'I must continue to give Rudi the injections every four hours,' she insisted when Duncan repeated his suggestion that she should get some rest. 'Whoever is on watch will have to wake me . . .'

'Don't worry,' he assured her, 'I will see that they follow your instructions to the letter.'

Morag had to admit that she would be grateful for the opportunity to get between the sheets after a hot bath.

Gordon arrived about ten o'clock, when she had already given in to her weariness and gone to bed. He took a quick look at their patient and found him lucid and clearly much improved.

'Where is Morag?' Rudi asked, when Gordon had performed all the usual tests.

'Sleeping,' he replied. 'You had her up all night.'

'Ah, yes . . . I seem to recall . . . such cool hands . . . such a soft voice,' said Rudi, dreamily.

'Contrasting very favourably with my own inept ways, I suppose?' Gordon retorted, amused.

'Did I say anything of the kind? But you must admit that she is much prettier than you!'

Gordon noticed the Sulphanilamide phials next to Morag's medical bag.

'Is this the famous miracle drug?' he enquired, casually.

'Whatever it is, it seems to be doing the job,' said Rudi with some satisfaction. 'I feel so much better, I don't think anyone should bother to wake Morag at midnight. I can do very well until morning.'

'I'm afraid that's not the way of things,' replied Gordon, scanning the instructions from Professor Murray. 'If you don't take the full dose every four hours until the whole lot has been used up, those nasty little bugs in your blood will simply shake off the drug and start multiplying again. What is more . . . the next generation may be immune to the effects of the Sulphanilamide.'

'It seems such a shame to wake her . . . she needs her rest,' protested Rudi.

'How will it be if I stay on for a bit, and give you the injection myself before I leave?'

Morag woke to a gentle shaking of her shoulder. Opening one eye to find the room dimly lit by a softly shaded bedside lamp, she shrugged off her tormentor. 'It's still the middle of the night,' she protested and turned over.

The middle of the night . . . MIDNIGHT!

She sat up suddenly and grabbed at her watch. It was four o'clock.

Dragging on her dressing gown, she barked angrily at McGregor, 'Why wasn't I woken at the proper time? You know how important it is to stick strictly to the rules!'

Without waiting for his explanation, she threw open the door into Rudi's room.

There was a single light which illuminated the chair where whoever had been keeping watch had been reading. A book lay open on the floor.

She advanced to the bed and examined her patient. He was sleeping peacefully. The flush of fever had disappeared, his breathing was steady and his pulse normal. Her hand flew to the syringe which lay ready in its kidney dish. She picked up a phial and plunged the needle in. Her hands were arrested in mid-air. According to the number of phials left, this was the sixth injection. Someone must have given him the twelve o'clock dose.

Relieved, she looked up as McGregor entered, carrying a tray.

'I thought you might like a cup of tea, Doctor,' he said blandly, apparently ignoring her earlier outburst.

'Thank you, John,' she responded, plunging the needle into Rudi's arm. 'Who gave him the midnight injection?'

'Dr McDonald called in after you retired, madam. He very kindly waited until midnight and gave the injection before he left.'

Of course . . . why hadn't she thought of that? Who was she to think she was the only one who knew what was going on in this case? And why was she suddenly so ready to accuse, and to lash out with her tongue?

Suddenly, Rudi opened his eyes.

'Fräulein Doctor.' He reached out a hand towards her. As she took it, she spoke to McGregor.

'Thank you, John, I can manage very well now.'

The butler turned to go but she called him back.

'I was very abrupt, John,' she apologised, 'please forgive me.'

'That is perfectly all right, Dr McRae. It has been a trying time for everyone.'

When Morag turned back to her patient, she found him regarding her with an enigmatic expression.

'Dr McRae?' he queried.

'Duncan and I were married at the beginning of the year.'

He nodded almost imperceptibly.

'Of course . . . I should have realised.'

'Realised what?'

'I found it extraordinary that such a beautiful woman could remain single. I should have known . . . that day in the garden . . . our host was so attentive.'

Morag had taken hold of his wrist, and pretended now to count his pulse while his words chased about in her head.

'At that time, marriage had not ever been thought about,' she dismissed the subject, and tried to concentrate on his condition.

'It is very good of both you and your husband to offer me your hospitality. I cannot help feeling that I am intruding upon your privacy. When Richard suggested we might be staying for a time with Mr McRae, I had assumed it would be in a bachelor establishment . . .'

'By rights, I should have insisted you remain in the hospital,' she told him. 'We don't have the facilities here for constant nursing supervision, but the treatment that you are receiving is a new drug which is being administered as a clinical trial. I began it, and it is up to me to keep a constant record of your progress. I shall have to be both nurse and physician for the time being.'

'I am a very fortunate man.'

Rudi lifted her hand to his lips, and smiled up at her as he kissed it. 'An outmoded custom which I have found hard to break . . .'

Morag recalled the last time he had said it.

'What drug is it?' he asked, as she turned away to hide her smile and picked up her stethoscope.

'Sulphanilamide,' she replied. 'It's produced by a German firm. Bayer, I think.'

'What!' he shouted at her, suddenly angry. 'You use products from those filthy swine on *me*!'

Had he been able to leap out of the bed, she thought, he would have done, but the pain in his shoulder halted him. The noise, however, had disturbed both McGegor and Duncan, each of whom raced to the scene, converging outside the bedroom door. They burst in to find Morag struggling to keep the patient in his bed.

'Rudi!' Duncan exclaimed, forcefully. 'Rudi Braun, what are you thinking of? Stop this noise at once.'

His sharp tone brought the Austrian to his senses. Weakness and frustration took their toll and he lolled back against the pillows, weeping helplessly.

Duncan looked to Morag for an explanation. She called him out of earshot before telling him of Rudi's reaction to the news of the German drug.

'I suppose it is understandable. We can have no notion of the depth of hatred that the Germans have engendered in people like Rudi. Leave it to me.'

Duncan approached the bed and sat down so that his face was level with the sick man's. For a few moments the Austrian ignored him but at last he allowed his glance to meet the other's.

'Rudi, you have been very ill . . . Gordon and Morag thought you might die. The drug you have been given is the only thing which could have saved you. You are very fortunate that Morag has a friend who was able to supply it. Think how angry the Germans will be when they find out it was a product of theirs which gave you the means to strike at them another day!'

The notion that Rudi, who prided himself on having been a thorn in the flesh of the Germans for a long time, should have been saved by the invention of one of their number, seemed to amuse him. He began to chuckle. 'One of these days,' he declared, 'I shall enjoy telling those bastards how they saved my life!'

Morag, clearing up the debris from her ministrations, shuddered at the thought of any circumstances which might bring him face to face with his enemy.

# *Chapter 22*

Once the wonder drug had done its work, Rudi Braun recovered quickly from his wounds and within weeks had again disappeared to some mysterious destination abroad, carrying with him Duncan and Morag's assurances that any further refugees he rescued would be given shelter at Achnafraoch.

Believing that he needed the company of the other children as much as anything, Morag had brought the crippled Johannes home to Achnafraoch after only a few days in the hospital, but it was many months before the boy's stump had healed sufficiently for Duncan to take him to Glasgow to be fitted with an artificial limb.

Meanwhile, Rudi and his companions made more journeys to the Continent each time returning with refugees. Now it was whole families escaping from the threat of imprisonment in Nazi Germany as well as Rudi's own countrymen.

Morag and Duncan were appalled at the stories told by the refugees but anxious to keep out of the spotlight lest the activities of Rudi and Richard should be jeopardised – they left the publication of these to the journalists and politicians.

It was not until late in January 1936, that Johannes took his first tentative steps on the new artificial leg. The child lacked the confidence to use it properly, and although both Duncan and Morag tried to persuade him to try, after only a few steps he would complain of the pain and give up. He was content to be confined to his wheelchair and as spring gave way to summer he would sit outside for hours watching the wild birds which flocked to the garden.

The boy's future was more doubtful than that of the other

children, for whom homes had been found with relatives or foster parents, some in Britain and others as far away as Canada and the United States. Johannes needed foster parents who were willing to take on a severely disabled youngster who was unlikely to be able to cope with his handicap, unaided, for a very long time.

It seemed as though the problem would never be solved. Duncan suggested that perhaps they themselves should adopt the child, but Morag had become convinced that Achnafraoch was not the best environment for him.

She had watched Johannes's wistful expression when other children were taken off to some new, exciting life. She knew that he questioned all the newcomers in his anxiety to find out what had happened to those he had left behind. Achnafraoch provided him with a constant reminder of the things which she most wanted him to forget.

During one of the quieter periods, when the dormitories in the west wing had been empty for nearly three weeks, Morag decided that Johannes could do with some company of his own age, and arranged a picnic tea in the grounds, to which she invited Gordon's family.

With Francis and Andy away at college, Anna's little brood seemed sadly depleted. Tim was now the responsible member of the tribe and his sudden changes of pitch when he spoke lent him a certain air of authority. The twins were boisterous as ever while Poppy, at the age of eight, was quiet and thoughtful, appearing much wiser than her years would suggest.

For a while all the children stayed with the adults on the terrace. Somewhat overawed by their surroundings and shy of the strange little boy who spoke only broken English, they were uncharacteristically silent until Anna expressed a desire to see Duncan's collection of water-colours and Morag led her away, leaving the youngsters to entertain themselves.

Melody could not remain silent for long. She looked hard at the little stranger who had not shifted from the chair where they had found him.

'Can't you walk?' she demanded.

'No,' said Johannes.

'That's a pity,' said Matt. 'You might have shown us the stables.'

'Why can't you walk?' demanded Poppy. 'Daddy said that they had given you a new leg.'

'It's sore to walk on,' Johannes replied.

'But it will get better the more you use it,' she insisted. 'It's like when Fran broke her leg. It was all stiff when she came out of hospital and it hurt her a lot to use it . . . but she kept trying, and now she's all right.'

'I'm going to see what's in the woods over there,' decided Tim. 'Who's coming with me?'

The twins jumped to their feet, eager to follow him.

'Coming Poppy?'

'No. I'll stay with Johannes.'

They ran off, laughing and shouting, leaving the two youngest children alone.

'You don't have to stay,' said Johannes 'Why don't you go and explore with them?'

'I'd rather stay here with you,' the little girl insisted.

'There are some puppies down in the stables,' he said. 'Joseph the gardener brought one up to show me this morning.'

'Oh, I'd love to see them,' said Poppy wistfully. 'Won't you take me? I could help you if it's hard to walk.'

'I'll come if . . .'

'What?'

'If you don't walk too fast. I hate it when they leave me behind.'

'I'll walk right beside you, I promise,' she told him. 'Come on, let's try.'

Johannes struggled to his feet and shuffled forward, putting his artificial limb down awkwardly.

Poppy lifted the walking cane which lay beside his chair.

'You use this alongside the good leg,' she explained, remembering how Fran had shown her. 'Put your good leg forward and lean on the stick. Now put your weight on the good foot and bring the stick and the other foot forward together . . . that way you always support the bad leg with the stick, don't you see?'

He found it difficult at first but with Poppy saying, 'Stick, now foot, now stick and bring the other foot up . . .' he soon got into a rhythm which carried him along so well that he hardly felt the rubbing on his stump.

Morag, glancing out of the window of the Long Room, watched in amazement. Poppy had managed in a few minutes what she and Duncan had failed to do in many months.

'I wanted to talk to you about little Johannes,' Anna said as they watched the children until they were out of sight. 'Gordon and I both feel that Achnafao is not the best place for him to be just at present.' Before Morag could interrupt she went on, 'I know you and Duncan are both very fond of him and in terms of comfort he lacks for nothing, but you are both professional people with many interests which he cannot share. Gordon tells me that much of the time he is left alone with the servants who, though well-meaning, are hardly the same as companions of his own age. Then again, Johannes is too intelligent and too sensitive not to be affected by the stories he hears from all the people passing through.'

'I couldn't agree with you more,' Morag agreed. 'Duncan and I have already decided on the kind of family he must go to, but until we can find the ideal foster parents, he will have to remain here.'

'Gordon and I have agreed that we can offer the boy a home . . . until he can be restored to his parents.'

Morag stared at Anna in surprise. 'But it could be years before he sees his mother again . . . if ever,' she warned. 'Don't you have enough responsibilities already, with your own brood?'

'Well, that's just it, you see,' Anna explained. 'Andy's unlikely to live at home again once he completes his medical training, and Fran started her course at teacher training college last autumn and it won't be all that long before Tim goes away as well. Poppy is very much on her own now that the twins have moved on to the High School . . . she needs a companion of her own age.'

'I think it's a wonderful idea,' said Morag. There was no doubt about it: Anna might be a somewhat unconventional mother but all her children seemed happy and well adjusted.

'Then there's the question of the boy's leg,' Anne added. 'Gordon can take better care of that than most dads, don't you think?'

'Oh, Anna, thank you.' It was as if a great burden had dropped from Morag's shoulders. 'I can't tell you how relieved I feel . . . and if Johannes is to live with you, we shall see him often. I don't think I could bear to lose contact with him altogether.'

'Whenever you want,' Anna answered, smiling.

They heard a commotion in the garden below and Morag looked out to see Johannes and Poppy on the lawn with a basket of puppies between them. As one more adventurous than the rest scrambled over the side and made off towards the woods, it was Johannes who hobbled after him and replaced him in the basket.

# Chapter 23

Morag scanned the headlines of the *Gazette*, her apprehension growing with every word she read.

'It seems that there is going to be a war after all,' she said sadly, as Duncan took his place opposite her and tucked into his bacon and eggs.

'It was inevitable,' Duncan assured her. 'That nonsense at Munich last year . . . no one was fooled into believing that it was anything more than a ploy to give us time to re-arm.'

'I know you're right,' she said, 'but one always hopes for a reprieve.'

During the past twelve months Duncan had spent more and more time away from home, supervising the retooling of one of his factories in the Clyde valley for the manufacture of tank components and another for military radio equipment. Morag knew little of the various enterprises which had created the McRae wealth, only that they had been associated with engineering since the early days of motor vehicle manufacture.

'Any post for me?'

She passed across a couple of official-looking envelopes.

'And there was this.'

She held up a small sheet of pink paper on which were written a few lines in a child's hand.

'It's from little Carl Rubenstein . . . Do you remember him? He's arrived in California and is living with his uncle.'

She recalled rather wistfully a mop of curly black hair and a pair of darkly appealing eyes and found herself choking on her words as she said. 'I hope he will not be too homesick . . .'

When they had married, it was on the understanding that

Morag's professional life would continue unrestricted, and in view of this they had agreed early on that there could be no children in this marriage.

For Duncan, already a father and by all accounts, soon to be a grandfather, this was no problem. Remembering the fearful outcome of his first wife's pregnancy, he was secretly thankful that Morag wished to remain childless.

To Morag, already blessed with a wonderful husband as well as a satisfying career, the absence of children appeared to be a worthwhile sacrifice. They had little enough time to spend together as it was and she knew enough about family life to realise that were she to become a mother, her children would absorb her every waking moment.

It was not that either of them disliked children. Quite the reverse. During the past years countless numbers of little ones had passed through Achnafao on their way to a new life. Morag had loved to hear the sound of young voices about the place and even now was thrilled to receive their carefully worded letters which arrived, sometimes as many as three or four in one week, from all corners of the globe.

'I have to go down to London next week,' Duncan announced, folding the letter he had been reading. 'There's a big meeting at the Vickers Works in Weybridge. Would you like to come? We could make a wee holiday of it.'

She hated to disappoint him.

'With the war likely to break out any day, I must stay here,' she told him. 'Several of the younger men are on standby for an immediate call-up and the hospital will be very short-staffed as soon as they go.'

He nodded, hiding his disappointment admirably. Folding his napkin, he took a final sip of coffee and got to his feet.

'Well, I must be off, my dear.'

He gave her a quick peck on the cheek and would have pulled away had she not grabbed him and kissed him more soundly on the mouth.

'Ring me if you have to take the late train,' she said. 'I'll pick you up from the station myself. There's a long list at the hospital today ... I doubt if I shall be finished before eight.'

McGregor was always available to collect Duncan from the station of course, but it was a task which Morag loved to undertake at the end of the day. They would pop in to the Long John for a drink with friends before driving home at a leisurely pace and, on a starry night, stopping to admire the view from the top of the brae. It gave them a few precious moments alone together in the midst of their busy lives.

As she stood in the window and watched McGregor close the door of the Rolls behind him, she waved, knowing that he would be looking back to catch a last glimpse of her.

She was startled by the shrill ringing of the telephone.

'Richard, is that you? No, I'm sorry but he's already left to catch the Glasgow train. He'll be back tonight ... not until quite late I suspect. How is Harriet? Look, why don't you both come over for lunch on Sunday, it's ages since we saw you ... Oh, I see, so you might have to join the regiment right away? Well, if it's that important, why don't you come over this evening? It will have to be rather late; Duncan will almost certainly catch the last train, but we'll both be back here by eleven o'clock ... Right, I'll see you about eleven then. Goodbye for now ... and give my love to Harriet.'

As she put down the phone she felt a shiver of apprehension for the second time that morning. Richard had already received his instructions to report to the barracks at Stirling Castle. All the many speculations of the past months had suddenly become a stark reality.

'So all this time, you and Rudi have been using the refugees as a means of setting up an underground network?'

Morag had listened in disbelief as her son-in-law related their activities during the previous years.

'When we began,' Richard tried to explain, 'our only concern was to get out as many children as we could. After a time we were approached by someone in the War Office and persuaded to carry messages, equipment too sometimes, to people in the occupied countries.'

'Equipment? Guns . . . explosives?'

He nodded. 'Radios mostly, and the means of committing acts of sabotage.'

'Does Duncan know what you have been up to?' she demanded, and when he nodded, asked: 'And Harriet? What about her?'

'There's no need to worry her . . .' he began. Morag silenced him with a glance.

'We women are made of sterner stuff than you think. Believe me, it would be better for you both if Harriet knows . . . and the sooner the better.'

Duncan had come into the room as she spoke.

'He's told you then?' he asked.

She nodded, still not sure if she was pleased or angry that, once again, Duncan had not shared his concerns with her.

'I can't tell you what a relief it is not to have to keep the secret from you any longer,' he said.

'And all these aircraft, flying low through the mountains, in the dark?' she asked.

'Lysanders mostly,' said Richard, 'practising putting down and picking up . . .'

Morag remembered the casualty burned in the mysterious plane crash. So they had been trying it out even then.

'What will the Army be using the house for?' she demanded. Large though it was, it hardly seemed suitable for a great number of soldiers.

'They will be training small groups of men for special assignments. The trainees will have to be one hundred percent fit and able to tackle the most difficult terrain in the worst weather conditions. They will learn to survive by living off the land and they'll be trained in all manner of skills, both on the water and in the wilderness.'

Remembering all the times that she had accompanied Adam and the rescue team out there on the mountains, Morag felt nothing but compassion for the young men who were destined to come to Achnafraoch in the future to train for their own very special kind of war.

\*    \*    \*

Conscription had been responsible for the loss of most of the household servants. The younger men had enlisted in the armed services while the older retainers, and the women, were engaged in war work. Morag had loaned her cottage in Canal Row to three of the maids who had taken jobs in one small engineering works in Feanagrogan.

From the start, Duncan had insisted that Morag should keep the cottage, even if she had no reason to live in it herself. He had no wish to deny her the satisfaction of complying with Magnus's Will.

Morag had retained her job at the hospital and her two days' consultancy had been extended. Duncan, who had thought his manufacturing days behind him, now found himself concerned not only with his own family businesses but also with co-ordinating the work of a number of small munitions operations which had been set up around the town. Much of the time the two of them met as ships passing in the night.

With only McGregor to maintain their household, they had moved into one wing of the house to make way for their military guests.

Over the years Morag had been called out many times to attend injured climbers, and her standing in the mountain rescue group was high, not only as its official surgeon, but also as an experienced mountaineer.

Duncan had never stood in her way over this or any other of her activities but when the weather was bad and the rescue mission dangerous, he died a hundred deaths in her absence. Only McGregor knew the torment he went through until he heard her car pulling up on the gravel outside the house.

'Morag!'

Rudi forced his way through the crowd, jostled and greeted in any one of a number of languages by the international membership of the Inverlinnhe Service Men's club. Finally he took a seat beside her and raised his voice to make himself heard over the background of noisy conversation. 'I'm so glad I caught you. They said I might find you here.'

She observed with interest his khaki uniform which carried little by way of identification other than a Major's crowns on his epaulettes.

'Duncan said he thought we might be seeing something of you again one day soon,' she said, smiling up at him. 'And here you are! Though I must say, I hadn't expected to see you in uniform . . . and a British uniform no less!'

'It's a long story, and I don't have time to go into it now. I have been searching the town for you,' he told her.

'I've been up at the hospital all day,' she explained. 'It was a longer list than usual.'

'So the girl said, the first time I rang.'

'Well, you've found me now!' She laughed, then seeing the seriousness of his expression, demanded: 'What is it?'

'Can you come . . . right away? There's been a very serious accident.'

'Of course,' she said, getting instantly to her feet. 'Do you want me to contact Gordon too?'

'It's a job for you, I'm afraid,' Rudi told her. 'A climbing incident.'

'I'd better alert the hospital . . .'

'That won't be necessary,' he answered. 'They'll explain when we get there.'

'I don't understand . . . *who* will explain?'

They're at it again, she told herself . . . more secrets. These men do love their mysteries!

'Look, I can't say anything more at present . . . you'll understand soon enough. If you're ready, I'll give you a lift. I presume you will have to collect your equipment?'

An army staff car awaited them outside in the main road. Rudi drove her to the mountain rescue-post, waiting impatiently while she changed into her climbing gear and checked over her medical bag.

'What about a stretcher?' asked Morag as he hustled her outside.

'All taken care of,' he assured her, and held open the door for her to climb in.

Very little was said as the car left the main road to Mallaig and took a lane, hardly more than a farm track, up through Glen Suileag. At the bothy which was situated at the head of the glen, the army vehicle drew to a halt.

'From here we go on foot, I'm afraid.'

The driver began to unload Morag's equipment, while from the bothy there emerged four men in regulation khaki battledress.

She regarded them critically.

'These men are not properly equipped for mountaineering,' she observed, surprised that Rudi should even consider taking them on the route that he had described to her.

'It's the best they can do . . . sorry.' He could give no further explanation, so simply shrugged his shoulders.

Morag noted the dark clouds gathering over the hills on the far side of the valley. 'It's going to be foggy very soon,' she observed, 'and probably it will rain heavily.'

'They have their groundsheets,' he replied, lamely.

'How are they going to climb in those uniforms?' she demanded. 'They are neither wind nor waterproof, and once wet they'll weigh a ton!'

'With difficulty,' he agreed.

'Why don't we wait for the proper rescue team to assemble?' she demanded. This way they were likely to be out for hours, gathering in inexperienced rescuers who would most probably become casualties themselves.

'No time,' replied Rudi curtly. Denying her any opportunity for further protest, he ordered two of the squaddies to take up the equipment they had brought with them, while a third hoisted Morag's special medical pack on his back. The fourth man carried ropes and an additional pack.

It was not long before her prediction about the weather proved to be correct. With the rain lashing almost horizontally, directly into their faces, their scramble along the narrow pass through the hills became a nightmare. A burn, which half an hour before had been a trickle meandering between the boulders in the river bed, suddenly became a raging torrent as a hundred rivulets gathered rainwater from across acres of impervious granite, and funnelled it into the main channel.

The rescue party was obliged to take to the slope above the river, and Morag found herself walking in that most uncomfortable of positions, with one foot higher than the other.

By the time they had reached the head of the valley and crossed over the watershed into the next, the rain had cleared a little and the going became easier. The men were flagging, unused to the rough terrain and weighted down by their soggy uniforms. The only thing that stopped them from voicing a protest was the sight of the woman doctor striding out ahead of them.

At 3,240 feet, Gulvain might not seem like much of a mountain to an alpine guide, but to the inexperienced men under Rudi's command, it looked very high indeed.

Above the treeline, the wind whipped around their bodies, drying out their wet clothing and making them feel even colder and more uncomfortable. As Morag had feared, the men were beginning to present the early symptoms of exposure, and they had not yet reached the casualty.

When at last they came upon the place, they found a number of soldiers gathered around a small petrol stove. Morag was relieved to see that they had water boiling steadily in a pan . . . at least they had had the sense to get themselves something hot to drink.

One of their number broke away and came over to them. He saluted Rudi.

'There's been very little movement from either of them for the past half hour, Sir,' he reported. 'I don't think they can last out for very much longer.'

'Very good Corporal,' Rudi responded. 'Dr McRae will be going down to them directly.'

The soldier regarded Morag with disbelief.

'But this is no job for a woman . . . begging your pardon, Ma'am. It's a job for a mountaineer.'

'Dr McRae is a member of the Inverlinnhe mountain rescue team,' Rudi explained.

The younger man coloured with embarrassment.

Morag had moved over to the cliff edge where one of the

soldiers was keeping an eye on what was happening below. She stood beside him and peered over.

The cliff was almost sheer. Some thirty feet below, two figures could be seen clinging precariously to a narrow ledge of rock.

As she watched, she saw an arm raised. One of them at least was still conscious.

Morag stepped back, nearly colliding with Rudi who had come up behind her.

'Best have a warm drink before you start down,' he suggested, handing her a soldier's aluminium mess tin. 'It may be some time before you get another.'

As she sipped at the hot sweet liquid, using the ungainly container with some difficulty, she listened curiously to the chatter which was going on around her. She had become almost bilingual in her dealings with the Jewish refugees, who mainly spoke one form of German or another, but here she could recognise both Dutch and French, something which sounded very much like Polish, and other languages which meant nothing to her at all.

Suddenly, Rudi called them all to order.

'Gentlemen, in the interests of safety we will now speak in English, if you please . . . I want no misunderstandings about what we are going to do.'

The men ceased their various conversations, turning to regard with interest the woman that their leader had brought back with him.

'Dr McRae has kindly agreed to go down and assist our casualty,' Rudi announced. 'She is very competent at her job, gentlemen. Let us show her that we know how to do ours!'

Has he got his fingers crossed? she wondered. His words sounded very much like a confidence booster to her.

'We will lower the doctor over the edge, just as we have practised. She will attend to the casualty and, when ready, you will haul him to safety. No one is to make a move of any kind until I give the command . . . understood?'

Heads nodded, and Morag detected at least half a dozen different forms of the word 'yes'.

She must have conveyed a little of the trepidation she felt

because Rudi put his arm about her and gave her a comforting squeeze.

'Don't worry,' he said, smiling. 'I won't let them drop you!'

Only partially convinced, she advanced to the edge of the precipice and peered over.

The injured man lay on his back on a narrow ledge, about fifty feet down. One leg was buckled under him and an arm thrown out at an unnatural angle.

Beside him crouched another of the soldiers. Sensibly, he had made no attempt to move the casualty, but had covered him as best he could. With no further means of helping his friend, he had remained loyally at his side for hours. Morag prayed that he would still be in a condition to lend her some assistance.

Survival, she thought, was very much a matter of will-power, coupled with a strong faith in one's fellow men.

'Do you have a flask or something, so that I can take the other lad a hot drink?' she demanded. 'He must be close to exhaustion, himself.'

She hauled the large medical pack on to her shoulders, adding to it the flask which one of the men had handed to her. Thank goodness for the aluminium splints which Adam had had made up to her design. Fraser's aluminium plant had turned up trumps there right enough. She had to smile to herself, for much as she detested the whole family, they had their uses.

'Ready?' she asked, as Rudi signalled to her to come closer to the edge.

'Ready now,' he said. 'You are to keep this rope about you at all times, no matter how much it gets in your way . . . promise?'

She nodded as he secured her rope and led her forward.

'Right then . . . off you go.'

It was a relatively easy descent; she had experienced far worse in practice. Looking down anxiously, measuring distances by eye, she reckoned she must be nearly there by now. She felt her boots scrape as they caught the edge of the shelf and slithered off the wet rock. Allowing her body to lean outwards from the cliff face in order to get her bearings, she picked a spot a little way from where the casualty lay and pushed off with her feet so that the return swing landed her, albeit somewhat clumsily, on the shelf beside the two soldiers. The uninjured man, who had got to his feet when he realised that something was happening at last, grabbed at her rope harness and managed to pull her in to safety.

'Thanks,' gasped Morag. 'That was a tricky landing!'

She was thankful to find that the ledge was not so narrow as it had appeared from the top of the cliff.

The injured man still lay as he had fallen.

'I not move him,' the other soldier explained in broken English. 'When I try . . . he scream.'

'You did well to leave him as he was,' Morag told him. 'You have done all that you could.'

In the absence of any blankets, a couple of soldiers' rain capes had been used to cover the casualty, and so far as she could see he was not suffering unduly from exposure. His companion, on the other hand, was in a very sorry state. He had become stiff and cold from crouching for so long beside his injured friend in an attempt to shield him from the chill wind.

Finding a safe spot close to the cliff, Morag off-loaded her pack and brought out an additional waterproof cape and the flask of hot tea. With the groundsheet fixed firmly around his shoulders, the young soldier took the cup gratefully, teeth chattering as he held it to his blue lips.

Morag crouched down beside him. It would save time if he could answer some of her questions before she removed the covers from the casualty. He began speaking rapidly in his own tongue.

'In English?' she suggested, hopefully. The colour was coming back to his lips now, and his cheeks were beginning to glow more healthily.

'I am very sorry, madame,' he began haltingly. 'I speak in Norwegian. I will try again in English.'

'If you understand me, just answer yes or no. That way we shall not take so long . . . OK?'

He nodded, then smiled apologetically. 'Yes.'

'Has he been unconscious for long . . . was he speaking to you?'

'Yes . . . some of the time.'

'His leg is broken?'

'Yes, I think so.'

'Any other breaks that you know of?'

'His arm . . . maybe.'

Morag nodded; she had suspected as much.

'He smack his head . . . there is much blood.'

A cracked skull as well! This poor fellow was going to know all about the inside of hospitals for some time to come.

'Thank you,' she said, smiling and patting the Norwegian on the shoulder. 'You have done well. Why don't you do a few exercises . . . try to keep warm?' She performed a few arm bends and squats to show what she meant and he nodded enthusiastically. 'I shall need you in good order when we set about getting him out of here.'

He could be no more than eighteen at the most, she judged, smiling at the soldier's burst of youthful energy as he began to strut about in the confined space, banging his arms against his sides, happier now that the main responsibility had been lifted from his shoulders.

Constrained by her own ropes, she crouched down with some difficulty beside the injured man. She paid out a sufficient amount to give her freedom of movement while remembering Rudi's warning not to disengage herself completely. Allowing her fingers to penetrate the layers of mackintosh sheeting in order to expose the man's tunic, she contacted the buttons and managed to undo the top two. Having exposed his neck sufficiently, she felt for a carotid pulse.

It was weak, but it was there.

Gently lifting his head, she examined a gash behind his right ear. He had bled a great deal, but the wound seemed superficial and the bleeding had already stopped. She reached for a bandage. Nothing to do there until they had him safe in the hospital.

'Let's try to get you straightened up a bit first,' she muttered aloud, and realised she was probably talking to herself.

She peeled back the groundsheets to expose a trouser leg, torn and matted with blood. So, it was a compound fracture of the femur. She would have to straighten out the limb in order to splint it.

She called the other soldier over.

'In my pack . . . lengths of metal . . . aluminium . . . for splints.'

He looked blank for a few seconds, followed the direction of her glance and then exclaimed, 'Splints . . . yes!'

As he crouched beside her, assembling the apparatus at her direction, she said, 'It would be easier if I knew your name. I am Morag McRae.'

'Lars . . . Lars Bjornson.' He smiled, exposing a set of gleaming white teeth which looked quite incongruous in a face covered in two days' growth of blond beard, the exposed flesh burnished to a deep crimson by the cruel winds.

'You will have to help me straighten this leg, Lars,' she said. 'It will be very painful for a few seconds and your friend is likely to struggle. You must try to keep him still.'

She showed Lars where to take hold, above the break in the thigh bone.

'Hold him tight so I can pull against you . . . OK?'

Lars nodded enthusiastically.

'First, I'll give him an injection to dull the pain.' Morag's ungloved fingers were already becoming numb. She fumbled with the syringe, taking far longer than usual to prepare the injection. As the needle slid home, the patient opened his eyes. Bewildered at first, he seemed suddenly to recall what had happened to him and struggled to rise.

Lars muttered a few words in Norwegian, and the injured soldier relaxed.

'I have told Niels that a beautiful angel of mercy has come to take care of him.' He grinned. 'He seems satisfied with that.'

Scarcely hearing his comment, Morag took her grip around the ankle of the injured leg and braced herself against the rock at her back.

'Hold tight, and continue to pull against me until I say . . . now!'

Lars had his friend in a vice-like grip around his upper thigh.

In one movement Morag swung the lower leg back into a more normal position, at the same time pulling steadily against him. Satisfied at last that she had got it right, she relaxed her grip and the two broken ends of bone came together. She reached for the metal splints and thrust them into place, one on either side of Niels's body.

'Now, keep him from moving as I tie his legs together.'

Beginning with the ankle, she tied a bandage tight around the aluminium splints, fixing both legs securely. Another bandage below the knees, and one above the fracture point, ensured that the damaged limb would not move.

'I will attend to the arm,' she told Lars. 'Will you give the signal for them to lower the stretcher?'

He did so, setting off a flurry of activity on the cliff top above.

Morag, meanwhile, slit the sleeve of the soldier's uniform jacket to expose his right arm. It was broken above the wrist, both bones probably, but nothing so serious that it could not be left until she could set it properly later. She bandaged the injured arm from wrist to elbow and supported it in a sling.

They lowered the stretcher, horizontally, on two ropes. Watching it colliding with the jutting rocks in its descent, Morag could see that Niels was likely to have a rough ride to the top. There was only one thing for it. They would have to haul him up vertically, and she would have to climb alongside, to protect him from any obstacles as best she could.

Morag was dismayed to see that the stretcher was a standard Army-issue contraption of heavy canvas and wooden poles. With such a cumbersome piece of equipment, it was going to be extremely difficult to get her patient to the top without further injury. If only they had provided themselves with one of the new devices which Adam Inglis had worked on with one of the town's small engineering companies. Manufactured from light canvas and steel rods, it folded easily for carrying but formed a strong, tidy, rigid structure when fully assembled. Webbing straps at intervals along its length made it possible to secure the patient without difficulty.

Oh, well, she decided, at least they have thought to send down additional rope to tie the casualty on with. I suppose we must be thankful for small mercies.

Lars caught hold of the stretcher as it reached them, and drew it in towards the cliff wall. There was barely enough room to lay it down beside the prone figure of Niels, but they somehow managed to lift him on.

Lars seemed to be well versed in the use of ropes, so she left him to secure his friend to the stretcher while she realigned the haulage ropes so that the contraption would be raised vertically up the cliff face, as though Niels were standing up.

She called up to Rudi.

'I've changed the ropes . . . you will be pulling him up head first. I'm coming with him!'

She wished Adam was there. This was an exercise they had performed many times, synchronising climber and stretcher alongside. She just prayed Rudi would understand what she was doing.

'They'll be back for you in a few minutes.' She smiled at Lars. 'Thanks for your help.'

Busy making a last check on his friend's lashings, Lars smiled up at her, squeezed Niels's shoulder encouragingly, and said something in Norwegian. 'Just wishing him a safe journey,' he explained.

With the stretcher hanging beside her, Morag made slow progress. When the cocooned casualty became lodged on a spike of rock, she eased him over it. When one pole of the stretcher became stuck in a crevice, she had them slacken off the rope from above, so that she could extract the pole and guide it past the obstacle. It was a painfully slow business, and an experience which she hoped she would not have to endure again.

A few feet before the top there was an overhang of at least eighteen inches. Relying entirely on her ropes now, Morag was obliged to free both hands in order to pull the stretcher outwards from under the lip, so that those above could reach out and grab it. As she glanced up to see that they had got a good grasp on

Niels before she let go, she found herself looking into the face of Adam Inglis.

'It was an incompetent bodge-up, and you know it!' Morag paced the library floor, venting her rage on all present.

Rudi and Richard Ashley Keynes looked shamefaced, Adam nodded his agreement, and Duncan struggled hard to contain his amusement. Lieutenant-Colonel Charles E. Vaughan put down his glass and leaned forward with interest.

'Could you be more specific, Doctor?'

'For a start, your men are not properly equipped for working outdoors in this climate. Oh, I know you are going to tell me that they are most of them used to such conditions and that is why they have been recruited for this training, but that does not justify a lack of attention to the most obvious requirements. The uniform clothing is not waterproof. When it gets wet it is too heavy for ease of movement. As it dries out in winds at sub-zero temperatures, valuable body heat is lost. These so-called waterproof capes are more of a hazard than a help when scrambling about on the side of a mountain.'

'Your criticism of the uniform provided has already been noted, Dr McRae,' Vaughan assured her. 'We have designers working on a more appropriate form of jacket and over-trousers for wet weather, lighter in weight than previously, so that it can be carried easily when not in use.'

Only slightly mollified, Morag moved to the next item on her agenda.

'These men have been given very little training in survival techniques for severe conditions. They carry nothing to keep themselves warm if they are obliged to camp out overnight on the mountains . . . and that's a very common requirement in such an unpredictable climate. Every man should have some kind of windproof covering, a blanket maybe but something lighter for preference. In this recent incident the casualty had to be kept warm with capes sacrificed by his comrades.' She turned on Rudi. 'You were lucky not to have further casualties on your hands . . . from exposure!'

He made no attempt to defend himself.

'It is not sufficient to have people out there on the mountains who can disport themselves efficiently on ropes and so on. No doubt they can shoot straight and use a knife to good effect . . .' Rudi and Richard exchanged glances '. . . but in every group,' Morag continued, 'there should be at least one man who has had proper instruction in rescue techniques of the kind which have been developed by Adam Inglis and his people over the past decade. Why don't you ask him?' She pointed to her friend who sat impassively, rather enjoying the effect that Morag the Firebrand was having on these chaps who believed themselves experts in the art of guerilla warfare.

'Adam's team has had as much experience of this kind of accident as anyone in the British Isles,' she went on, directing her remarks directly at Rudi, 'and I can tell you now that I was actually *praying* for him to be on that rope when you hauled young Niels up the cliff. I wake up at night in a sweat, thinking of what might have happened if he hadn't turned up when he did.'

She didn't ask how Adam had come to be there, just in the nick of time. Instead she turned again to Rudi, less angry now she had had her say.

'I knew immediately I saw that stretcher descending that your people had absolutely no idea what they were about. That was why I took it upon myself to reorganise the roping. Even then it would have been hazardous had not Adam turned up when he did. We have practised that manoeuvre a dozen times. How often have your men attempted to get a casualty off a cliff under similar circumstances?'

'Never,' Rudi admitted, sheepishly. 'We have been concentrating upon battle tactics.'

'Is there anything else?' asked the Colonel, sensing the tension between these two.

'Yes, since you ask,' Morag replied, shortly. 'This is the scenario. A man falls down the cliff. His friend descends to help him and decides to stay until further assistance arrives. At the very most, a couple of men should have been left at the top of the cliff to guide the rescue party. The remainder should have been instructed to make their way to a safe place where they could keep warm. Instead, the person in command leaves his entire company, ill-clothed, ill-equipped, with virtually no means of keeping themselves warm other than a pitiful little stove, waiting at the scene until he can summon help.

'It must have been four hours, at least, that those men were hanging about on that cliff top, quite unnecessarily. I am amazed that there were no further injuries from frostbite, exposure or an accident of some other kind. Surely in such circumstances it is as important to conserve the condition of the fit troops, it is to alleviate the suffering of the injured person?'

'These men are not out on the mountains for recreational purposes,' grumbled Rudi. 'Their main priority is to be able to fight over this kind of terrain.'

'All the more reason to pay great attention to the points I have mentioned,' she retorted. 'A soldier with frostbitten fingers will find it jolly difficult to squeeze a trigger.'

At this point the Colonel nodded to Richard Ashley Keynes, who got to his feet, expectantly.

'I think that just about wraps it up, thank you, Mr McRae,' the Colonel said to Duncan. 'I wonder if I might have a few words in private with your wife?'

Duncan ushered his remaining guests into the drawing-room, leaving the other two alone.

'Another whisky, Doctor?' asked Vaughan striding to the tray resting on the library table.

'I think I need one,' said Morag, accepting the glass gratefully. 'I'm afraid I upset Rudi, but I do so hate to see senseless waste of any kind. My father often speaks of the terrible things which happened in the last war, and the tragic consequences of using people who were unprepared and ill-equipped for the jobs they were given to do.'

'It is because of the excellent reports I have had, both of your own work and that of the Inverlinnhe Mountain Rescue Service as a whole, that I asked Duncan to arrange this meeting,' the soldier responded.

He sat down in the winged chair opposite Morag and stretched out his legs comfortably before the roaring fire.

'You cannot have failed to notice that the men we are dealing with are no ordinary recruits,' he commented.

Remembering the variety of languages spoken, she grinned. 'They certainly seemed to be a very mixed bag.'

'I have been given the task of forming a Special Force,' the Colonel explained, 'whose members are to be recruited not only from amongst our own troops, but also from many of the occupied countries of Europe, as well as a number of volunteers from Canada and America. Their job will be to go into any part of occupied Europe, to carry out specific tasks and give assistance where necessary to the guerilla fighters in those countries.

'In defence of your friends,' he went on, with a wry smile, 'both Braun and Ashley Keynes have been bending my ear for weeks about the state of their equipment. I have a thick file filled with their memos on my desk at this very moment.'

'Then why . . . ?' Morag could feel her temper rising again.

'I had to be convinced, Doctor, that you really did know something about the task which confronts us. Your forceful exposé of our weaknesses tells me you are exactly the right person to take responsibility for the survival training which we have decided to include in our courses. If you agree to take up my offer, you will be required to act as Medical Officer to the training division, and attend incidents of the type in which you have just been involved. More importantly, you would be responsible for designing training courses in survival techniques, and possibly carrying out research into the effects of exposure and stress upon our young men, under battle conditions.'

He allowed his remarks to sink in for a few moments, then taking a document from his briefcase, continued, 'You will appreciate that what I have already revealed to you is highly secret, I shall require your assurance, on oath, that you will not divulge any of the information you have already received or that you are about to be given.' He handed her the document to read.

It was headed 'Official Secrets Act 1911'. Morag attempted

to sift the meaning of the words from a plethora of legal jargon.

Puzzled she looked up at Lieutenant-Colonel Vaughan.

'All right,' she said, 'I'll sign this if that's what you want, but I can assure you there's no need. I would never mention what you have just told me without your consent.'

'If you join our Special Service, I'm afraid you will have to sign it,' he replied, bluntly.

Morag was overwhelmed. Never once had she contemplated enlisting in the armed forces. There were plenty of male doctors lining up in the recruitment offices. Female physicians and surgeons like herself were now in great demand on the home front. She had already put her name down to join a mobile emergency force which could be transferred to any trouble spots if required, but had considered that her main responsibility lay with the people of Inverlinnhe.

'But my work at the hospital . . . There has to be someone there . . .'

'I have already made a few enquiries in that respect,' Vaughan said. 'It seems that one of the local GPs has offered to give assistance as a consultant surgeon . . . a Dr McDonald? They think they can manage until further help is forthcoming.'

Morag stared at him in astonishment.

'You will carry the rank of Major, Dr McRae,' Vaughan continued smoothly, then grinned as another thought struck him. 'And while you are discussing combat clothing with our designers, perhaps you had better give some thought to a uniform suitable for yourself and other female recruits to the section . . .'

An additional outcome of the conference at Achnafraoch was that a date was at last agreed when Lieutenant-Colonel Vaughan would take over the greater part of the house.

Within weeks the Special Forces Training Battalion was established in its new headquarters. Outbuildings were converted to classrooms, the long corridors and lofty rooms became dormitories, and the basement kitchens which had once been the stronghold of

Cook and her scullery maids, was now re-equipped as a canteen. Nissen huts clustered at the rear of the stable block and a firing range was set up on the open hillside behind the house.

Morag was amused by the notion that hers must be the only case in which an enlisted officer had had the Army brought to her instead of going to it!

Adam too was recruited as an instructor, leaving his civilian job to be carried on by an ageing band of public servants who, but for the war, would have been spending their days digging their gardens and walking their dogs across the hills.

Morag enjoyed this phase of her life almost more than any other she had experienced so far. The camaraderie of the servicemen appealed to her and she understood for the first time the strength of friendships formed under such conditions. She thought of the little band of men she had come to know and love: Duncan and Gordon, dear Magnus and Charlie Stewart – men with nothing in common but a muddy trench in Flanders, whose friendship had bridged a quarter of a century.

She enjoyed the training exercises, gaining great satisfaction from knowing that her surgical skills were rarely called upon now that experience had taught the men to move warily across the mountains.

Her hardest moments came when she had to say farewell to each class of recruits, young men honed to a peak of fitness and trained to perfection, whom she would never see again. It was then that she recalled the terrible aftermath of war: the men with their lungs choked, their bodies mutilated, and their minds damaged so badly that their only solace was to be found at the bottom of a whisky bottle. She thought at these times of Magnus Glendenning, of Laughlan McNeal on his daughter's wedding day, and of her own father, though one unexpected benefit of the war had been to bring Hugh Beaton back into the practice where work kept him too busy to worry about his own personal nightmares.

'The most important rule to follow when the mists come down is to stay put. Don't wander about blind. That's the easiest way to go over a cliff . . .'

Hearing the sound of tyres tearing up the gravel, Morag wandered over to the window. An army staff car had drawn up below the steps. She wondered vaguely who it could be.

With her back to the light, she continued, 'Remember, a search party will have the same difficulties as you, so don't expect anyone to come looking for you until the mists clear. If someone's injured and you can't move off when you are able to see, then again, stay put and use your whistle. Regular blasts once every five minutes will alert the rescuers . . . If you've lost the pea . . . shout.' There was a bubble of deep-throated laughter from the twenty marines gathered about her in the Long Room classroom.

She turned back to the window, curious about the visitor and her heart missed a beat. She recognised the uniform. Could it be Rudi? It was just like him to go missing for months on end and then turn up out of the blue . . . just like that.

The man turned to show his full face and she realised that she had been mistaken. He was taller than Rudi, indeed he was obliged to stoop a little to hear what Duncan was saying to him.

After a few more minutes, the soldier stepped back, saluted smartly and returned to his car.

Watching Duncan return to the front door, she was suddenly struck by a feeling of dread. She could tell by her husband's manner that he had heard some dreadful news.

Conscious of twenty pairs of eyes upon her she stammered, 'You'll have to excuse me, gentlemen. That will be all for today.'

As they shuffled to their feet, chairs scraping on the polished woodblock floor, she hurried down to the library, one of the few rooms in the house which remained their private territory.

Her worst fears were realised when she saw Duncan slumped in his chair, an untouched glass of whisky in his hand.

'What is it?' she cried, aghast.

'There's been a message . . . from Richard. Rudi's dead.'

Her hand flew to her mouth to stifle her cry.

'How?'

'It was in Yugoslavia, apparently. There was a pitched battle

430

between the Partisans and the Germans . . . Rudi was caught in a fusillade of withering gunfire . . . he died immediately.'

She sat down, receiving the glass he handed to her, in silence.

'Poor, brave, foolish Rudi,' she said a few minutes later. She swallowed the whisky and tried to smile through her tears.

'At least it was quick . . .'

Each time their friend left on one of his clandestine expeditions she had worried about what would happen to him should he fall into German hands. Frequently during his absences, she would wake in the night terrified by some nightmare scene her fertile imagination had conjured. At least this way he had been spared the torture and imprisonment which others were known to have suffered before execution.

'It was only a matter of time before he was caught,' Duncan murmured. 'It seems ironic that he should have survived until now only to die just as the tide is beginning to turn.'

He set down his glass on the day's *Gazette* which lay, unread, on the library table.

The banner headline read:

### GERMAN ARMY RETREATS FROM STALINGRAD. GENERAL PAULUS SURRENDERS!

\*    \*    \*

'Morag . . . Morag!' She could hear Duncan calling from the front hall.

She went to the top of the stairs.

'Here's a friend of yours, wanting to say goodbye.' He waved her down.

The tall young man at his side was familiar but she could not recall him. She recognised the insignia on his uniform however: the Norwegian Forces.

'Dr McRae.' The young man spoke perfect English with only the slightest hint of an accent. 'I felt I could not leave without first thanking you for saving my life.'

Now she knew him. 'Neils . . . Neils Bergen.' It was the boy

431

she had picked from off the cliff on that first brush with Vaughan's Special Forces.

'How are you?' she asked, making a professional survey of his outward appearance. He stood straight enough and when he moved it was without a limp. As she watched he flexed his wrist for her.

'You see, everything as good as new . . . thanks to you. I am eternally in your debt.'

'It's good to see you looking so well, Neils,' she exclaimed. 'And Lars . . . what about him? Have you seen anything of him?'

A shadow passed across the eager, youthful features. 'Alas, my friend is missing. He was sent on a mission to Norway a few weeks ago and has not been heard of for some time . . .'

'Oh, I'm so sorry.' She thought of that brave boy, frozen half to death as he clung to the cliff, ready if need be to sacrifice his own life for his friend . . . She felt the tears coming and brushed her hand across her eyes.

'So, what will you be doing now?' she asked hastily. His injuries probably meant they would have found him a desk job somewhere.

'I'm ready for active service,' Neils told her excitedly, 'and I think I can safely say that this time next week I shall be in Stavanger.'

Morag caught her breath and tried hard to smile as he bent over her hand and kissed it, reminding her for a moment of Rudi.

She and Duncan stood side by side at the top of the stone steps, watching the young man taking them two at a time before jumping aboard the lorry waiting to take the rest of the men to the railway station.

Duncan put his arm about Morag's shoulders, hugging her to him.

'It's as if they were our own children,' she said quietly, waving until the lorry pulled out of sight around the bend in the drive.

'I know,' he answered. 'I know.'

# Epilogue

## Spean Bridge, 27 September 1952

$\frown$

'Raised in urgent, clouded days, the Commandos hardened themselves for battle, by land, sea or air, in which nothing was certain except the hazards which they would have to face. To them, danger was a spur and the unknown was a challenge . . .'

Morag studied the ranks of men in lounge suits, many wearing bowler hats, some carrying umbrellas, with nothing to distinguish them from the passengers on the 8.27 but the rows of medals proudly disported on their chests. Could these really be the same stalwart lads whose blisters she had treated after toughening-up hikes across the mountains, with whom she had scaled the precipices along the Nevis range, and whom she had revived when they were fished from the icy waters of the loch after their canoes capsized?

She noticed a group of women, many of them in black like Her Majesty, some with their children gathered about them. The widows who died a little more each day . . .

Queen Elizabeth the Queen Mother was coming to the end of her speech now.

'It is in their honour and for their remembrance that I unveil this memorial.'

Her Majesty stepped forward and pulled the golden cord to release the giant Union Jacks which covered the memorial sculpture.

Mary Withall

The crowd remained silent as the Queen Mother stepped back to survey the work.

A lone piper began his lament quietly and then, with the notes swelling on the autumnal air, and with his kilt swinging to the rhythm of *Flowers of the Forrest*, he marched slowly once around the mighty plinth. Turning away, he moved down the slope, parting the crowds as he went. The notes faded to nothing as he disappeared over the brow of the hill.

Now it was the turn of the bugler. *The Last Post* was followed by *Reveille*, when wreaths were laid at the foot of the monument.

There followed further speeches before, at last, the Queen Mother moved off to meet those responsible for the setting up of the Memorial Fund, and other distinguished persons. A small shelter, like an open-sided shepherd's bothy, built of stone and thatched with heather, had been built nearby, to shelter Her Majesty while the dignitaries passed by.

She had a smile for all, a word for many.

Those outside waited, shivering in the strengthening wind. Soon it would be their turn . . .

Morag was glad she had chosen to wear her suit, for despite the bright sunshine which had woken them that morning, there was a definite nip of autumn in the air. The moss-green A-line skirt in soft wool fell to just above her ankles and her neatly tailored jacket, which barely reached her waist, had the cut of a military uniform . . . most appropriate in this setting.

When the moment came, she executed her curtsey with some trepidation, but responded quite naturally to the smiling lady who held out her hand in such a friendly manner.

'I must congratulate you, Dr McRae. I have been much impressed by reports of your work here. Such a wonderful example for women everywhere.'

'Thank you, ma'am.' Morag blushed charmingly, and the Queen Mother passed along to the next in line.

She herself showed no sign of discomfort. Her elegant outfit, in black silk chiffon, appeared to defy the vagaries of the Scottish weather, for she lingered over her task, chatting freely with each of the men. Colonel Vaughan introduced the ex-Commandos as though he had known them all personally; Morag suspected that, in fact, he had.

During the exchanges, she caught the sound of an occasional phrase in French or Dutch, Danish or Norwegian. What a talented woman she is, Morag thought. Widowed only months before, the Queen Mother appeared today as though her only concern in life was for the well-being and comfort of those about her. She was such a tiny figure, dwarfed by the men beside her, yet she radiated a charisma which made her a giant personality in any company.

Morag studied the line of veteran Commandos with interest. Could she recognise any of them? There had been so many of them . . . so many, who could not be here today.

Lars Bjornson had disappeared on a clandestine visit to his homeland in 1942 and his young friend Neils was shot by the Germans in 1943.

The Queen Mother was moving away now, walking slowly between the ranks of presently serving Commandos, who wore their famous green berets and badges of rank so proudly in this august company. From time to time she would stop to speak to one of them and the young man would have to bend his head to reply to the little lady. She walked on through the huge crowds of ordinary people gathered on the windy hillside, smiling and waving her hand in characteristic fashion. Lieutenant-Colonel Vaughan paced slowly at her side, with Major Richard Ashley Keynes one pace to the rear. Behind them walked Lord Lovat and MacDonald of MacDonald, the Lord-Lieutenant of Lochaber, both resplendent in full highland dress, together with the Reverend John Armstrong in the robes of Chaplain to the Commando Regiment.

The pageantry was over now. The vast crowd – some said it was as many as four thousand people – broke up into a kaleidoscope of colour as groups formed, disintegrated and reformed, while old friendships were renewed and new ones made.

Morag moved closer to the magnificent monument to get a better view of the artist's work. The three men depicted could have been any of the hundreds whom she had met during five years of war. They wore the special uniform which she had envisaged during that strange evening with Vaughan in 1940, including the woolly hats which they had all laughed at when she suggested them. They had come to wear them proudly, and gratefully, as time went on. Small packs, carefully distributed around their bodies, allowed the men to carry everything they needed into battle, while providing a freedom of movement denied by the ordinary soldier's back-pack.

The figures, greater than life-size, gazed out across the hills which the Commandos had come to know so intimately. The faces were tough and rugged, the bodies strong and their stance determined. This magnificent work, the sculptor, Scott Sutherland, had captured the spirit of these men for all time. Morag studied the central figure more closely. He might have been any age under thirty, any nationality. He might have been Rudi . . .

She felt the tears spring to her eyes, remembering their last meeting. She and Duncan had seen him off on the train to Glasgow, knowing that his destination was to be Yugoslavia. It had been a mission from which he was not likely to return . . .

She glanced up to see that her friends were beginning to gather to one side of the memorial.

Adam was there, looking extremely handsome in his dress uniform. Late in 1942 he had been transferred to the RAF in order to set up the first military Mountain Rescue Organisation. This had been retained at the close of hostilities, and he had found himself in the enviable position of retaining his RAF rank and carrying out his duties while remaining at home with his wife and family. A Wing Commander's insignia now sat impressively upon his broad shoulders.

Mary looked radiant in a fashionable blue dress which complemented Adam's uniform. Her hair had gone prematurely grey, but the colour suited her. Their two children were looking very grown up. Peter was the image of his father. Morag wondered if he could possibly be as talented.

Allowing her gaze to travel around the group, she spotted Gordon and his wife deep in conversation with Harriet. Richard's wife was heavily pregnant for the third time and Morag had expressed doubts about her attending the function at all. In characteristic fashion she had poured scorn on Morag's fears, insisting that she should witness the unveiling.

The war years had taken their toll of Gordon McDonald. Morag was pleased that her departure from the hospital had forced him to take up surgery again, but to have undertaken the burden in addition to the demands of his own practice was too much for any one man. He had worked under intense pressure, only relinquishing his hospital post just as Morag was released from the Army in 1946.

She moved across to join them.

When he saw her approaching, Gordon fished an envelope out of his pocket.

'News from Johannes,' he called. 'There's a photo too.'

'Has he graduated?' she asked eagerly. Their protégé had insisted that he must gain his medical training in Vienna, despite the devastation wrought in that city by the war.

'With distinction,' Gordon assured her, proudly. 'Poppy is beside herself with delight. A year or two as a registrar, and he will be fully qualified.'

While Johannes undertook his medical studies in Austria, Poppy had trained to be a nurse in Glasgow. Morag knew that they planned to go somewhere in the world where they could do some good . . . Africa maybe, or South America. It didn't matter, so long as they were together.

'Will she join him in Vienna, after the wedding?' Morag asked.

'I expect so,' Gordon replied . . . a little wistfully, she thought. His youngest daughter had always been Gordon's special favourite. Morag knew how much he must dread losing her.

'But the wedding comes first,' he continued. 'They're planning to marry on New Year's Day.'

'Good,' said Morag. 'I have a feeling 1953 is going to be a very special year . . . they could not be marrying at a better time!

'Look.' Gordon displayed the photograph of Johannes in his academic robes, proudly holding his diploma. At his side stood his mother, a tiny, frail-looking woman, who had miraculously survived many years in Auschwitz before her release in 1945.

'How can she bear to lose him again?' asked Morag.

Anna, overhearing the remark, surprised Morag when she replied, 'She has not lost him so far, and nor will she now – provided she lets him go. Apron strings should be made of elastic . . . children tied to them can go as far as they like. They will always come home when the time is right!'

There had been times in the past when Morag had considered Anna to be too flippant and superficial a wife for Gordon. Deep philosophical thought was hardly her usual style. In recent years, however, Morag had been forced to change her opinion of the flamboyant wife of her best friend. When things had got really tough during the war, Anna had shown her true mettle, and her work as an artist had improved dramatically as a result. A recent exhibition in Edinburgh had been highly acclaimed.

Linking arms with the two of them, Morag led them towards Duncan's Rolls-Royce, suddenly very conspicuous amongst a collection of more modest vehicles, now that the Royal party had left.

'Won't you both come back to Achnafraoch for the evening?' she suggested. 'We have quite a little party arranged. Adam and Mary are coming, a few nurses from the hospital and some of the veterans . . . you can help us to entertain them.' Her entreaties were addressed to Anna, who was always reluctant to be among strangers. Morag knew that Gordon would only consent to join them if his wife wanted to come.

Anna glanced across at her husband, sensing his eagerness to renew old acquaintance. 'We'd love to,' she replied, and Morag squeezed her arm, gratefully.

Duncan got out of the car as they approached, greeting Anna and Gordon while apologising to his wife.

'I'm sorry, my dear,' he said, giving her a kiss, 'I became rather chilled standing for so long . . . I hope you didn't mind my going on ahead?'

She regarded him anxiously, thinking he might be unwell, then relaxed. Today was her day. How like him to see it as the cue for him to retreat into the background while she held centre stage.

'Anna and Gordon are coming to the party, dearest,' she told him. 'We had better get along now, or our guests will be there before us!'

Gordon and Anna made for their own car, while Harriet went off to find Richard. Duncan settled into the back seat of the Rolls beside his wife. He tapped on the glass screen and Roberts responded by steering the sleek, black limousine out of the parking area, between crowds of visitors queuing to board their coaches and buses for the long journey home.

Very soon they had joined the stream of traffic, and were heading slowly back into town.

A mile or two down the road, Roberts made a left-hand turn and headed the car up the road towards Achnafraoch. They turned in at the gates, left permanently open now. After the old gatekeeper had died, Duncan had not bothered to replace him.

'I thought I would offer Poppy and Johannes the use of my cottage while they are here,' Morag said, watching the hedgerows on either side for glimpses of the heather fields beyond the trees. 'They won't have much opportunity to be alone together at Gordon's house, and once they get back to Vienna . . . well, I understand that living accommodation there is so cramped it's like being in a Russian commune.'

'I'm sure they'll be very grateful.' Duncan placed his hand over hers. 'I was proud of you today, my darling. Did you enjoy yourself?'

'Yes . . . in a way.' She was hesitant over her reply. 'It's a beautiful memorial, but . . . well, I just wish it had never been necessary to build it. All those young men . . .' Her voice trailed off.

Suddenly she leaned forward and slid back the glass panel behind the driver's head.

'Pull over on to the verge, please, Roberts,' she ordered. 'We'll walk from here.'

She could scarcely wait until the vehicle had come to a halt before leaping out. Hurrying through the trees, Morag made for the heather-covered hillside beyond, coming to a halt beside a great boulder which perched precariously on the slope, defying gravity.

As she sank down upon a mossy clump and leaned back against the rock, gasping for breath, from behind the clouds emerged a lone aircraft.

She shaded her eyes to see if she could identify the 'plane.

It was one of the old Lysanders.

Duncan caught up with her just as the aircraft appeared to dip in salute above the spot where the new memorial had been unveiled that afternoon.

'Someone paying his own personal tribute to lost comrades,' he suggested, as he crouched down beside her.

A cold wind sprang up suddenly as the sun disappeared behind a cloud, and mists began to roll down from the top of the Ben. Morag shivered and Duncan put his arm around her, drawing her close.

'I thought a lot about Rudi this morning,' she said, picturing again that gentle giant with a procession of children in his wake.

In silence Duncan and Morag gazed out over the loch to the mighty peaks beyond. It was a scene of autumnal splendour, a multitude of colours slashed like some demented artist's brush strokes, across the wide canvas of Lochaber.

Above the crags behind the house a golden eagle hovered. With a sudden rush of air and a ponderous beating of its giant wings, the magnificent bird swooped down to where a flock of sheep grazed lazily in the meadow beyond the road.

Within seconds it was back, soaring on the upward currents of air, a full-grown rabbit held firmly in its huge talons.

Duncan and Morag turned, their gaze following the eagle in its flight until it disappeared from sight, high up among the cliffs.

'That's freedom for you,' Duncan observed, quietly.

'But why must it cost so very, very much?' demanded Morag, a sea of boyish faces dancing before her tear-filled eyes.

'Come along, my dear,' he urged her, clambering to his feet. 'Our guests are waiting.'

Arm in arm they took the path through the woods to the edge of the lawn. As they approached Achnafraoch, the setting sun emerged from behind the clouds, and bathed the grey stonework of the old house in a warm, ruddy glow.

Someone had wheeled a table out on to the terrace, and an ancient gramophone was belting out dance music. 'Tommy Dorsey,' Morag cried delightedly. 'I wonder where they dug that out from?'

She took the steps to the terrace two at a time, dragging Duncan after her. 'Come on,' she cried, 'let's show some of these young things what *real* dancing is all about!'